The Secret GUY

A NEW ENGLAND DIARY

The Secret GUY

A NEW ENGLAND DIARY

A Fictional Diary

JOSEPH T. COLEMAN

ARPress
45 Dan Road Suite 15
Canton, MA 02021
Hotline: 1(888) 821-0229
Fax: 1(508) 545-7580

Ordering Information:
Quantity sales. Special discounts are available on quantity purchases by corporations,associations, and others. For details, contact the publisher at the address above.

Printed in the United States of America.

ISBN-13: Hardback 979-8-89676-088-7

Library of Congress Control Number: 2025915346

This is a work of fiction. Some of the locations are real, but all of the characters are a product of my imagination. Similarity to real persons, living or no longer among us, is coincidence.

Author's Note

My heroine thinks of herself as a tomboy. She dwells more deeply in the world of men than is typical among her peers in the world of women. Sometimes, she finds it useful to think and express herself in the manner of her contemporaries of the male gender, thus to understand instead of to misunderstand. Her words in full womanly voice are echoes of messages internalized by the author over a lifetime, whenever he took the time to listen.

Prologue

It does not matter who he is, my Secret Guy. The only thing which matters is that he is mine. We meet in private. Nobody can comment. No one can interfere. If it becomes necessary to meet in public, we require anonymity within a crowd of strangers. When our story is finished, then finally, others may know it. Future readers of these pages will know it, in due time.

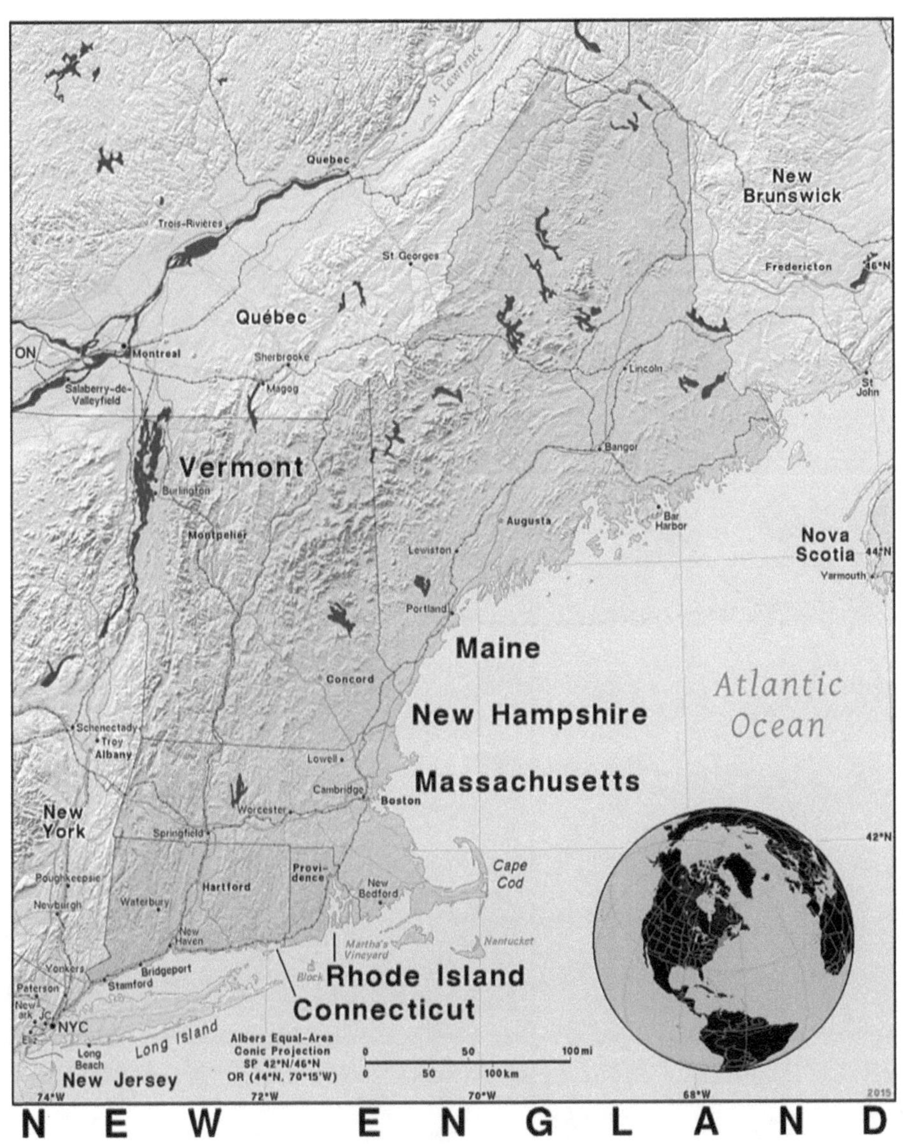

N E W E N G L A N D

https://ian.macky.net/pat/map/neng/nengblu2.gif

THE DIARY OF SARAH JANE POWELL

Saturday, January 1

Dear Diary, I am so depressed. Plus, I am hung over from last night. I can't hold my liquor, as usual. I went home alone, as usual. What is wrong with me? People say I am really cute. I think I am. I have my assets, no pun. I have a good job with normal hours. I have a little money. I have friends. My car is a junker, but it's good enough to take me most places. In April I will be 39 and nobody loves me. I sit here neglected and unloved.

It's been so long since college. Phil seemed to love me. He said the words at least but he didn't love me quite enough, I guess. I miss him so, so much, way too much. He is the only one so far, the only one I think about, but he is gone, gone, gone. Mom made sure of that. Before that, puppy love. When was my last date? I can hardly remember his name. One dinner and out with no chemistry, Charlie, over a year ago it was.

I have sealed and locked away my 2010 diary. I must not go on that way. This year has got to be big time better and totally different. I am getting my love life off of the ground, one way or another, by hook or by crook, straightforward or devious. This is my one and only New Year's Resolution. Now think, think, think. I am a smart girl. I can, I must think of a way. One thing is for sure. Mom will not know anything about it. First step, hmm, let's see, what if I recycle? From all of the rejects, pick one. Give him a second chance. Rick perhaps, the guy from the coffee shop, what was wrong with him? He seemed a little too old plus he was divorced, with kids. Too much talk about the ex. It would have been complicated. But maybe he has upped his game. He is still around, I think. I resolve to take a second look. Thoughts of the ex will be exploded and banished and vanished into thin air. He will be thinking only about me, night and day, every day and all night long. Who else? Maybe Dave, my uber guy on retainer. He might be secretly in love with me. All over Boston, there might guys secretly in love with me. Sleep and dream on it, Sarah. Pray. Make it happen.

Sunday, January 2

Dear Diary, Mom wants me to meet some guy she has picked out for me. She should know that I am automatically going to reject all of her choices. They were inviting him over after church. I say that she can give him my work phone number but say I have other plans for this Sunday. Sometimes, I attend Lutheran services just for fun. I am far past the worry of being damned to hell for missing Mass.

After church, I hang out for an hour at Café Paradiso on Dedham Square and read from my current novel, *Jude the Obscure*. Compared to the heroine, Sue Bridehead, my life is quite minimum misery. I pick out a DVD for later, Doctor Zhivago. Believe it or not, I read the book first. I take my book and my DVD across the street to the bagel place. I get the last bacon cheddar scone and wait for Rick. He didn't show. Snow begins to fall. They make me a pot of green tea. Their pastries are tempting. I fail to resist the raspberry tarts. I look up at each entry. A mother and daughter sit near me, both named Charlotte. They just returned from Europe. They speak both French and German. We chat. We decide to meet next Sunday so I can dust off my High School French. This could be very rewarding, to be in their network, that is. The two Charlottes go on their merry way as daylight begins to fade.

Late Sunday's winter afternoons are a sad time. I phone in a pizza order and pick it up on my way home. My Calico cat, Felicia, and half a bottle of Pinot Noir are waiting for me, plus a sink full of dirty dishes. Snow continues to fall. A few birds hop about the bird feeder outside my kitchen window. I replenish Felicia's dish of cat kibble, put on my apron and take care of the dishes. The first glass of wine and a hot shower cheer me up a little. I dive into my thick terry cloth robe, refill my glass and settle on the sofa. Felicia joins me. I fall asleep halfway through the movie. Some crazy dream wakes me at 2 am. Things are happening to me under water, some dark ocean. I light a vanilla scented candle and turn out the lights. I stay on the sofa to make my diary entry. Already, my entries are better than last year.

Monday, January 3

Dear Diary, Today is day two of my quest for love. I write my own story. I control my destiny. In a way, I still leave it all to chance but I improve my chances. My morning rituals unfold in the usual way. Felicia stares in endless fascination at the bird feeder. Maybe I should get a dog, a little dog and they can play while I am out. Walking your dog is a great way to meet guys. I saw in the rescue shelter, dogs and cats together in a large enclosure with furniture, just like a family living-room.

I choose a better than average business suit today, something snug at the hips. Whoever walks into the office will take notice. It's time for a new coiffure. Make your appointment at lunchtime, baby doll. I hear Roger's voice saying, "If I had to switch teams, it would be for you honey. You are a little tomboy and that would make it easy." He always gives me a hug if I need one. He smells nice. I tip him well from my meager budget. He is always happy to see me. He understands me. He knows secrets about me. I may hint but I will not tell.

No more day-dreaming or I will be late. I brush snow off of the car. I proceed on my usual circuitous route from West Roxbury to Chestnut Hill. There was a message there from Robert, the guy Mom corralled for me. I may string him along for a while. He can come to the office and the other girls will give their opinions. His voice was just okay. He sounded a little shy. I should leave the office for lunch once or twice a week but where? I have been lulled into a safe and comfortable rut.

I take a different route home. There is a bakery. Take a number. Get in line, in a crush of people. One never knows who might get crushed up against you. This could be my new bakery, pastries and marble rye, during the busy time. Snatch up all of the day-old stuff. Fill out that figure. More jiggle wouldn't hurt. I am home later than usual. It's dark already. Cat, novel and movie comfort me for one more lonely night. I meditate in my bathtub. I need a mantra, something that doesn't sound like a mooing cow. I hear movement upstairs. I don't even know who lives there. How convenient if someone really nice is up there.

Tuesday, January 4

Dear Diary, Mom calls at work. To make her happy, I said I would meet Robert but not sure when, not at church, that is for sure. I do not mix romance and religion. If you are a Catholic, they kind of cancel each other out. It has been a long time since I confessed an impure thought and I am going to keep it that way.

At lunch, the girls talked about our financial conditions. We compared our credit scores. Mine was dead last at 625. My savings was dead last as well at $2000, which is barely more than 1 month's living expenses. I waste it on too much take-out meals. Too many store credit-cards, all near limit. Too many impulse buys on Saturday shopping. I am going second hand and vintage. I was told not to cut up the cards. Keep them for emergency. Pay them down. Use will power.

A guy on the make once told me that he loves the dressed down look. He said that he can always tell when there is something really good under those loose-fitting Plain-Jane outfits. He said he has never been wrong. That is a pretty smooth line, I must admit, but I did not fall for it. I told him I can do the same with guys. I told him I detect musculature. I said go hit the gym and a year from now you might have a chance.

I may even try on some of Mom's old stuff, if it doesn't smell like moth balls. I think she has some cashmere, some nice woolens and linens, all made in USA, high end labels. I may even flaunt some fur. I will just say it is faux fur. If the mink died 20 years ago and the fur was preserved, I do not see the harm.

Seven buyers and two lessees were in the office today. One of them pinged my radar. On further inspection, a wedding band was detected. I drove home slowly. I have decided to get a second cat, another neutered female, then I won't feel so guilty about leaving Felicia alone, so often. I feel good. I feel calm. I have a plan. My weekend is wide open. Anything can happen. Something really good could be just around the corner. On arrival home, I find some vodka in the back of the freezer. A toast to my future is in order. I make it a double mixed with cranberry. That's good, buzzed and mellow.

Wednesday, January 5

Dear Diary, Robert can't meet me for lunch. He works in Norwood. It's too far away. We'll have coffee in Norwood on Saturday morning.

I'm wearing winter business casual outfit number 3 today. These are the same ensembles I wore last winter. The Malibu got new brakes a month ago. I got a new coat and scarf. Dad gives me scarves. Mom gives me hats and gloves. She is still dressing me up like a Barbie. It is fun to accessorize. We agree on that. At work, Susan is my same size. We raided each other's closets once. It was a swap meet. "Hey, it looks a lot better on you," we told each other.

Some children move far away from their parents, from where they grew up. I seem to be stuck here, just a few miles from Dedham High School. I dream about far-away places, usually populated by palm trees. It's time to make a move, but not alone. Partner up, baby girl, for business and pleasure.

Husband and wife with separate careers, different hours and different daily commutes is high risk for estrangement. Yes, I read regularly the column entitled "Can this Marriage be Saved?" in *McCall's Magazine*. It is in our waiting room and it ends up in our break room. I will avoid the pitfalls. First, some kind of partner, any kind. Every weekend is a casting call, an audition. I will keep an understudy waiting in the wings for back up. It could be fun. Action every weekend, big game or small game.

Wednesdays are Yoga. I have my gym bag packed for flexibility and total body tone up at 10 bucks a class. By the time the lesson is over, traffic has cleared a bit. I stop at the Greek International Food Market. I see a decent guy there. I say something spontaneous. We wait in line together at checkout. I manage a weary smile and some small talk. I offer my first name. I get a first name. I make shop talk about work. We exchange business cards. How difficult is that? Not very. Bingo! The card puts Steven Sandler, life insurance, into my network. Will he ever call me? Eventually someone must or else spinsterhood could become permanent.

Thursday, January 6

Dear Diary, After a deep dreamless sleep, I am up early today. There is no more hitting the snooze alarm. That is just avoiding life. Instead, I hit the shower. I let the bathroom fill with steam. I wrap my wet hair in a towel. I dive into my terry cloth robe and fluffy slippers. Felicia is waiting in the kitchen. She gets milk with her kibble. It is still dark outside. More snow has fallen. I start the old-fashioned percolator, the same as my parents used as I remember from childhood. I like the way it sounds. Today is a good day for slacks.

Halfway to next hair appointment, I fix the low chignon in the back and a necklace in front. My favorite is the lab created emerald on a silver chain. It draws attention to my top line. I have got a remote starter for my car, one more luxury bought on credit. Windshield is defrosting while I have my second cup.

I love my little apartment. I have it fixed up just the way I like it. It's an older style blond brick four-unit building with windows facing south and west. There are shade trees. My neighbors are quiet. Some low rumbles of conversation penetrate the walls. I have been here for five years now. Who is the new tenant upstairs? Maybe a cute guy? I turn the heat down for daytime. With keys and purse in hand, I am out the door.

I am at my desk early. Maybe I will score some points with the boss, Maggie. I could use a raise. Flat screens have been installed. Every kind of app is one click away. Surfing is forbidden. E-mail only. Texting only on break. My guy and I will be very discreet. At lunch there is a message from Steven Sandler. Maybe I should buy some life insurance. Maybe I should take a meeting at his office. Maybe he just wants to see me again. Maybe he would love to have my private phone number.

I crunch some figures for the boss such as occupancy rates, repairs costs for last quarter, scheduled move outs. I handle some tenant complaints. I make appointments to show units. One neutered female waits for me, but no man, yet. Steven wants to do lunch sometime but our offices are too far apart. He never mentions dinner. Dead end?

Friday, January 7

Dear Diary, Thank God it's Friday. I am wide awake earlier than usual. I begin my entry while the coffee is percolating. With these first sentences, the aroma alone is helping me to think clearly. Felicia remains in bed. She tolerates no such change in her daily routine.

Something is going to happen today. I can feel it. Bitter cold is predicted. I should stay inside, but where? Not necessarily at home, but somewhere with a fireplace seems right. Napper Tandy's, in Norwood, has one. I am pretty sure of it. Should I bring back-up? Susan might come. She has a boyfriend. Do they have plans? We should share a taxi, thus no worries about alcohol, nor police, nor parking. Okay, that is settled. Later tonight, I will tell all. Stand by for my late-night report.

At coffee break, it's only 10 am and already there is a snag in my plan. Susan and boyfriend are staying in at her place watching the Celtics play the Lakers. If the Celtics win, he does anything she wants in bed. If the Celtics lose, Susan is the consolation prize. Quite a system, that is. Never let sports interfere with your love life.

I go home. I take a little nap. From the last of my clean clothes, I choose jeans and a nice snug sweater. There is no smoking inside. My perfume will be noticed. Tonight, I choose Poison, the nastiest stuff I have. The musky bottom note lasts until well after midnight. My Uber driver is Dave. He notices the fragrance and approves. He agrees to pick me up at midnight for my return trip home. He drives into the wee hours every weekend. It's how he pays for college. He is a little young for me.

Inside the bar, it's as I expected. The fireplace is there. I spy 3 girls barely legal at a table for 4. They let me join them. There are 2 bartenders and a waitress circulating. I have got my Irish Coffee with whipped cream. I stand and take off my coat. I turn a few heads in the process. One of them is Robert. He recognizes me from a photo Mom showed him. He just got off work at Norwood Hospital. Robert orders me a second round. He has spent money on me already. It is too noisy to chat. We stare into the flames.

We are totally mellowed out. We play a game. While I am in the powder room, Robert must go and talk to at least one other woman, the cutest one in the room according to his taste in women, then report back to me. While he takes his bathroom break, I will go over to the most interesting man I see, and say something, anything just to get noticed. What is the worst that can happen? He may look through me as if I was not there, which is no great harm. Robert has got his girl picked out. She is a blond at the end of the bar near us. "Off you go," I say. "I will be back in 5." Off he went. I made sure of that. "Well?" I said when I got back. "I asked her the score," he reported. "It was all I could think of. She said that the Lakers were up at the half." Then I added "That is not the score I meant." She looked at me a moment and said, "You are down at the half." "Good one," I told her. "Then I ordered another drink, a double, and made my retreat. Now it is your turn. Off you go."

Robert watches me move toward 3 guys who seemed to be debating a serious matter. On his return, I gave my report. My line was "Guys, can I settle your debate for you?" They said that they were talking about muscle cars. I said that I had a '70 Malibu, 307 cubic inch V8. I lied. I asked them if I seemed drunk because the bartender just cut me off. I lied. I said that I was with someone but where is a good late-night place to eat because we don't know Norwood too well. They told me about a place. One of the guys asked me my name. I said that I'm Sara Jane and I'll be over by the fire if you need me. Robert and I looked toward the trio. I waved. One of them waved back.

I switched to Guiness for the second half. Robert nursed his Johnny Walker Black. The Celtics lost. I began to wonder just what kind of consolation Susan was delivering at that very moment. Dave, my driver, pinged me at midnight. Robert said he was on foot and it was not far. I told him to call me tomorrow. He was a good sport. As a reward, I gave him my private number. I will keep him as a pal. It's good to have a Platonic pal. Did Plato have one? I will ask Roger. My head hits the pillow at 1 am.

Saturday, January 8

Dear Diary, Here I am, once again hungover on a Saturday morning. Felicia is not going to allow me to sleep any longer. The sun is bright on the snow outside, that's nice. I have a lot to do. I had better get busy. Today is laundry day, a load for down below in the creepy basement and a load for up here by hand are both lying there in a pile, staring at me. The kitchen is a mess. I will start there. There is some cold coffee in the percolator. I said I would meet Robert at noon to compare notes.

Someday, from my rocking chair, I will relive this ordinary day down to the tiniest details which I record here. On my way out the door, I search for my gloves in my coat pocket. There is a bar napkin there with writing on it as follows. "I want to see that '70 Malibu but mostly I want to see you again. Call me, Roy (the one who waved at you)." There is a phone number. I copy the number into my flip phone and stuff the napkin into my purse. I am 15 minutes late to meet Robert. He is there at Perks, not exactly patiently waiting. He is flirting with one of the baristas named Cameron. "It's easy to flirt when you know you have no chance," he said. True, she seems impossibly young. I tell him about the note. Since I went over to 3 guys, I had 3 swings and 1 was a base hit. "I only had one swing and it was a foul ball," he replies. We survey the room. "Will you take any more swings today?" I ask. "Maybe tonight, after work. I go in at 2. I'll stay here with my book until just before. A book is a conversation starter," he continues. "What about you and I?" he wonders. "Pals, that can last longer. Boyfriends come and go. If you like me, you will be a pal and that could last a long time," I offer. Pals can do hugs and before I depart, I offer one, without my coat on. Some rough hands go up and down my back. I do not mind.

Back home chores consume the afternoon. Evening descends. What to do? Of course, I shall call Roy but when? A text will do for starters. By text we agree to talk Sunday afternoon at 4 pm sharp. I give my private land line number. I have almost a full day to prepare for the phone call. Tonight, it will be Dedham Square, my usual lounge lizard routine.

I call Dave, who picks me up at 8. Randy is behind the bar at Oscar's, my upscale hang out. Randy and I go way back. I have asked him to marry me several times. He plays along. I am spending a lot of money this weekend. I'll save a little by sticking to soft drinks tonight. I say goodbye to my old life tonight. I am going all in on Roy. I tell Randy about it. "You mean we're through?" he whines. "Yes, our fantasy love affair is over, for now, I'm pretty sure," I reply. "You'll be back," he quips.

I am at my usual bar stool where I typically order just an appetizer or just a dessert or just coffee or just one drink after going to a movie alone. I look around at the affluent couples.

Some of them seem content, some seem bored. A few give a nod of recognition from once upon a time I chatted them up. I never sat at a table. Next New Year's will be my triumphant return at a table for two. They call it a self-fulfilling prophecy.

I look at the dessert menu. I settle for vanilla ice cream covered in bar cherries and coffee on the side. The coffee here is the best. I have tried it with every kind of shot poured in. All too soon comes 10 pm. Dave has pulled up outside. Randy comes around the bar for hugs and a kiss on the cheek. "You'll be back," he repeats. He smiles and waves goodbye.

Waiting for me is a warm leather seat. I sit in front. It's nice to look at the night city from the passenger seat for a change. Dave waits until I get to my door. I look up at a clear winter sky full of stars. I take a deep breath of the bitter-cold, pine-scented night air.

I leave a trail of cap, gloves, coat and boots leading to a bathtub filling fast. Can two fit in there? What a thought. I've never done that before. I stare at the never married, no kids, sporty little body I've still got. I check the rear view. All systems go, a bod for sin. I step into the tub. Felicia goes after some bubbles pouring over the side. I realize I have been selfish. I'll get my wing-man, Robert fixed up also. If worst comes to worst, we'll console each other. That's too easy. That is settling. Have faith. You were just too passive all those lonely years. Have faith. I tell myself.

Sunday, January 9

Dear Diary, Get up, Sarah. Go to church. See Mom and Dad. Be nice to them. You are still their little girl. I tell them I met Robert. Yes, he is nice. That is all. I have lots to do today. Finally, I get back home at noon. Laundry is sitting there waiting. I get a ragout started. It is clean out the ice box day. Every not so fresh veggie will go in there. Simmer them down while I work.

Roy calls at 4 pm. I pick up on the third ring, out of breath like I am so busy. I tell him we are on a secure land line and my place has been swept for bugs. He laughs. He does not have a room-mate which is perfect because neither do I. I tell him I need a nice serious boyfriend. He loves girls who make the first move, just as I did. I tell him I will give him a one-year tryout. He lives in Canton. We agree to meet again on Friday. He will call me at lunchtime every day on a secure land line phone number at my work. Our flip phones should be text only and then delete the text. It is more fun this way. I am confident that I will get him to agree to a lot of stuff before the year is through. I tell him I need little talk but lots of action. He laughs and says, "Okay, Sarah Jane Powell." I say I have to go.

The ragout has simmered down nicely. There is enough to last all week. The clothes are in the dryer. I have a few blouses to iron. There is drip dry hanging in the bathroom. Such has been my life for all these many years, just waiting for something to happen. I walk to the corner store. A box wine will be fine. It is 3 liters, enough to last the rest of the month. Hundreds of times, some little item, a late-night consolation could be had there.

Sometimes just fancy cat food for Felicia. Cold, it's so cold outside. I shiver. Soon there will be a man to keep me warm, a guy, my guy, a secret guy. Everybody else butt out. This is private. This is going to be really good. I am not leaving it to fate. I have a plan and it is going to work.

That's about it for another forgettable Sunday except for one detail. I have got my guy. I have reeled him in. I have a really good feeling about this one. I didn't tell him my age yet. "39? No fucking way!" he'll say. Oops! I forgot about the 2 Charlottes.

Monday, January 10

Dear Diary, Normally, I dread Mondays in winter. There is such a long week ahead and not much on the weekend horizon to look forward to. Now I can put all kinds of adventures in there.

A normal morning flies by. Roy has the break room extension which he can choose right from the phone menu. He rings in at 1 pm. I do not say his name during our chat, in case of eavesdroppers. We agree to meet on Friday, come as you are, directly from work. He has a sister who might like to meet Robert. We agree to meet in Walpole, somewhere he is not known. I tell him I need him on Saturday as well. There will be no first date anxiety, no dumped after one date. He is a little younger than me, only 36. I didn't get that close of a look at the guy but he seemed to be better than just okay, a presentable type, average height and build. We don't waste time in idle phone chatter. The date is set with four more days of anticipation.

During afternoon coffee break, I search Walpole night life. It's a boring provincial suburb complete with town square and gazebo. That is fine with me. No one I know lives or works there. Once again, I will have Dave to drive me. Susan notices a change in me. She wonders what's up. Too early to say, I tell her. I am not dishing anything yet, not for a long time.

I go out in the parking lot. There are a few smokers out there. Suddenly, I want a smoke. I smoked in college. My mother could smell it on my clothes. Just be glad it's not reefer, I would tell her. I was up to a pack a day before I quit. Phil got me started. We were at Providence College, a short train ride away. I won't compare my new guy to Phil.

Susan catches me humming my way through reports later. Mom knows Susan. My secret will not be secure with her. Maybe I can make up a misdirection. She can wonder if I have fallen for a married man. Married men come on to Susan all the time. She flirts with them, but that's all. True confessions a year from now, I tell her. Good things come to those who wait. I have waited almost all of my young life. I think I am playing my cards just exactly right. No pressure. No pressure at all.

Tuesday, January 11

Dear Diary, I just realized that today is 1/11/11. Is it a sign of something? What do the five ones portend? Eleven is a prime number, divisible only by itself and one. I remember that from math class. In spite of the unique numerology, it seems like an ordinary winter day. I am awake early and busy with my morning routine. I have time for a proper breakfast. No more rushing out the door, running late, forgetting stuff. I brush and floss while the Malibu is warming up. I check the bathroom mirror. My cheeks are rosy, my slouch is gone, pleasingly plain, some might say, someone solid, not moody, not trouble, not going to scare anyone away.

I will be doing credit checks today on new tenant applications. It is sad but some new tenants will require large deposits. I think the deposits should earn interest, then it won't hurt so bad. I open my window a crack on the way to work. I wind my way through old neighborhoods at a leisurely pace. I wonder who lives in some of these fabulous houses of old construction. It is fun to do the title searches and find a place that has stayed in the same family for several generations, owned and maintained. I only know about rented.

Already, I see Roy and I looking to buy and we have not even had our first date. Roy calls at lunch again today. We keep it short and sweet. He says he likes my voice. He says he wants it in person as much as possible. The anticipation is building. We won't be shy. We won't be nervous. We are going to have so much fun together. I just know it. Susan hears me humming as the afternoon drags on. Once again, I quash all inquiries.

I work a little late. Maybe I can somehow earn a raise. I totally clear my desk. I let the rush hour traffic thin out. Twilight is beginning as I leave. I get a flirt from a guy I never saw before, also working late. His name is Phil. Do I need a daily remainder of my old flame, Phil. I will tell Susan about this to deflect her curiosity. It's only 3 miles to home, on VFW Parkway. I go super slow due to patches of ice. I see Felicia in the window as I park. There is a light on in the unit above me.

Wednesday, January 12

Dear Diary, I show furnished demo town house units today. The morning flies by and suddenly by noon, we are over the hump, halfway to 5 pm Friday freedom. I am getting really excited. Calm down, baby girl. Stay all self-assured just as you were last Saturday. How brazen you were when you walked up to those 3 guys and you made an impression on one of them. One is enough. He can't get you out of his mind. He can't wait to take a closer look. I think I will go no bra with a peek-a-boo blouse. We who barely graduated to the B-cups can get away with that. More than a handful is a waste. I have heard that kind of locker room talk many times.

After lunch, I calm down a bit. The other girls want to know what I'm doing this weekend. I told them I need to wash my hair. They laugh. "Are you sure that is all?" they wonder. They suspect something but mum's the word. Previously, I pretended a lot of plans that fizzled. Now I pretend I am resigned to old maid, until one day I show up with a rock.

I clear my desk. I am on salary so I can leave early. I beat the rush hour traffic along Hammond St. I am home super early. I need some relief, some private self-love with my favorite devices, some of them battery operated. Afterwards, I study the bush. A trim around there is in order. Will I get naked this weekend? I better hold off on some of those fantasies. I check the expiration date on the just-in-case Trojans stashed under my bed. To do list for tomorrow: Buy a fresh supply of rubbers and some K-Y. There it is, a big post-it right on my fridge.

I go outside at twilight. I need a brisk walk. I need the cold air. People are walking their dogs. I find myself humming that George Michael song, the one banned from aerobics class. "Sex is natural. Sex is good." Mom would be horrified. Sorry, Mom. I have grown up. On return I am really hungry. Kitty gets fed first. I feel like a big salad with every veggie. I want to remember this ordinary day full of simple pleasures and anticipation. Oops, now it's Carly Simon singing. I am so old school. Can I make it in the modern world of Love? "You can and you will," I command.

Thursday, January 13

Dear Diary, Holy Macaroni! I am awake but it is still dark and exceedingly quiet out there. Traffic noise wakes me if my alarm fails but last night was a blizzard. My digital alarm is blinking and stuck at 0335 am. I am not going anywhere today on my all-weather tires slightly worn and front wheel drive. I stay in my slippers. I call in at 9 am. Recorded message says that the office is closed. A text from the boss says work from home and report for work on Saturday, if possible. I open all of the curtains. It is beautiful out there. I will clear snow from my car later.

It's just you and me, Felicia. It looks like we got enough food. We got power. I better set the faucets dripping. Pipes might freeze. Staring out my kitchen window, I see action at the bird feeder. Life goes on. Mainly humans get stuck. I wonder what Roy is doing. He is a school teacher. I forgot to mention that. It is likely that he also has the day off and will work from home.

I switch to office software on my Apple. By noon I have processed the usual emails which hit my desk daily. Roy calls on my land line. We agree to stay safe and snug. By afternoon the sun has broken through. I check online. Walgreen's is open. I put on my army boots, grab my ski poles, and don my heaviest parka and gloves. I can hoof it over there. It is only 7 blocks. I want to get those personal items on my list and a few other things.

By 2 pm I am home. I get the car cleared off and the sidewalk shoveled and the bird feeder filled. Today is my big chance to watch *The Young and the Restless*. I gave up on taping it long ago. I get updates at work. Mom calls. Yes, I am okay.

She wants to know about Robert. I say we start as friends. Then I shut down her inquiries. Robert meets Darla. Perfect.

Hot chocolate! Yes, that is what I need now. Come on, Felicia. Let's get back in bed. Jude Frawley and Sue Bridehead have decided to forgo marriage and live together unwed, in Victorian England, no less. No way! This will not have a happy ending, unlike true life Roy and

Sarah Jane. The power of positive thinking is kicking in. The power of prayer couldn't hurt either. Perhaps they are somehow related.

Friday, January 14

Dear Diary, The office opens at 10 am today. The Malibu is plenty warm and totally defrosted on my departure. I spend most of the morning dispatching maintenance crew to sand the stairways and hiring extra snow plow service for the parking lots. Roy calls at lunch per usual. He also reported late for teaching. We decide to meet at Clyde's Road House on US 1 in Walpole 'round about 5:30 pm. It's a dive bar. It's come as you are. We agree to come direct from work. He works a little late on lesson plans to get us synchronized.

I freshen up a little before departure. Felicia has her weekend feeder and extra scratch box in place. She knows the drill. Roy is waiting at the bar. I check him out before he sees me. It's not too late to run away. Now he sees me. He gives a wave and a hint of a smile. I zoom right in for a hug, like chums who have known each other forever. We get a table way in the back. It's early. The music is loud, oldies and some country. To hear each other, we sit side by side. Truck drivers like the place and they tip well. Service is good.

We start with beer in a frosted glass. No sipping, down the hatch. "You get the face to go with the voice, finally. Stare all you want," I tell him. "You'll do very nicely," he replies. "We'll never be nervous with each other. I guarantee you that," I add. "Now let's order. I am really hungry. We'll go Dutch. We'll pool our resources. I like cash. How 'bout you?" He checks his wallet. He's got 5 twenties fresh from the ATM. I've got $80 and change, my cash back from Walgreen's. "I think we're good," he says. We order appetizers, 3 kinds to share. I pocket my cash and check my coat and my purse. There is a postage stamp size dance floor. One other couple is out there. A slow dance begins. "Let's dance off that beer," I insist. "It's just a hug set to music, like so," as I proceed to put his hands just where I want them. Our appetizers come. I ask him about whiskey. He knows a little. We each have a shot of Johnny Walker Black. "Nice smokey taste," I say and then "It's getting a little warm in here." This is my cue to strip off my sweater and underneath, of course is the peek-a-boo blouse, no bra required. I can't stop smiling. "You have an infectious grin," he reports. "You've got me halfway mellowed out." Another slow dance should finish the job. He is melting in my arms. Main course arrives. They have a super "Surf and Turf", side salad, baked potato, sour cream. We linger over it. We dance it off. Coffee, ice cream, another drink, this time Jack Daniels. I go to the Pandora jukebox. I dial up George Thorogood: *One Bourbon, One Scotch and One Beer.*

We promise not to talk about anything serious. We do not question each other about past partners. The main compatibility question is already being answered. He is at ease and my Tomboy body is working for him. Never married, no kids, no stretch marks, almost a virgin.

By now it is almost 9 o'clock. The place is getting crowded. Under the table, I put a hand on Roy's thigh. "Let's get out of here," I say. "I have an idea." While we are getting our coats on, I remote start my car. "Let's sober up in my car," I add. "Are you with me?" "Roger that," was his reply, my man of few words. We get in back. We keep each other warm. We count our money. We got $70 left. "Let's camp out," I suggest. "Our campsite is right next door, The Boston View Motel otherwise known as "The View for a Few". It's $40. They take cash. I asked them to show me a room once. They are old but clean. We can park in the back. We'll be safe there from cops and drunk drivers. After we pay the room, we'll have $30 left for breakfast."

We park my Malibu and his Jeep, discreetly in back. We register. "We've had too much to drink," I say. "We need a room." They have a room in back second floor, number 9A. It's quiet, no traffic noise, no parties, but cold. We turn on the heat. The towels are threadbare. The mattress is lumpy. The color TV can display only green and white pixels. MeTV channel has Perry Mason. We buy toothbrush and toothpaste from a vending machine. We freshen up. "Do we agree this is not a one-night stand?" I ask. "Two nights, at least, for sure," he says with a grin.

"Take your clothes off," I command "We'll shower together to conserve water." The view was not bad. He must work out.

"Get the bathroom steamed up. I'll join you in a minute," I promise. Then it's "Ready or not, here I come." Inside the shower, the steam puts me in soft focus. "Lather me up," I say. "Then I'll do you." By the time I got done with the private parts my new man confesses: "That's the best hand job I ever had, including the ones I gave myself," he quips. "We can save the B.J.'s for next time," I tease. "Those will always be a special reward," I add. Now warm up the bed and turn off the lights. I will join you in a minute," I promise.

The room is dark except for some parking lot lights through slits in the curtains. We leave the tv on low volume for a bit of ambient light and sound. I sneak under the covers from the bottom kissing legs up to balls and then up to chest 'til I reach the face. I give tongue in the ear with hot breath. "I like to ride on top," I announce. "No pressure, I'll get myself off. First, the rubber, which I have placed conveniently under the pillow." I get myself off. I keep the vocalizations soft and sensual. After a quick clean up, I announce that I am ready to sleep but please get a soda from the machine in the hall, anything will do. He comes back with a Dr. Pepper and a Ginger Ale.

Perry Mason solves the case as we drink. The secretary did it. I've seen this one before. "Are you happy?" I ask. "Are you glad you met me? Can we make it a hundred-night stand?" "Yes, yes, and yes!" he replies. "Hand jobs and blow jobs and horsey rides, your basic stuff, no kink, no three ways. That is what I offer. Are you in or are you out?" I demand. "I am in. We can put it in writing, if you like," he affirms. "I sleep on my stomach. I require a back tickle. Try not to snore. Look at that. It's exactly midnight," these were my final words. I vaguely remember a back tickle proceeding ever downwards to my bare ass. I wake up once. He is using my ass for a pillow.

Saturday, January 15

Dear Diary, Everything is wonderful on our first date. We enjoy afterglow in the morning from the spoon position. He was behind me. I feel a big boner there. Why waste it? A hard man is good to find. "Care for a refill?" he asks. "Fill 'er up," I reply. The sex is turning out really good. I have read about this. We make the pleasure bond first and the love comes along little by little. He is already in love with my ass.

My hero runs across the road for coffee at the Shell station while I finish dressing. I watch him from the window. My life was so simple. Now it's 'gonna get complicated. Over coffee, I explain why I want everything we do to be secret and totally private. It's because of Mom always running interference and it's simply more fun this way, sneaking around that is, even though we don't need to. "Works for me," says my hero.

He lives in Canton, a duplex, not far. I follow him there. It's a dump but I don't care, as long as no roaches. There are dishes in the sink. He washes them once a week. The place is a mess but he knows where everything is. We do laundry. We put down clean sheets. We test his bed, a quickie. Good thing I brought lots of rubbers although certainly his potency must be getting depleted by now. I draw him a map to my apartment. We agree to meet after Church, afternoon delight at my place. "On the weekend," I promise, "you get to screw your secret girlfriend as often as you like. You don't even need to be romantic. Once you are totally in love with me forever, then you can be romantic." As I am leaving, he turns on football playoffs. There are 2 dried pieces of pizza in a box on the couch. He offers me one. I decline. "More for me," he says with a grin.

Felicia is waiting for me. I take care of her and give her love. Suddenly, I want to head over to Dedham Square. It's a beautiful day. I go to Café Fresh Bagel. Rick is there but he can't recall my name. After a while, Charlotte and Charlotte appear. "Ravi de vous revoir," I tell them. They help me with pronunciation. I start with phrases for food.

We enjoy patisseries. I bid them au revoir. I soak up winter sunshine. It feels good.

Sunday, January 16

Dear Diary, I go to Mass at St. Theresa's here in West Roxbury, instead of St. Mary's in Dedham where the whole fam-damily always goes. I tell Mom I made some friends at St. Theresa and it's closer and I want to walk to an early Mass. I tell her I'll see her for dinner and rang off quickly. I enjoy the walk of 1.5 miles. Roy likes Dos Equis beer. They have it at the Speedy Mart on my way home. I get a 6 pack and two frozen pizzas. I am home by 10 o'clock.

I find my old cheerleader outfit from Dedham High, 21 years ago. It still fits. After a Woolite wash and rinse, it is good as new. Roy calls at 11 o'clock. He is just getting up. He was binge watching something 'til 2 am. He had vegged out all the remainder of Saturday since I left him. I tell him that I'll be waiting, unless I get a better offer. He shows up at 1 pm, unshaven. He never shaves on Sunday. He does shower, though. I can smell the Irish Spring.

We shove the pizzas in the oven and set a timer for 20 minutes. We are all over each other on the couch for the full 20. We crack 2 beers while the pizza cools. He says he requires a frosted glass. I put 2 on ice. He is comical in one of my old over-sized terry cloth robes. My TV is pitifully small compared to his giant Sony. "Only 20 more payments on that," he notes.

The Steelers are playing the Ravens. At half time, I come out in my cheerleader outfit. "I've never done it with a cheerleader," he confessed. "Well, here's your big chance," I announce. "Beg for it. Kneel down and beg and I'll let you get under the skirt." He begs. We clear away the coffee table and pretend that the carpet is the 50-yard line. He is done ravaging cheerleader Sara Jane sometime during the 3rd quarter. Then I tell him that I am due at my parents for dinner. I say, "Here take the leftover pizza, and get out now or I'll be late and questions will be asked.

You'll be home in time for the late game. You can screw me a bunch more times next weekend. Off you go." "Agreed. Screw a bunch more times next weekend. Got it," he repeats. I watch him drive off. He seems very happy indeed.

Monday, January 17

Dear Diary, I am pleased with myself. Can it possibly last? Wow! I am a little sore this morning. That sure was a lot of action over the weekend. We were both overdue. What if I get knocked up? Maybe I should get on the pill. Does Roy ever want to be a Dad? Do I ever want to be a Mom and when is too late? Should we ever live together? So many burning questions but we've given ourselves a year to answer them. For now, let it be carefree. I still have a career path to plot. Maybe I can get a promotion.

Roy calls at his usual time. I ask him if he is sore because I sure am. I tell him we got it on four times over the weekend and does he care to try for five? He says, "I'm man enough, if you're woman enough." "Eat your Wheaties," I advise. He admits "Yes, I'm sore because you're so wonderfully nice and tight." After lunch. Susan says she heard me saying something about being sore. I told her I need more stretching at Yoga.

I go outside after lunch. Today is partly cloudy. Phil is out there smoking. He asks if I am seeing anyone. I tell him yes and she's very jealous. "I'll believe that when I see the two of you kissing," he replies. Now I'm thinking about that song by Katie Perry. If Roy asks me to kiss a girl, I might do it just for him. Girls are always kissing. It's no big deal. I saw some lesbos kissing in Dedham High School locker room. It didn't bother me.

I ask Susan about Phil. She says she thinks he's married or maybe separated and he smokes too much. There is time for plenty of gossip this afternoon. Joni, the part timer wants to fix me up with a guy. I tell her I never do blind dates. We all agree that we should have girls' night out on Super Sunday.

I am home early again today. I have time for a walk over to Bellevue Hill Park. I come home ravenously hungry. Maybe I should try some recipes. Roy says he likes leftovers. I'll cook for two and save him some. We'll be needing lots of energy. Pork chops and sauerkraut tonight. I try one of the Dos Equis. I believe they call that an ass-kicking beer. Lights go out early tonight but I find it hard to sleep. I put a pillow between my legs, hug another one and rock myself to sleep.

Tuesday, January 18

Dear Diary, Do you like what I am writing? Would anyone ever enjoy reading my secrets? Or am I just jerking off? Decades from now, this book will be boxed up in a dusty attic somewhere. A teen-age girl or maybe a spinster like me will find it, start reading and think "Holy Shit! This is really dirty, but in a good way!" I just realized that yesterday was MLK Day. I thought traffic was lighter than usual.

Roy called again at lunch today. He is really proud of himself. Yesterday, on the no school holiday, he cleaned up his man cave, his garage. He parks outside except when he is changing his oil. He doesn't want a garage door opener. The signal can be hacked. He doesn't want people to see what he's got in there, tools and such. He keeps the garage securely locked down and alarmed. He only goes in there from the kitchen door access. The way he has got it, bugs can't get in from outside either, which is a good thing. He is very pleased that I don't mind slumming it with him. When I took him to a zero-star, Mom and Pop, truck stop motel, that was his first clue that he could just relax and not worry about expectations. He is Tarzan and he needs his Jungle Jane who will not complain about things like the toilet seat being up. In the man cave, he's got an old leather couch which he bought at estate sale. He wants to do me on that old leather couch. The gossip topic of the week is now: Man-caves we have seen. Did the man do you there and was it only because you were drunk?

I work late until traffic clears. I need to get a head start on the new tenant move-in packets. Also, there will be a meeting about a new advertising campaign. I do not work well at home. As soon as I get home, maybe some cooking, but otherwise, total laziness. I make a shopping list. On my way home I make a detour over to Centre St. to shop at Marino's Market and Deli for all kinds of sandwich stuff, fresh greens, and pasta ingredients. I am fixed for the week. I have never put much effort into my cuisine, but now, cooking for two, it could be fun and Roy can be my prep-chef. Or just stare at the sex object soon to be love object.

Wednesday, January 19

Dear Diary, The forecast is for warm and overcast. I drive to work with the windows down. Right away there is a crisis at work. A tenant has moved out without notice and left his cat behind. In the key drop box is a note. "I know I lose my deposit. Please use it to take care of Fatima. She was stray and I can't take her with me. Beware because she will get out if you are not careful." The housekeeping crew brings her over to the office in a cardboard box. She is a kitten, long-hair Calico. The girls love her on the spot but I am only one who can take her home. We give her some half and half from the coffee bar. An ex-employee left a can of sardines in the lunch room closet. We give her just one minced sardine. If she eats too much, she will likely throw up.

Several people call looking for the missing tenant. We give no information per protocol. Fatima sleeps away the afternoon. The girls give her a hug and kiss goodbye. They take pictures with their flip phones. I put the box on the passenger's side floor. Are my maternal instincts flowering this late in the game? I skip yoga so I can go straight home. Felicia is very curious about the contents of the box. In the neutered Felicia, does there remain any remnants of maternal instinct?

She had just the one litter before her operation. I put Fatima in a big plastic laundry basket with a fluffy towel. She is wary. Felicia stares intently and circles the basket, then stands guard during the remainder of my evening routine. She routinely stands guard daily at my windows against outdoors cats lurking about.

Roy calls on my private land line. It's nice to talk with no fear of being overheard. Just think of it. I have got a boyfriend who calls me every day without fail. I have waited a long time for that comfort and security. We are both sleepy. It's quiet. It's late. We are 10 miles apart but connected. We have our secret. We finally say goodnight. I light a candle, lavender scented. I look through the curtains at the empty street. The little one is asleep and safe in her new home. Felicia jumps up. She nuzzles me. She settles in beside me. She knows she will always be number one.

Thursday, January 20

Dear Diary, I am awake early, 6 am, per usual. Traffic noise starts at 5:30 am. I hardly ever need the alarm. My girls are hungry. I set up separate food and water bowls for each. The new arrival will complicate weekend plans. I bundle up, all woolens and faux fur against a sudden cold snap. I have time to stop at Recreo Roasterie on Centre St. to replenish the break room with fresh grind. I connect over to VFW Parkway on residential Corey Street. I have a pleasant commute almost every day. It's just about 4 miles, depending on which route I choose. I can even get there on the Number 51 Bus when the car is in the shop. I have got it made. There is no reason in the world not to be happy, now that Roy is on the scene. What could go wrong? Don't even think about it.

At work, I am dispatching the maintenance crew today. There are a few frozen pipes, but none have burst. Someone has filed a missing-persons report on our tenant who skipped out. His rent was paid up. He doesn't owe us anything. We pray it is not foul play. I only met him once, when he moved in almost two years ago. Here is a fresh topic for office gossip. Other than removal of the cat, the efficiency unit has not yet been cleaned and inspected. The Police are there looking for clues. Susan once dated a police detective. He never talked about his work.

I proceed homeward early on my new favorite, mainly residential route. I have got to do this weekend on the cheap. My girls are waiting for me. I'll make some kitten toys from whatever sundry items I can find at home. Cooking for two, tonight is lasagna, with plenty left over. While it is baking, I stare out the window. I have got a sticky bird bell hanging from a tree. It is packed with seeds, nuts and dried bugs. The Blackbirds have located it. It won't last long now. I call Roy to see what he is making for dinner. It's a stir fry. He is trying out sesame oil.

Wow! Who would have imagined? In his dump of a kitchen, he actually has some ingredients. He plans to give me a math test when I come over. I had statistics in college. That might help.

Fatima is using the scratch box. The girls are getting along nicely.

Friday, January 21

Dear Diary, I sit up in bed at six. I stretch and greet the weekend. I know good stuff is about to happen. Fatima is trying to get up in the bed but she can't quite make it yet. Felicia is getting used to her new companion although sometimes she wearies of the endless playfulness. I pull the curtains open wide to see first light. Today is payday. I bring bagels to work.

Police are in the office again asking about everyone who called looking for the mystery missing tenant. One was a woman who would not give her name. She said his phone is disconnected. Maybe he owes child support. Everyone wants to solve the case. We become amateur sleuths. I think he has gone into federal witness protection or deep undercover.

Roy calls mid-afternoon between his Geometry and Trigonometry classes. He likes to use the old-fashioned phone booth at the main entrance to Canton High. Inside a phone booth is private and he can speak freely. He had his Wheaties this morning. He thinks we can establish a new personal best of the wild thing times 5, starting tonight. He works in his office until 4:30 pm. He meets me at my door at 5 pm sharp. He brings an overnight bag including a bottle of Chianti, the kind that sits in a decorative wicker base. I dig around in my closet and produce a checkered tablecloth I once found at a church rummage sale.

It is nice and warm in the kitchen. I decide to cook topless. My tits are the appetizer. Roy makes the salad. His grandmother is full blooded Italian. In her kitchen as a boy, his job was to make the dressing from scratch. He says don't expect him to dine with a giant boner. While the tomato sauce is thickening on low heat, we have a quickie in the semi-privacy of my walk-in pantry. It is the first time in my sex history that I get off standing up. We linger over dinner for an hour. I set a timer. I will see if my personal porno star can be ready again in an hour. He freshens up first and comes out in tighty-whities. Obvious from the bulge, it is time for scene two. The porno stars schedule scene three for early morning. Meanwhile, on this sleep-over the leading man enjoys the luxuries of a plush, fresh scented woman's bedroom.

Saturday, January 22

Dear Diary, On weekends with Roy, I write to you after he falls asleep. I write in the kitchen. I need a drink anyway. It's Saturday night and I have custody of my man except it seems I have to share him with Fatima. We finally let her up on the bed after sex scene number five. Felicia is loyal to me. She is beside me as I write. Roy and I celebrated our feat of sex prowess with the last two beers. They knocked him out but not me.

We had a lot of action today. It turns out it's easy to screw five times in two days if they are all quickies. We went outside before each time today. The morning excursion was to Speedy Market. We tried the salted caramel coffee. We walked home on side streets. The afternoon excursion was by his car to Turtle Pond. The evening excursion was the Saturday Vigil Mass, where Roy and I pretended to be strangers. He followed me home, saying he saw me at Church and it was love at first sight and could he be my boyfriend? I said I would give him an audition.

Cold air delivers oxygen more efficiently, I have heard. We fed on leftovers I had piled up. Then he had his audition. I said wait for a call back. I had to deal with Mom, of course. I told her to meet me for bagels after her Mass on Sunday. We finished watching Dr. Zhivago, a chick flick. I said I liked the Klaus Kinski character, Kostoyed. Roy called him Klaus Kinky. He says he doesn't care much for Julie Christie as the blond, Lara. He much prefers Geraldine Chaplin as the brunette, Tonya. He complains about what are you showing me this for, there's no nudity. That's when he gets bored with Zhivago and goes muff diving for hot breath on the full brunette bush. I ask why doesn't he want to see the end because it's so sad. He replies, "I'm busy." I eject the DVD. He comes out from under the sheet and asks, "Bring me a beer, dear. I need it bad," He slams the beer and adds, "Roy needs to sleep, right now." Then he gives me a peck on the cheek, rolls over and is fast asleep in no time flat. So here we are, Dear Diary, just what I was hoping for, and even more, but now how do I make it last? Just be myself, maybe, fun-loving spontaneous, and walking around naked a lot.

Sunday, January 23

Dear Diary, I hear Roy showering. He appears with towel around waist. He was watching me sleeping a few minutes ago. He says I look like an angel while in repose and the under the cover curves were tempting but he has to go. I say, "No! Don't Go! You're mine!" He says he'll call me later. I ask him to pick me up and deposit me at the kitchen table otherwise I'll get lazy. Another fantasy comes true. My man carries me in his arms. He smells good too. Dove shower scrub works for guys. On the table is my Math Test. He says it is open book test of all High School Math and he will correct my test next weekend.

My girls and I have breakfast. In the shower, I decide what to wear at Dedham Square. It's 'gonna be jeans, flannel shirt, army boots and parka. Mom won't like it but she's got to love me as I am per my whim of the day. We meet at Big Bear Cafe on High St., 11 am. Of course, she goes on about Robert and did we meet and how he would be perfect for me. I say maybe too perfect and yes, we met and we're kind of just pals and anything more is private. I change the subject to church activities and how for winter, I want the Saturday Vigil in my neighborhood. I tell her I've got to have my own territory not much overlapping with hers. For the first time I begin to feel in control of the encounters with Mom. She is glad I seem to have a healthy glow, not depressed. By noon, she is gone home to start dinner.

I call Charlotte, the daughter. I leave a message. I call Charlotte, the mother. She answers. I ask her if she is coming over. That's a yes and we agree to meet across the street at Cafe Paradiso. I study the two of them. Is it possible that I could actually enjoy meeting Mom, instead of dreading it? The daughter will be going to college next fall. I tell her about Providence, what it was like there but that was 20 years ago. Charlotte, the mother is 45. She got married straight out of college. What was that like I want to know? They leave to go shopping. I walk around the square in cold air. Roy calls just before Packers at Bears. He says he misses me already. I read one more chapter of Jude and his love, desperate and doomed.

Monday, January 24

Dear Diary, I bring my math test to work so I can puzzle over it at lunch all this week. I seems like I am not very good at solving for "X". There are no more calls for Reggie, the missing tenant who left behind his cat. The Police are finished snooping around. We hope it was not foul play. What if a private detective is on the case also? I predict we have not heard the last of this.

Meanwhile, we are free to rent the unit to someone new. After the cleaning crew is done, I go there on inspection. It is Building 6, Apt. G. Maybe I will find a clue. These units were built in the 1950's. A long litany of prior occupants are associated with 6-G. A little piece of each of them might remain. What have these walls seen? I take photos of minor damage with the office digital. Probably it is time to replace the appliances. I check the mailbox. There is a hand-written personal letter. We do not have a forwarding address. It will be returned to sender. I take a picture of the letter in case it becomes significant. I return the letter and the camera to Sandy, the office manager.

After lunch, I prepare empty ink cartridges for FedEx pick-up. We always check out the FedEx guy. Susan and I have time for a mid-afternoon coffee break. She says that she is in love but cannot say more. I told her I am in lust with a guy but I, as well, can't say more. We touch on the biological clock. My brother, James and sister, Sally both are younger and both have kids. Do I really need to have some of my own? I could get pregnant, accidentally, recklessly knocked-up. Mainly, I just want to keep my man. He is good enough and getting better by the day.

Sunset is 4:48 pm. I drive home surrounded by snow turned deep blue at twilight. Tonight, is salad night. My girls are getting along. I have 2 sets of yellow eyes staring at me from under the bed when Roy calls at 10 pm. There are no football games this weekend so the possibilities are endless. Saturday night, dinner and a movie would be nice. "I choose the theater, you choose the movie," I say. "You're on," he concurs. Friday is still wide open, play it by ear, some kind of spontaneous adventure, no need to plan it, with my wonderful almost too good to be true Secret Guy.

Tuesday, January 25

Dear Diary, I woke up with the ticklish whiskers of the kitten, Fatima in my face. She has become one of multiple alarms which ensure that I am up by 6 am daily. I let her follow me to the shower. The under-sink cabinet is empty. She likes to sit it in there and watch my morning rituals. In the shower, I shave legs and armpits. I have got plenty of time to let my hair air dry. A hair dryer in the bathroom is scary. I do some poses, robe open, in the full-length mirror. I think I am ready for my first nude photo shoot, the old-fashioned way. Nothing digital. On the fridge is a new reminder. "Get the old Pentax from Dad."

It's super cold and clear outside. Plenty of birds are at the feeder. The Sparrows are making a racket. I whip up a full breakfast. I take the longest, slowest, least traffic route, five miles, 25 minutes due to red lights and stop signs. It's a typical, routine, boring, forgettable day at work until I reveal my modeling aspirations. I wonder if Susan or Sandy have done any kind of photo shoot in reckless youth or full maturity. Sandy says that she was an artist's model in college. "It was kind of fun being naked, like a two-year old with no shame," she admits. Sandy ordered a new stove for 6-G. The new tenant, Sheila, will move in on February 15th. Since there was a cat there, the carpet will be removed and the unit will become one of our new hypo-allergenic units with hardwood floor restoration. Wait a minute. That gives me an idea. Maybe there is a future for me in Interior Design. How much school will it be? Maybe night school?

We do pretend job interviews on each-other, starting with the old stand-by: "Where do you see yourself in ten years?" Susan replies, "I see myself as CEO of a Fortune 500 Company." "Let's not waist any more time. You're hired," I pronounce. Tammy, the temp asks me, "So, Miss Powell, how would you handle the co-worker with a difficult personality trait, like talks too much, won't shut up?" "I would ask an expert," I reply. "All of us would follow the advice of the expert." "Okay, interviews are over. Shut-up and get back to work, you chatter-boxes," orders Sandy.

Wednesday, January 26

Dear Diary, I dreamed I was an artist, a painter, making a portrait in oils, of myself, full length, full frontal nude, no modesty, no shame. I want to paint 6-G, make it all fresh and cheerful for the new tenant.

Why am I fixated on this unit? It's the mystery of Reggie, the man who disappeared, and Sheila, the woman who is moving in. What is her story? Maybe we can help each-other. I begin to think of tenants as family. I have files on all of them. Contact persons, background checks, credit scores, birthday, marital status, how many pets and how large, make of vehicle and license tag number, how many children and their ages. Some are divorced and the children come on visitation.

In my kitchen, Felicia and Fatima sit and stare at me. "Okay, girls, be good," I say. It's time to go. I roll down my driver's side window. It's warm enough. High of 40 predicted today. I take temporary distraction in the mindless chatter of the FM morning wake up show. Right away I find out that 6-G will be a full remodel. The guys have pulled up the old shag carpet. They found a necklace smooshed under a corner in the bedroom. They pulled out the old stove and fridge. Behind were more traces of tenants past. Under and behind, what wonders one may find.

Roy calls at lunch. He says he is getting really horny for me by mid-week. At 16:30, the remodel crew brings a cardboard box with the found items. The necklace is sterling silver chain and Maltese cross, with 4 small emeralds. On the back is the inscription: "To Sylvia, All My Love Forever, James, 7-1-52." "Holy crap, that's really old," Susan comments. We must store this item in our lost and found for 1 year. We wonder how long it was there. The rug was last replaced 4 years ago. Under the fridge and behind the stove the following were found: A match book with a local phone number inside, a pencil, a pen from a hardware store, 3 pennies, a dime, a cigarette butt with lipstick and a Dunkin Donuts receipt dated March 10, 2010, for a small coffee and a buttered bagel. One or more of those items could be a useful clue for Nancy Drew.

At home food bowls are empty and litter boxes are full.

Thursday, January 27

Dear Diary, I am so ready for the weekend. I might have to limp my way through the day. Roy calls in the morning, not like it is his duty but just to hear my voice. The cold air outside helps me wake up. It must be winter doldrums. Brighter lights and sheer curtains for the kitchen might help plus more time outside during day, like maybe a winter beach stroll.

Yoga will help. I have been neglecting my yoga. Yesterday, I snatched that matchbook with phone number from the trash. I am tempted to do a reverse lookup on it. I'll leave it in back of my top desk drawer for now. I box up old records for scanning. I compile occupancy stats for all of our properties. I volunteer for clean out the break room fridge duty. All have been warned. Once a month, if it needs it or not. I mask up against moldy left-overs stuck in the back.

My desk is clear. I leave at 16:15. I can make the 5 pm Yoga class at the Blissful Monkey. I keep my leotard and mat in the back seat. During stretches, I check myself in the wall mirrors. I like what I see. Leggings are on my shopping list. They are max comfort, form-fitting. Roy will go wild at the sight. Back home, I make meatloaf with mashed potatoes and gravy. I finish "Jude" while doing laundry in the basement. What a tearjerker!

Lindsey from upstairs comes down with 2 loads. She is even more tomboy than me, younger, in her twenties, kind of brooding and sullen. I ask her if she likes cats. I bring them down during dry cycle. They like to snoop around down there. They rub against Lindsey's legs, recognizing a kindred spirit. She gives Felicia a chin scratch and Fatima a cuddle. She says she does photography, fine art. I say knock on my door if you ever need something, like quarters for the dryer. My girls ride back upstairs on top of the towels.

I treat myself to a bubble bath. My girls have fun with the soap bubbles. I get in bed early. I want this day to be over so I can sleep and wake up to my Friday, my weekend, my Secret Guy. He misses me. He loves me. He wants to keep me, indefinitely, or until his dick wears out, ha!

Friday, January 28

Dear Diary, Roy calls at 7 am. I tell him just come over about 7 pm. I got lots of food, don't need to spend money. But there is bad news. I am on the rag. It started this morning. The good news is he should get ready for blow jobs and dry humping. The pad will stay on. Is it a turn off? He says he can handle it.

At work, now I find they are ripping out the old water heater in 6-G. It will be inline water heater. It will be the first energy efficient ultra-modern remodel, including LED lighting and new windows. The extra space allows an over-under laundry unit. The workers let me watch daily progress. I call Sheila and ask her what color paint she prefers.

Susan and I go walking after lunch. The sun comes out. It seems we are both expecting company tonight. At home there is a post-it on my door from Lindsey. I go up there to see her place. We make a deal. She will be my first interior design customer. I will redecorate her place if she will do my figure studies.

It's pretty obvious that she is gay. She wants her love life all secret and private, same as me. She can meet Roy, but not know his name or anything about him. She can meet Robert also, same deal. She can just guess the status of each and if I might even be a pro. I ask her if I can use her as forbidden fruit because, she is Roy's type, not far different from my look, except younger. She can show my nudes to some of her girlfriends, then I will be the forbidden fruit in their horny minds. We agree this is an innocent way to spice things up. It's nice to be on good terms with the upstairs neighbor, some support in crisis, an extra solid in my network.

Roy arrives promptly at 7 pm. I answer the door topless. The cold air makes the nipples stand up. We do our dry humping in the pantry. He creams his jeans in no time flat. He cleans up and comes back commando. We have dinner, 3 kinds of leftovers. We go outside for a walk around the block. Lindsey takes a look through her curtains. On return, one vodka shot makes me slutty enough for Roy's first blow job, him standing, me sitting. I blindfold him and tell him to whip it out.

Saturday, January 29

Dear Diary, Roy is there in my bed at crack of dawn. We wake up with cuddles. I make him a big breakfast and off he goes. He has stuff to do in his man cave. I have some quality time with my girls. Hours away is Saturday Night, date night. We already have our plan.

It is Roy's choice of movie, Kon-Tiki, a recreation of a 1947 Pacific crossing on raft by Thor Heyerdahl. It's at Dedham Community Theater, right there on the square. This theater is known for arty independent and foreign films. This is definitely a guy flick, action and adventure on the high seas. It is my choice of restaurant, Oscar's just a few doors down from the theater. We plan to do the early show and late dinner.

My girls are happy up on the window ledges while I shower. I come out in my robe just in time to greet Lindsey at my door. Already I am like her big sister. She wants to check out the lighting in my apartment. She takes some meter readings at the various windows and doorways. Like me, she prefers all of her lovers to be secret. Like me, there have been very few. We take a walk together to Walgreen's. I restock my rubbers. She says that lucky for her, she never needs those which allows extra money for film.

On return, Roy calls for an update. I ask him to come by Taxi because of parking and possible cocktails on board during dinner. We meet at 6 pm to get our tickets, then we go get coffee. We endure extreme bitter cold. I take Roy's arm. He holds me tight under the Saturday night city lights. We jostle along the crowded sidewalk. At 18:30, we get our giant tub of popcorn, popped in olive oil and soaked in real butter. We look at paintings in the lower vestibule. It is the notorious MOBA, aka "The Museum of Bad Art", art too bad to be ignored, collected from second hand shops and trash heaps then nicely curated and hilariously reviewed with faint praise by genuine art critics. I love the movie, anything about the ocean. I promise to take Roy to Cape Cod, Martha's Vineyard, Nantucket, and Rhode Island beaches, along the way, stopping at Providence, my old stomping ground.

Randy is on duty at Oscar's. The bar seating is nearly full. We check our coats. Roy agrees to pretend we are strangers one more time. I put on my fake wedding ring. I grab a solo bar stool. I order a draft and joke around with Randy. He has seen me in here solo many times. Roy comes over at a standing room spot and pretends to watch the Bruins Hockey game. A couple is called to a free table for second seating. Roy says, "Do you mind?" and grabs the newly vacated stool next to me. I give him barely a glance and say, "It's a free country." Randy is watching me operate. I order an appetizer. Roy says, "That looks good." He orders the same. I tell him "I'm married." Roy says "Well, I won't hold that against you." Because of the movie, we both want seafood. Eventually, we both order dinner at the bar. He has shrimp. I have salmon. Roy says, "Let me guess your age." That's his excuse to look me up and down. "I would say 29, not a day older." Randy suppresses a laugh. I show my driver's license, holding my thumb over the name. "No way!" Roy acts amazed. By now, it's 10 pm. We have after dinner drinks. I pretend to be tipsy. Roy says, "I'm a divorce lawyer. I can spot a jilted woman from across the room. We should go somewhere for a consult this very night." "The only consult you are going to get is a Psychiatric consult," I reply. I nod to Randy and he brings the bills. Roy says, "At least let me pay for this." He throws down cash and adds "Keep the change." I close my purse and say "Well if you insist." Roy is coming up with some really good stuff here. He helps me on with my coat. Finally, he says "I usually don't beg, but now I am begging you for just one kiss." He takes me by the shoulders and gets ready to plant one. I turn my head so that he only gets a kiss on the cheek. I leave. Roy goes back to the bar. Randy says, "Fella, you worked hard and paid a lot for just a kiss on the cheek." Roy slams one more drink and says, "It was worth it!" We meet up outside. Our driver, Dave, is there. I tell Dave "This is Derek. We're drunk on a one-night stand." We can't stop laughing. At home, Roy plays with the cats while I write all this down. We do chastity for a change until morning.

Sunday, January 30

Dear Diary, It was worth the wait for me to get astride my stallion. We shower together, washing the other's back, towel each other off.

We walk to 9 am Mass, sitting in separate pews. I wear my little gloves and hat, just for church, all dainty and prim. After mass is glorious full sun and blue sky on fresh overnight snow. I take Roy's arm. I tell him that he is my hero, the first to flirt me at a bar and he did it super cool and smooth. He says that I am the first to go home with him after the flirt.

No football today, no NFL, how strange. What to do? What to do? I know! I drive Roy home. We get coffee at Speedy Market followed by the traditional Sunday drive after church. I take a scenic route, dead reckoning through Boston southern suburban sprawl. He shows me houses he likes. I do the same. Further out is more affordable. We see one we both like in Sharon. It is for sale. Today is open house. We take the tour and imagine what to do with each room. It has a full basement with man cave written all over it. A seed of jointly owned domicile is planted. Will it flourish?

I have my math test. I left it in my car. Roy clears off his kitchen table and gets out his red pen. It's not looking good, a lot of red. I end up with a 25% on my High School Math Test. I blame Dedham High Math teacher there whom I hated, Mr. Hesse. He was mean, plus I was never very good at solving for "X". I did well on all of the Geometry shapes. Roy congratulated me. I remembered the Parallelogram, the Rhombus, the Trapezoid and The Pythagorean Theorem. "Oh yeah," I told him. "Pythagoras and I go way back. He was my boyfriend in a previous life. Don't be jealous. It was a long time ago and he wasn't near as good as you in bed. We got tangled up in the toga too often." We exchange some deep wet winter kisses and off I go.

Sunday afternoon includes girl talk with Lindsey. She explains what it's like in her world of woman love. Mom gets a routine call. My secret remains safe, it seems.

Monday, January 31

Dear Diary, Is it too good to be true? Thirty days ago, I was in Purgatory. Now it seems like I have died and gone to Heaven. What could go wrong? Plenty! We'll head all that off at the pass.

Meanwhile, got to work, work, work, for my felines, for my man, for me, myself and I. More snow means drive slow. First, stay alive, survive. All else is a bonus. Work at a deliberate pace. The minutes tick by. Morning break is gossip. Lunch break means go outside. Phil is there on his cell. He winks at me. He thinks he's got me figured out. Maybe he does. In no time flat, it's afternoon break and Roy calls. He says I look like an angel, sitting there in church.

At home, I finish all leftovers. I look outside. Not a soul to be seen and vehicles are a rare few, proceeding slowly. My book and bed are calling me. No more tragic heroines for now. Tonight, it shall be Sherlock Holmes, an old edition, his best mysteries, yellowed pages, intricate plot lines, a gift from Grandpa Powell, with an inscription thus: "To my Dear Sarah, May you solve all of life's mysteries. Happy Sweet Sixteen. From Grandpa Powell".

This book has followed me from the bedroom where I grew up to dorm rooms to now my sixth apartment. There are a few tales still unread. My girls are beside me. Fatima has gotten up under the covers forming a curious lump which migrates from time to time. Sherlock could certainly solve the enigma of Apartment 6-G and the Lost Necklace. It sounds more like a "Nancy Drew". The National Inquirer might look into it, or the "Unsolved Mysteries" TV show. Maybe it is best not to know what became of the poor slob, Reggie. He wanted to get lost, it seems. So be it.

I begin "A Study in Scarlet". Just about the time the story leads back to the early Mormons, my eyelids get heavy. "Sleep, perchance to dream." I can barely finish this entry, Dear Diary. I do it while it is all fresh in my mind. It's a good thing you are conveniently under the bed. I do not want to forget these happy days. Sleep, Sarah, now you may sleep, says the sandman.

Tuesday, February 1

Dear Diary, I had a dream. I scribbled it on scrap paper as soon as I got up. It is a recurrent dream which winds up being some variation on stuck at the bottom of the ocean. This is ever since the Titanic movie. There is no sound there. It's too far to swim to the surface. I am aware that somewhere down there are those passengers, dead and drowned. I may spot a glow worm crawling about or a phosphorescent squid or a blinking jellyfish looking like a UFO. I search endlessly within the netherworld. I will ask Roy to interpret my dream.

Meanwhile, there is work. Earn your happiness, Sarah Jane, and maybe help someone else along the way. Already, I helped Fatima. Maybe somehow Reggie has found out that his kitten is well cared for. In the blink of an eye I am already parked. I turn off the key. I survey the grayness of the winter morning in my familiar urban landscape and sigh. Let me save this quiet moment alone in the warmth and safety of my Chevy. Twenty years from now, I can look back at this moment and realize that I was happy. Roy would call that extrapolating. I remember that from my experience with graph paper, straight-edge, compass and protractor.

Inside, the phones are clanging. By 10 am, I have cleared my desk. What will be the girl-talk topic of the day? During coffee, we decide to discuss the typical stuff of boyfriend fights. Sandy says the usual fighting is about money, but that's when you're married. Susan has had plenty of boyfriends going all the way back to middle school. She can remember them all. What was the usual theme of all of the fights? "That's easy, jealousy, of course," she declares. I have not had any fights with Roy yet. We should do a practice fight so that a real one won't be too hurtful. I'll be jealous of Cameron, that barista he flirted with. We can't fight at my place. I don't want my girls to see us fighting, even if it is just pretend. There are forbidden words. We talk about this when Roy calls at 10 pm. Roy can't call me the "C" word. I can't call him a douche bag. We'll have make-up sex the same day. There will never be a freeze out. Good plan, Sarah!

Wednesday, February 2

Dear Diary, You have got a live action feed today. Breaking news! Sarah is home sick. I called in at 8 am. Joni, the part-timer will cover. It's fever and chills and sore throat. It happens to me once every winter. Mom comes over with chicken soup and some flu powders to drink with hot tea, honey and lemon. She met Fatima. I gave her some of my old stuff from college days. Phil finally fades away along with the heavy nostalgia. The old stuff all still fits, but it brings back too many bitter-sweet memories. Mom will sell it all at the next church rummage sale. Lots of room in my closet now. I for sure kept the cheerleader costumes.

I take a long hot shower. I really steam the place up. I stay in bathrobe and slippers all day. I prop myself up to watch "The Young and the Restless." I start another Sherlock Holmes tale. This one is titled "The Sign of the Four". Lindsey comes down for a few minutes at supper time. She makes me a hot toddy. She makes friends with Fatima and Felicia. She volunteers to cat sit if needed. I tell her where I hide my extra key.

I make my appointment with "Dr. Roy" to interpret my dream. He will see me on his Saturday morning office hours. He has a Psychology Minor from U Mass. He may even write my "Case History", an appendix to these diary entries. Maybe he will call it "A Case of Nymphomania in an Unmarried 39-year-old". That's me, closet nympho.

What a lazy day. I need some fresh air, just a few breathes standing outside my back entrance. I look up at the stars and vast infinity, such emptiness, the way I felt just a few weeks ago. By the time I sit to write, I feel a little better. I find my scented candles. I turn the heat down. I breathe better in a cool room. I invite my girls up beside me, one on each side. I turn on the radio, NPR, It's a classical music program, Respighi: "Ancient Airs and Dances". Once again, I am aware of how happy I am but also a bit nervous about how easily the bubble could burst. Thomas Hardy is not writing my story. It need not be a tragedy or indictment of society. I am writing my story.

Thursday, February 3

Dear Diary, It was a 24 hour bug. I feel much better today and fit for duty by 10 am. I think about my career ladder. Am I going anywhere upwards or maybe sideways to new territory then upwards? Am I at my final destination? This question could be in my dream somewhere.

On my late lunch I check the 6-G remodel in progress. The hardwood floors are being sanded prior to staining. We have a trendy hypo-allergenic unit, no more replacing of crappy carpeting. More of these units will follow. I will do a demand projection and cost analysis, with some help.

I take a deep breath. The air smells nice. It's good to be outside. My world is opening up. I look south toward Canton, 10 miles away. If I sent up a flare would Roy see it? He is over there trying to teach some young skulls full of mush. What's in store for our Friday? I predict mutual satisfaction. It will be our 4-week anniversary, 4 weeks since the day we met.

Back at my desk, I check on overdue rents. You lose your job and you can't pay your rent. I know what that is like. Five years ago, I lost my job with Remax. There was recession. Not everyone enjoys a 2-income household, nor Mom and Dad to take you in. I took a pay cut to come here but I learned to live with less.

I leave work late, after traffic has cleared. I head home on Lagrange St., stopping at Star Market for my usual essentials. At home, Roy calls in his kitchen report. He is making 4-alarm chili. If we were together 7 nights a week, would we get on each other's nerves? We can test that next summer. I have 2 weeks of vacation in August. I better get to bed early tonight. There is a big weekend coming up. But I am restless. I decide to go upstairs and check on Lindsey. I thank her for the hot toddy. She makes me another, packed with Vitamin C. She confides that she is 100% pure Lambda for Lesbian, never been with a man. She prefers 40 something sophisticated blondes and the most recent was almost a year ago. She meets them at art galleries, where my upcoming nudes will hang. The plot thickens.

Friday, February 4

Dear Diary, My morning is a blur. My workday is a blur, all routine. I can only think about tonight, together, me and my man, my main man, Roy. We do his plan for tonight. He wants to camp out again at The Boston View Motel, "The View for a Few", "The No-Tell Motel". Our secret is safe. It's fun to sneak around even though we don't have to. He has ordered take-out from Clyde's Roadhouse. Lyndsey will babysit my girls.

Dave drops me off at 7 pm. It's bitter blizzard cold. I'm wearing jeans, sweatshirt and parka. We have 9A, same as our first overnight with same threadbare towels and lumpy mattress. He wants to show me the frosted windows where he wrote "I Love You," with a Cupid arrow through the "O" of Love. The "L" word! Already the "L" word is afloat. The last time it came from a guy other than Dad was 17 years ago. Dad adds the title, "Princess". I am Dad's princess. I am Roy's sex goddess.

Sex is primary. Food is secondary. Neither of us brought rubbers. In my eagerness, I forgot. "Should we take a chance?" I queried. "Not to worry, Doll. I had myself fixed years ago. Babies are factored out of our equation. Is it okay? Am I disqualified?" Roy blurts out. I think about it for a minute. "No way," I say. "I'm keepin' you the full year and your contract will be up for renewal exactly 49 weeks from today, the anniversary of our first fuck. Now that's settled, let's get busy. Whip it out. Show me what I'm dealing with tonight. Now that there is no protection, suddenly I wonder how do I know where that thing has been. "This unit has serviced only nice girls, no skanks," he promises. I examine the unit closely and pronounce it fit for duty. I play "Come Together" by The Beatles on my I-pod. Without the rubber, he is a little early but my nails dig in and I get myself off as usual. He turns over. I kiss the scratches on his back and spank his butt. I will save a fortune on rubbers.

We watch our green and white TV while demolishing our take-out. I write "I Love You, Too," in the frosted window. The maid who cleans will see it tomorrow. Her opinion of the clientele may improve.

Saturday, February 5

Dear Diary, Early Saturday morning, while still dark outside, the first sounds are traffic. I feel body heat! This is a test. When we go camping, will his body heat be enough for me, I wonder. Yes, if we stay together under the blankets. Roy gives me five more minutes of his hot body. Then he is gone, across the street for coffee. I get the bathroom steamed up and dress in there. Only 60 in the room, zero outside. The baseboard heater couldn't keep up. I peek out the window. There he is, my man, blowing steam out of his mouth like a bull moose. His truck is warming up. It will be clear and cold. He sees me watching. He motions me on down to meet him. I grab my stuff and drop off the key.

His cab is all defrosted. The coffees and sticky buns are in there. We'll watch the sun rise on Edge Hill Road, halfway to his place. I tell him I've never done it in a pick-up truck. "All in good time," he says. His duplex is on Ames Avenue, a short walk from the Canton Waterfall. We check the pipes. The couple on the other side of the wall are away. Roy has the key. We check those pipes. We keep the water dripping.

I help with breakfast. He has a den which will double as a consulting room. There is a leather couch in there. My appointment with Dr. Roy is for 9 am.

"The doctor will see you now," he says. "Make yourself comfortable on the analysis couch. You are safe here. You may hug this pillow and pull up this fleece throw blanket. Now, how may I help you?" He sits at his desk behind me. He is peering over some ridiculous half frame glasses.

"I keep having this dream about being stuck at the bottom of the ocean. There is a shipwreck, like the Titanic, with skeletons inside. Some deep-sea glowing fish like squid and jellyfish and electric eels sometimes come to look at me. I don't know what to do. I am stuck there. I have been stuck there for a long time. What does it mean?"

"Beats the hell out of me," he says. "No seriously, let us ponder this a minute or two."

"How do I feel when I wake out of these?" I feel sad, nervous and frustrated.

"Which glowing object is the most appealing?"

"The Squid, with its waves of neon colors."

"Anything on my mind in my waking hours?"

" I worry that I am becoming a nymphomaniac."

All the while Roy seemed to be making some sort of diagram. He shows me what is called a mapping. It's something from higher math.

"Recurrent dreams are asking one or more questions about something unresolved. When you answer the questions, once and for all, the dream will cease. Eventually, you would figure this out on your own but my probing speeds it up. The shipwreck is your far past, possibly college years, a guy you loved then, you keep it near and dear to you. To go to the surface, you would have to leave it behind. Your Mom is the jellyfish. She has controlling tentacles. She is watching over you. The eel is a sperm which could give you a pregnancy. The Squid is me. Will you go to the surface, live in the present with me or any new guy? We have only been together 3 weeks. Can you trust me? Will you ever have a baby? The biological clock is ticking. Your active sex life now seems like nymphomania compared to the empty years after college. To answer the question, you keep having sex and see what happens. Your body is saying you must do it now before it's too late. That could make you hornier than average. Answer the questions. Decide. That will be $75."

"Okay, Dr. Freud. Let me write down those questions and stare at them. Will you take a check?" I write a check just for fun. I know he will not cash it. Roy leaves the room. I take a little power nap. I love leather couches. I smell bacon. Roy has served up some more food. I sit on his lap. "Hurry up and eat. The nympho wants to do you in the man cave," I say.

We are back at my house by noon. Lindsey is there. My girls want some love. I check in with Mom. I check in with Robert. I am evasive with both. I thank Lindsey. "We'll do your photo shoot next weekend," she announces. "Her ass is almost as good as yours," Roy comments. "It's a forbidden ass," I notify him and tell why.

Sunday, February 6

Dear Diary, Here is some leftover stuff from Saturday. The days, nights and mornings after are bleeding together like free running time. We go grocery shopping at the Star Market where everything is cheaper. His basket for him and mine for me. We make spaghetti and meatballs. We walk to Church, sitting separately again. Mom probably has spies. I pray about the questions in my dream.

We shower together to save hot water and scrub each-others back. We find some nice FM with love songs. Whitney Houston sings "Hold Me". Vanessa Williams sings "Love Is". George Benson sings "Love is Here Tonight". I go on top first. One hour later, Roy goes on top. By now it's midnight, officially Super Bowl Sunday, Packers against Steelers. Roy wants the Packers. So does Dad. This is a good sign. I don't care who wins the stupid game. We have bets down at work just for fun. We watch some ESPN. We have a bedtime snack, those crazy individual pies, mine is blueberry, his is pecan. We add ice cream. We put a shot of Jack on top. I am pretty mellowed out. I have decided about the dream.

Sunday morning, I pop out of bed like a kangaroo. I start the coffee. I brush my teeth. I declare that am ready to announce my decisions. I pull the covers off of the bed. Roy gets up, rubs his eyes, get his coffee and proceeds to the bathroom, all the while walking around naked. This is so much fun for me to see. The butt cheeks jiggle and the tool flops around and the jewels are "one hung low". He's mine. I'm keepin' him. "Well?" he says while brushing his teeth. "Yes, I trust you. I trust you got no one on the side. I won't even waste $29.95 on a background check. If Canton Schools trusts you, then so do I. Yes! Take me to the surface, take me with you, away from the shipwreck. No! I don't need a baby of my own. If you're shootin' blanks, well that's fine with me. It's destiny. So there! I think we are clear on all current controversies. Now let's fuck! The nympho needs a quickie and then off you go." I give him a light breakfast leaving plenty room for Super Bowl super buffet.

Monday, February 7

Dear Diary, Yesterday, the Packers beat the Steelers. Dad was happy. Roy was pleased. Mom and I watched Figure Skating. She likes the old-timey pro skaters in Champions on Ice. Her mom once upon a time saw Sonja Henie in Ice Capades. Today, I won a little bit at the office Super Bowl betting pool. Overnight there was no dream I can remember.

At lunch, I compare myself with one year ago. What would I tell my one year ago self. Maybe I would say, "Keep your antennas up. Your guy may be just around the corner." Is today what happiness is? If so, I will take it, today or any day of the week. There is bright sun. Snow is melting. There will be black ice. I ask to leave early, before dark. At home it is time to start cooking. I use all ingredients which won't stay fresh for long. Hot house tomatoes for salad and sauces. Cut 'em up, dice 'em up. They were marked down for quick sale. I took them all.

I act like a wife with kids, penny pinching, all from scratch instead of ready to eat. Bread, home-made. Knead that dough. Watch it rise.

While it rises, I go up and see Lindsey. She shows me her portfolio, all fine art black and white. She is doing some framing. I will be in her next show entitled "Aphrodite Reborn". Some of her self-portraits will be in there. I must say, I am impressed. I ask if she is in love. She was, but it's all over. Strange, but she has a land line also. Sometimes, she can faintly hear my land line ringing and I can hear hers. This is turning out nicely. She is like a sister without sibling rivalry and envies. I hear my phone ringing. I say goodbye.

Roy lets it ring just long enough for me to get there all out of breath. The phone has a long cord. I bring it to the kitchen and cradle it in my neck while pounding down the dough for its second rise. We are all just small talk. He is happy to hear me chattering on about matters of no great significance. He says my voice is musical, music to his ears. "That is so sweet," I tell him. I am so happy. He is too. This must be love. My girls sit there staring at me. It's easy to make them happy. Nightly rituals ensue, followed by purring in stereo.

Tuesday, February 8

Dear Diary, Roy says I should get new tires. Dad has been nagging me about that also. I say find me a pickup truck, one with 4-wheel drive. A Bronco would be perfect. An old beat up one would be fine. No one messes with a girl driving a Bronco. I'll get my credit score up. Maybe by springtime I'll have transpo befitting my new more active than the typical spinster lifestyle. The roads are slick. I get up early and take the bus. The old Malibu can rest a day in the driveway. On the bus I daydream about going to Cape Cod with Roy next summer, 2 weeks of heaven alone together, just us and the seagulls and the odd crab staring at us.

At work, the girls and I shop online for swimwear. Should we show cheek? Hell yes! Looking in my desk, I see that matchbook with phone number found in Reggie's apartment. We have a scan of his photo ID still on file. I can't resist. I print a screen shot on the pretext of returning the lost necklace. I have a feeling it means a lot to someone still alive. This activity is not really in my job description. I had best be careful.

I find out that another unit will be stripped to make it hypoallergenic. I want to be in on this. It is possible to configure a fresh modern interior design on desktop applications. I get permission to download and tinker with this on my spare time.

Lindsey can tell me about the cutting-edge stuff she may have heard about at her Alma Mater, RISD, Rhode Island School of Design.

Career Development means "Where can we go from here?" My co-workers are a think tank at my fingertips daily. I call Dave for my return trip home. I ask him about trucks. I think I can operate shift sticks. "It's stick-shift," he corrects me. "Go practice with a four-on-the-floor is my recommendation, maybe in a big empty parking lot," he adds. I can't wait. At home, I bake the bread. The dough rested all day. It smells wonderful. I bring a loaf to Lindsey. We are on hugging terms now. Man she has got some girl muscles under all those loose boyish outfits. At home, I dive into my Sherlock Holmes.

Wednesday, February 9

Dear Diary, Wow, winter is flying by! Less than 6 weeks to go. We have a false spring. At work, we have lunch outside at our office picnic table. We feed the birds and squirrels. Can I make it through the week without my guy's arms around me? I stare wistfully into space. Susan is sure that I am in love. "Maybe it is a tenant. You know that is forbidden," she reminds me. "That guess is not even warm," I tell her and remain evasive. Last year I hated myself, I hated my life at least. I forgave myself, kicked myself in the butt and now things are looking up. We talk about blue collar versus white collar guys. They watch me closely for a clue. "They're all just a bunch of horny sons of bitches," according to Joni, "high maintenance, spoiled by their Moms, wanting someone to service them daily."

This reminds me that I have a service appointment at Nick's Parkway Auto on the way home. I can afford new front tires because I paid down my Visa. I promise a full report on the blue-collar beefcake on Thursday. It is getting dark as I wait for my car. The waiting room is all stale coffee and tattered magazines but I like the smell of new tires. They rush to get done before closing. I drive away with a feeling of renewal, just like after Confession, for which I am overdue. Rear tires next month, maybe.

That night I tell Roy to find me an old Bronco, any color. He says that sure, lots of girls drive Broncos these days. He promises to find me one with a roll bar, tells me to save up and then laughs. I say I want to tow things and pull people out of ditches instead of being weak and helpless. "That's my girl!" he adds. There are so many adventures in store for the two of us. I say that before long, I might need him mid-week. He says he was thinking the same thing.

My girls are pestering me. I refill their bowls of kibble. I calm down by washing dishes and making the kitchen sparkle. I run a bubble bath. The legs get lathered for their weekly shave, the arm pits too. I leave the soft as moss full bush alone for Roy to rest his head on while he hugs my hips.

Thursday, February 10

Dear Diary, I hear Lindsey's alarm a few seconds before mine. Are we getting synchronized? Some women even sync their periods, I've heard. Maybe we should car pool. I am not even sure she has a car. Fatima is pouncing on my toes poking up under the covers. My girls are active early. They can hear the sparrows. I keep my thermostat at 65 to save on heat. I guess I am penny wise and pound foolish, thinking I can buy a truck. I open my little frosted bathroom window and stick my head outside in the cold air to help me wake up. I take some deep breaths.

The air smells nice, like I remember from childhood, going off to school in winter when it is still dark out, all bundled up with snow boots and mittens pinned to my sleeves.

I want a pot of tea for a change, cottage cheese and cling peaches. I put out the last of the bird seed. My girls are watching from the window. I make a snowball and throw it at the nearest tree. I think I am regressing to childhood. I stop at the Speedy Market for newspapers, the Globe and the Herald, plus the Dedham Times. I will be searching the classifieds for trucks. At work, the renovations on 6-G are almost finished. At lunch, I go over and take some more pictures. The walk does me good. The monthly rent will be $1800, Chestnut Hill is somewhat exclusive. Sheila can afford it.

I give my blue-collar beefcake report. The only candidate I recall enough to describe is Jason at Parkway Auto. He might be worth a test flirt for the others but not me. I want to make it a habit at lunch to go out walking. I read that if you have a sedentary job, after several years, your ass gets really big and horsey, guys too. We should try the standing desks.

I can't resist. I call the number on the matchbook. I ask for Reggie. A woman answers and asks, "Who wants to know?" I tell who I am and about the lost necklace. She says, "Damn, I figured it might be there. It was a one-night stand last summer and I was drunk. I took it off because it kept getting tangled in his chest hair." I feel really good now that I solved the mystery. I had a feeling it was important.

Friday, February 11

Dear Diary, Delores, the woman who lost the necklace in Reggie's apartment, is there waiting upon opening of the office at 9 am. She describes it perfectly, including the inscription. It is a family heirloom, once belonging to her mom and given by her dad when they were courting. Reggie was a mistake is all she would say about him, but she did like his unit, his apartment, that is. We laugh. She wants to see the model. She takes a rental application with her after the tour.

Lindsey calls me at lunch. She needs a ride home. She works not far away at the Boston Museum of Fine Arts. It turns out she does not have a car. On the way home, I tell her about Delores, who happens to be blond and 40ish. Maybe we can invite her to an art opening or something.

Roy is waiting for me when I get home. His weekend began a few hours ago. He has got sandwich stuff from Santoro's Sicilian Trattoria in Dedham. I tell Lindsey to wake me early tomorrow morning. "Go ahead, have your hetero fun," she says. "I'll be upstairs planning our shoot." My skirt is up and panties down in less than a minute. I stay standing. His face is buried deep at my pleasure zone, paying tribute. He gives a good muff job. He turns me around kisses both cheeks from bottom to top and across the crack. "If I found out you were a pro, I would pay for this," he declares. Standing up, he finishes me off from behind. "I knew you would be perfect tomboy tight right from the start, and plenty horny," he adds.

We shower quickly and change into bathrobes. I eat with my robe open and my tits hanging out. "I'll be fluffing you vertical again as soon as we're done here," I declare. The cats get some attention and then we lock them in the kitchen, knowing their protest will be paws reaching under the door. I give him the warm wash cloth treatment. As promised, I work my magic with the unit to get it ready for action. Fifteen minutes of missionary later, we are satisfied, probably at least until morning. We squeeze into the tub. We let the cats in. They always want to see what people do in the bathroom, the little pervs.

Saturday, February 12

Dear Diary, Roy is out the door by 7 am. He has stuff to do and so do I. Lindsey says that the light is better upstairs. I tip-toe up to her flat in robe and slippers. I stand on a pedestal. I will be Aphrodite reborn, totally naked or partially draped. I mimic the poses of the Goddess from four sculpture replicas in alabaster, each about 10 inches tall. My favorite is the total nude, "Aphrodite as Phryne". We take a break. We do some full-length mirror formal poses and then some candids, which simply depict a young woman at ease in the nude at home, for example, on her toes reaching for something on a shelf.

We repeat the mirror work with Lindsey as the model. She shows me how to use the camera. Our bodies are very similar but hers is 15 years younger. She will have a show in April at a small gallery. These will be framed 8x10s, with at least one, the centerpiece to be 16x20, and colorized. Her previous show, of self-portraits, sold out. After this show, she could be published. It feels so normal to be naked now. I must be careful not to walk out the door that way. This was a strangely hypnotic experience.

Roy is going to give me the night off but we plan a fun trip to Providence for Sunday. I admit I am a little sore after yesterday's action. I walk to my Saturday Vigil Mass at St. Theresa's. It is so nice just to walk outside, breathe deep and feel alive. When have I ever been so happy? Now is the best time ever. Is it just because of one guy, someone who loves me? Is it just because I waited so long for this? Who cares? "Enjoy it, Baby Girl Sarah," I tell myself, "while it lasts." It will be at least a year. We are on contract and neither is getting out of it.

Lindsey sees me from her window. I open my coat like a flasher. She grins. What we have here are two women who are happy with their bodies. No changes needed. After Mass, I do stretches at home, some crunches. There are leftovers plenty. Have I gained weight? Nope, 125 pounds, same as usual. I dive back into Sherlock Holmes, the conclusion of: *The Sign of the Four*. Murder, revenge, treasure, a helpless young woman, and good old fashioned detective work solve the case.

Sunday, February 13

Dear Diary, I meet Roy at 830 am at Canton Junction commuter rail station for our Sunday excursion to Providence. Dave, my Uber Guy, is busy so I get Lindsey to drive me there. She needs the car while I am gone so she can get the darkroom at Tufts University during off peak hours. We could make a deal to share my old Chevy on a regular basis. She has never had a traffic ticket. Her driving record is spotless. I am sure she will be fine.

We hit the pavement of downtown Providence by 930 am. This is my old stomping ground from my first years of independence. It is snowing lightly. I take Roy's arm and stay close. It is just like "The Freewheelin' Bob Dylan" album cover. We walk several blocks to my favorite quirky café called Olga's Cup and Saucer. The baked goods there are incredible. We are in a crush of strangers, just the way I like it.

Afterwards, we taxi over to Providence College campus. My parents spent a fortune to send me here, private, Catholic and near home. Almost nothing has changed. Some of the Copper Beeches seem larger. Saint Dominic Chapel is open. We go inside to get warm. Way in the back, we kiss in the style of secret lovers enjoying a stolen moment of privacy. Next stop is the Phillips Memorial Library, cozier, less cavernous. I see exactly where I sat on many Winter Quarter Sundays such as this. We stroll on the quad and catch a bus back to downtown Providence Place Mall.

I make a wish list of stuff there. We decide to lunch inside the semi-creepy Old Biltmore Hotel. We enjoy grand views of the city from the 18th floor. Street lights are beginning to turn on. At a place of an old happiness, I return in the euphoria of a new happiness. It is all a little overwhelming. I begin to cry. Roy comforts me. He seems to understand. He offers me a handkerchief. Few men carry these in recent times.

Back on the street, our final destination is The Arcade shopping complex, dating from 1828, built in Greek Revival style, the first enclosed shopping mall in the USA. We find postcards and souvenirs of the day. We catch the final inbound commuter train. By the time we reach Canton Junction, snow is falling heavily. I call Lindsey and say to stay home. I tell her that Dave, my Uber guy is coming in his Toyota Tundra. The parking lot is empty except for a few forlorn vehicles, already shapeless behind windswept drift. Roy's Jeep heats up quickly and we wait inside. Dave is due in 15 minutes. This is plenty of time for a major make-out session in the soft glow of dashboard lights. Minutes ago, we were in college again. It is so easy on this magical day to take a step even further back. We are in high school again with our French kisses, roamin' hands, rushin' fingers, buttons, bra straps, zippers, first base, second base, third base, the ingredients of falling in lust. Roy says the sweetest thing. "I believe I have solved an equation comprised of equal parts of Lust, of Love, and of the Look on Your Face. What should I do?" "What to do? Maybe save for a ring?" I blurt out. "Save for a ring? Hmm…, what an idea! If I do, that means we are unofficially engaged, starting right now," Roy confirms barely missing a beat. Now come the tears. As he hugs me, he goes on something like this "After unofficially engaged comes officially engaged. There is a ring. We keep it secret just the way you like it. Engagement is the happiest time of all, according to studies. We'll have a nice long one. We can even keep the marriage secret for a while. We can elope. 'Let's get lost, lost in each-others' arms. Let's get lost. Let them send out alarms.' It's an old Jazz tune. It can be our theme song."

All too soon we see headlights. Dave sends out alarm. He toots his horn. I cry all the way home. I tell Dave not to worry. They are tears of joy. At home, I hug my girls. I sit at my kitchen table and try to comprehend what has just happened. There is a soft knock. Lindsey has the final touch to add to my magical weekend. She has contact sheets and some automated prints. Through her lens, I look very nice naked, naked and unashamed. "Guess what?" I tell her. "Aphrodite is engaged. Can you believe it? Lindsey looks me straight in the eye and affirms, "I can believe it. Very much so, indeed I do believe it. Your Secret Guy is a very Lucky Guy."

Monday, February 14

I arrive at my employee parking at 8 am. Already, flower trucks are there. Many women work in the building. It is Valentine's Day, I just remembered. Who will get the most extravagant bouquet? There is a van from Stephanie's Flowers. Stephanie knows me. I sent flowers to myself last year. I chose them in her shop. The lobby opened early. The security guard has custody of the fragrant deliveries. As my desktop is booting up, Stephanie's driver comes straight to my desk. Orchids require special handling. On the card is written "From Your Secret Admirer". The girls can speculate but I am still not telling. Some of the girls are left out, like I used to be or maybe they get home delivery. Early is okay but late is not okay. Sandy allows the hen party to last a little longer than usual today. Some boxes of chocolates are opened. There is chocolate with every coffee break today.

Eventually I get to work. My desk is piled high. I process the scheduled move-outs. Sandy must handle the unscheduled ones which are much trickier. She may have to do some tap dancing to satisfy corporate on those. Reggie was unscheduled. Do Police suspect foul play? Was he in trouble with people not as understanding as Sandy is. Lindsey says that if he was a wedding photographer and one of his brides didn't like her photos, then he might as well leave town. How would Sherlock Holmes proceed? I only have one more clue. The Dunkin's receipt. Maybe he still goes there in disguise. I table this question for later.

At home, I call Roy and say how happy he has made me. The orchids he sent will flourish in my office. They need special care. I better read about it. It is almost like we have a child already. Just as I ring off Lindsey is arriving home late on the last bus. She has some 8x10's. We are similar enough nude for her to be young Aphrodite and for me to be the fully mature Goddess. They are definitely suitable for framing. Her ass is skinnier, mine is maximum luscious. I suggest a jeans and cowboy boots photo shoot next, me and my pick-up truck. A Honky Tonk and a Country Waltz are coming up soon. Yee haw!

Tuesday, February 15

Dear Diary, I wake up early. What is my next move? Get money for my Ford Bronco pick-up truck, that's it. I will need about 5K for a decent used one, Roy tells me. The kitchen is stuffy. I crack the window. Hearing the birds at the feeder, my girls are up there pronto. My head begins to clear at the smell of the coffee percolating. The wheels are turning. Sell some stuff? Work overtime? Do more modeling? Save on gas by carpooling? All of the above, I think. Okay, that's settled.

Lindsey and I share the ride starting today and as often as possible. I drive today. It is only a short detour over to Huntington Avenue to drop her off. She wants the Classical Station, WCRB, 99.5 FM. That is fine with me. She takes out her sketchbook, all nice and quiet and introverted, a deep well, part of her mystique. I ask her about the modeling. It pays about $15 an hour for amateurs, she says. That was enough to pay for groceries during her starving artist years at RISD, Rhode Island School of Design. For me, it would be enough for cat food. Still, my girls must eat. I give them the premium stuff. They turn their noses up at the cheap stuff. The date is set at Friday, April 8th for "Rites of Spring" art opening at Lindsey's trendy little boutique gallery. Lots of people will be sipping Champagne as they view my curves.

Roy doesn't care. He is no prude. "The world is a happier place when babes are showing off their bods," he informed me. The large, framed prints will be $900 and the smaller ones priced at $500. People bring their checkbooks and we expect to sell all. I will also appear in the catalog. It is very exciting. When I attend in person, will people realize that I am the model? Only for Mom, would it be a scandal. We won't advertise among my family.

By 9 AM, I am at my desk and booted up. Plenty of chocolate remains from yesterday but it definitely won't last until Friday in this office. Later, I have time to bounce some design ideas off of the bosses. I am allowed to keep the layout app on my desktop. I let Lindsey drive home. By 7 pm the weary workers return where two fur balls await.

Wednesday, February 16

Dear Diary, Lindsey drives today. She is in my kitchen. The Malibu is warming up. Whoever drives gets free coffee. She comments on my perk brew, which seems bitter compared to her press pot, but more aromatic when brewing. We are out the door at 06:45, a new record.

The traffic is light. Along the way we discuss our weaknesses. "Human frailty makes you more lovable. Don't try to be perfect," she states. I was too often, too passive, say I. All my life until recently, I wait and see what happens and hope for the best. She says it is hard for her to trust people. These are all kind of vague. In the coming weeks, we task ourselves to name specific bad habits, the kind which annoy people. She will be hanging a photo exhibit today, giant high resolution photo-journalist prints with dense colors. All are unframed. They require a specific sequence. The curator wants the room lit for maximum impact. She has notes on this from one of her seminars at RISD.

I am at my desk by 07:05. I dive right in. At coffee break I go outside. I want to see if Sheila has moved in. I knock and she answers. Her stuff is all in boxes except for a Lazy-Boy recliner where she sleeps until her futon arrives. She will have an open house on March 4th.

Back in the office, I feel energized from my few minutes in the cold. I wonder again about Reggie. My final clue is the Dunkin Donuts receipt from the location at 15 Commonwealth Avenue. Did he go there often enough to be remembered? In my next life, I will be a detective, major case squad, like on TV. I will track down missing persons.

I want to see what Lindsey is working on. Susan drops me there. Holy Shit!! It's giant crime scene photos, entitled: "Houston, Texas, Capital of Crime." The exhibit is on tour. I get just a peek from behind the ropes and that was enough! We stop at my Dunkins of interest. I ask the barista if she has seen Reggie lately. She says "No, don't know no Reggie." I buy a pound of whole bean, French Roast and a grinder. It will be fun to grind my own, a new element to my morning ritual.

Thursday, February 17

Dear Diary, Roy is up early like 6 am and calling in his horniness report. On Monday he is totally satisfied. On Tuesday, he starts thinking about my pieces and parts again. By Wednesday, he is planning where and when and how many times to ravage me over the weekend. By Thursday, he wakes up with a big boner and has to pound the mattress, pretending it is me. "That's so sweet!" I replied, "Tonight I will pleasure myself to sleep, thinking about you." He wants to pick me up from work tomorrow and take me to a surprise somewhere.

I drive today. Lindsey is making some last-minute calculations in her notebook about lumens and color temperatures and viewing distances. I do not disturb her with small talk. It turns out to be an otherwise forgettable, normal, routine day. I realize that this is happiness: just get up, get dressed, go to work, talk to your boyfriend, gossip with the girls, take a coffee break, see what's left in the fridge, fill my tank, check my oil and cuddle with my kittens.

Mom phones in for an update. We arrange to meet. I am still her little girl, her first, her oldest, her love child with Dad. She is sure of the night I was conceived near to 40 years ago. She wrote it in her diary.

At work, I check the little weather station in our break room. The humidity is too low for orchids. I read about how to create a micro-environment with higher humidity.

On our drive home, Lindsey and I do a little shopping for the weekend at the Star Market. I tell her she can have the car all weekend because Roy is taking custody of me right after work. She will work overtime on Saturday while I am off on my adventures but she will have time to feed and water, plants and felines. "What if someone takes custody of you on weekends?" I wonder. Blond, sophisticate hairstyle, educated, chauffeur driven, woman of independent means and off you two go for a weekend at Cape Cod. "I guess I need a hug," she replies. It is like hugging an earlier version of myself. "I will surely miss you some day when we go our separate ways," I predict.

Friday, February 18

Dear Diary, I pack an overnight bag. I hug and kiss my girls goodbye. I might not see them until Sunday. Lindsey is driving. There is wet snow. We commute in silence.

All the girls are excited about their weekends. Mine will be impulsive, report to follow, I say. Susan has her suspicions. Five o'clock finally rolls around. Roy is late. He proceeds slowly in his 4-wheel drive. Lindsey will stay overnight at the Museum. I have stayed over at the office a time or two during winter storms.

By 6 pm, I am in the custody of my man, approaching North Station. We have a roomette on northbound Amtrak to Saco, Maine departing 10:30 pm. There is plenty of time for dinner. We walk over to Tavern on the Square, no reservation required. At our table, without further ado, Roy does the whole kneel down and offering of ring to make our engagement official. He has had the item for years. He bought it at estate sale. It called out to him. Who wore it before, he does not know. It is a rock, encrusted with emeralds. I hold it up to the light. Be still my heart, I gasp. I try it on. It fits. He stole one of my bling rings and resized my rock on the sly. He waits while I savor the moment. I drain my bottle of Dos Equis. I say yes and we kiss for the benefit of onlookers. Then I hiccup several times more, providing entertainment for the room. A shot of Jack stops the hiccups. I ignore the "Beer before Liquor, Never Sicker" general alcohol advisory. We both share a basket of fried seafood. We have time to linger. We get congrats from the wait staff. Roy leaves a "C Note" for a tip.

I have never had a roomette on any kind of train. This will be a first. We settle in 15 minutes before departure of the Downeaster, Northbound. We freshen up. Of course, we do the wild thing without any further delay. We have 2 hours, most of it naked. Naked on a train. The porter brings us coffee. I believe they call this the feeling of well-being. Is it a dream? I pinch myself. By 12:45 am, we are on the platform at Saco. A taxi is waiting. We arrive at The Allouette Beach

Resort, oceanside by 1 am. On our balcony, the air is cold and clean. I begin to cry.

Saturday, February 19

Dear Diary, Barely past midnight, Roy and I steam up the bathroom, wrap ourselves in luxurious terry cloth robes and crash. My next awareness is noisy seagulls. My hero, with coffee in hand, escorts me back to the balcony. Breakers are churning below. We do deep cleansing breaths, no need to speak. Our future is on the horizon, uncharted waters, cheerfully sparkling in full winter sun. I look at my ring. Can I let anyone know? Some can guess, but no one will know. We swear to keep our secret.

He carries me across the threshold. I drop my robe and assume some of my modeling poses. Aphrodite looks kindly on the desires of her current companion. She grants him his carnal wishes, which are quickly, albeit temporarily satisfied.

Off we go to join other winter weekenders in the village of Saco. We seek souvenirs at quaint seaside shops including the usual shells. I want a conch, a big one. I want a fistful of post cards. Next is more seafood, fresh caught, for lunch. I post a card to Lindsey and one to myself. I want the Saco postmark with date, to attach to this diary as proof that this happy time was not a dream.

We have a kitchenette. We shop for a few things. Our room is warm enough, so I cook topless. The front desk allows us some candles, kept in case of power failure. Pasta is easy, with crusty French bread and fromage. We have a rhubarb pie warming in the oven. We settled on a Chianti in the wicker basket style bottle. "Your tits look amazing in candlelight," announces my fiancé. Roy brought a point and shoot. He understands lighting. I will let Lindsey critique these topless candlelit candid shots.

We have a radio, but no TV. I have heard of such resorts which limit intrusion from the outside world. We find a program of Jazz for the wee hours. Once more, I feel like crying, tears of joy. Roy pours me another glass and gives his best neck and shoulder massage. Time on the balcony clears my head a bit. Shower and steam prep us for bed. We leave the music on. There is a Fox Trot rhythm. Our vertical dance to Fox Trot rhythm ends up horizontal. Now I can't stop giggling.

Sunday, February 20

Dear Diary, It's a lazy Sunday Morning without Mass. Will I burn in Hell for the omission? I say a little prayer, thankful for this blessed weekend. Maybe I have already died and gone to Heaven.

I stick my head outside for another gulp of ocean air. Coffee is ready. I serve my man. He yawns, rubs eyes and smiles. I stand in front of him, robe open and get my hip hug, a long lingering one, including hot breath at the bush. We need one more screw. This one is a horsey ride. I can always get off first that way. There is mirror behind me. Roy gets to enjoy both the rear view and the bouncing-tits front view. We have a cuddle afterwards then steam up the shower one last time.

We have four hours before departure. We pack up, check out and deposit our bags at the station. We haunt the historic homes on High Street, cheerful in winter wood frame Colonial white, then we cruise main street shops with their red brick facades. I can't resist the antique stores. I show the shopkeeper my stone. It's okay since he is a stranger. Back outside, I am in fur trimmed wool. Roy is in leather Bomber Jacket and scarf. He offers me his arm. We have a hot chocolate with marshmallows. I end up with a whipped cream mustache. He kisses it away.

Finally, we catch the 2:05 pm southbound Downeaster, in coach watching winter landscapes on our two-hour return. We sip on some dry red wine from the club car. At 4:15, we sadly survey North Station once more. Roy brings his pickup from indoor parking. It's all warmed up for me curbside. We take a slow route home through the North Side twilight and South Side dusk. It is near to 6 pm as we approach West Roxbury. "Well, everything can't last forever," I suppose as more tears well up. Roy pops in a CD. His parents said that this was their song. I hear the band Chicago who seem vaguely familiar from the misty past already retro during my college days. The song is *Beginnings*, vintage 1967. As we kiss goodbye, Peter Cetera is singing "...only the beginning, only just the start, only the beginning, of what I want to feel forever..."

Monday, February 21

Dear Diary, Lindsey took good care of my girls. They keep me warm early on my frosty Monday morning. Fatima is getting big. Should I wear my ring to work? Better not. I put it back in its velvet case and hide it under the mattress.

I start work at 9 today. Lindsey drives. She made cheese biscuits. We eat in the car during our mid-morning leisurely commute. She said my phone was ringing a lot over the weekend. Because I have the old-fashioned cassette tape voice recorder, she could hear the voices of the callers leaving messages. Most were from Mom. Others were from Robert, just checking in, Roger, confirming a hair appointment, Sandy telling me to come at 9 am, and Charlotte, the Mom, my vast network. Comes a day everyone leaves a cute message, I save that tape and attach to you, Dear Diary, at years end.

Lindsey and I both manage to survive without cable TV. That saves money and time flipping channels. We are focused instead of distracted. Mom is on Facebook. I say no to social media. Mom married early, 20 years old, an office romance. I explain that Mom experiences her lost bachelorette life vicariously through me. Lindsey's Mom is a retired nurse. Her Dad still drives truck. They live up in up in Brattleboro, Vermont. They are due for a visit on the Dad's birthday in March. She invites me to come along. I agree.

At work, I handle the move-outs. There are 3 in all. One place is trashed, no refund of deposit. I take photos. One has pet damage, partial refund. One is immaculate. It even smells nice. This restores my faith in humanity. I recommend full refund. All keys are accounted for.

No kittens were left behind but lots of furniture is at the dumpsters. Lindsey wants a beautiful lamp shade we spotted on a broken lamp. I grab it quick and stick it in the trunk. The girls at work want to know about my weekend in Maine. I tell them it was romantic but I don't say who with. I leave some of the shells in the break room. I tell them about the beach near Saco. Susan still thinks it must be a married guy. Smooth Jazz on FM in the Malibu carries the working-girls home.

Tuesday, February 22

Dear Diary, The working girls are temporarily derailed. The battery in my Malibu is dead. Dave to the rescue. He drops Lindsey first. I am a little bit late.

There is a staff meeting today. We talk about vacancy rates and customer complaints. Maggie indicates small improvements in both departments for the corporate suits to look at. At lunch Dad calls. He has replaced my battery. He will pick me up later which will be for him a fun diversion from his daily routine. I am the daughter who did not move far away. Roy calls also. He just wants to hear my voice. How sweet of him to say.

Afternoon is routine background checks. Eight new tenants are to be cleared by March 1st. Dad arrives as darkness falls. He gets to meet my co-workers and practice his charm. It's National Bring Dad to Work Day, I decide. They all like the idea. Lindsey is working late. She will catch a late bus as she often did before our carpool began. Should I let Dad in on my secret, on our drive home? Better not. I tell him simply that I am happy with my career and social life, plus I am saving for a Ford Bronco. I listen to his advice on vehicles. He has done many of my repairs over the years. The Malibu is only my 4th car since High School. He gets to meet Fatima. He will meet Roy all in good time.

My girls are with me while I cook. Soup and salad sound simple enough for tonight. I call Roy to see what he is cooking, which is a mountain of spaghetti and meatballs with lots leftover to get him through the week. We talk about weekend plans. This coming weekend, I will surprise him.

By 9 pm I am in bed with my head in a book, more adventures of Sherlock Holmes, which reminds me of Reggie. Was he made to disappear by the Deep State? Did he know too much? Was he a victim of the underworld? Will he sneak in one day and reclaim Fatima? Probably I will never know the answers to these questions. He is gone and that is all. Why should I care? Am I starting to feel like the tenants are children in my custody. Both Susan and I have been mentioned in Yelp comments as being "nurturing".

Wednesday, February 23

Dear Diary, I was never much of a morning person but suddenly I am up almost every day before sunrise. Remaining in robe and slippers and staring into the coffee mug, I do my best thinking. I put on my ring. Nine more months of engagement lie ahead. I plan Sunday for Mom and Charlotte. I hear voices overhead.

Does Lindsey have a guest? As I am dressing, I hear a car leave.

I drive today. The Malibu starts at first crank with my new battery. On the way I find out it was a photog, as the models call them. It got late. She put him on the couch. "So close and yet so far," he told her. He saw our photos. He wants us both for Mata Hari, Lindsey for early career and me for late career, including the day she faced the firing squad. It might require two sessions. He will pay $50 an hour. There will be a hair and make-up artist. He needs us on Saturday, May 21st, in Providence. My double life as a nude model continues. I am sure Roy won't care. I tell her okay as long as we have a warm dressing and undressing room.

Our route is a winter wonderland under old growth trees. There are some patches of blue above. I look at Lindsey, my adopted kid sister, today as usual studying her notebooks. She is just one of several new people in my life this year. Someday, I will be looking back at this year,

2011. "It was a very good year," I will say, just as Sinatra sang. I've got my "city girl who lives up the stair, with all that perfumed hair, and it came undone". This gives me an idea. What kind of seductive perfume could Mata Hari possibly have worn way back then, circa 1910. I will research it, maybe recreate it.

We occupy ourselves with more mundane matters on our workday, me with reports for management, she with some multi-media for upcoming exhibits. Back home, we have dinner upstairs and do our perfume research. Possible French perfumes from the era of the tragic heroine were *Spring Rain, Paris Rose* and *Vintage Gardenia.* I want to wear the Gardenia. L. has some red wine. We get a little tipsy. We say good night with a hug and a kiss on the cheek, similar to what I do with Mom, but somewhat more pleasant.

Thursday, February 24

Dear Diary, I am slightly hung over from that wine last night. I take extra time steaming up the bathroom. I let the girls come in and satisfy their endless fascination with everything I do. When I come out, there is a message from Roy. It's a cute one. I am going to save it. He wonders what surprises I have in store for him. I call back and get his machine. He knows he can reach me on my lunch break as usual. Where will I be living one year from now during our domestic bliss?

First get through today, I say. An early start is in order. My car pool partner has the same idea. She is ready, notebooks in hand at 6:30. She heard me remote start the car and that was her cue. I made tea this this morning, Jasmine, just for a change. We grab our mugs and go. FM radio is playing Scheherazade. We agree to grocery shopping after work.

At work, the girls go on endlessly about their weekends. I need a cover story. I feel like a spy, like Mata Hari herself. Anything I say could get back to Mom. She knows Susan and Maggie. I say maybe I will go cruising with just friends Robert again. It was great fun the first time.

After work I take Lindsey to the Greek International high-end deli and grocery where I chatted up that guy Steven Sandler. There is one blond sophisticate there who gets a second look from Lindsey. "Your style?" I ask. I decide to find out her name. In the cheese section, I ask her if she grates her own cheese and makes her own pasta sauce from scratch. I tell her once a month I allow myself the luxury of this place. We introduce each other.

Her name is Desiree. I introduce Lindsey. None of us is in a hurry. We all shake hands and sit down for a Cappuccino. My side kick is as usual all quiet and mysterious. Desiree chats her up, learning about her upcoming show, offers her card and asks for a mailed invitation. Desiree is a Dermatologist, we find out. There is an address for her office.

In my kitchen, we toast our new acquaintance, Desiree, from whom Lindsey felt a nice vibe, enough to stimulate fantasies, she admits.

Friday, February 25

Dear Diary, Winter is flying by. I track the extra minutes of daylight. The sparrows wake me today. They are reminding me to buy birdseed. It's payday. I'll get a big bag. Enough to last until spring. What to do for my man today? I puzzle over this at my breakfast table. I stare at my teapot lately instead of my coffee cup. As I replace the tea cozy, it hits me. I will buy a spa day for my man. While he is getting his treatments, Lindsey and I will get our hair done. Then I will cook for my fiancé. On our overnight, we can act out some more romantic fantasies.

I am glad I moved my hair date to Saturday. Roger has an introductory offer for my city girl who lives up the stairs. We take our most scenic route today, Centre St. to Arbor Way to Pond St., allowing us 30 minutes of drive time to plot our Saturday. I drop Lindsey at 7. I am at my desk at 7:30. At lunch I notify Roy to meet me at my place at 7 pm for candlelit dinner. I ask him to dress formal. We stop at Roche Brother's for a few more delicacies. At home, I just need to put a casserole in the oven, toss the salad and set the table.

I hear the rumble of Roy's truck at 6:50. He is cowboy formal straight out of the Ponderosa Ranch. He stomps the snow off his boots. I take his Stetson and Low Rider Duster. "You look good enough to eat," he tells me. "I will be the dessert," I promise. Luscious, that's me, maximum glammed-up. He has never seen me this way, hair piled up, boobs pushed up, slinky black velvet dress plus my best matching necklace and earrings. My 3-inch pumps make me taller and leggier in my silk stockings. I light the tapers. We have white tablecloth and napkins. We douse the overhead lights. We open the curtains. It is clear and cold. The winter moon is waning but still bright enough to sparkle the back yard snow. I serve him beer in a frosted mug to wash everything down.

By 7:30, it is time for dessert. We take the candles into the bedroom. I push him into a chair. I stripped often for Phil. I know the moves. By 8:00 pm, I am buck naked and dragging him into bed by his bola tie.

Saturday, February 26

Dear Diary, Saturday Morning is just be lazy and sleep late. So cold outside, so warm beside my man. I see two lumps. The girls have gotten under the covers. Roy plugs in the percolator and hits the shower first. He towels off in front of me. I ask him to turn around. I enjoy the view. He is mine, all mine. By the time I finish my shower, my man is outside, shoveling snow. I start some toast and eggs and bacon.

When the abominable snowman returns, he is all grab-ass with cold hands. I fight him off. I instruct him to sit. I explain that at noon his spa day begins. He is booked for the full treatment at Inspiration Salon and Spa on LaGrange Street. Meanwhile, Lindsey and I will be at Loose Ends in Arlington. I am glad I rescheduled for today. We have our side-by-side shampoos given by Natalie and Roger, followed by our side-by-side cut and blow dry. For Roger, Lindsey is an unknown quantity. She is a case study. They decide to go for a look which matches her usual calm and quiet dignity. A look which says, "Handle with care." Roger creates an elegant low chignon with loose curls in front. Looking in the mirror, Lindsey admits that she has never been this girly-girl, that this is timeless. This could work for young Mata-Hari. For me, Roger does my usual tousled textured layers well below shoulder length, hair I can hide behind or toss about. When we return, Roy is having a shot of bourbon in the men's lounge area at Inspiration. He is totally mellowed out. He has re-booked for another foot treatment in 4 weeks.

Because it is cold and windy, Roy takes one lady on each arm all the way to his truck. On the way home Roy gives his review. "Ladies, let me tell you one thing. If anyone is ever mad at you, just deliver one of those foot treatments and all will be forgiven, totally and forever. A shot of bourbon, scented candles, dim light, a comfy chair, a sudsy soak, apricot scrub, hot towels, trim, polish and buff, followed by hot oil massage. I never knew what I was missing." I said I'll keep that in mind, a handy get out of jail free card to have just in case.

Sunday, February 27

Dear Diary, I awaken early. Roy is still sleeping. I can finish the story of yesterday. It has a happy ending for both of us, massage happy endings. It is our latest foreplay. We stayed home with our scented candles and lotions. It was too cold and dark outside. I woke up at 1 AM and blew out the candles.

Today is just another ordinary happy day. Roy came with me to late Mass at St. Theresa. We had brunch at Rox Diner. We waited patiently for our table. This is a super popular place. We try the Tahitian French Toast with Mango and Coconut.

Afterwards, Roy drops me in Dedham Square. He goes home. He has guy stuff to do. I grab some new videos at Café Paradiso, some old black and white Film Noir tough guy detective stuff, stuff that guys like, stuff with dames who are trouble. I could be trouble, if I wanted to be, so be careful, Roy.

I meet Mom and the two Charlottes across the street at Café Fresh Bagel. We have cheerful idle chatter, nothing too serious, mainly encouragement to the younger Charlotte, who wants to be a lawyer, a defense attorney for the downtrodden. I tell her about my old book "Clarence Darrow, Attorney for the Damned". I promise to bring it when next we meet. Mom and I shop some specialty items at Santoro's Sicilian. I get something for Dad, my other hero, who fixed up my new car battery. I get him a mess of his favorite salami.

Mom drops me at home. Time for a bubble bath. The girls come in of course. They play with the soap bubbles. They sneeze when the bubbles touch their noses. I clean up the kitchen in my robe and slippers. Tonight's feature is "The Glass Key" with Alan Ladd and Veronica Lake. There are queens and princesses and wives of millionaires who are not as happy as little old me tonight. It seems like it is going to last. Thank You, Lord. Praise the Lord! Halleluiah! Good things come to those who wait. I find a little Rosé gone flat in the back of the fridge. Fatima sniffs at my glass. She tastes a drop on my fingertip. She doesn't like it. "More for me," as Roy would say. I drain the glass and douse the light. I hug my pillow. Amen.

Monday, February 28

Dear Diary, It has been a very happy month. Sometimes, I read you just to remember and relive the highlights.

I drive today. Lindsey takes a catnap along the way. There is fog this morning, a wintry mix. We depart at first dim light 6:30 am. On my Bronco, I will be sure to have fog lights. We take our usual route, Northeast along Centre St., stopping at 7-11 in Roslindale. I need more wiper solution. There are many more messy days to come. We get our coffee refills. To help us perk up we tune to WJMN, JAM'N 94.5 FM, a favorite at RISD during Lindsey's college days. We be jammin' the remaining few miles.

I am at my desk all powered up and logged in by 7:30. I will handle phone calls and walk-ins today. In the break room there are some left-over doughnuts from Friday, including a raspberry jelly one. It is still soft. I can't resist. I have my mouth full when Roy calls in on the break room phone. He can't start his week without me chiming in cheerfully, he says.

The rest of the staff show up just before 8. The hen party lasts longer than usual. Susan talks about her new guy, and no, they haven't done it yet. Her flip phone takes good snaps. I use my flip only on Wi-Fi, which we have in the office. Four years of my life are on there.

At lunch, I check on Sheila in 6-G. She loves her renovated unit. Her furnishings are sumptuous. I think we should offer some furnished executive units in similar décor. She says a strange man knocked on her door on Saturday, asking for Reggie. He was well dressed and charming but with an accent she could not place. She told him what little she knew. After peeking into the bedroom and bath, he seemed satisfied and departed in some high-end car. She thinks it was a Bentley, dark blue. He said he needed to return something he had borrowed months ago. This is all very vague and suspicious. What does it mean?

The two car-poolers are home by 5:30, each lost in thought along the way. By 8:30, I am propped up in bed with Sherlock Holmes in *The Valley of Fear.*

Tuesday, March 1

Dear Diary, I rose from the valley of fear at 6 AM. I slept somewhat restlessly but free of nightmares. I am anticipating springtime. March, April, and May I designate as spring. All of the corresponding Liturgical Calendar stuff is there to guide me. I can feed off of the passion already flowing this wonderful year. I wait for first light, 1 or 2 minutes earlier every day. March is the cruelest month, they say. It gives hope then knocks you back down. The next sunny day, I will get the girls at work to do our stepping on coats ceremony in the parking lot. Flowers at work, that will be nice. Maybe my potted plant will bloom some more. It's Jasmine Tea again today. I think I will brew some more at work. Coffee is mainly for winter.

I hear the remote starter engage. Lindsey has the key fob. It is a selling point. When I get my Bronco, she will have her '99 Malibu beater. No one will ever try to steal it, that is the beauty of it. There is plenty of room in there for all of her stuff which is beginning to fill the back seat.

We arrive just on time today. I will be sending rent reminder notices and tallying incidental charges. The bean counting, bookkeeping is my least favorite part of my job. If the eagle flies on Friday, better pay on Friday or a cute crow, me, will serve up the late charges. Don't shoot the messenger, please.

I go out at lunch, searching for a patch of blue. I have my flip phone. Office Wi-Fi blasts out to the parking lot so I can talk to Roy. At Canton High there is discussion among teachers about bullying, which now includes cyber bullying. I got teased a lot during my early awkward years. I counted it as payment for my sins such as impure thoughts which were starting around grade 7. Later, I was goody two shoes, the virgin. I was the tease. "See if you can be the first, if you are man enough," I said, just for fun. When we get home, Lindsey and I, have dinner upstairs. We tell our stories of the first time. Mine is in an old diary. Her story got me a little bi-curious, just a wee bit, enough to understand. Her first was Leslie, candle-lit, in a dorm room, a blond, above and below.

Wednesday, March 2

Dear Diary, It's hump day. I get to start late, 10:00 to 18:30. I drop Lindsey at 9:00. At mid-week, I am already horny. I need my man. That reminds me. Time to restock the K-Y.

I get to show units today. The first appointment is not until noon. It's a sun worshiper who needs third floor south facing. He has waited a long time for a suitable unit. No curtains needed, no one can see in, edge of the complex with a tree line view. Kind of a strange guy, an accountant, I think. He works from home. He wants the carpet pulled out. That will require a 2-year lease and an extra week to refinish the hard wood floors. We aim to please. He asks about food delivery and hiking trails.

Roy and I should look at more places this weekend. We may need to get on a waiting list. Then there is our summer rental. We need to reserve that soon. I am out of the office four more times that afternoon. That helped to keep my mind off of you know what but it also made me really hungry.

We stop for Chinese on the way home. We demolish it in my kitchen. Lindsey goes upstairs. She has designs to work on. I call Roy and tell him how much I need his services. He wonders why don't I have a dildo, vibrator, something. We decide to order one online. He confesses he did a pantie raid last time he was at my place. I was looking for those pink lacy ones. I call him a perv and laugh. I think I need to check his apartment thoroughly next time for evidence of closet kink.

I get the tub running. My girls keep me company. I check my front and rear view in the full-length mirror. Satisfied, I test the water. Suddenly, I want some wine. I will give it up for Lent but for now let me have some. I almost forgot I bought a small bottle of Saki to go with the Chinese. I left it in the car. I bundle up and go out there. I look up at the sky. It's clear and cold but I am sure I can smell spring. A dog is barking nearby. Cars pass with a hiss on the slushy street. Lindsey is watching from above. I bring her a glass and get back to my tub. Keep my story safe, Dear Diary, so that someday I may relive it minute by minute.

Thursday, March 3

Dear Diary, I am up super early, zero five hundred hours, as Dad used to say. Sometimes he played Drill Sargent and us kids were the soldiers.

I tidy up, make a big breakfast and pack a lunch, including a pear, 2 sandwiches wrapped in wax paper, and Hostess Cupcakes all in a paper bag like Mom used to do for the school age soldiers at her command. The girls have to settle for cat kibble today until I restock on Fancy Feast. Their disdain is immediate and obvious.

Lindsey overslept. She is grumpy today. She is entitled to her moods and doesn't want to talk about it. I drive, trying not to be too annoyingly cheerful. She drops me off and is perking up a little as she takes the wheel of the car which soon will be hers.

The hen party lasts until 09:00, weekend plans, spring fever and such. We decide March 15 will be stepping on coats day. We draw straws for cleaning out the break room fridge. I get the short straw. By noon a lot of nasty stuff that's been in there all winter hits the dumpster. By mid-afternoon, long forgotten items locked in freezer ice get excavated. I am in such a good mood I get to handle tenant complaints. Some tenants are much more needy than others. Sometimes they ask for me because I'm nicer, they say.

Roy calls pretending to be a tenant. He complains of being neglected by his girlfriend. The girls can hear me talking to him so we use coded references to his plumbing problem. Last duty today is get with the maintenance super and have his supply order approved. He went over budget last month. I love my job but I make it a stepping stone. Interior design is my future. I request Friday afternoon off if I stay late today.

Lindsey is up against a deadline. She picks me up at 7 pm. We want more Chinese. It's easy to get hooked on it, so convenient, so satisfying. Is it the MSG? We have our fortune cookies, from yesterday also, still unread. Hers are as follows: "You are wise beyond your years." and "A routine task will turn into an enchanting adventure." Mine are thus: "Plan for many pleasures ahead." and "You will be very happy with your spouse."

Friday, March 4

Dear Diary, The young career women hit the road at 06:30, eager to accomplish their tasks and start their weekend adventures. We have got our tea mugs, Jasmine with lemon and honey. We have our sandwiches packed. We bring changes of clothes. Phil is in the parking lot as Lindsey drops me off. He is deep into his first pack of smokes for the day. He looks at us and shakes his head. "Those things will kill you," I say. "What a way to go!" he replies. It's a running joke we have. Each time he has a new come back. I have a short stack of folders on my desk. Joni is handling the phone. I clear my desk. I check in office supplies.

I have an e-mail from Roy at my work-related address. He wants to meet again in Providence. He has a room booked at the fabulous Renaissance Providence Downtown. I tell the girls where I am going. They remain quite certain that I am meeting a married man.

Lindsey arrives at 13:30. She comes in to meet the girls. They like her style. They ask where she shops. She deposits me at the Harvard Square Red Line stop. Tonight, she is buying art supplies and cruising the coffee shops. I hit South Station by 14:30 and Downtown Providence by 15:30 on commuter rail. I wait for Roy in the sumptuous hotel lounge. I tentatively take a booth. The bartender, Julian, is restocking. He asks me if I am lost. I say that yes, I'm a 'Stranger in Paradise' but my guide will be along soon. I ask for Ginger Ale with 3 cherries. In short order he returns announcing "Here is your Shirley Temple Miss...?" "Sarah Jane Powell," I inform him as if to establish an alibi. With great formality he deposits my drink on a bar napkin. I sip, sigh, and relax. I close out in cash and wave off the change. As I exit my weekend way station, Julian waves me back. "Miss Powell, a call for you here at the bar," he announces. The other bar patrons show no interest, as I would hope. It's Roy, summoning me to our room. "At this very moment?" I tease. "That will cost you extra." I wink at Julian and whisper, "It's my fiancé." I flash my ring. He regards me curiously as I depart.

Saturday, March 5

Dear Diary, At 03:00, I slide out of my silky sheets to get a drink. There are all kinds of nice juices in our mini-bar. Roy is on his stomach, dead to the world, hugging 2 pillows. A few hours ago, he was much more active attending to my desires, with room service for an intermission. I peak through sheer curtains at the cityscape five floors below, a peaceful pallet of muted colors mirrored on wet thoroughfares nearly empty, the traffic lights winking compulsively in case of rare vehicle. There is a man on a bicycle. He looks up at our window. That's a little scary. I close the curtain and sneak back into bed, content just to snuggle. Roy turns over. Now it is me on my stomach with left hand free to wander the manscape. I delay further gratification until first light sometime after 06:00.

I do my woman on top routine, a great way to start the day. On top I can delay the full climax and instead have some little ones first. Roy reaches for the remote. I snatch it away from him. "On Saturdays, I make you my submissive," I declare. He lies there smiling for a while, checks his wristwatch and sighs. "Okay enough," he finally asserts while rolling me over and concluding the morning action to our mutual satisfaction. I give him back the remote and sashay to the shower naked, diverting his attention from ESPN. I deliver what he pays extra for, the show which includes Sarah's ass in action, live, on stage, front row VIP seating. So many simple pleasures, must I list them all?

I make the in-room coffee while Roy does his grooming. I open curtains. I crack windows for fresh air. Both of us are in jeans, his rear view nearly as nice as mine. We take our coffee to the 9th floor lounge by stairway. We check out the vista south towards Newport. Sun is trying to break through. We find a stairway to lobby. The gentleman proceeds in front in case the lady stumbles. Our step aerobics concluded, we pause in the cheerful Greek Revival foyer. I make mental notes on how the effect is achieved. Will it always be this way, contentment simply being together?

Brunch begins with Mimosas in a quiet booth. We order from the menu. Table-side service is so much more fun compared to buffet. Our waiter is Anton. His service exceeds that of Julian in formality and quiet dignity. I love it. Avocado toast is for me. Southern Boy Delight is for Roy. We share a bowl of blueberries and whipped cream. We try a pot of Ginseng Tea. I can't stop smiling, about what exactly, I am not sure. At first it is Roy's whipped cream mustache, which he doesn't bother to wipe away.

We check out at exactly 11:00, taking every minute allowed to us in this fabulous place. Exiting arm in arm on Francis St., I go for a big passionate kiss, arms flung around my man's neck. I warn Roy a minute in advance. He plays along, like an actor under direction and here we are, young and in love, on location, Providence, Rhode Island. "I believe that is a cut and print, first take, baby doll," he declares. Strangers, namely, two senior couples and one young woman walking her dog, comprise our limited audience, as is fitting.

By 12:30 we are at Canton Junction, where Roy's pickup sits in a corner of the lot beside some dirty half melted snow piles. He drops me at Perks in Norwood. He has guy stuff to do. Robert is there. He has a shift later at Norwood Hospital. He is content with Darla, probably a passing fancy and he still has the hots for me, he admits. He continues to tell Mom that we are just friends, which is true, but we don't confide too much, not yet. He likes to flirt with barista Cameron though. Everyone likes to flirt with Cameron, hoping for a smile.

Lindsey arrives at 14:00. We catch up on the way home. She has met someone, her type if only not so young and so straight. Details follow as we share housekeeping chores at home. The young woman's name is Jessica. They shared a table at Blue Bottle Coffee on Bow St. in Cambridge, a place that attracts a nice mixed crowd. Jessica had just come from an AA meeting. She checks the bulletin boards for jobs that pay cash. L. tells her about the caterers who serve art openings and also tells her about Art School Modeling and her own private projects. Jessica does not even have a phone. We decide to stay home tonight, except that I will do my evening vigil Mass.

Sunday, March 6

Dear Diary, Little brother James, the brat, is in town from North Adams. His wife, Trudy stayed home with the kids. My presence is required at the parents for lunch. His old bedroom is now Mom's sewing room. I shared with little sister in the upstairs corner bedroom. We could climb outside onto the roof of the side porch and sneak a smoke. I manage to escape before dinner.

Roy has let himself in. My girls are used to him. They stay in the kitchen watching his every move. He is making spaghetti. He brought some Chianti. I brought one of Mom's apple pies. I get busy grating some Parmesan. We also have sourdough rolls and butter, a head of iceberg, and some Klondike Bars. What a feast! Basketball is on TV, March Madness. We set the table and wait for it to get dark enough for candles. We stretch out on my bed and trade massages. This could be a normal Sunday evening once we are married. By 21:00 the wine has worn off and my man has to go. It's light up full in the kitchen for dish-washing.

I hear a knock. It's Lindsey, of course. I set her a plate for company and confidences. We did our shopping for the week at Star Market that morning. She makes our sandwiches for tomorrow.

She tells me about guys who thought they had a chance with her. "Try it. You might like it," one of them said. Another offered to pay $20 for just one kiss, if it was a wet one in a clinch and lasted a full minute. Others wanted to hang out often and try to get her tipsy to see if maybe just maybe once in a blue moon, but none ever got lucky. She played strip poker in mixed company mainly to see the girls go topless. Yes, men have seen her naked. They looked but did not dare touch.

Thus, we finished the Chianti. The more we drank, the better the stories became. After years of inhibition, I rediscover how much fun it is to be starkers, the same fun I had as a 2-years old, running around the house naked and unafraid. Once, I even got outside, naked an unashamed. While I still have it, I don't mind flaunting it.

Monday, March 7

Dear Diary, Time marches on for two career women, two love lives, one broken down Chevy. We are on duty in our respective workplaces by 09:00, content to trundle along on our weekday routines.

I send Roy a hand-written thank you on company letterhead, with a lipstick kiss signature. I thanked him with my body already and now with all my heart. This is it. This is being in love. How long will it last? None can know.

Thankfully, the morning starts out slow. We have got our full crew in the office today except for Maggie who is in meetings at corporate offices off site. Sandy gets Tammy and Joni busy on overdue projects, while Susan and I run the rest of the show at our side-by-side desks. We have Tammy for 5 more days. Friday will be a goodbye party. Susan has decided to be secretive about her love life also. I won't dish about Roy so she won't dish about her secret guy either. We say only that our secret guys are not married and it is not Phil, the parking lot flirt. We simply hint and one-up each other on how super fine and expert he is in bed.

By afternoon, we have a balmy 42 F. The car poolers cruise home at a leisurely pace on one of our scenic routes including Pond St. and Arborway. We roll the windows down. We are not much for idle chatter. We compare ourselves with one year ago. We decide that things are looking up.

Our "Rites of Spring" exhibit will open on Friday, April 8, at Galerie D'Orsay on Newberry St. meaning we have 4 more weekends to finish printing and framing. Later we look at virtual framing on Lindsey's software. Her negatives have been scanned for such manipulations. Later in my bubble bath with my girls staring at me, I conjure up some fantasies for the weekend. Simple pleasures with a surprise twist. I call Roy while he is correcting math tests. He is happy to take a break from that. Later, in bed, I dive into another Sherlock Holmes mystery. I flip to "The Sussex Vampire". Later, in my dream, Susan's secret guy is a vampire and now so is she.

Tuesday, March 8

Dear Diary, Snow fell overnight, just a dusting, maybe the last of the season. The bird feeder is near empty. I pull on some jeans and deposit the remaining seeds from the sack I bought in February. The air smells nice, not the usual city air. My girls watch me from the window. Sparrows and Blackbirds are first to swoop in.

I drive today. We take Centre St. Lindsey needs a power nap on the way. She was up late choosing frames. She has decided to hang without glass or plexi, but just a dust-able spray finish. She will be unpacking sculptures today.

At our desks, I tell Susan about my dream. She has a totally different fear. What if we are dating the same guy, a two-timer, and then when he gets found out, he wants a threesome? A fine Hollywood sitcom that would be. We decide for sure we will not share. Susan wants the model apartment tours today and I am stuck in the office alone at lunchtime. I look online for some new rental furniture people. The stuff we have in the demo units looks kind of old fashioned 1980s cheesy to me. I solicit some bids and work up a proposal. Someday, that is what I will be, an Interior Designer, good and married for life. I have had my single years. They were bittersweet.

On the way home I let Lindsey do the talking. It is time for me to just listen, to be a pal. We have some tunes turned down low. She thinks she can buy my car after the Art Opening. She has never had her own car. It could open some possibilities for her. She likes that it is a girl's car, first mine, then hers. I will be gone, living with a man, but she will have my car. She confesses that she has become very fond of me and because of me maybe she will not always require a blond for a lover. I will be very careful with her feelings and just in general the fragile artists' temperament. She will be one of my bridesmaids and perhaps we can arrange diversity among the other bridesmaids. "Yes, do it," she says. We decide to have a slumber party tonight. I have a DVD of "Pillow Talk" with Doris Day, Rock Hudson and Tony Randall. It is fun to see her giggle.

Wednesday, March 9

Dear Diary, It's Ash Wednesday. Mom reminded me. I walk to church. By 7:30, I come out all ashen square in the middle of my forehead. Lindsey is there waiting. I give up chocolate for Lent. That is an easy one. Last year it was Pizza. We are on duty punctually as usual.

At lunch, I drop hints with Roy about weekend activities. Leave it all up to me, I guarantee. The afternoon drags on. We plan Tammy's going away party on the sly. Sandy has the card already and we all sign. After work, Lindsey and I find that we are overdue for Yoga. It will be nice new ingredient in our weekly routine. The Blissful Monkey on Centre Street is convenient and has a vibe that we both like. There is a staff of 12, including the owner. We do a beginner class and get schedules to hang on our fridge. "See anything you like?" I inquire. "Close," she replies with a grin. At home, I find out that Doris Day is Lindsey's main fantasy.

I give her "Send Me No Flowers" to enjoy privately for tonight. It seems like both of us need some relief soon. I am barely getting through 3 days without my man. Tonight, it is just a quick shower then I fish out my bag of toys from under the bed. I have fun until the batteries wear down. I call to see if the horny young woman upstairs has any spare "D" replacements. "I was going to ask you the same thing," she replies. We'll just have to make do without, it seems. I channel the sex energy into housekeeping. I make sandwiches and tidy the kitchen. I take out the trash in my robe and slippers. I gaze at the stars.

The hot water kettle is whistling on my return. A nice pot of vanilla and chamomile tea at bedside will calm me. I switch on the radio. Delilah is spinning love songs. Lindsey calls. "Can I come down?" she wonders. "Go ahead, what the heck," I agree. Roy says I can screw as many women as I like. That is not really being unfaithful in his logic. In 2 minutes, my partner in photo nudity is there beside me under the covers. We might as well get this over with, perhaps one time only or in emergency, as long as Mom never knows.

Thursday, March 10

Dear Diary, At 06:00, I roll over half asleep. I reach for Roy or a pillow or something to hug and end up with a handful of one of Lyndsey's A-cup boobs. I give her a kiss between the shoulder blades and slide out of bed on my way to the shower. "It's okay, no regrets, our lives will go on as before," I say with a smile on the way to the shower. She joins me in there. We have always been comfortable with each other naked. It's just a girls locker room type shower. We dress quickly while the Malibu warms up.

We stop for breakfast at Harry's All American on Centre Street. Lindsey is looking at me a little uncertainly. For reassurance, I explain that Roy has already imagined us together. He is not worried about it. We agree to keep each other in case of TLC emergency. I let her know that she kisses very nicely and that we certainly got each other off. It seems I am now at least 1% bisexual. Her boyishness and general love-ability made the experiment pleasant and guilt free, I explain. We can use the "L" word. "I am your first and maybe only bi-curious? I like the sound of that," she chimes in, suddenly cheerful. I drop her off at 08:00. She seems very happy. "Here comes the L word. You said I could use it. I love you, Sarah Jane," I hear. "I love you, too, Lindsey. It feels nice," I reply. Will you forgive me for marrying that guy Roy? I add with a grin. "I suppose. We'll see," is her playful response. She is off to work with a bounce in her step.

I am at my desk by 08:30. Susan suspects something. I ask her in private if she ever lip-locked a girl. "That's a no but Katy Perry has, at least according to that song she does, you know the one. Is that an invitation?" she wonders. "Maybe on New Year's Eve, if we are both drunk," I tease. "We'll talk more about this later. I suspect something," Susan whispers in my ear. I catch her staring at me later. I simply shrug my shoulders. When I pick up my female lover I blurt out "How's about we sleep in your bed tonight and maybe the cats can come along? But then, I'm giving you up for Lent." "Fair enough," my emergency lover replies.

Friday, March 11

Dear Diary, It was strange to wake up in Lindsey's bed. She sleeps with the curtains open. The street light shines in. We sit up and look outside at the empty street. It is still dark but we hear bird song. I want her to know that the previous night was not an aberration, that she is desired without regret. She has a long love life ahead of her and I am just one who happened during this early period. It was mainly hugging and kissing and playing with her tits. I smothered her with my pair which are slightly fuller. Her hands are very ticklish. I prefer to be the one with the wandering hands. She has got some apricot scrub for the shower which is fun. Her kitchen has less stuff in it, but we make do.

At work I tell Susan that Lindsey is a sweet kid. She needed a hug and we added a big kiss. "Aha! I figured her for a Lesbo straight off, that day you brought her in here." says she. I have still got her wondering about me.

Roy calls at lunch. He will let himself in and start cooking at 16:30. I get there at 17:30. Lindsey takes the car and goes off to the darkroom. Roy has set the table but first I am the appetizer, all of my pieces and parts which he can't get enough of. During dinner, I tell him how terribly much I missed him all week. We leave the dirty dishes and take a walk. We do a bubble bath. At 5 foot 10, he can barely fit in there with me. Later, in bed, we hear Lindsey come in. I decide to bring the cats up there to keep her company.

On return I admit "Yes, I slept with her. It was bound to happen eventually. We were both so horny." "I knew it. What else? You know us guys are endlessly curious about this girl-on-girl stuff," he demands. "She kisses very nicely; her tits are luscious; and she taught me scissoring," I explain. "Enough! Now spread 'em. It's my turn," he declares. That was the last of the talk as we make up for lost time. We clean up the kitchen. I make the sleepy time tea with honey and lemon. We douse the lights.

I deliver some of Lindsey's tongue technique. "Heavenly, heavenly," are my man's last words.

Saturday, March 12

Dear Diary, Coffee is perking at 09:00 when we hear a knock. Lindsey is there with a cat in each arm. A family of five sits down to milk in a bowl for two and coffee for three. The part time Psychologist, Roy, asks Lindsey about her family. She grew up in Brattleboro, Vermont. Her Dad is a truck driver, often absent on the road. Her Mom is a Nurse, often absent doing shift-work evening, nights, weekends and overtime. She has an older brother and sister. Quite often breakfast was the 3 children fending for themselves, sitting at an old-fashioned Formica top kitchen table just like mine. "Welcome home," Roy chimes in. "What was your favorite breakfast cereal?" It turns out it was Lucky Charms but we are all out of Lucky Charms today. Our pretend kid sister gets up, heads for the door and gives me a look like: is it ok? I nod and give her a kiss goodbye. She is off to the darkroom again.

Roy is shaking his head. He reminds me that seeing girls kissing is an instant boner for him which means back to bed for another hour. By noon we finally make it to Canton for spring cleaning at Roy's duplex. We get under and behind everything. We throw open the windows. He gets the bathroom. I get the kitchen. We team on the living room. We dust with lemon pledge. He sees me bending over and here we go back to bed again. It's a good thing I keep K-Y at his house also.

Dinner is whatever was left in the freezer. It has turned cold and windy. We take a short walk, enough to redden my cheeks. He finds some Jack Daniels tucked away in the garage. We blow the dust off the bottle and make hot toddies to take to bed. We are spending more time horizontal than vertical this weekend. I remind him how much, so terribly much I missed him all week. How long can we go on like this? He admits that he probably would not get much work done at home if I were there every night. We agree that I will get a job in Canton and move in next January but exact wedding date remains uncertain. Next, we make up stories about us being monogamous porno stars.

Sunday, March 13

Dear Diary: I am awake first. I look around at Roy's bedroom. Sure, it is clean and fresh but a little sad and depressing all the same. It's too tacky 20th Century. Roy's den can be transformed the easiest and cheapest just with paint, curtains and a different desk. I work in an office, why not start with office space. I will consult with Lindsey and other advisers on this. Is there room for a partners' desk? The creative juices are flowing.

We decide to go to Mass in Canton then attend estate sales. I bring Roy breakfast in his office while he looks up churches and sales. We make it in time for 10:00 services at St. Oscar Romero, the closest location. It is very cheerful modern architecture. I say, "Let's get married here." "Fine with me," says Roy. To him, that is a minor detail.

The estate sale is in Norwood. Most of the stuff there is wishful thinking for our budget. There are a few desktop items marked down half price for the last day of the sale, such as an inkwell with fountain pen, a desk blotter, a paper weight and a letter opener. We offer $25 for the lot. Sold!

Parting is such sweet sorrow. We say goodbye at Perks in Norwood. We decide to arrange a mid-week tryst. I meet Mom at the Cedar Lebanese Market on Cottage Street. I get stuff from the deli. Mom gets mixed olives for Dad and some of their luscious French Pastries for guests. I tell her about my career plans. I tell her not to worry, I will not be an old maid. "Just believe in me, Mom. I'm tough. I'm solid. You raised me well, you and Dad. I will be nearby arranging all of my own affairs privately. It is more fun for me that way. Please don't snoop. All will be revealed to your delight in due time." This elicited a reluctant okay from Mom. She dropped me home by 16:00. I promised to visit next Sunday.

My 3 girls are waiting for me. Lindsey had coffee with Desiree. It turns she is married but she has had woman love in her history. They had a nice chat including hints about seduction and a promise to come with friends to "Rites of Spring".

Monday, March 14

Dear Diary, I have to settle down a little. I am becoming annoyingly cheerful at work. The girls are the grumpiest on Monday mornings. We take afternoon coffee break outside. There is a picnic table. Joni, the part timer is working, as usual on Mondays. She is having a nicotine fit. She is trying to quit smoking but the patch is very expensive and she is all out of the Nicorette gum. Phil offers one of his Marlboros. He thinks he has a chance but Joni already has a boyfriend. I think he likes to flirt just to get a smile or a smart-aleck come-back. I work late so that I can get off early on Wednesday.

L. meets me at 18:30. She has taken some of her negatives to a pro lab. The 11x14's are very difficult to get just right. She is a little stressed out. She feels like the success of our show could be a turning point in her life, personally and professionally. She feels like she can take some risks if I remain the net under her high wire act. I send her off with a hug and a kiss and some "D" batteries which Roy gave me. "Have fun," I say. "Think about me if you like," I add with a grin.

I call Roy on the land line. We plan our mid-week tryst.

Where can we meet if we have to sneak around? We decide to sleep on it and be guided by our dreams. For deeper sleep, I decide to exercise, sit-ups and girl push-ups, 100 each, also my soft dumbbells for every kind of arm thing I can remember. It takes 90 minutes. I still have some lavender soap and lavender scented candles. At 22:30, I let the girls back in. I fall asleep to their purring.

About 02:30 I awaken briefly to blow out the candles and drink some water. It seems like a dream was starting and I have to get back to it. I was going to confession. I couldn't think of any sins. My kittens are with me. We can all dream together, so warm, so cozy, so quiet. What are my sins? I have lots of dirty thoughts about doing stuff with a guy not my husband yet. We're engaged, that's my excuse. The priest wants to hear all of the dirty thoughts. I say "Wait, are you really a Priest?" He vanishes. Poof! Then I wake up.

Tuesday, March 15

Dear Diary, All of us girls decide to report dreams daily. Lindsey woke up once last night. She felt like she was falling. "Things are happening. I should let them happen?" she mused. I reached out and squeezed her hand. Maggie dreams of a big fat bonus at the end of the year and early retirement to Aruba but that is just a daydream. Last year she got a 20-year plaque from corporate that hangs on her office wall. The last dream Sandy remembers is about riding a horse bareback in the dark and she is holding on for dear life. She rode a pony once as a child but the pony was in a bad mood that day. It tried to brush her off and she started to cry. The family still tells the story. We suspect a deeper meaning.

All of Susan's dreams happen at her Grandma's house. Sometimes she is there playing hide and seek but nobody comes to find her. I save my dream for afternoon coffee klatch. "We know your dreams will be the dirtiest, Sarah Jane," they all agree. A life of fantasies and impure thoughts and nobody came to find me neither until I changed my game to seek and you shall find. At lunch I look up the quote from Matthew Chapter 7, Verse 7.

Maybe I heard it at Mass late last year and it stuck in my head. I quote it to the lunch room. "Ask and it will be given to you. Knock and the door will be opened to you." I post it on the break room fridge.

It gets busy. Afternoon coffee break happens kind of late at 15:00. I tell my dream about the Priest who is maybe the devil in disguise. "Who did he look like?" Sandy wants to know. "Kind of like Reggie, now that I think about it," I admit. "Poof! Up in smoke. Now we know where he went, into Sarah's dirty mind," laughs Sandy. We decide that Sunday will be girls night out at Loretta's Last Call, near Fenway.

Lindsey is up against deadlines. I agree to close up and wait for her here. I use the time to design Roy's office make-over. We have our Yoga gear in the Malibu. We do the 7 pm Reiki variations class. We balance our chakras and meridians. By 20:00, it is late supper in my kitchen. A girl crush hug and a kiss conclude our day well spent.

Wednesday, March 16

Dear Diary, The young artist and her not so young pal downstairs hit the pavement early in their trusty Malibu. 'Tis warm enough to roll down the windows. Lindsey must work late to finish her printing in the darkrooms of Tufts University. She drops me off and keeps the vehicle for the rest of the day and night. Sandy is cracking the whip today. The girls demonstrate their max efficiency. I am out the door by 14:00 on route to my secret rendezvous.

I have a pleasant 20-minute walk along Centre St. to meet the No. 37 Bus. After 10 stops, I transfer to the No. 30 Bus at Washington St. After 17 more stops, I arrive at Mattapan where I transfer to the No. 716 Bus. By 16:20, after 10 more stops, I am at Canton, all in all 90 minutes, to cover 15 miles via 3 buses, 37 stops, and $3.50 in swipes of my Charlie Card. A short walk along Washington St. brings me to Canton High School, where I am expected.

Roy is in his office on the first floor, correcting some quizzes. We close the door. "I had to see you!" I declare. Then he said something like, "Delighted you came. You smell wonderfully springtime all fresh like a bouquet of blossoms." He picks me up and sits me on his desk where the major make-out session begins. A tour of the school proceeds through deserted stairwells with stolen moments at many stops along the way, not as many stops as the bus, but plenty enough for wandering hands to find their favorite intimate places. I am sure we are not the first couple to use these stairwells for such. Going upstairs, I am in front offering flashes up the dress. By 18:00, I am close beside my roughneck man on the bench seat of his pickup. He takes me to Norwood and after a passionate kiss goodbye, I wander into Perks Coffeehouse to decompress.

By now, the baristas know me by name. Cameron is there. She clears her throat. Oops, my blouse remains untucked and unbuttoned. "Afternoon delight?" she inquires. "Yes, it definitely was," I affirm. I'll tell you about it sometime. We can compare notes." "High School seems like yesterday," I add with a wink.

Thursday, March 17

Dear Diary, Dave delivered me home at 20:00 yesterday. I heard Lindsey come in late at 22:00. We meet at breakfast in my kitchen. We both had a deep, dreamless sleep. I tell how I went back to High School. She tells me a little about Brattleboro Union High School, where she was Class of 2004. She went to the Prom with a guy named Wesley who agreed to be "the Beard". He was a charming escort. They looked good together. They were pals within her limits. "I just want to be with you, someone different, someone deep." he once avowed. He's married now, she found out at the 5 Year Reunion. They danced once for old time's sake. "You're still in love with her, I bet" she heard the wife say. "Maybe just a little," she heard Wesley say. "That is so sweet. That is priceless," is what I say.

We "lively ourselves up" with a Reggae tape on the way to work. We are both in a really good mood. What could go wrong? A flat tire could go wrong, that's what. It's a good thing I have Triple A. Dad insisted on it. We end up with two new rear tires, and alignment per Dad's advice. Career girls need trusty transpo. We are late to work so we both stay late.

I tell Susan about my make out session in a public building. "Next time, get a room!" she declares. "Tell me a trashier true story about you.

Think overnight." I challenge her. "I can out trash you any day," says she.

The working girls are home by 19:30. I let Lindsey cook and flop on her bed. Grilled cheese sandwiches are her specialty. Felicia and Fatima come up to visit while we watch a little TV. I go crash at 21:00. I will be well rested, fully energized for weekend. I do my exercises. I shower instead of bathe. I light my candles then off into dreamland where anything can happen. I dream of ambulances and fire trucks. I don't like this dream. I wake myself up. A siren is fading away in the distance. Then I hear birdsong.

This calms me. I have a Guardian Angel of sorts right above me. It's too bad we can't just summon each other and climb up and down at will, as needed through a secret trap door.

Friday, March 18

Dear Diary, Boing! I pop out of bed like a Jack-in-the-Box at 06:00 hours. Dad likes the military time. Many was a morning he rousted the teenage me out of bed to fight for bathroom time in a crowded house. If he had bacon in the skillet already, that helped. The radio, AM talk radio, that helps. I am enjoying every hour of every day now that I got my kittens and my guy and my gal pal and new tires.

It feels like the Malibu can drive itself on our favorite route along Lagrange Street and VFW Parkway. I get dropped off, curb service style. I can't wait to hear what wanton woman tale Susan has come up with. She keeps me waiting until afternoon break. Sandy says to keep the locker room talk to a minimum. It is a place of business after all. Susan takes me aside and recounts the night her boyfriend went missing at a party. Assuming the worst, she got revenge sex with some other guy she just met. Later her boyfriend came home in custody of his pals who found him passed out on the lawn. She dutifully screwed her boyfriend, it being the rare opportunity to screw two guys in one night. "Within hours of each other! You are a bad, bad girl!! That beats my wicked ways," I concede.

At home, Roy is cooking. We do dinner for three. Afterwards, Lindsey is going out to The Blue Bottle just to hang out and see what happens. She goes up to change and returns in the look that Roger gave her. "Very nice and modest and your curfew is midnight," Roy renders his approval.

She has her sketchbook with her. We watch her drive away. "Let's keep her forever," I suggest. "Fine with me, anything you want. Now get those clothes off. I can't wait any longer," my man demands. One hard core hour later the bedroom is as big a mess as the kitchen. We need some fresh air. We take a walk to Speedy Mart for beer because my man has built up a powerful thirst after an hour in the saddle. Roy is sleeping as I write this. From the fog of my beer buzz mini-hangover emerges the memory of a shower, fluffy robes, frosted glasses, foam tickling my nose and falling asleep with my head on a hairy chest.

Saturday, March 19

Dear Diary, "It's cold out, honey. Let's stay home and do nothing," is my man's request. "Yes, you're mine and I keep you prisoner under house arrest," I concur. "Does the prisoner get any breakfast?" he wonders. "Maybe a piece of dry toast and we'll stay home all day until we get sick of each other." The warden exits to the kitchen leaving the captive to fend for himself. He discovers the prison library.

I look out at the bird feeder. I notice the Malibu is not there. I plug my flip phone into the charger. There is a text from L. indicating, "accepted overnight invite, details 2 follow". We breakfast in bed and hypothesize about the details to follow. We flip my 8 channels of antenna TV. We settle on cartoons, Looney Tunes. The girls jump into bed. They get max attention today. This is domestic bliss. Fatima will need her operation soon. We get her used to the cat carrier with the cage door open.

My prisoner can earn his lunch if he goes out on work release. Trash, that needs to go out and there's recycling. They pick up today. Breadcrumbs for the feeder, let's see what else? Can't think of anything. On return I fling my arms around my man all fresh air infused and wet leaves stuck to his boots. Then I turn away, angry. "I saw you flirting with that girl who walked by," I hiss. "Aha! Jealousy rears its ugly head. It was an old granny," he protests. "Okay, never mind, I forgive you, I will always forgive you. It's our first fight, a pretend fight. Was it good for you?" I inquire. "Yes, indeed. It was my big chance to give you my best Rhett Butler attitude." Rhett Butler earned his hot lunch consisting of soup, BLT sandwiches and coleslaw.

We hear a car door slam. Lindsey has returned just in time. She joins us all excited. She has been with her new pal Jessica in a drafty triple-decker in Dorchester. Jessica was too much for her parents to handle so they sent her to live with Grand-dad. Lindsey sketched the old guy, which gave her an idea for her next exhibit called "Worn to Perfection" which is pretty much the opposite end of the spectrum from Aphrodite.

Sunday, March 20

Dear Diary, Saturday evening was all about make up sex after our first pretend fight. We're getting cabin fever so we made the 10-minute walk to Saturday Vigil Mass at St. John's. We crashed early and now, oh, the luxury of a lazy Sunday morning with the man you love. He gets the prisoner rations of some toaster waffles with jam chased by my percolator brew Sumatra fresh ground. I stay open robe with the tits hanging out. It seems we need one more for the road. He performed well enough for me to grant the captive parole. But he must meet with his parole officer, me, next Friday.

I watch his truck drive away. Straight off, I am depressed. I tidy up the place. I freshen up myself. When in doubt, go shopping. Lindsey wants some old wood frames from second hand. We go to The Thrift

Shop of Boston in nearby Roslindale. She has decided to present one digital print in 16x20. We score some bling and old furs for possible use with Mata Hari. As darkness falls, we zoom quickly through Star Mart. We are stocked up and ready for our exciting week to come.

At my place, we watch the DVD movie "Bound" starring Jennifer Tilly. We hold hands, with one cat each for the free hands. I examine the right hand of the artist. It's a workers hand, active daily with many tools of the trade. This movie is intense. We require an intermission. I serve the leftover Dos Equis from Friday evening. There is a happy ending. Spoiler alert: the ladies team up, use their wits and have their way in end.

The party finishes early with a promise of breakfast at 06:00 upstairs. It was comforting to hold the hand of my gal pal as we proceed on our quest for Love and Success. Now I am depressed again. My little ones are staring at me. They get their Fancy Fiest. I manage a few more pages of Sherlock Holmes. I dream about tall buildings in yellow brick. I am getting a roof top tour. People are jumping off like lemmings. I read that lemmings are not really committing mass suicide. They are high divers and that is the quickest way to get to the water below.

Monday, March 21

Dear Diary, At first light 06:40, the career girls are finishing a breakfast of fruit cocktail, toast and butter. My hostess serves Maxwell House instant. Saves time, she says. We check the view from her higher vantage point. We hit the remote starter on the Malibu and watch it defrost as we drain our cups.

We have time to take the scenic route following West Roxbury Parkway and Grove Street. We are in work mode and not much to say. I drop my passenger at 07:30. I am at my desk all booted up by 08:00.

Full crew will be here today, including the maintenance boys, who have already made their first sorties in golf carts loaded with tools. Those guys get dirty. They brave the elements. They dealt with two lock-outs over the weekend. I attach the fees due with April rent. We girls got it made, safe and warm inside, ergonomic desks, morning and afternoon coffee breaks, a lunch that need not be rushed, free parking, time to socialize. How much will I miss all this, one year from now when I am happily married and living in Canton. I could stay as a part-timer, the old life bleeding into the new one. How would that feel? Strange, I think.

Roy calls in at lunch. He misses me already. Friday seems so far away. Just being apart is heartache. A year ago, there was no heartache, just emptiness. Today is spring solstice. We are not planting anything yet. At least let's buy some and prepare some pots indoors. Nature Girl Joni has sprouted some Avocado pits at home. She agrees to bring them in. We will get them rooted here in the office.

At lunch we search for wildflowers in the grassy areas. I found some patches of Bluets. Sandy found some Crocuses emerging. As the only single women in the office, Susan and I admit that love has blossomed but we must, for personal reasons, keep all details private.

Lindsey and I detour over to Whole Foods to buy seeds and potting soil on our way home. I want to grow some peas. Lindsey wants to try Shasta Daisies. We dinner at my place. The little ones get lots of love.

Tuesday, March 22

Dear Diary, I start my peas in the bathroom where they will not be molested by cats. The fluorescent lighting in there should be sufficient. Lindsey is driving. I look at my budget. Payday is Friday. Tax refund will be a few hundred more fairly soon. That will help. Somewhere, a pickup truck is waiting for me. I start humming "Somewhere" from "West Side Story". There is the lyric about "peace and quiet and open air wait for us somewhere" which prompts me to suggest a stop along Arborway after work to watch the sun go down. It is agreed.

The morning flies by as I update our waiting list and make notifications for those still waiting. Roy can't talk. He is in a meeting about cyber bullying and suicide prevention. His work group is preparing recommendations for the school board. School buses discharge children in our complex daily and it always reminds me of Roy.

Susan and I sit outside for lunch. Phil is there. We decide to find out what his deal is. He works in the next building but here is a nicer place to smoke, protected from the wind, plus there is a chance for pleasant company. Yes, it's a great way to meet people, especially other smokers. Some say smokers are more sociable. I used to be one myself. Susan and I say we each have secret boyfriends and we're pretty sure it's not the same guy. He laughs. "Someday, all will be revealed," he says with a grin as we all go back to work.

By 17:30, I am on my way to Boston MFA. By 18:00, Lindsey and I have found a park bench facing west on our homeward bound scenic route. We huddle together against the chill. The sun is setting on our magical winter. We will remember this moment at the end of every winter to follow. At twilight we are nearing home on Centre Street, moving slowly. We cut across Roslindale Village to Washington St. We dine at Pleasant Café, my treat, all cozy in the crush of many, but private in our booth. We share a fish, chips and 2 sides. We park at home by 20:00. "Your bed or mine? I ask. "Mine," says she. "Kittens or no kittens?" I further inquire. "Kittens," says she.

Wednesday, March 23

Dear Diary, At 06:00 my eyes pop open with the sound of early traffic. I give my slumber companion a kiss on the forehead and a whispered message to meet me downstairs. I grab the kittens and tiptoe downstairs. Lent is 40 days. I only lasted 14 days abstaining from the comfort of Lindsey's bed. If only she weren't so adorable and so near, it would be simpler. At least the abstaining from chocolate remains continuous.

I try one of Mom's vintage dresses from when she was size 7. The pleated double breasted lapel collar outfit in burgundy could create a stir. I saw Maggie wearing something similar one day. I am almost finished with our sandwiches when Lindsey engages the remote starter. My percolator has stopped just as she knocks and lets herself in. We are in work mode once more. There is not much to say. We drink silently and stare out the window.

I drive. My companion finds classical music. We have our favorite stations saved. I drop my passenger at 07:40. I am logged in by 08:00. Sandy has brought doughnuts to help us over the hump. Susan is grinning at me with powdered sugar on her face. "There was only one jelly donut. First come, first served," she explains. Thus, begins the happiness of another ordinary day. We reschedule girls' night out at Loretta's Last Call to the coming Sunday. The sun breaks through and we lunch outdoors. My man rings in at afternoon break. He misses me terribly. Next week, perhaps another Wednesday tryst, I propose. "Leave it to me," he assures.

I have time to create another variation for our future furnished units. I see how much of the work our own guys can do. During return commute, my partner and I have smooth jazz on low volume. We discuss our weekend plans. Saturday, I will be in Canton. L. will go to Colortek Pro Labs downtown to pick up the digital prints. "Last night was wonderful," she tells me. "Yes, it was," I confirm. "Let's keep it spontaneous." "That would be very nice," says she. "We'll always kiss goodbye?" I wonder. "Like signing a painting," is her reply.

Thursday, March 24

Dear Diary, What new ingredient can the career girls add to their Thursday? We decide to visit Galerie D'Orsay after work thus to preview our wall space. Could we configure our space to look like a boudoir painted by Maxfield Parrish? I had his painting, Ecstasy in the back of my mind during one of my poses. Mitzi, the gallery owner is a RISD graduate and happy to promote a talented fellow graduate such as Lindsey. She will advise us.

I play with some designs on my lunch break. I'm thinking fresh, modern, cheerful, and high key. There should be a chaise lounge, maybe even a fragrance, something like Sweet Woodruff or Lilacs. We grind out the usual tasks of our standard workdays.

By 17:30 we proceed on our route from the Museum of Fine Arts, first on Fenway Drive, with a view of the Back Bay Fens on the left. Storrow Drive takes us alongside the Charles River to Arlington Street, which leads to our destination on Newberry Street. We manage to find a parking spot two blocks down. Mitzi is there to meet us. She feels Gardenia is right for Aphrodite. She has a chaise lounge in her office. We discuss how to mimic morning light. We will have a corner enclosure with an extra portable wall on the right. We have tea and cookies in Mitzi's office. She has seen the previews and she is confident all items will sell on the first weekend.

We retrace our path to the MFA, thereby back to our usual homebound route along Jamaica Way to Centre Street. We are finally home sweet home at 20:00. The kittens get their dinner first while leftovers are heating. "Are you happy?" I inquire. "Very," says she. We have dessert upstairs. I found some ice cream. We trade shoulder massages. A hug and a kiss goodnight feel nice.

A hot shower and shampoo feel really nice. It's a small bathroom, easy filled with steam. My lights are out at 21:30. There is a big weekend coming up. Come along baby girls. Keep Mama company. I must call my man. He is watching basketball, so easy to please. I tell him get ready for some more fun pretend fights on our weekend of domesticity.

Friday, March 25

Dear Diary, Because of my pretend fights with Roy, neither of us will go on defensive in a real fight. It just occurred to me during a half-awake minute.

The career girls have been getting good sleep. We are both full of energy. My partner in artistic endeavors hits my door with a smile today. She boosts herself up and sits on the countertop to sip her tea while I pack our sandwiches. With her up there, she gets to be the taller one for a nice hug.

It's only 06:30. We have time for the scenic commute, western route, along Lagrange Street and VFW Parkway. The outside air smells wonderful. We have windows rolled down and Reggae on the radio. We are at Chestnut Hill by 07:30 and I relinquish the Malibu into the trusty super safe driver hands of Miss Lindsey.

I am first in the office. The maintenance guys are buzzing about outside. I wonder why I never gave any of them a second glance. They obviously have skills. Mostly they are married.

Some are way too old. Plus, there has always been that "Don't fish off the company pier," advisory in place. I am the official greeter as the staff trickles in, all perky and TGIF. It's casual Friday with dress, jeans and slacks on parade. I am cheerfully on phone duty with a few folders to process in between calls.

We finalize details for Sunday girls' night out. Before I know it, it's 17:30. Lindsey is there in the office. She breezes through to the break room with confidence and bit of a smile, there to wait for me while I finish up. Susan whispers in my ear, "Okay, I admit, if I kiss a girl just to drive guys crazy, she would be a good choice." "A wet one?" I inquire. "The wetter and deeper, the more the guys would go wild," she replies with a grin. L. is happy to hear me recount this exchange. Her confidence is growing.

There is a message waiting at home. Roy wants to meet for dinner in Needham. He will meet me at the train station. By 19:00, I am ready. I wear my ring so dazzling. L. will stay home to frame her 8x10's in my kitchen which is more spacious. Dave, my transporter, whisks me away in style. Details to follow...

Saturday, March 26

Dear Diary: Okay, I'm back from my date with Roy. It's just a little bit past midnight. I am in my robe and slippers. Lindsey is still busy in the kitchen. My man took me to Sweet Basil on Great Plains Ave. This could become "Our Place". Roy wants to have dates, instead of just crashing at his place or mine.

He picks me up, spins me around and plants a big one right on the kisser. I take his arm. Our table is waiting a mere two-minute walk from the train station. We scan the room. It's all strangers. The coast is clear. The atmosphere is wonderful, similar to Oscar's except a bit more spacious. He does the Shrimp. I do the Salmon. We linger over Strawberry Parfait. He stares at my peek-a-boo cleavage the whole time. In a clinch on a park bench in the square, we wait for Dave. It ends up being a tantalizing ten minute make out session. He cops a feel at the chest. I cop a feel at the package. He strolls over to his pickup in his cowboy walk. Looking back, I see him tip his hat and wave goodbye.

The framing is finished. I take a look. OMG!!! Two sex bombs are we. I grab the younger Goddess under her hips and pick her up. At just over 100 pounds, it's no sweat to carry her around. She looks down at me. "Let me shower here," she pleads. "Be my guest," say I. She comes out towel wrapped around at armpits. We share the final beer in a frosted mug followed by a beer foam kiss, the kind of kiss Susan mentioned. "You know this can't last forever," I sigh. "Yes," she sighs in return. "but stranger things have happened."

We douse lights then it's candles, kisses and cuddles 'til the break of dawn, four way, including felines. We laugh ourselves to sleep. We left curtains open to catch first light. My guest sits up and smiles, waiting for breakfast in bed. We have tea and toast, topless. By 07:30, we bid farewell until tomorrow. Gal Pal has consented to join girls night out Sunday.

Roy rings up at 08:00 asking my ETA. He will take me to more estate sales. We stick to a budget of $100 each. I get two wicker chairs and matching end tables. The wicker could work at the gallery. Roy found one of those desk lamps with the green shade, cylindrical bulb, and pull chain, very subdued quiet dignity retro upscale classy. My man is a class act. I tell him so. I ask him what is the worst thing a woman can do. He says that would be the silent treatment freeze out. We promise never to do that. No matter how exasperated one may be with the other, we will always work it out in the bedroom. This brings us to our pretend fight of the day. It goes something like this.

-You don't really love me. You're just using me as a sex object, a jack pack.

-That's lucky for you, 'cuz I'm the only guy who gets you off.

-Except for the times I'm faking it.

-You're just using me as a pole to ride.

-Whenever I run out of D batteries.

-My pole is ready for another ride. See how well you can fake it today.

After 20 minutes, the two sex objects disengage for long enough to start dinner. Roy cooks. It's his kitchen. I set the table and make things romantic. I wonder what L. is doing? She seems a member of the family, kid sister still under my wing. We give her the Malibu and freedom. She gives us privacy.

Roy is even washing dishes. I dry and put away. We take out the trash. He waves to a retired couple across the street who sit on their deck. "That's us 40 years from now," I foresee. "Boring," says he. "We'll be having a fun fight. We stay sharp by matching wits." That's Roy, once again the Psychologist.

I take his arm for a stroll in a not far city park. We search for wildflowers in bloom. We find wild violets. These have a scent. I don't want to pick them. They are too delicate. Let the bees have them all. On rising from flower inspection, I fling my arms around my man's neck and declare my love for all in earshot to hear. It's like the song "Secret Love" by Lorrie Morgan. I heard it on the radio. "Now I shout it from the highest hills," she sings. Maybe not quite yet. Secret is fun. Secret is safe.

Sunday, March 27

Dear Diary, No practice fighting today. I don't want it to be daily. Roy makes breakfast. It's his kitchen. He can rule there. We sit outside on his deck. It's barely warm enough. A hot shower together takes the chill off. We go to mid-morning Mass. My man is happy just to sit beside me. We take a scenic route to Norwood via Neponset Street. It's bike-able, mostly flat, only 5 miles. L. is waiting for me at Perks. Roy waves goodbye and blows me a kiss. He has planned a surprise for Wednesday. I wonder what he has dreamed up. L. has her sketch book. She has sketched Cameron who is on duty. L. is smiling. She got her 16x20 digital prints. She is very happy with how they turned out.

I have to check in with Mom. I tell her I will see her next weekend. She suspects there is something I am not telling her. She can wait, like most everyone else. Can I trust Robert? Even he doesn't know about the engagement. Mom could certainly be pumping him for info. Best not think about this too much. Tonight will be fun. We'll see who all shows up for Ladies' Night at Loretta's Last Call. Some of us can try a two-step, gender free.

We go home to get ready.

We have cowboy boots and jeans. Guys will be there, wondering if they have a chance. This will not be a problem. We have plenty of ways to decline and give the brush off all cool and smooth.

When we arrive, Susan and Joni have already staked out our table. Tammy, Sandy and Maggie are the late arrivals. The group agreed to do ponytails with ribbons and bows matching the blouse making us 7 delightful Easter eggs in red, pink, blue or yellow. Maggie, our leader, is first to get out there on the dance floor. She is able to lead L. very nicely. I trade lead and follow with Susan. Our share of guys who say Ma'am show interest which we limit to a one dance flirt. Margaritas, Martinis and Daiquiris decorate our table. L. chooses beer. One Coors Light is enough to loosen her up. She wants to lead which turns out just fine since we practiced at home. Susan has been sitting for a while. L. comes over and off they go, with a wink and a smile.

Monday March 28

Dear Diary, The Cowgirls got home at a decent hour and hit the hay without delay. The evening was a success. My guy had fun watching basketball sweet 16 at Matt Kelly's Irish Pub in Canton. Two of his teams were still in the bracket of the betting pool among teachers.

The avocado sprouts have done well over the weekend. We can root them soon. It's warm enough to have lunch outdoors. We drop breadcrumbs for the Sparrows. The sun breaks through from where it was hiding that morning. I emerge from just such a cloud, a dysphoria of fifteen forgettable years duration. Was it worth waiting for? Yes!!! Subconsciously, I must have been saving myself for the really great guy that I have found.

The crew hum-drums their way to 17:30. I am the last to leave as I wait for my transporter. We have a pleasant drive home in full daylight. We divert a few blocks to Star Market. We pool our resources. We restock our staples, the usual stuff. We are home before dark. I check on my peas. They will sprout soon. We flip to see who will cook. I win therefor L. will cook and we eat upstairs. We talk about signage. There is a shop on LaGrange Street, Jan Boyd Calligraphy and Illustration. It is worth a look.

The tea kettle whistles. I set the orange and spice tea to brewing. From the limited menu at Chez Lindsey, we have grilled cheese, tossed salad, and tomato soup. Lorna Doone cookies go nicely with the tea. We trade neck rubs. "I must go below for my bubble bath and quality time with the little ones," I announce. "If you need me, just come down" I assure. One hour later, I am in bed with Sherlock Holmes' secrets and mysteries. They help me stay tuned to what is going on out there instead of just what is going on inside me. Reggie, what happened to you? Why do I care? I have your little girl, Fatima, maybe that is why. Roy calls to thank me for the wonderful weekend. How can he be real? He seems too good to be true. I intend to ferret out his human frailties. There is a tap, tap, tap at the door. L. stands forlornly under the dim hallway light. "I need you," says she.

Tuesday, March 29

Dear Diary, Overnight Sarah Jane and Lindsey pledge to remain something like family members, kissing cousins. We pledge to never move far away. Because of this connection, neither one of us will ever be needy or insecure. We have a stabilizing influence on each other. She is gay. I am straight, but not too straight.

We are quiet on our inbound commute. I have time to think. What is my purpose beyond simple survival? I work. I get paid, but what exactly is the result of my work? People find a home they can afford. They are happy there. My agency operates at a profit. People call with their complaints and needs. I satisfy them. I am a cog in the Real Estate mechanism. I can be replaced. This is a stepping stone for me. I can do more, but what exactly?

At lunch, Sandy drags out an old photo album. She has a bunch more photos she has printed out of her phone from various events such as Christmas parties. We get a few laughs out of these. There is me from 6 years ago. I had my health. I had my Yoga. I was saving for the Malibu. I had a future far better than I imagined.

I get a head start on tomorrow's work while waiting for L. They are letting her frame the 11x14s in Museum work areas. By 18:00, we cruise along on return commute. L. has an outlook different from mine. She is immersed in the world of Art. She creates it and presents it and sometimes she sells it. She gets her share of the funding. It happens for her as naturally as taking a breath. Art for Art's sake.

We stop at the Calligraphy printer on Lagrange. She is open late. Many people stop after work to pick up their orders. She will show us some possibilities on Thursday. A few minutes later, we throw open the windows in my kitchen. Ah! Springtime at last.

We have waited so long. We have sandwiches left over from lunch. We chew on a very important question as we stare at each other across the table. Do we sleep better in two beds or together in one? My girl crush catches on quickly. "You mean use each other as a sleep aid? Yes, use me, please do," says she. "It seems so natural with a girl like you," say I.

Wednesday, March 30

Dear Diary: This is all about sleeping, I tell myself. Who has the best bed? The kittens certainly don't care. Extra rooms are there for them to explore upstairs and an extra person to watch over them. It's cold downstairs. I forgot to close my windows. Start that percolator. Steam up that bathroom. L. brings extra toast. "Here, eat this while I button you up. We're running late. Don't forget your Yoga stuff. I'll meet you in the car," says my domestic partner, all super organized this morning. We're just two career girls taking care of each other.

I am the passenger. I am in charge of the tunes. Lately, I want Reggae. I pretend we are going to the beach. We arrive at Chestnut Hill a little later than usual. At 08:15, Susan is already on duty. She is inspecting a flower delivery, a springtime bouquet including Irises, Hyacinth, and Gerber Daisies. "To my Darling Sarah, Happy Birthday in advance from your Secret Admirer," is the note. Friday is my birthday. Now the girls are reminded of that plus they all get to enjoy the blooms which should last a week or so.

What other surprises has Roy got in store? He knows that our Yoga is at 6. We are home at a little after 7. He is there with all kinds of Chinese take-out, plenty for three, a bottle of Saki, and Sapporo Japanese beer in bottles. We eat with chopsticks.

He has some sort of oriental music playing on a little boom box. I think it is Japanese. There is Zither and Harp. I guess we have Asian Fusion. By 9, he has to go. We have a big smooch under the stars as I walk him to his truck. "You're mine," he declares. "Mine, all mine. See you Saturday." Then off he goes.

"A guy can come in handy sometimes, I suppose," admits my roommate. We replay the Oriental music, creating our pretend Asian Massage Parlor with incense and candles. At 02:00, we wake up thirsty, perhaps due to a Soy Sauce overdose. The Sapporo is calling us. We can't stop laughing. We don't know why. It's just a school girl slumber party flash back, I suppose. I write in my calendar. L. has her birthday on June 1. Now must sleep, must sleep....

Thursday, March 31

Dear Diary, I am awakened by whiskers. Felicia is on my shoulder making bread. The other side of the bed is empty, but still warm. Let's see how quickly I can be ready. The little ones get what they need first. I have a red pants suit laid out. It's one of Mom's. By 06:30 tea is brewing and sandwiches are done. I have time to refill the bird feeder. L. gives me a wave from above. It's my turn to drive and we need gas so there is a brief stop at Speedy Mart.

I get a lot done on my early arrivals at the office, before the chatter, before the phone calls. I send my enthusiastic appreciation to Roy's work email for his wonderful surprises. Background checks are done by 09:00. I take my coffee cup outside to stretch and daydream about things to come. One year from today, where will I be? Driving my truck to estate sales?

Working from a home office? Giving bids to clients?

At lunch the chatter is summer plans. My vacation will be early August. Susan gets July. Maggie and Sandy take winter slots. Our next hypo-allergenic unit is almost ready. I take a look after lunch. Very nice, I must say. This one will come furnished.

On the return commute, we stop at Jan Boyd Calligraphy. She agrees to create the Aphrodite Reborn Price List and Artist Bio on Linen Paper. L. chose a Calligraphy Style and Ink for each. I am the Chef tonight. L. has stuff to do. Tonight, is stir fry including the leftover Chinese. L. finishes her tasks. She comes down in her jammies. We have a late supper, including the remaining Saki. "I'm getting a little nervous. Show time is delayed to one week from tomorrow," the Artist reveals. The Saki is making us tipsy again. We decide to play Scrabble but limited to words of Love, Sex, Marriage, Procreation and Sensuality, that is anything in the domain of the Goddess. L. opens with Tits. Our Tits are going to be out there for all the world to see. So is the Bush, my first word. Hips go on the hanging H. I make Lips out of the hanging P.

So far, it's all 4 letter words. The game will continue over the next week. Roy can help. For now, it's beddy-bye.

Friday, April 1

Dear Diary, Friday, fun day, rolls around. Okay, I have to work a little first. My partner and I saddle up. I drop the Artist early so she can frame the 16x20's before she goes on duty out in the gallery.

Susan is in the office first with a grin and powdered sugar all over her face. She is rearranging my bouquet. "I'm resigning today," she quips. "I'm sick of you and all of your flowers, and boyfriends and girl crushes." "Then I quit also," I shoot back. "So there!" "On second thought, let's not quit. Here, have a jelly doughnut. I saved one for you," Susan goes on. The practical joking continues with Susan telling everyone that she is pregnant and she doesn't know who the father is because she was too drunk. She has Sandy going on that one before announcing "April Fools!" Sandy replies that "It's not nice to fool Mother Nature." From now on we refer to her as Mother Nature. I mean, she did have 2 children by natural childbirth. Susan gets to give tours today. One guy, George something, is cute and he's single. "It's forbidden to date tenants," I remind Susan on her return. "Especially when you are already knocked up." Eventually, 5 o'clock rolls around and Maggie releases us from bondage.

L. is waiting for me. She leans her head on my shoulder. "Let's just go home," she pleads. We take a nap after work. It's dark when we wake up. Roy calls. We meet bright and early tomorrow for more adventures. I tell him we are killing the last of the Sapporo. We are under a lot of stress. We need comic relief. We can't remember whose turn it was supposed to be on Scrabble. I add Lesbo to the hanging L. That gets taken down and changed to Lamda.

We go to see what's left in the upstairs kitchen. Cheese, crackers and pepperoni, that's about it. I've got olives. We make a Charcuterie plate. We go outside and look at the stars. "I was jealous when I saw you kissing Roy outside on Wednesday," my girlfriend complains. "It's my turn. Hint, hint," adds she. Girl kisses, guy kisses, for so many years, I had none, now I got both. Aphrodite gets her kisses under the heavens, thus reborn.

Saturday, April 2

Dear Diary, I bring you with me to Canton for another weekend of domesticity, just to be together with my man. He meets me in Needham, our safe place. We go on scenic Route 27 passing through Medfield, Walpole and Sharon. Most of the trees are still bare.

At the duplex, my man makes me waffles. He makes me a Mimosa with grapefruit juice. We get a little landscaping done outside. He has got a couple of rose bushes in a root ball. We plant in a bare spot out front. We leave our dirty boots, jeans and gloves in the combo garage and man cave. We are in our undies. The leather couch is conveniently there. Why not make use of it. That George Michael song plays in my head. The one that goes "Sex is natural, sex is good." But I also wonder who else has been naked on this couch. "None," he swears. "They all thought my man cave was creepy. They didn't want to slum it. You do.

That is how I know you are the one." That makes me very happy. I assure him he is first in my bed at Heron Street. We are almost like virgins, if you redefine it.

We get cleaned up. We get some music on. We take a before picture of his junky office. Then he lets me get to work using just what we have already. I focus mainly on the lighting including his new desk lamp. I make his bookshelves look nice. I dust a little.

Before long something is smelling really good in the kitchen. It's just a frozen pizza but he has doctored it up with lots of extras and a nice wedge of iceberg on the side.

We walk to the Canton Waterfall, a significant place in our love history. On our way home we divert to St. Oscar's for Saturday Vigil. Back home we decide what to fight about on our pretend practice fight of the week. He left the toilet seat up again, so inconsiderate. I put things away where he can't find them. It drives him crazy. We do the pretend yelling. I say "Stop yelling at me." Even louder he says, "I wasn't yelling, but you were screaming." Then I pretend to cry. Then he says that he's sorry. Then we fuck each other's brains out, upon which we are ravenous. We fight over the last slice of pizza.

Sunday, April 3

Dear Diary, It's 3 AM. I get up for a glass of cold water. My man is sleeping quietly face down. We agree that if either one of us snores, the other will facilitate the necessary repositioning to achieve more peaceful repose. I compare the night sounds here with those at my place. Both abodes are near Washington Street, here being the far South extremity of that thoroughfare. Traffic noise is somewhat less. Maybe the population of backyard birds is not exactly the same. My man, with his many skills, can certainly build a fine feeder for me. I sigh and slip back between the sheets.

At 7 AM, I return to you, Dear Diary. Roy sees me writing. I tell him that years from now we can read this together. In case of mismatched memories, I have my documentation. "We'll sell it as a screenplay to Hollywood," he quips. He wears an apron for comic effect as he presents breakfast in bed. "I have my documentation also," he replies. "In a span of a few short months, I have screwed you more times than all other sex partners combined. Men keep track of these things." This is quite an amazing statistic. It makes me smile. "Ditto," I reply. "I have screwed you more times than all other guys in my sex life combined. So we're even. It's all good. Plus, I faked the climax fewer times," I tease.

I yawn, stretch, drain my juice glass and let out a satisfied "Ah! Ain't love grand?" Roy doesn't miss a beat. He gets the last word, "We're gonna have so much fun together, me and my brazen, Tomboy, smart-ass, side kick. Now get dressed. It's time to go outside and play. Let's see if you can pitch a soft ball, then we can go to the track and have some races. Finally, we'll see if you can kick a 15-yard field goal."

So, Dear Diary, we arrive at 11 PM. I can report that my attempts at athletic prowess were humorous. One of my softball pitches landed on the street, bounced off a car, and into a storm drain. While Roy covered his eyes as the holder, I managed to get some of my place kicks off the ground. The main event, our 100-yard dash, was a tie, with only a 20-yard head start for me.

Monday, April 4

Dear Diary: It's breakfast at the crack of dawn once more for me and my gal pal. She is a little brighter than usual for a Monday morning. All of her printing and framing is done plus she had fun with Jessica over the weekend. They had a slumber party upstairs. The kittens got lots of attention. First, get a lot of girlfriends. Later comes the lover. She is only halfway through her lease and already two women inhabited her bed, plus two cats.

We stay with the island tropical theme for our driving music. She really has a very nice smile which people seldom see. I drop her and proceed to my office in custody of our vehicle, a total ten-mile commute. We take it nice and easy does it. We avoid the pitfall of starting the day all stressed out from traffic.

Susan and I, the two single girls, start their teasing straight off and all day in between tasks. We are really spicing things up for the long-time married ladies. "You look a little saddle sore there, young lady," is Susan's first wisecrack. "Isn't that the same outfit you wore on Friday? It looks a little wrinkled." Is my comeback. "I have two of these," says she. "I keep an extra in the car." There is plenty to keep us busy. The day flies by. I eat lunch at my desk. My bouquet is fading just a little. I add fresh water.

Five PM finds me on Boylston St. heading east. Six PM sees the happy commuters nearing home on Centre St. It is Springtime and all is well, including my pea patch which has sprouted. Over dinner downstairs, I get the details of the weekend adventures of Lindsey and Jessica. They toured coffee houses. Alcohol gets you in trouble. J. does not have a boyfriend. Financial security first, romance later is her plan. Her Grand-Dad is training her up well. L. and J. plan to partner up and back each other up on weekend adventures. On weekdays, I remain the main squeeze. Our dirty words scrabble board got messed up by the cats. So much for that. Also, no big surprise, our monthlies have got synchronized. Three days of purification and abstinence ensue. We don't do the wild thing when we're on the rag.

Tuesday, April 5

Dear Diary, The suspense builds about our Rites of Spring exhibit Friday upcoming. I am only one of the models but I am emotionally invested in the success. There is significant printing and framing investment also. The artist and I succeed in getting Friday off, but meanwhile, there is work to do at our main occupations. No time for gossip or teasing today. Joni and Sandy simply tell about their kids. Maggie tells about her grand-kids. Phil winks at us at lunch. He likes to shake his head as if he knows something. We tell him to get those cancer sticks away from us. For our entertainment he blows some smoke rings. It's a comic relief before back to work. This week I do four 9 hour shifts.

My transporter sweeps me up at 18:30. She wants me to drive. She is flipping through sketches. Most of her co-workers will come to the opening. Some have seen previews. Something like "Wow, very nice!" is the typical comment. One guy asked for my phone number and got a big laugh. One of the women said, "You go, girl!" Her boss, John Lowery, assured that nudes will always sell. Don't you worry about it." We don't want to go home yet. We decide to sit in church and decompress. Candles, Chandeliers, and Icon reproductions complete the atmosphere of reverence. There will be reverence spoken and checkbooks opened for the Goddess we created.

At home, kitties need attention. Fatima gets her operation next week. She will never know motherhood. We cook in my kitchen with windows open and curtains aflutter. We get laundry started while pasta is boiling. Before dessert, we get the dryers started. I remind Lindsey that here is where we met, 27 of January, deep in Winter. I wrote it in my diary. We have a hug and a kiss, a wet one to commemorate the occasion. We trade back rubs. I find some lotion, an ambient music CD and some incense. L. sleeps beside me on top of the covers. When we wake at midnight, I see her face in the dim light. The look on her face says, "Love me. Love me forever." She rises and slips silently from the room.

Wednesday, April 6

Dear Diary, I woke up alone today, except for cats, that is. Other than some cramps, I feel good. I call Mom. It's her job to worry. She gets up early. I have time to reassure her. I grab a soup, chips and an apple for lunch. Maybe I'll trade something with L. I throw on my dark blue shift in clingy cotton. Susan and I can walk the fashion runway for fun at work. I grab an optional belt. Oops! The armpits need a shave. Did Aphrodite shave her legs, I wonder? Roy hasn't seen this outfit yet. It's the type of outfit that leaves just the right amount to the guys' imagination, the kind with shifting curves and jiggle.

I start the Malibu. L. waves from above. She needs 5 minutes. I fill the feeder with seeds, nuts, worms and bugs, the deluxe mix. We stay quiet on our commute, as typical.

Meanwhile, the fantasies are flying. Saturday, I will give Roy a Barber style hot towel shave. Then he can shave my legs. Once I saw unshaved legs under nylons. Yikes!

Susan is there early today. She has done something with her hair, very nice I must say. I try to imagine the maintenance guys complimenting each-others' appearance as in "Hey, Ben, somebody ironed your shirt. That's a nice look for you." It's a routine day. I find myself daydreaming a lot. The girls go out walking at lunch. We spot a car with a flat tire and no plates. Here is another mystery for Sherlock.

By 18:30 the Yoga girls are suiting up. Today is Reiki method. It opens blocked energy pathways if practiced diligently. There is time to socialize. We post a notice about "Rites of Spring." Monica and Lydia, two college students from Tufts are curious. They will try to come. We decide to continue with the Reiki. Let the energy flow unchecked.

For our home-bound commute, streetlights are twinkling, suffused by a light mist. We move along slowly, all cozy and dry. Back home, we want dessert only. Upstairs, L. has some angel food cake, frozen berry mix, and Cool Whip. It goes good with Green Tea. We trade quickie back rubs then off to our separate showers. Quality Time. Can't beat it with a stick.

Thursday, April 7

Dear Diary, The two living visions of the Goddess are up and about at their usual time. I go with pleasingly plain-pants suit today. I modestly stay outside myself. Be warm and nurturing like the sun and the soil. I make a date with Mom for Sunday. It's just another normal day. Go about your business. Be cool. Drive serenely. Give hugs and kisses all around.

I tell Susan that she is in full bloom. She gives me a kiss on the lips and she doesn't even need to be drunk to do it. Kisses from men are like Rocky Road ice cream. Kisses from women are like Tangerine Sorbet. The delight comes from the situation at hand. Tunes pop into my head to hum the morning away. I am on Cloud Nine. I almost need a chill pill. It is a smooth glide to 17:30. Weekend plans are the buzz, except for Susan and I. We do not kiss and tell, at least not yet.

Home-bound, we park at West Roxbury Commuter Rail. We ride to Needham to meet Roy. He has bouquets of wildflowers for both of us. We eat some take-out under the gazebo of the village square. He wishes us good luck and sends us off before sunset. We arrive at West Roxbury Station's near empty parking lot. L. wants to drive. She starts the car. We look at each other. We smile. We sigh. We are home by 20:00.

The kittens are asking for Fancy Feast. They have a special vocalization for that. We walk to the Speedy Market. We need the exercise. At home we flop on my bed, sip some tea and explain the manifestations of Aphrodite. One is virginal youth. The other is full sophistication womanliness. That works. Of course, buyers will want both. It is like Cupid Awake and Cupid Asleep by M.B. Parkinson.

With the 8x10s, a diptych is possible. We have extra prints. We light candles. We turn off the bedside lamps. We fall asleep with our clothes on.

I wake at 02:00. I cover L. with a throw fleece. I have some cold tea, undress and slide under the covers beside the virginal Goddess. She looks like an angel. Her Mommy and Daddy love her dearly; I am certain; and so do I. Twenty four hours from now we celebrate success. This, I foresee clearly.

Friday, April 8

Dear Diary, At 06:00, my love object is sitting up in my bed wondering "Where am I? What time is it." I get her oriented to time and place and how she slept 9 hours solid. I have some fruit cocktail for her. The gallery walk begins at 18:00 so we have lots of time. We decide to let traffic clear, no rush. By 09:00 Baby Girl is ready. Mitzi says we can come to the Gallery at 10:00.

We stop nearby at Breyt Photography to buy variations of the 8x10 diptych which they may have in stock, wood, metal, and leatherette. Good thing I got paid today by direct deposit to my TD checking. The trip to Back Bay is 9 miles. I offload the artist and her wares. I find a parking deck. By 10:30, I am admitted to help with the hanging. It is not easy to get everything just right. I stay mostly in the workroom. The calligraphy on parchment paper catalog looks classy. Some of the other artists are here. The place is all abuzz. I meet Jessica for the first time. She is working with the caterer. She will be serving Champagne. The first case is being chilled and the flutes lined up. Our booth has a sheer curtain, table lamps and a mantelpiece for the diptych array.

We break for lunch. We go out on Newberry Street. I'm grinning and it must be infectious because L. does the same. Our booth looks very appealing, even better than first imagined by the artist. We just need to hang the 16x20s. At 16:00, Lindsey changes clothes to something more semi-formal, dark tones, serious artist look. I get out of the way.

Back Bay, Newberry St. on a late Friday afternoon and early evening provides the aromas of steaks and seafood from restaurant kitchens. It is the weekend. No one is in a rush to go home or off to any beaches. It is too early in the season. I go to the Thinking Cup which offers coffee and sandwiches in a hip atmosphere. That's me, very hip in more ways than one. My full mature cheeky sensual woman hips are on display in hand tinted black and white, trendy and archival, gazed upon in a private gallery 100 years from now; I hope.

By 20:00, the gallery is filled with just lookers and a few buyers. I enter discreetly, snag a flute of bubbly, a nibble of a canape and survey the various artworks. I take a peek inside Lindsey's booth. There is a "Sold" sticker on the 11x14's. It seems like some of the diptych pieces are packed up and gone. I see my "Artist in Residence" in the vestibule talking seriously with a distinguished older gentleman. I stand off to the side. I touch Mitzi on the arm. She says it is going swimmingly. She says to come back at 21:30. Darn, that Champagne was top shelf. I trade in my flute for a full one. I look. It is Perrier-Jouet, the one with the flowers on the label.

I call Roy on my flip. He is out with his buddies, bowling, of all things. His buddies complain that he has been neglecting them. They suspect that he is p-whipped. He gets a phone smooch and a promise of carnal pleasures tomorrow. Outside is cool and crisp. Of course, a smoker is there. He says I look familiar. "In a previous life, perhaps," I tease. He wants to see my profile. "Holy Shit!, It's you! In there! The Goddess!" he erupts. "I want the 16x20." "Save up," I add. "Will the artist take payments? Layaway? Can we do a layaway?" "No layaway," I advise. He gives me his business card. He is a little light just now but he will be back in a month. I am to contact him about anything which did not sell. His name is Roger Quinn. He is a buyer of antiques at Estate Sales. He has a warehouse in Portland. Just for fun, I tuck his card down into my bra. He puts his smokes away to take one more look inside.

I take a little walk in the night air at nearby well-lit areas. I wait in the work room. The caterers have coffee and tea back there. I tweak my little buzz with black tea. The last buyers depart at 22:30. Jessica gets paid cash. Lindsey will get a check for her sales in one week. Mitzi's husband escorts us to the parking deck and we drop him back. Lindsey drives. Jessica will sleep over. We are home by eleven. We are ravenously hungry. Snacks are combined from both kitchens. The new friends depart to upstairs by midnight leaving me a little deflated. Shower and kittens, that is all I really need. Plus, Sherlock will keep me company for a page or two.

Saturday, April 9

Dear Diary, Ah! I feel really good, but it's only 07:00. I hug my pillow for a snooze. I hear a tap at the window. Roy is standing there, grinning at me. It's early Saturday morning. The dew is still on the grass. It's time for the Tomboy to go outside and play with one of the neighborhood boys. I can hear some children out there. That helps.

I grab my robe and slippers and let my playmate into the kitchen. My robe is open and the boobs are hanging out. Roy pours himself a cup of cold coffee and enjoys the view. He has the newspaper. Estate sales are listed therein. He follows me into the bathroom to watch me shower and gargle. "Why is it so much fun to watch girls in the shower," he wonders out loud. "Because you are a Peeping Tom Perv. That's why," I assert. "Maybe I've got secret cams all over this place," he snickers. "It's better than me watching porno, isn't it? Now I get to watch you get dressed," he adds. On the way out I knock upstairs. The door opens a crack. To a sleepy eye behind a curtain of dark hair, I suggest cat sitting in return for custody of the car. I get a nod of assent and off we go in Roy's machine.

The estate sales are in Dedham and Needham. We seek a desk, lamps and end tables. We bust our budget right away on a pair of Vintage Art Deco Glass Boudoir Lamps. I brought my money and I snapped them up pronto. I could resell these to Mr. Roger Quinn for a profit perhaps. All the desks are too pricey. We check Goodwill in

Norwood. We find an Ikea corner desk slightly damaged. We truck our treasures to Roy's man cave for closer inspection. We take a breath.

"I need you," says he. "Here is the perfect place," say I. "What is it about that body of yours? I can't get enough of it." Roy keeps up the chatter as he unzips and unbuttons. "It's just the perfect fit for your arms and for that thing you have down there which wants to deliver a payload as often as possible. That's my guess," I giggle. By the end of the day, 3 payloads have been delivered in 3 different rooms, by 3 different hook-up positions. We have a smoke, just for fun.

Sunday, April 10

Dear Diary, Sunday morning seems like cuddle time; no boner today. That thing takes the day off. Roy just wants to study me, all the pieces and parts, starting with the belly button, but there is a problem. The legs need a shave. This is going to be fun. I get to sit in a comfy chair, munch on my toast and sip my tea while Roy goes to work. He uses his after-shave face balm from the knees down. Of course, my crotch is right there snug under pink cotton panties. I get a hot breath love bite full on the pleasure zone. He worships at the Mount of Venus until I rise and get the hot towels ready for his shave.

I proceed slowly and ticklishly from the back of the neck and end with the upper lip, holding his nose up for the final touch up. I wrap with another hot towel and watch him sitting there like the Mummy. I give a facial massage with the after-shave balm. I finger comb his hair until I notice that it is time to get dressed.

Roy drops me at 10:15 at Perks in Norwood. He comes in and sits apart from me. Mom comes in at 10:30 and gets a coffee to go. As we leave, I point to Roy and question her, "What do you think about that guy?" "Hard to tell," says she. "Maybe if he's Catholic." Mass is my weekly ritual. It is a structure, something solid and predictable. People you know are there, like an extended family. You can depend on them. There is a homily.

What is the moral of the story? It is important enough to be reminded of. Socialize a bit. How else will you ever see these people, members of the congregation? A christening, a wedding, a funeral? We mark time together on the liturgical calendar.

I have dinner at the home where I grew up. Dad and Mom are there but for how much longer? Unknown. Have to go. Dad drops me. He has a peek at the Malibu, checks the tires and oil. I tell him I love him. I tell him things are looking up. He'll find me a Bronco. He gives me a kiss on the top of the head. Inside there is a note on the kitchen table inviting me upstairs. I interrupt the fun the felines are having. Lindsey has saved me some blueberry pie and some bubbly.

Monday, April 11

Dear Diary, Mondays are not a downer. I don't just work for the weekend. I meet challenges and have fun every day. Making plans is fun. Vacation, where to go? The coast of Maine is the most practical. We should book it this week. I drive today. L. learns about Roger Quinn. He wants the 16x20s bad, especially mine, but I don't add that detail. I wave goodbye to the young artist at 07:30.

Susan is at her desk already at 08:00. She is taking pages out of my book. If so, kudos to her. She checks to see if I am saddle sore again from weekend activities. I am, a little. No pain, no gain. My core is getting really strong. Anyway, it is work first, speculation later. I meet with Maggie. She will take some of my recommendations to meeting of corporate suits tomorrow. I am more in touch with renter issues. I am on the front lines with the revenue base. Sandy brings potting soil today. On lunch break, we go outside to get the Avocado pits rooted in pots. There are 5, one for each of us. Mine will stay on my desk.

After picking up L., we go home-bound along Fenway, Riverway, Jamaicaway and West Roxbury Parkway, a 7.2 mile trip, normally about 25 minutes. As we rejoin Washington St., We divert to Dunkin Donuts for some fresh ground. Like a private detective, I continue to canvas

Dunkins locations using the time stamp on the receipt I still have in my desk to narrow the search. I sit while L. is paying. There is a bearded man at a table opposite. He looks familiar. I stare. He notices. He puts his finger to his lips. I nod my head. I write on my napkin that kitten has found a loving home. He sees me writing. The napkin falls near his feet as I leave. I look back and see him reading it. I am glad that Reggie is still alive and in the area. I will keep his secret.

With workday finished, L. begins to relax and relate her weekend activities which include 12 medium format black and white photos of the grandfather. Jessica is self-taught. They visit her favorite library. They research the life of Mata Hari. The Artist imagines the Firing Squad Death Scene.

Tuesday, April 12

Dear Diary, L. wants to drive. She is talkative today. She wants to create something high impact about the tragic heroine and how beauty can be both a blessing and a curse. Something about survival in a cruel world. A spectacular life and a dramatic death. I begin to see inside the mind of the artist. I see the wheels turning. She is getting into a creative frenzy. I just tag along for the ride.

At 08:00, I am first at my desk. I water the baby Avocado trees. Amazingly, dried but colorful remains of my birthday bouquet can be rearranged nicely. No detail is too tiny to record from this full year of living, Dear Diary, and you will keep them preserved for me. The clock on the wall says 08:45. I am booted up and logged in. I remember life before computers. Is it really that much better now? Do we really need them to be happy? I say no. People found ways to live fully before the Pentiums.

Only 3 girls today, Sandy, Susan and I. We can do it all. We show team spirit. Fifteen buildings, 180 units, plus some off-site properties, fast turnover, only 8 empty units, 4 of those being remodeled. Maggie gets the credit. Could I do her job? Maybe.

The sun is setting as I wait for my transporter. I am her package. Such happy days we have. Enjoy it, Sarah Jane. They may not last forever. There is no guarantee. Reggae on the radio gets me out of the reflective mood. I get to see a smile from my driver. Three miles, 3 songs, 10 minutes and we are home. It is time once more for girl-girl domestic bliss.

Do I need Roy every night? No. I keep the tunes going while I cook. L. does some work upstairs. She comes back down in an hour to be my guest. We can't stop grinning. Life is good. Fatima and Felicia just stare at us. They are sizing up the situation. I guess it's going to be a foursome again tonight. Sleepovers remain random, when the mood is right. I made Spanish Rice. I also made a mess. After clean-up, straight to communal shower. Two terry cloth robes fall to our feet. If I was a guy, I would want us both. Shampoo the hair, lather the bush, scrub the back, thirsty towel and flop on my bed. Amen!

Wednesday, April 13

Dear Diary, Anything earlier than 06:00 seems depressing, to be dragging about when still dark. Not too extreme seems 06:15 when aromas from the kitchen activate the junior member of the girl power team. She grabs a mug of tea and a slice of toast on route upstairs. She announces her impending return by remote start of our Malibu. One cat on each lap, we have time to stare quietly at the morning scene outside my kitchen window where oblique rays of sun penetrate tree lines, creating dappled appearance on grass wet with dew. Robins are having their breakfast as well, though I don't much care for the vermiform avian bill of fare. Two women in pants suits enter the waiting vehicle and buckle up.

L. is focused. She wants to drive. The normal day in the life of two law abiding citizens of Boston Metro begins with a right turn onto Heron Street. Our workday ends much the same, southbound on Washington Street, making a right turn onto Heron Street, where two tenants live happily one above the other.

At Boston MFA, L. helps to relocate some of the permanent collection. I have quarterly reports to finish. I am tucked away in a cubicle where I can put my feet up, stand or stretch as needed. Storm clouds roll in at mid-day. The girls avoid the wetness and wind. We conduct our hen party in the cluttered break room at lunch. If Maggie is out of ear-shot, the subject matter is unrestricted and spicier. Sandy's and Joni's children have learned some curse words, the vocalization, but thankfully not the full meaning of the "F Bomb", for example. These words are for grown-ups only is the lesson to be taught. How to keep things lively in the master bedroom comes under debate. Sandy has some dominatrix items from the Adam and Eve catalog sent discreetly to a post office box. Joni gets household cash bonuses by providing "services" for her husband.

The services I enjoy tonight are a clean out the icebox buffet at Lindsey's kitchen table, and two on one making bread massage from little paws. They love me in their own special way.

Thursday, April 14

Dear Diary, How are you? I'm fine. I want to put a face to you, the recorder of my thoughts and impressions. Someday, a reader unknown to me at present will understand those thoughts and visualize those impressions. Two people in particular are making a very deep impression this happy year 2011. One of them is in a bad mood this morning. She is processing something. I say nothing to distract from the processing. I drive without tunes and leave her to her daily tasks by 08:00.

At my desk, there is the sad news that a ten-year resident has gone to nursing home. At 10:00, I supervise the removal of personal items and disposal of food items. If this wheelchair accessible unit, 12-F, can be turned over quickly enough, this means favorable terms for discharge of the lease. I inform a suitable retired couple on the waiting list. Fritz and Kitty Hennig have sold their country home in New Hampshire. They need the conveniences of an urban dwelling near to their specialists.

They can afford a furnished unit. They need June 1st move-in. Maggie gives the green light for full speed ahead on the remodel and furnishing. I am designated project coordinator. I assemble my team.

L. has some suggestions to offer. She remains otherwise quiet on return trip. She says it's complicated, a family matter and to just be there for her if she needs a hug. I surf onto 107.3 FM, K-Love, out of Westborough. Amy Grant is singing "Lay Down Your Burden". Tears start to flow. We have to pull over. I drive the remainder. At home, she feels a little better. She wants to take a nap. At 21:00, I hear her walking about up there. I bring her a bedtime snack. We watch some of her antenna TV on a small HD flat screen. MeTV has the Alfred Hitchcock Hour in cool, crisp, extra sharp black and white. This appeals to the aesthetic of the fine arts photographer. A sleepover seems appropriate. L. goes down to fetch the felines. They happily accept her transport to their upstairs playground where extra cat treats and cat toys are waiting. We fall asleep holding hands, kittens at our feet.

Friday, April 15

It's Friday, Dear Diary. It rolls around once a week. April showers continue. The bunk mates make the best of it. We splash our way to work well before the school children appear. L. discloses that her mother is sick. She will tell me more later. How many people are getting dressed right now, little knowing they will not make it through the day. This is a sobering thought. First, survive the day. Everything else is a bonus.

We survive our commute. Susan winks at me from her desk. We have fun guessing each other's secrets. By mid-morning the sun breaks through. We go outside for some stretches. Phil is there smoking his Chesterfield non-filters. He says he had a dream about Susan and I blowing smoke rings. "Nice," I said. "We're very flattered." He just grins. He's harmless.

L. gets paid today. She prefers a paper check. On our return commute we stop at Galerie D'Orsay. We replace the items which sold with new prints. Her revenue from last weekend is a little over a thousand. She signs on for another week's run. We are home by 19:00. We go to our separate offices to confirm weekend plans. Fatima goes to Vet. Roy comes here. L. goes to Dorchester. Tonight is wide open. Freedom! We should go out. If only for an hour or two. Somewhere new. Somewhere walk-able. We have each other for back up.

We proceed aimlessly South on Washington Street. We can afford appetizer and dessert at Viva Mi Arepa Venezuelan Restaurant. We feed each other some grilled shrimp. We try the Arepas, savory corn flour patties, stuffed with cheese. We savor the Golfeados, flaky pastry, for dessert. We look around for anyone we might talk to? Will anyone chat us up? I am quite brazen recently. Girls only seems right, if anyone at all, a couple of extra friendly acquaintances. People go out to socialize. I ask two girls, Casey and Kelsey, at a nearby table what is good for a cocktail and can we join you? They say yes and we must try the Cinco de Julio and the Purple Banana. One has Tequila, the other, Gin. They live in Roslindale. After small talk, we exchange numbers, easy as that.

Weekend, April 16 and 17

Dear Diary, Saturday and Sunday are all blurred together. Roy brings a new type of cat carrier. It's like a cradle, with tilt back dome lid. We endure some heart-rending vocalizations of dread on route to Bond Vet, in Chestnut Hill. Tawney, the vet assistant, is able to comfort poor Fatima somewhat during her pre-op exam and prep. We are to return at 16:00. We head to Star Market to get all of Roy's favorite stuff, including the brews. I get all the best sandwich bread, cheeses and lunch meats. We no sooner unload then look at the time, just enough to express how much I missed my man with reckless abandon.

We collect our patient on time and receive post-op care instructions. She hates that cone collar and is strong enough to express complaint. She is happy to be home with sister Felicia. All of this simplifies our weekend since I am required to stay home and watch over my patient.

I will even skip Mass. Some kind of maternal instinct is awakening. I leave the bedside to partake of Roy's pasta creation. If he only makes me a PB&J, it would mean more than a gourmet meal from any other man. After I wash and he dries, the kitchen is tidy. I serve my patient some milk in a jar lid held up to her chin and my man his brew in a frosted mug.

We surf my limited number of channels. I can back rub and observe the little one at the same time. She seems to be resting comfortably. Now I get my back rub. We stay up really late watching Mannix, Barnaby Jones and Canon. We don't last through Petticoat Junction.

An extra loud commercial, rouses me at 05:00. The little one gets an assisted trip to the scratch box and some soft food then we all doze off until 08:00. Nursing assistant, Roy looks in on the patient. She wants to play. "I think she'll live," he pronounces. He goes out to run while I make breakfast. I open the kitchen window. The air smells really nice. I can stream Mass from St. Patrick's in New York City. They have a choir. I sing along. The runner reappears carrying The Boston Herald, Sunday edition. He heads to the shower. A few minutes later, we sit side by side. He grabs the sports. I have the comics. Dilbert is all about the office. It's a good thing we have a big kitchen table to spread out. Beyond crinkling of newsprint, blessed silence is ours until we hear the rumble of the Malibu.

We crack the door for easy entry. My soul sister enters after a soft knock. She drops her knapsack. I fix her a plate from our brunch buffet. She sprawls at the table with head between hands. She stares into her coffee mug. She picks at her plate. We find out that the gas tank is full, that Jessica is a wild thing, and that not much sleeping occurred on the sleepover. Roy recounts the overnight vigil here in our love nest. Fatima has the strength to seek attention from her alternate caretaker lately arrived. They touch noses. "Mom is coming for chemo once a week," is the final announcement. "She will stay with me. The prognosis is not good." Lindsey needs a hug. She cries on my shoulder. "I'm going up for a nap," she says quietly. Roy adds his hug. She picks up her backpack and treads softly upward to seek an hour or so of oblivion.

Kittens need fresh air too. Are there fleas out there? To be a cat and never get to sneak around outside seems cruel. For today we keep them in arms. In the limited green space surrounding the apartments are some benches, mostly for smokers, I suppose. We have this wonderful time to do nothing but just to be together. We look up at the sky. We feel just the slightest sense of the world spinning 'round. Time is passing, and it's a very precious time. This is it. This is what I have been waiting for all my life. It's getting a little chilly. My hair catches a bit of a breeze. I have my man's arm around me. It is still all so brand new.

We have a light supper of tossed salad and soup. We get naked afterward. Suddenly, today for unknown reason, I am inordinately fascinated with the tally wacker. "Give me that thing to play with," I start will the balls, which stay in jail 99.9% of a guy's life. They are free now and they deserve some attention, followed by the legendary no hands blow job. The hands come into tickle. When he can't stand it anymore, I turn around and he gets to thrust against my long-neglected, full sumptuous hips.

Later he gets the standard question, "Was it good for you?" "Probably too good. Now I'll be wanting one of those every day," he admits. "Okay, you're on," I agree. "I am into it now like never before. Your dong will never be lonely, not even for one day," is my promise. "We can even put it in our marriage vows." On that humorous note, we enter the shower where I get my muff dive. I wouldn't mind getting my muff dive on a daily basis as well. Two sex addicts we are, but only for each other. How long can it last? I see no end in sight. We towel each other off and there's the boner again. The guy is insatiable. "I cannot leave you, tonight" he declares. "I'm staying overnight. Even if I lose my job. Even if my career is ruined. I have to have you. I'll pay anything. I'll do anything. I'll even beg." "Just say please. Ask and you shall receive," I assure him.

He does some of his school stuff online. He prints. He staples. He collates. He is suddenly all very organized. That takes about an hour. He logs out and packs the papers away.

"Now I want your tits, please, tits only," is his plea. "As you wish, but wait here just a few," I require. I change into my bra with maximum number of hooks and my silkiest polyester blouse with the maximum number of buttons. "Now you must work for it," I explain.

I sit on his lap. There is no silly ripping apart of the beautiful blouse. He must unbutton slowly with reverence. He fumbles in back until fully unhooked. The hands return to the chest, a nice handful for each. The blouse and bra finally fall to the floor. He can see my bare back in the mirror. I smother the guy full in the face. I get him re-smothered flat on his back in bed. "You must suck my tits, kiss my ass and muff dive me every day for life, from this day forward. Do you agree?" I declare. He shrugs his shoulders. "Okay, seems reasonable," he laughs.

It's time for a beer. We get our frosted mugs. For my amusement, he quaffs his first beer in one long gulp, foam running down his face. Wiping his chin, he lets out a satisfied "Ah!" I require 4 gulps to achieve the same result.

Monday, April 18

Dear Diary, Roy sneaks away at 05:00 like thief in the night. I work from home today. Fatima remains under observation. Maggie says it's okay. I send Lindsey off like a Mom sending a schoolgirl. She gets a hug, a kiss, a bag lunch and a wave goodbye.

There is no going back to bed. My online activity will be monitored. Susan calls at lunch to tease me about playing hooky. Roy calls just to hear my recorded message. I let him record and save it with other fun messages of the year. It is strange to stay home on a spring day, not sick, no storm. I catch an episode of "Young and the Restless". I stay close to my phone. Crunches and stretches, that is what I need. I have my soft dumbbells at my desk. I check in with Robert. They are killing him with overtime. Darla hasn't dumped him yet. I pay some bills online. I crank up the radio. I am hooked on that island music. The beat keeps me going. Maggie sends me some continuing education work modules. I log out at 16:30.

It was a productive day at home but I prefer the spaciousness of the office. I feel like I should start dinner, just like a housewife. I find myself staring at the clock, waiting for my dear girl to come home. At 18:00, supper is ready. Salad, green beans, mashed potatoes and pork chops. Tea is brewing. Sun is setting.

At last, I hear the rumble of the Malibu. The tailpipe may need attention. Dad will fix it. My girl knocks and enters. I offer her a chair table-side. I give a quick neck rub and kiss on the top of the head. The novelty of the situation releases a wee smile on her face. I say "Grace". She stabs a pork chop. I tell her I missed her and watched the clock all afternoon. She admits that it was strange commuting alone. She will need some extra love this week. "Tomorrow, I cook," she promises. "Can I stay here, tonight?" she pleads. "It's so lonely up there. Let me just go up and change." She returns in robe and slippers. We trade back rubs. I end hers with a smack on the butt. "It was just such I nice target," I explain. "Yours is bigger," she reminds me.

Tuesday, April 19

Dear Diary, It's back to normal, our comfortable routine. I find out that Casey has called Lindsey which seems right. They are similar age. They will do brunch this coming Sunday. Wild thing, Jessica, will always be a fun but exhausting alternative. On my lunch I leave Roy an unfiltered voice message telling him he is the best possible boy-friend, he is a Prince and he gets me off really well. I thank him for coming over so many times and helping in the kitchen. I do not take these things for granted and I miss him already.

Okay, back to work. The new furnished unit plans are approved. Our guys start tomorrow on clean up and retrofit. As project coordinator, I am very excited about this. By 17:30, I have L. with me cruising on home. I hear that Casey is blond enough but too young and probably too straight, but she is a person of interest. Keep her in your network is what I suggest. I ask, "How do you feel, just in general, all things considered." "I am really worried about Mom," she admits "So much that I get distracted at work. We have a lot to work out and we may not have much time." "Starting Saturday, you will have weekly quality time for all of that," I assure her.

We are home. We unbuckle. "Let me have a nap. Then I'll make supper. Come up about 7:30 ok?" she proposes. "7:30 it is," I affirm. At the appointed hour I arrive upstairs with my overnight bag. L. smiles when she sees it. She perks up quite a bit. We have wine and some sort of Charcuterie Plate she has created including grapes, olives, nuts, cheeses and slices of apple. We have more wine and sprawl on her love seat. "I know you are basically straight and you love your man but we have kissed and you seem to like it. Would you mind being full on Lambda for me, just for tonight?" she pleads. Without hesitation I tell her, "Let's not limit ourselves. I am going to marry Roy, but I love you too, full measure. Whatever you have in your fantasies, I am happy to make them come true." We change into loose fitting sleep-wear. Her pillows are cedar scented. She holds me tight. We love ourselves to sleep.

Wednesday, April 20

Dear Diary, I prefer my man but I must admit that last night was very nice until of course 06:00 and quickly back into work mode. We prepare separately. I drive. On route, L. Is humming. Her window is down and her arm rides the breeze. She looks at me once. There is a hint of a smile there. She continues her humming. "What is that tune?" I wonder. "I don't even know myself," she confesses.

In the office, we are all serious. By lunch tasks are nearly complete. Susan and I go over to the maintenance workshop for a surprise visit and appreciation in the form of buckets of KFC. The domain of the grease and grunge gang looks like a disaster area. "A messy workshop is a busy workshop," they explain. One guy has a giant old-fashioned thermos that looks like it has been through two world wars. "Spend a day with us and find out what real work is," they challenge us. "Maybe we will," says Susan as she twirls a hammer like a six-gun. We need to keep on their good side.

A bit more work, a coffee klatch at 2 pm, a bit more work and finally, Maggie sets us free. My partner and I arrive at The Blissful Monkey early. There is time to socialize and set our intention. All the girls look fine or well on their way. Monica and Lydia are there. They wonder if our show is still hanging. "Two more weeks," we say. Feeling nicely balanced and aligned, we exit the studio in the fading light of one more happy day.

All along South St. and Washington St. we wind our way homeward. We make a wish list of places where we can step out just girls, what a power we are. Sophia's Grotto Classic Italian in Roslindale is at the top of the list. We have time to peek at the Patio seating with its lovely atmosphere.

Our kittens need us. Our maternal instincts kick in. Lindsey gets the cooking challenge while I tend to scratch boxes and food bowls plus keep the little ones from tripping up the Chef. It's fun to see L. in an apron. If we were married, she would stay home and have the babies. Does she want a baby?" I ask. "Of course, I do," says she.

Thursday, April 21

Dear Diary, I slept with only the sheer curtains. The streetlights flickered through branches waving in nocturnal breezes. It was nice to rouse at first light, sit up, stretch and hug my girls.

Almost weekend. Almost my man in my arms. Okay, let's get going then.

I seem to be the designated sandwich maker. L. is wearing a fragrance today which is unusual for her. It is Jean Nate, body splash, so fresh it makes me feel 20 something again. Off we go, windows rolled down. Are these our days of heaven? Later, I am stuck completing and filing folders of move-outs. Banker boxes go to archive closets and beware of spiders.

Susan and I go out wandering again at lunch. We compare our secret guys. Mine is taller at 5'10". She wants us to measure that other private dimension of the secret guys. We will measure biceps also. We agree to use metric. Maybe we should sex objectify ourselves as well. Susan, with her C cup, has got me beat at the top line. "But maybe it's falsies," I tease. She shows me a topless selfie which she sent to her guy. "Maybe, it was photo shopped," I challenge. "Tomorrow, casual Friday, we should all just show up for work topless. That will settle the matter," is Susan's idea. We return laughing but we don't say why.

Tenants are in the office. The whole office seems to be giddy. We have spring fever. Maggie just shakes her head. The car poolers take Washington St. home bound again today. We stop and roll, windows down. At Roslindale, aromas from the various restaurants are tempting but our maternal instincts prevail and we continue onward without diversion. We park. L. wants a new thing in her love memory bank. She wants to kiss me in the car. I say to go ahead, practice taking initiative which she does. I will never brush you off, I assure, neither in public nor in private. This is the kissing cousins promise. We take care of Felicia and Fatima. We take them upstairs. Thinking I will cook tonight, I inquire, "What sounds good for dinner?" Her reply is "You. I want you for dinner. Main course is the muff dive. Get ready for a good one."

Friday, April 22

Dear Diary, I wake at 02:00 for a cold drink. My girlfriend is sleeping on her tummy. As usual, she looks like an angel. I may as well admit it that I am a full on bi-sexual. The nymphomania has spilled over into same sex. Will I always be this way? Is it only because L. is so adorable? That's it. I will always be this way but my body given exclusively to the most lovable. My body, so long neglected, now being adored by two lovers and the general public in a museum of fine art. I guess good things do come to those who wait.

At work I come out as "Bi" to Susan, 90/10 in favor of men. "I always suspected you had lesbo leanings," she quips with a grin. Could a Friday go any slower, I think as I watch the clock. L. is keeping the Malibu to meet her Mom post chemo at Brigham and Woman's Hospital.

At 17:00, Susan takes me to Back Bay, a slight detour on her way home. I want to help Mitzi at the Gallery tonight. Roy is coming to meet me. He hasn't seen the exhibit yet. He is taking the commuter train from Norwood Depot. I meet him at Back Bay Station. We have dinner at Cafe Nero. It is lovely on the terrace. From there it is short walk on Newberry St. to the Gallery.

I just realize this is Good Friday. I feel like Mary Magdalene. I will be forgiven my lack of modesty and all of my indiscretions. I check in with Mitzi while Roy makes the tour. He buys one of the diptych in leatherette, the seated pose because he is in love with my ass. I hang replacement prints in place of those which sold. I tidy and dust in our booth. I hand out brochures. I answer questions about the artist.

One potential buyer says that I am even more sensual in person because the voice and movement are there. I thank him profusely and give him a kiss on the cheek. I tell him it is just recently I came to full bloom. I wipe away a tear. I hear him telling his friends that he got a kiss from the Goddess. I think that helped sell one of the 11x14s. When we get back to my place, I see that the cats have been fed. There is some activity upstairs. We settle in with beers and back rubs.

Saturday, April 23

Dear Diary, It's just another lazy Saturday morning with my man and my girls and my pea plants growing up strong. On such a wonderful spring day, I fling the windows open wide. Birds and a bit of traffic noise provide accompaniment. Guys seem to have their max boner at wake up so now is the perfect time for the measurement I promised to Susan. I guess 16 cm is about average. We stay in bathrobes because now we trim the hedges. I take care to keep the nut sack up and out of harm's way. Then he does me, just a trim because he prefers the full bush.

By noon, we are finally ready to go outside arm in arm. The vehicles get a rest today. The only downside is the illness in the family upstairs. L. has heard me exit the building. I look up from the street. She is there in her window. We wave to each other. Streets are named after birds in my neighborhood. We take Heron to Grouse to Thrush to Eagle. Maplewood gets us back home where there is an unfamiliar Dodge Ram pickup in the parking lot.

We get to meet the Mom, Sylvia, and the Dad, Bob, who has come to fetch his wife and return her to their home in Brattleboro. Roy and Bob talk about trucks. There are hugs, handshakes and waves goodbye. We three who remain freshen up for my genius plan. We embark northward on Washington St. for 4 pm Holy Saturday Mass at St. John Chrysostom. We have a short walk of barely half a mile to the church which is filled to capacity. A Cantor chants the Nocturne Service. After services, a further 1.2 miles northward brings us to Sophia's Grotto. Roy walks closest to traffic. I take his arm and Lindsey takes mine.

We proceed at a leisurely pace under the protection of our chivalrous escort.

We get an outdoor table. The lights strung above are just coming on. It is my idea, therefor my treat. By now we are really hungry. We start with Sangria. We each try a dish we have never heard of. I can't remember the names. We end with Raspberry Drizzled Cheesecake. Our waiter, Rosario, takes a snap of the happy threesome on Lindsey's flip.

Sunday, April 24

Dear Diary, Today's entry must include a wrap up of our happy Saturday. We were a little tipsy from Sangria so I rang up Dave to transport us home. It was not even 9 pm and the streets were still full but we were ready for home. We watched TV at my place, something mindless. Then L. wants to borrow Sherlock and both kittens to keep her company. She has some calls to make, Jessica and Casey perhaps. By the stroke of midnight, my lights are out.

We keep the windows open a crack, cool air to breathe, hot man to hug. This is bliss. Roy is up early for his run, with Sunday newspaper in hand on return. We split the sections and lounge around with our coffee until 09:00. L. rings on my land line to announce that Casey is coming for brunch. We are invited. Taking a cue from me, the curtains are pulled cheerfully all the way back. Pastel throws are the color palette for her little parlor. A tablecloth in white completes the Easter vibe. We are fully risen from winter depths.

I can do chocolate again starting with Casey's chocolate frosted donuts. She wants to do a blessing, something she made up, all Christian, innocent, and overflowing with joy. She giggles, tosses her hair and tells funny stories. She is young and she likes to party. We may be seeing a lot more of her. 'Round about noon, Roy has to go. I watch him drive away. Now I want to cry. My girls console me. I get hugs from both. It's time for me to go see my own Mom and Dad.

Sister Sally, the brat, is there with her kids, a boy of 8 and a girl of 5. I take the Malibu. I am far different than last year. Sally says I seem different. I have my secret. Spinsterhood no longer seems my fate. I stare at Dad as he carves and at Mom as she serves. They seem content. Sally's kids are running amok. I take them outside for games. They are kicking a ball around. Sally comes out to watch over them. They mustn't run into the street. I play soccer goalie. There is pie and coffee on the side porch. I tell Mom about the Greek Orthodox services. As the light begins to fade, I feel I have to go. Someone is waiting for me.

Monday, April 25

Dear Diary, Right away I ring up Roy and thank him for the happy weekend. L. did not get too stressed about her Mom's condition. They had good quality time one to one in a place different from the home growing up. There is a chance of a remission. I will pray for Sylvia. She and Bob seem very nice. And so now it is just a matter of another day of productive work. The biggest challenge is commute safely, about 16 miles round trip daily, depending our route and detours.

There is a light rain. We proceed slowly with classical music on low volume. I get the early drop off and my kiss goodbye. The staff stays seriously into their work until coffee break. Joni is with us. She is processing the move-outs. There will be 5 this week. Susan brought doughnuts. Some of them can help with my post Lent chocolate deficiency.

Susan and I take lunch outside. The extra brightness and cool moist air revive us. Comparing notes, we find that her guy's unit beats Roy by 2 mm, not much to brag about. We sigh, get our minds out of the gutter and get back to work, maximum serious and efficient. I love my job, but it offers a career path and I am moving along.

When she picks me up, L. is worn out and doesn't want to talk shop. We divert to Star Market, our cheap practical grocery. We both have a list, allowing no impulse buys. We are disciplined. At home, Bill, the photog from Providence, is there waiting. He wants to meet me in person. I will be one of a number of studies for Mata Hari death scene. He and L. agree that existing photos of Mata Hari alive, done by photographers of her era, cannot be surpassed and need not be re-imagined. He asks that I grow my hair longer. Meanwhile, we study reports of the execution, recreate her prison garb, and place a moral to the story. Bill wants a model less fantasy than were Greta Garbo or Jeanne Moreau playing the part in cinema.

We flip to see who cooks. Heads, I cook. I can be the Mom again tonight while my little girl does her homework. Once again, we create domestic bliss.

Tuesday, April 26

Dear Diary, When we are married, Roy wants to get a dog. I say make it two and mutts are fine. Could a neutered male and a neutered female fall in love? One will be my favorite and the other will be Roy's favorite. This is a fun peek into our future. Our home will be teaming with life, animal and vegetable. We will be less likely to fight because we don't want the animals to see us fighting. It would cause them distress. Such are my ponderings over my early morning Ginseng Tea.

L. breezes in and grabs the last wedge of buttered toast, slams the last cup of tea and off we go. Her creative juices are flowing. On the way, while she sketches, she is humming again. This time, I recognize the melody: "Softly, as in a Morning Sunrise" by Romberg, a rather obscure tune. It must have played one morning on WCRB 99.5. There are jazz versions as well, I seem to recall. This is perfect for our morning drive. The only downer is when I see roadkill, a deer, a cat, a dog, a fox, sneaking around at night, minding its own business, and "wham!" a horrible death. I hit a bird once. I still feel bad about it. Can't we commute without killing? In a perfect world, maybe but life is not fair, so beware, all you winged ones and four legged ones, if you choose to live alongside humans.

What's to note at work. Maggie treats for lunch. She got good feedback from corporate. We get Stromboli with a giant plate of Ante Pasta, nice choice. At afternoon break, I stare at my hands, bare of rings. Moisturize, I need to moisturize. I want to wear my ring. I ask Susan if she has a ring from her secret guy. "Any day now," says she with a wink.

Who offers who a ring between two Lambdas? "Either one or both," quote Lindsey then dives back into her drawings. We stop at St. Theresa and say a prayer for Sylvia. Maybe we should meditate daily. At home we make a plan to nap, freshen up, and meet for antenna TV and a late supper. I look at the sketches for death of Mata Hari. Did she ever actually harm anyone? What kind of a future had she if not a casualty of war at the age of 41? She was loved by many but love was not enough to save her.

Wednesday, April 27

Dear Diary, Why did Tuesday bring thoughts of death, roadkill, executions? This is not the domain of Aphrodite. Let's get back to the "Rites of Spring". Wednesday is Hump Day in more ways than one. Life affirming fantasies prevail. My passenger and I agree to provide each other some relief from the itch we need to scratch.

Phil does his usual flirt on arrival. Susan does her usual grin and wink. Later she admits "I'm so horny I could almost do you right here at work. No man nearby? You might be better than nothing." "What about Phil?" I wonder. "Can't do the ash tray mouth. I would rather do you," she laughs. Now that we have secret boyfriends, we are hornier than ever. Focus, Sarah Jane, focus.

I knock my work out, mouse clicking and keyboard tapping the hours away. By 17:00, I am at the Museum. I stretch while waiting for my baby girl. I stare at the partly cloudy sky occupied by random flocks of blackbirds. Suddenly, I feel familiar hands around my waist. The reverse hug is very nice. A request is whispered in my ear, "I want to kiss you here in public in front of everybody". I am happy to comply. Nobody pays us no never mind.

We take the maximum green scenic route passing Arnold Arboretum leading to West Roxbury Parkway. We pause at St. John Chrysostom for another prayer and meditation. We are holding hands. Maybe the prayer will be more powerful that way. Ten minutes later, the spiritual turns to carnal. This is something I have heard about and want to try. Can we get each other off dry humping? We trade who is on top. Her on top does the trick. It counts as a quickie. We have very busy active lifestyle. Sometimes it's got to be a quickie. Not much time for afterglow with whiskers in our faces. We flip to see who does the scratch box. Tails, it's me, a solitary task. The woman at the can opener gets the audience. We wonder if these cats can meet other cats on a play date? Perhaps not. Soon they may have dogs to play with. Roy calls. I tell him my day, leaving certain parts out. Oops, we forgot Yoga. Instead, is massage and early to bed.

Thursday, April 28

Dear Diary, I wake up to an empty bed. I hear L. upstairs doing stuff. Those busy, busy serious sounds of workday bustle help to activate me. Within minutes, I am up to full speed, brewing, sandwiching, hair fixing and the like. I even make the bed. Why not use some of my White Linen perfume before it goes stale. It is appropriate for the professional woman in the workplace according to the ad campaign. The top note will be there in Malibu. The middle note will be there at work to make the office more cheerful. The base note remains for whomever wants to love me after work. L. says she wore "Poison" in college to get noticed, when she wanted to get noticed.

On my drop off, my kiss goodbye comes with a whispered "I love you" and hot ticklish breath in the ear. It came as a surprise since she is all business typically on workday mornings. I respond in kind but I spell it into her hand, which brings a smile. Susan is taking a personal day so Sandy is out in the main office. I am at the phone desk all day, inquiries, complaints, and repair requests. My left ear still tickles from this morning. The phone handset stays on my right ear.

L. is a little late. I am alone in the office when she arrives at 18:30. She says she will help me finish up. We fill all of the printers and copiers with paper, requiring a trip to the clerical supply room. Why waste the opportunity? A make-out session in the workplace. This is like when Roy and I met at his school after hours. I am deep into probably my only ever affair with a woman. I may as well give her everything she wants, except for the babies. She will have to go beyond me to get the babies.

We stop at St. Theresa again for prayer and meditation. At home a 4-way cat nap seems right followed by a late light supper. I call Roy and we talk while I am getting my back rub. I tell him I want more sports. He can coach me one or two clicks closer to athletic female bod. He has already had the cheerleader version of me. My training starts Saturday but for now, it's 'gonna be happy endings on the massage. Why hold back?

Friday, April 29

Dear Diary, Windows are cracked. I hear the birds. Boing! I pop up in bed like a Jack-in-the-Box. Stretch. Yawn. Hot shower yourself, but quickly. Time is a wastin'. So much life to live. Go. Go. Go! How can I lively up the office today? We should plan another girls' night out. I'll see what kind of ideas L. can come up with. We are not going to create babies together, but ideas do come to fruition from our partnership.

We take the western route today, LaGrange St., with Baby Girl at the wheel, windows down, and warm breeze in the face. We pass Bellevue Hill Park on the right. I look out at the greenery. I let my mind wander. I sip my hot tea. "Please, don't let this feeling end. It might not come again and I want to remember..."-the Theme from Ice Castles. Everyone deserves a time, however brief, of exquisite happiness. I waited for it. I earned it. Today, L. is wearing a skirt. I write my drop off love message on her inner thigh. No one else will ever think to do that. It will be remembered fondly. "Pieces of April, in a memory bouquet..." old soft rock tunes resurface.

Susan is back. She had a 24-hour bug. A little cough remains. "Stay away from me!" I warn. Sandy is off on a 3 day weekend. Roy calls on the break room hot-line. He has booked our summer vacation in Maine, which is one week in a cabin in the woods, one week at the beach. Susan wants Martha's Vineyard. Her secret guy is already there. Which couple will have the most fun? At some point all will be revealed. A Brainstorm hits me. Why not turn the demo unit into Airbnb, for just weekends? It just sits there generating no income. Maggie will present the idea to corporate. L is early today at 17:30. We stop at St. George Orthodox on LaGrange. We will pray to every possible saint on Sylvia's behalf. Cool, quiet solemnity fills our souls. Thirty minutes later, lust is filling our loins. We progress in our expertise at getting each other off. Mitzi calls. Roger Quinn has purchased both of the 16x20s. A customer wants them for his cigar bar in Portland. Sometime in May, Lindsey will buy the Malibu.

Saturday, April 30

Dear Diary: My Cowboy arrives in his truck at 07:30. I am ready. Overnight bag is packed. Kitchen is clean. I wear jeans, athletic shoes and sweatshirt. I kiss the girls goodbye. He is leaning against the passenger door. I run to his arms. I tell him how much I missed him which was mucho, mucho. He opens my door, helps me step up and kisses my hand. He saddles up for our 20-minute ride to Canton High Memorial Field.

I ask him about his week. He teaches Algebra, Geometry, Trig, Statistics, Home Room and Gym Class. He is pushing to get a second school Psychologist, one just for the boys. He is working with the drama Club to put on play about ways to handle a bully, about learning assertion. You don't push anyone around and no one pushes you around. He has got to get the School Board behind him. I told him in Dedham High there were snobs, mean girls and cliques. The boys betting on who could deflower me was a type of harassment but it was so juvenile. It was water off a duck's back. I liked my reputation.

"Be True to Yourself, That's it. That's what we'll call it, a series of vignettes acted out by the students themselves. Thanks honey. You are good sounding board for me," my hero replies. Today I get gym class for freshmen, an athletic aptitude test. First comes stretching, not too different from Yoga. The grass is wet. We stay on the track. We will jog the 400 meters. He helps me get a longer, smoother stride. I was sucking wind at 300 meters. He shows me the kick at the end. I manage a pitiful kick and come in at 2 minutes and 20 seconds. He promises to lower my time a little each try and see where I level out. Next is soccer penalty kicks. I am getting them into the goal with no goalie. When Roy is playing goalie, I get one of ten in the net. Then we see how far I can kick. I manage 20 yards in the air. Softball is next, bunting only. I try it left-handed and right-handed. I get the hang of it, how to splat the ball down so it trickles away. Finally, throwing, how far can I throw the softball overhand. Right-handed is 35 yards, Left-handed is 30. I copy how Roy throws. Monkey see, Monkey do.

We head home for lunch. He makes me a Reuben with pickle, chips and soup. He gives me a little rubdown then out we go for second session. He has a tennis racket for me and some balls to doink against the garage wall. He shows me the grip. I do little bounces on the driveway or taps in the air. I manage to keep the ball in the air for about ten taps at a time. We retire to the man cave. He has a little putting green in there. I start missing at 5 feet. Back outside, he has sponge balls. I manage to get a few of them up in the air, but one goes over the fence to the neighbor's yard. The final event is basketball bounce passes, free throws and dribbling. My first bounce pass hits him on the foot. Most of my free throws are air balls. I can dribble though. We had a hoop in Dad's driveway growing up.

We hit the shower. I suppose you could call screwing a sport, but how would you score it? I score Roy good on endurance plus he gets style points for the foreplay. We have dinner at home like an old married couple. We have some beers to get ready for our pretend fight of the week.

This week we fight about money, what he wastes it on and how what I waste it on is more important. I pretend cry as he pretend cuts up all my credit cards. Maybe we won't ever fight over money except for "Oh! You shouldn't have!" when he buys me expensive anniversary, Christmas and birthday presents. He shouldn't but he does because I'm worth it. So there! Now what program do we watch? "How come we always have to watch what you want? You make me watch war movies when you know I like Lifetime Movie Channel best. You don't love me anymore. That proves it." "I love you most of the time, except when you nag," is his smart-ass reply. Just for that he gets a tickle torture.

Unfortunately, two can play that game.

We break for more beer. I belch a little tiny girl belch, not much more than a burp. It's okay for guys and everyone just laughs. It's so not fair. After my man overcomes the horror of that unexpected sound, we go for a nice cuddle and snooze. I wake up to find him kissing my ass. "It's just too luscious, those cheeks and that crack. I can't resist," are his words of love.

Sunday, May 1

Dear Diary, I wake up with my head on a hairy chest. I can hear the heartbeat, the heart that beats only for me. Just as I expected, it doesn't take much to get the boner activated, boing, standing at attention pronto. I take my time on top. He reaches for the remote. No way, not today. I use him for my pleasure until I notice my wristwatch. I'm like, "Oh gosh, look at the time." He's like, "Not so fast, I'm not finished with you." It doesn't take long. A minute or two of hard pounding seals the deal.

We get to St. Oscar's late. We sit in back. We remember Sylvia. We close our eyes and see her wan face. We hold hands while I whisper a prayer for her remission, may it be soon, may it be long. We leave quietly. It's barely 9 am.

We do coffee at Copper City Espresso inside the old Canton Junction Train Station. We find a discarded Boston Sunday Globe. The money we save on that, we can put in our cookie jar. We share an apple fritter. I stuff it in his face so he gets the bigger bite. We get a refill and sit outside. I study the classifieds for Ford Broncos used, but none today. I have $3200 saved. He studies the sports.

I get my coaching report. He picks running as my best aptitude. We should give swimming a try also. Later, we look online for the female triathlete swimwear. Swim, bike and run. I become a triathlete. We can start with 4 lap swim, 2 mile bike ride and half mile run, the Cupcake triathlon.

At home there is a special request for the blow job because I am so good at it and I promised it whenever needed. I get to sit in a chair this time. "Why hold back," is my motto I give my lovers whatever they like, within reason. The nympho I was destined to be is out of her decades long confines and going wild. "Are you sure you want to marry a nympho?" I want to know. "Pretty sure," he smirks but then "very sure!" when he feels the teeth. "Ok, I'm glad we got that settled," I declare. At 19:30, we are back at my house. Sylvia has just departed with Bob. She takes her chemo on Saturdays now. My girls are glad to see me, all three of them.

Monday, May 2

Dear Diary, The nympho is able to abstain for one night. Last night was only about sleep. I get a big hug and "I'm glad you are home," as the working girls pack their lunches. We proceed along our 20-minute eastern route through Jamacia Plain. We have time to talk about our future. My lease expires end of November, meaning we can be together 7 more months. After that, we still have shopping, yoga, modeling and girl's night out. L. admits "I probably will move also, possibly to Roslindale. I don't want to live in that building without you. It would be daily heartache." At drop off, I whisper in her ear, "Seven more months, can you handle it? They are going to be really good ones." She nods her head and gives a wet kiss goodbye, my Tangerine Sorbet kiss.

Susan and I go walking at lunch. I ask if she gives her secret guy blow jobs. "Whatever he wants," is her reply. "What if he wanted to watch you do me?" I wonder. "Whatever he wants," she affirms with a laugh. "Mine trims his hedges or we do each other's," I brag. We are both maybe too horny, but it hasn't gotten us into trouble yet. "Sex is natural. Sex is good." George Michael sang it, so it must be true.

Okay, work, focus, filing, late charges, schedule tours, clear waiting lists. Occupancy is high. Feedback is good. We deserve a bonus. At 18:00, I gather up my passenger for our return trip. We have our quiet time at St. John's. We go home to have our nap. It's been a long day. We have a nice cuddle. I assure her that I will never love another woman. "You are the only one," I promise. "The only one," I repeat. Suddenly, I want to see if she is ticklish. She is. We have a tickle tussle which turns into a passionate clinch.

Some chilled beers remain, but not for long. She likes to drink out of the bottle. Guys in college would buy her beers just to see her work the bottle. She has to go upstairs for some design work. I have a soak.

My muscles are still sore from Saturday's tryouts. No sooner are lights out but I hear a tapping at the door. "I need you," pleads my visitant. Those are my thoughts as well.

Tuesday, May 3

Dear Diary, I wake up with my arms around my dear one from one floor above. It's becoming such a normal and natural way to start my day. We have quiet time with Fatima and Felicia. It's still dark. My bedfellow slips upstairs to prepare herself. I whip up our usual breakfast and lunches. At first light, tea is brewing. L. returns for more quiet time. We compare notes. It seems like we both enjoyed blissful oblivion.

On route, we find our island music. I ask if she runs, bikes or swims. She has access to the pool at Tuft's. She has a bike, seldom used. She once ran a 5K, ending near the back of the pack. I pledge to find the next 5K charity run. My coach, I explain, advises me, for the safety of the general public, to participate in sports which do not involve a projectile. We are now routinely delivering wet kisses at drop off. Phil caught the show. I tell him we just do that to drive you wild. He just stands there, shaking his head.

I tell Joni about the 10K. She knows about one in Norwood on May 14. She and her kids attended last year. There are minor events for all age groups. Susan wants to come. I check on the progress of the upcoming furnished unit. The guys have gutted the place. New furniture for the model unit has been approved. That unit will be offered for weekenders. We are choosing a website for marketing the unit. Homeward bound, we stop at St. Theresa's. We sit there quietly in the cool and dark. She rests her head on my shoulder. At home, we change and go for a jog, just our street, a dead end, with little traffic. After 2 laps, we barely break a sweat. We go for 2 more. Our designated girl's locker room is upstairs, just the two of us. We can take liberties with scrubbing each other. "You really have the best body I have ever seen in any locker room shower," my lover declares. I could just cry.

There is no need to get dressed. We have lust in her bed before dinner and a date for lust before sleep in mine. "Are you happy?" I whisper. "Very much so, indeed," says she.

Wednesday, May 4

Dear Diary, A hard rain wakes us. We leave early, taking Centre St., coffee mugs in hand, headlights on and wipers flapping. L. likes this route the best. It's coming down hard. We pull over at the 7-Eleven. We may as well refuel. We have 5 miles to go. Prompted towards caution by sirens, we wait it out. We share an Almond Joy with our refills. "Okay, Danica Patrick, pit stop is over," I prod. "You're much cuter, I add as we pull away. Danica merges smoothly coming out of pit row. I slide over at the museum employee entrance. I roll down the window for our kiss goodbye. I watch her trudge away in her raincoat and boots, umbrella in hand. She swipes and waves from the entry.

Susan brings doughnuts again. She is showing off cleavage today. On her face is that mischievous grin we see a lot of this year. "They're real," she informs me. Maggie brings pizza for lunch. Not much action today. I prepare toner cartridges for FedEx pick up. I unpack some deliveries.

Roy phones on our hotline. He is welcome relief from the estrogen overdose. He wants to come and get me from work on Friday night. He has Celtics playoff tickets. The afternoon drags on. We have entertainment when we go outside for a stretch. I get an elbow in the ribs. Susan warns me that Phil is coming over. He blurts out, "I adore you, Susan. Will you marry me?" "Oh, that's sweet," says she. "But I guess not. Don't worry, you'll find someone." Back inside, she explains how she likes to let them down easy.

I am glad to get on the Yoga mat. We are on time for the Reiki Class. We set our intention, which is focus and creativity, plus a bit more flexibility. We will be toned up nicely for our athletic endeavors. We are famished by the time we get to St. John's for prayer. I am able to delay gratification. At home we inspect the leftovers. Most are edible if heated up and doctored up with spices. Our stir fry smells wonderful. By 8 pm, we are on the couch, reading. I have my Sherlock Holmes. She is more Goth. She prefers Edgar Allen Poe. We play footsie. We douse the lights and drift off right there on the sofa.

Thursday, May 5

Dear Diary, Our week is flying by. I cherish these happy days. My couch guest moves to the bed sometime in the wee hours. Both cats are still with me. On our morning, we want tea. I have some loose-leaf Earl Grey. I dress as it infuses. I take my mug upstairs to watch Milady prepare herself, so organized, so efficient. Now she is brushing her teeth. Then she is gargling. How can anyone be so adorable, no matter what she is doing?

I stare out her kitchen window which offers a much different perspective from what I see from my window. I become her, staring down at me. I wave up to myself. Strange and unexpected how we merge into one thing, united and residing in the quiet and shade of 14 Heron Street. Some philosophers debate whether the past still exists. Yes, it does. We will always be here on the time continuum, happy together, in the 11th year of the 21st Century.

I am in an unfocused mood. L. is driver on our scenic western route. She is in her usual serious morning mood. Our kiss goodbye is warm and fragrant, on both cheeks and slightly open mouth. We can see the love in each other's eyes.

I open the office, at 07:15, all alone with yesterday's doughnuts. I grab a powdered sugar jelly. I make fresh brew. It drips while I boot up. Susan is next in the door. Giving me a strange look, she wonders, "What is the matter with you?" "Love sick, double shot!" I explain. I was neglected for so many years, but now seems a near overdose. Sandy arrives next. It's just we 3.

A packet of mail drops through the slot. I see hand-written personal mail. It's for me, from Roy. Susan tries to look but I stuff it in my blouse. I read it and lock it in my desk. On Friday, I will have him recite it for me. At 18:00, I am all alone once again. My lethargy suddenly evaporates when I see our Malibu turn the corner. My transporter looks a little tired. Our prayer vigil is at St. Theresa. We hold hands. She rests her head on my shoulder. My vision rises above us. I see us together below, in front of Jesus, Mary, Joseph and all of the Saints. I see our prayers offered up, for Sylvia, Lindsey's Mom in Distress.

Friday, May 6

Dear Diary, We have ourselves a crisis. Coming home yesterday, we notice a problem with the left front wheel. Dad thinks it is the CV Boot. Dave is our backup transporter while Dad takes the Malibu to his mechanic. The working girls enjoy Dave's leather seat limo service to MFA. We sit in back, holding hands. We have our wet kiss goodbye. L. likes it when we kiss in front of others. I move to the front on route to Chestnut Hill. Dave asks if I have changed teams. "More like a switch hitter in the Game of Love," I explain. "She sure is cute. I'll give you that, and kind of young too," he observes. "What am I, Grandma Moses?", I shoot back. "Ageless and timeless, in my book," he offers. "Good one. You get a kiss goodbye also," I concede as I plant one on his cheek.

I tell Susan about my flirt of the day. She reminds me that she got proposed to twice, her Secret Guy plus Phil. I remind her that I got the ring, which I am wearing, but I have yet to see hers.

The last late rents come in before lunch because "The Eagle Flies on Friday." All afternoon, people are calling in. I must meet Roy at Tavern on the Square 'round about 19:00. It's the place where he took a knee in front of me. Dad says the Malibu will be ready Saturday afternoon. Lindsey gets a ride with her boss, John Lowery to Back Bay. She gets her final check from her gallery sales. I get a ride with Susan to South Station. Thus, we are off on our wild weekend which we worked so hard for with the sweat of our brows. Susan drives a Toyota standard trans. She is giving a leg show working the gas, brakes and clutch pedal with dress hiked up nearly to the crotch.

I catch my train to North Station. Roy is there at our rendezvous location, waiting outdoors. "I missed you terribly," he declares. We spy two seats open at the bar. Some of the wait staff recognize us from February. At the Garden I hold Roy tight in the crush of the crowd. We are in the lower bowl. I forgot how loud it can get. The Celtics get a decisive win over D. Wade, Lebron, and the rest of the Miami Heat. Roy's truck threads through late night traffic. At home, the lights are on upstairs.

Saturday, May 7

Dear Diary, Saturday's action begins early, like just after midnight. Roy and I get an invitation to join the group upstairs. L. is hosting a slumber party for special guests, Jessica, Casey, Kelsey and her boyfriend, Chad. They sip Champagne. L. is recreating her strip poker parties from college. Jessica is the only one who missed out on college, instead attending "The School of Hard Knocks." Chad is an actor; as such, he has been on stage nude many times. Casey went streaking on a dare once at Spring Break. The novelty of nudity in mixed company lies solely with Kelsey. The game is 5-card draw. Each player starts with 8 items of clothing. Roy declines to join, at least not today. To say never implies disapproval. He likes better the idea of Strip Black Jack downstairs, just us two. I agree. We stay sipping Champagne long enough to see 4 out of 5 lose their hats.

Our Black Jack game concludes with Roy retaining his jockey shorts and one sock. I am tipsy enough to say, "Release the Kraken. Claim your prize." How comical to see his pleasure probe busting out of the confines of the jockey shorts through the fly. While Roy is claiming his winnings, the nudists upstairs are losing their socks one by one.

At breakfast, we find that Kelsey was first to lose it all. The guests depart early in Chad's SUV. L. has time to tidy up and prepare for her Mom. Roy and I jog over to Speedy Mart. We return with the Globe and some items for Nurse Lindsey in her role of post chemo care of her Mom. We greet Sylvia on arrival. She likes to sit at the kitchen table and share the paper just as Roy and I do. She looks ok, maybe just a little pale.

Lindsey shows us her bike. She rode it all the way to work once. We get the seat adjusted and the tires inflated. I am up in the saddle for the first time since grade school. Staying on my street, I have my first bike and run. We shower and head back to bed for afternoon delight. I deliver rewards without limit. I watch my lover getting dressed. Sadly, Roy must bid me adieu. Dad arrives at 16:30 with the Malibu and a bill for $176. It's fun to write him a check. I wonder if he will actually cash it.

Sunday, May 8, Mothers' Day

Dear Diary, It's Mother's Day. From our Aphrodite shoot, we have some head shots. I put one in a cameo for Mom. It's a cropped print from the Ecstasy pose, a profile where my hair looks quite luxurious. L. has a cameo for her Mom as well. I go to early Mass at St. Theresa's. I grab a dried flower arrangement from Star Market. Back home, I make a hand-written card to go with the flowers. It's only 10 am. I am due at Mom and Dad's at 16:30.

Roy calls to say he misses me terribly all over again. He tells how his mother passed when he was just a boy and the Dad, who lives in Maine, never married again. We plan to visit her grave and his dad on our vacation in August.

I hear activity upstairs. L. and her Mom soon appear on the sidewalk having a fresh air promenade. Shortly after their return, I hear the rumble of Bob's truck. He is come to take custody of his wife. We do a meet and greet outside. Bob takes a look under the hood of the Malibu. He listens to the engine. He will advise on the proposed purchase. We wave farewell.

L. wants to meet my Dad and to sketch him. I call Mom and tell her to set one more place. Mom has done her hair up nicely for her special day. She loves the dried flowers. They will last forever, as few things do. She stares at the cameo, exclaiming, "Wow, that's my little girl!" She reads the card in which I wrote, "To Mom, Thanks for raising me good and strong. From your Firstborn, on Mother's Day, Year of Our Lord, 2011." She dabs her eyes and delivers her usual big bosom smothering hug.

L. has been watching Dad and sketching. She takes a bow as the creator of the cameo. She wants to see my childhood bedroom. It is not much different from my High School days. We greet the evening with a swing under the backyard Oak. We say our goodbyes just before dark.

Homebound, we stop at Oscar's on Dedham Square. We want an after-dinner coffee. Randy makes it the best. "And who might you be?" he inquires, seeing Lindsey for the first time. "Randy, this is Lindsey, the woman I love. You'll be seeing more of her," I declare. "The mystery deepens," says he as he pours.

Monday, May 9

Dear Diary, So much happened over the weekend that to process it all, L. and I retire earlier than usual last night and get up earlier today. Sure enough, at 05:30, I hear my Dear One, moving about. We have breakfast upstairs. I like to stuff the toast in her mouth. It's a nice view of first light from up there. By 06:30, off we go on another full week of commuting adventures.

L. is chattier than usual, inbound on Centre St. Her dad gave a thumbs up on the Malibu. He can maintain it at low cost, which is what fathers like to do for their daughters. While the radio plays Reggae, we make a deal. L. will be the third owner. The sticker price new was $18K. I got it 6 years old for $12K. The odometer shows 120K miles. Experts give it a life expectancy of 150K miles. We settle on the price to her of $2.5K. She will need one more month to save up. It is her very first car and she is super excited. She has a possible investor, namely Jessica.

I open the office at 08:00. Susan is not far behind with more doughnuts from Dunkins. She knows my weakness. We compare our secret guys before the others arrive. "We did the wild thing on the beach," she brags. "I was naked outside. No one saw us, I guess. It was night but we had a campfire. "Congratulations, you're one up on me there," I admit. I tell her I am inventing a new kind of wedding vows. I don't like that business about 'til death do us part. "That's morbid, plus he can't get rid of me that easily. Even on the other side, one or both of us, he is still mine."

We have an extra box of doughnuts for the maintenance guys. It's fun to pop in on them. They grab them with their black, greasy hands.

At 17:30, L. is waiting for me, employee entrance, per usual. She wants to drive. It will be her baby soon. The kittens and the car are practice, if she is going to be a mom. I request that she never sell it or junk it. Instead, garage it and use it for storage or park it on some land and camp out in it. She agrees. It will always have big sentimental value. We will always be connected that way. Naturally, we sleep together tonight. My bed offers more luxury for the two Goddesses.

Tuesday, May 10

Dear Diary, The younger of us needs more sleep. She gets 15 bonus minutes. I grab the shower first for a quick, cool wake up followed by KP duty in robe and slippers. L. takes her tea upstairs to finish dressing. We renew our prayer vigil early at St. John's.

Our route is mostly stop and go on Washington St. but we enjoy this time together. Both of our usual routes wind through scenic areas. Boston, due to its terrain, cannot possibly submit to a grid. We view sunrise from Roslindale Wetlands Urban Wilds to the right of Centre St. Our North-South routes never lead to glare from rising or setting sun. A kiss fare thee well 'til eventide with something whispered in the ear for spice, accompanies our drop off.

Susan beats me to the office. The others are there including Joni but lacking Maggie. Sandy is allowing a little more latitude for chatter. I see the others looking at me while I am busy on the phone. Susan is wearing her mischievous grin. She is trying to decide if my secret guy is really a girl. Little does she know I have two secret loves, and only one of them is a guy.

When Roy phones in, I float the idea of getting married twice, a secret civil ceremony followed by the public Church Wedding for Mom and Dad. I ask him to write alternative vows. We can compare them on the weekend.

L. is extra chatty on the way home. One of her lighting ideas for a new sculpture exhibit was accepted. At home, we are quick into our running gear. We stay safe on our own little street. We follow with crunches in our designated gym upstairs. Girls' locker room is the fun part. We towel each other off. The back is hard to get at alone. Eating upstairs is our version of camping out, the food choices and equipment being relatively meager there compared to my kitchen. We raid freezer-burned remnants and fry them up.

It's easy to go to bed early with someone so cuddly. The subject of pillow talk is moods. When she is in a bad mood, I should be no demand and say nothing but when I am irritable, she should question me and get to the bottom of it.

Wednesday, May 11

Dear Diary, My tits are getting some attention to help wake me. Oops, there goes the nipple erection. A tease to start the day? Why not? No big delay. We are out the door by 06:45. Itinerary includes prayer vigil, gassing up and Dunkin's detour. L. is on duty by 08:00 and I as well by 08:30.

Right away, I want to stuff a jelly doughnut in Susan's smirking face. We get another glowing report from Maggie's meeting at Corporate. What a team we are! We can be proud. Susan and I walk at lunch, being quiet for a change. On the afternoon, I am stuck with inventory. Usage has been normal. The standing order need not be altered. I have some filing and presto! It's 5 pm, time to pick up my little girl from school, except that she is all grown up.

Grove St. begins the usual Brookline traverse. Things slow down at Rt. 9. We make it to Yoga on time. Monica and Lydia are there. We exchange phone numbers. L. need never be lonely. Her network is expanding.

At home, after kitten care, it's back rubs and a power nap. We light candles for twilight supper. Afterward, I want to do some snaps with my old Canon point and shoot. L. poses herself full nude under subdued lamp light, seated at my vanity. She shows me how to bounce the flash. Her hair is tossed forward over her left shoulder. She turns to her right exposing one breast in profile. Her hands are palms down on the vanity bench which is cushioned in red. She looks like an angel. After 24 frames, I toss the camera aside. I put my hands on her shoulders and kiss the top of her head. She lets me brush her hair, fifty strokes. "Some of those will be suitable for framing, lover girl" I predict. "Quite possibly," she agrees, her reflection smiling back. We are packing much pleasure into just 1 day and it's still early, only 21:30.

Time out for Lifetime TV, the usual charming but evil husband. Roy calls in. He is coming to get me Friday evening. Jessica calls in. She wants to visit some late-night places that same evening. We are equally popular. We stay booked. It's all good. Snuggle time.

Thursday, May 12

Dear Diary, With my Angel beside me, every day is a joy, even when she is moody. She is up first, tossing two cats on the bed, saying, "Here, these two creatures want something. I have to go upstairs." She pulls on her clothes from yesterday and exits. Thirty minutes later, I hear the Malibu engine crank. We are efficient on our workday mornings. I am almost ready for the debut of one of Mom's pants suits from the 1980's. L. is out there, wiping dew from the windows. I grab our mugs and lunches. I relax to Mozart the entire trip, no need to speak, just sip my Earl Grey and watch the people out there, going about their business, business as usual in our fair city.

We arrive at MFA early, time enough for me to exit the passenger door, cross to the driver door, open it and offer my hand, a standing hug and kiss, a lunch and the mug of honey and lemon hot tea. "I had a bad dream," she reveals. "I have a magic wand that banishes bad dreams. Poof! Up in smoke," I proclaim with a wave of my hand. This releases a hint of a smile.

Susan also seems gloomy. There is no teasing of each other today. She gets a flower delivery in the afternoon. Someone was thoughtless and has come to his senses. She leaves them in the breakroom. We have a nice collection of vases in there. She is prepared to do the 10K on Saturday. Joni signs us up. We can run off all of those jelly doughnuts. I am able to leave on time to gather up my partner in prayer.

We spend a little extra time at St. John's. At home we stretch and do 8 laps up and down our street followed by crunches. I envy her leaner than me almost a six-pack tummy. I find out that Casey is hoping they can be roommates. Chad is moving in with Kelsey. It will be too crowded there with only one bathroom. She has a big car payment so can't get her own place. She works at Rockland Trust near Jamaica Way. It could be very practical for all three of us. The move in would be June 1st. "The more, the merrier. I can handle it," is the opinion I express. I feel very confident about relationships these days. With that, it's locker room time once again, my second favorite time of day.

Friday, May 13

Dear Diary, We do our prayer vigil early. St. Theresa is conveniently along our western inbound route. I have an overnight bag just in case.

The cloud L. was under yesterday seems to have vanished. She is meeting Jessica at a North End bistro on her evening.

Susan opens the office before me. She has freshened her flowers and moved them to her desk. She plans an early escape to Back Bay to meet her secret guy. We could lose her if she marries the dude. By years end, all will be revealed, we agree.

We don't have our minds much on our work. Sandy does the tours. She is best at sales. I do the phones. Susan processes lease applications, all very routine. We are like school children waiting for the bell to ring.

I end up alone for 20 minutes waiting for my man. I stare out the window, daydreaming about our future until I hear a familiar rumble. Roy rolls down his window. He is wearing a sailor hat. He has a really cute ladies sailor hat for me and a spare wind-breaker. He gives me the all aboard. We are going on a sunset cruise aboard a schooner departing at 19:00 from South Boston Waterfront. We are there in no time flat on I-90.

By 19:30 we in full sail out in the harbor. We may take the helm for a few minutes each. We are offered typical sailor's fare, slightly upgraded for modern times. The hard cheeses, kipper snacks, ship's biscuit and ale made for a nice light supper. A close hug inside Roy's hot tent windbreaker protects me from chilly gusts. By the time we are back to shore, stars are glimmering, a perfect evening for a pleasant waterfront stroll to our parking. His right arm stays around my shoulders, my left arm around his waist. A little after 10 pm finds us safely home in my kitchen. We already have lights out when L. and her guest, Jessica roll in around midnight. We hear some music faintly from up there but nod off again quickly. I dream that I am back at Dedham High and Roy is the coach of both boys and girls track teams. We have mixed practices. I run 880 relay and magically, Lindsey is on the relay squad. I pass the baton to her. She takes off like a rabbit.

Saturday, May 14

Dear Diary, At 07:00, the young ladies upstairs knock as the athletes downstairs have their pre-race power breakfast. Jessica rides with us to Norwood Depot while L. prepares for her Mom.

We are at Norwood High in time to watch the children's sprints. In the 4, 5, and 6-year-old group. Some of those kids can fly, while some get overwhelmed and run to Momma in tears. It's good to have my coach with me at the starting area. We stretch. We apply tracking chips to our running shoes. Roy has some high-end New Balance. I have my old Nike cross trainers. We start in the last group. It's 3 miles out and 3 miles back with elevation changes. Roy stays with me for our first mile, a 12-minute walk and run. I feel good. I feel light. At the 2-mile mark, Roy is way ahead almost out of sight. I pass a few people here and there. At least I won't be last.

I catch up with Susan. She was in the group right before me. We decide to stay together until the last 100 yards, then sprint it out. We hit the Gatorade booths whenever we find one. She shares some sunblock with me. I am wearing my sailor hat from last night. We are both getting wolf whistles galore. At Peabody St. we get a second wind. We are able to maintain a jog. I swat her jiggly butt to ignite our cupcake version of a sprint to finish line. It's a photo finish. Too close to call. We are tied for 620th place out of 750 starters. We'll do better next year. We rest in the shade for a bit then off to find our "coaches".

Back home, beers are waiting. We give our sports report to Mother and Daughter who are getting some sun in lawn chairs. They had fun earlier, shopping at Star Market. We enjoy our Dos Equis inside. Roy doesn't always drink beer, but when he does, he drinks Dos Equis. He identifies with the Gentleman in the ad campaign. I sit on his lap while he drinks. We go for a nice cool shower. We towel each other off. I have to be careful with "the family jewels". We have our siesta with fur balls in attendance. Near to sunset, we are outside again to walk off the stiffness. At home, something is getting stiff again. This will require more exercise, in the missionary position.

Sunday, May15

Dear Diary, My hero takes me to Church early Sunday, just down the street to Good Old St. Theresa's, and the congregation therein. Now it is my turn to lay my head on someone's shoulder, in a place of sanctuary, within a mist of chanted prayers repeated weekly since childhood, first in Latin, later in English. It is a nice way to take time out, even if you are not a serious true believer. We harmonize with the choir in our modest muted tones, not too shy to lift our voices upward, despite they be slightly off key. Feeling uplifted, we proceed homeward, where more fornication may happen, sinners that we are. We are engaged to be married, civil and religious, and we are in love. This is more than enough to banish feelings of guilt.

Sylvia is finished with the Sunday Herald, which we inherit minus the coupons. Bob is expected at 1600 hours. He also likes military time, just as my Dad. Sylvia notices how much happier her daughter is recently, compared to her baseline gloomy goth temperament. She thanks me for taking care of her little girl. "We just have fun together, almost daily," I explain. L. begins to blush. "It started simply with folding laundry, boring alone, fun together," I elaborate. At 16:30, we wave goodbye to Bob and Sylvia. Bob likes his Sunday excursion, previously aimless, now purposeful. It is a drive of a little over 2 hours to Brattleboro, with roadside stands along the way featuring eggs, honey, produce and flowers.

We discuss the possibility of adding Casey to the household. Roy agrees with me, "The more, the merrier, except I will be way outnumbered." The main question is whether on Saturdays Casey can stay with me. Since, quite often I will be in Canton on Saturdays, seems like no problem. Roy has to leave soon. He likes to get home before dark. L. conveniently has some work to do on her desktop. I have time to give my appreciation to such a great guy and what a prince. I do it privately in my boudoir of erotic fantasies come true. Later, over beers upstairs, I pose the question of where to sleep. L. points to her bed which she made up with fresh linens while waiting. "You're mine now," says she.

Monday, May 16

Dear Diary, First thing, I ask my partner if she is happy. She says she gets pulses of happiness. I tell her about my dream of us on the 880-relay team. She definitely likes that. We get dressed separately on weekdays. We would slow each other down otherwise. Inbound, I drive the western route while L. stays in a serious and thoughtful mood. I do not disturb her thoughts. Why talk and analyze our affair. Less talk, more action, enjoy to the full while it lasts.

At my office, I wait while L. comes around to the driver's side. She opens the door. I get out for our standing kiss but there is no one to witness. I notice bright sun. There will be glare driving east to MFA. She agrees to come inside for a while. It's early. We are alone for a morning make out session in the office. Making out in public places is a thrill. A mini-climax just from getting into a clinch fully dressed is a nice way to start the shift. We keep it spontaneous. Susan is arriving just as L. is leaving. They greet politely. Susan alerts me that my blouse is cross buttoned which leads to more teasing about my B cup versus her C cup. So begins another workday recorded in tiny detail, each detail a tasty tidbit.

By 18:00 my transporter and I glide along W. Roxbury Parkway, windows down, communicating by means of body language. We stop at St. John's. Our prayer vigil ends with a seated power nap. Our at home checklist is cats, run, crunches, shower, bathrobes, soup and salad. I call Roy. She calls Casey. Casey will move in on Sunday, May 29. To allow more space, they will do bunk beds. We can take a deep breath. What's left to do? Backrubs, of course, after which L. needs some time alone upstairs. There is activity upstairs until late.

I fall asleep, book across my chest, felines at my feet. L. has a key. Sometime after midnight, she slips in silently. The bedside digital clock displays 04:07 as I get up for a drink. I light a candle to watch my angel sleeping. She is talking in her sleep, just some whimpers and murmurs except for the words "no, no, please no".

Tuesday, May 17

Dear Diary, At 06:00, my guest is sitting up in bed, rubbing her eyes and sipping the first pour of our teapot. I open the curtains and crack the window. The birdsong is mostly sparrows. She refills her cup and heads upstairs. By 06:45 we are northbound on our eastern route which is preferred from now on. That way, the last leg of the commute has the sun at my back.

L. has a straightforward day of exhibit tear down. As usual, I wait while she swipes in. She blows me a kiss, au revoir. Susan precedes me with macaroons, the cookie of the day. She made them herself. We have the model booked for the weekend. I go to stock it with bottled water, muffins, coffee, tea, sugar and creamers. I make sure the TV remote and A/C are working. The new furniture looks wonderful, a cheerful modern look, similar to Ikea brand. I set the time on the microwave and stove. I install the Keurig. Joni is on duty today. On Saturday, her 8-year-old won the sprint in his division. Sandy reports on her 2 kids, both in High School. Prom is next Saturday. At afternoon coffee break, Sandy and I share the last macaroon. Her kids seem happy at Brookline High. They are able to walk to school and practices, which is huge. At 16:30, I complete the last of my credit checks. I breeze out the door. Phil gives me a wink. He's a girl watcher. By 17:15, my girl and I have moved from the mundane to the spiritual at St. John's. We sit in front which seems more cloistered. After our quarter hour of solemnity, we rise and proceed homeward for our usual mini workout, locker room and light supper. We share some of the Jägermeister L. keeps for emergency lightening of the mood. Mellowed by this elixir, she is ready for her back rub in my boudoir of wishes come true. Her fondest wish is for me to spend a weekend with her in Brattleboro. In grade 6, she reported to her parents about boys and girls kissing and how she wanted to kiss girls. Bob was relieved. "Less worries for me about trouble with boys," he flatly stated. "That thing that boys have, I don't like it," she confided to her mom. Her nightmares are not a sex thing. She'll explain later.

Wednesday, May 18

Dear Diary, At breakfast next morning, we look at a calendar. We circle June 11 and 12 for our Brattleboro adventure just us two. On the way to the car, I happen to mention, "By the way, that thing that boys have, I never much liked it at first, but I guess I have kind of got used to it. It depends on who it is attached to." We laugh. Crank up the Reggae! It is a high key morning. At drop off, after our kiss goodbye, I suddenly realize and report, "Guess what? We are young and in love. What a thought for a weekday workday morning." She smiles, swipes and waves farewell.

All fully nurtured, we tackle our tasks. Vanilla wafers are the cookie of the day. Chatter is at a minimum. Susan and I power walk at lunch, barely breaking a sweat. Next thing I know I am at The Blissful Monkey once more setting some really nice intentions alongside baby girl Lindsey and our newest pals, Monica and Lydia. We linger at the juice bar. They are rising seniors, having just passed spring semester finals. They are looking for summer jobs. The Boston MFA takes interns. It will be good for their resume. They agree to meet Lindsey tomorrow morning to fill out the application.

St. George's is locked for the night. We find an outdoor grotto from which to send our prayers. We stop at Speedy Mart for a frozen pizza. We shower while it bakes. L. sets the table while I talk to Roy. I ask L. if Roy can see the nudes which I shot last week. "Sure, guys can look but may not touch," he hears in the background. "Music to my ears," he responds. I finally get back to the dinner table after making my secret horny guy 10 times hornier. I whip up a salad while Milady dishes the Fancy Feast. We feed each other bites of pizza. We brush and floss scrupulously, as usual. My guest enters the "Boudoir of Wishes Come True" which sounds like a great title for our next project. What is her fantasy wish? She is shy about asking in so many words. It involves a full frontal nuzzle and hug around the hips with her standing facing me. I give my lovers all they request. Compared to dongs staring me in the face, Lindsey's little love nest is artistically pleasant to behold.

Thursday, May 19

Dear Diary, If every love affair has a peak, then yesterday could be our peak, as good as it gets in love with my darling little neighbor upstairs. I write this at 22:00. L. is already asleep on her tummy, clutching her pillow, one cat on either side. I sit at my desk, scribbling away under dim lighting. The windows are cracked to permit a slight breeze. What happened today? Just more ordinary time, steady as you go, pilot and co-pilot, to and from work.

Cookie of the day was Vanilla Wafers. Lydia and Monica applied for their internships. It rained in the afternoon. We stopped at Color-Tek for the color prints "Nude at the Vanity". The low angle shots, including a leg show were dramatic, kind of a cat's eye view. We ordered some 5x7's, suitable for framing. We had time for prayers, a jog, shopping and a candle-lit dinner.

We studied about the last days of Mata-Hari. Her prison accommodations were fairly nice. The French provided special treatment for their high-profile prisoner. She made public appearances during her show trial. She had a roommate in her cell. They enjoyed meals much better than the typical prisoner. Therefore, she was not shrunken and gaunt for her execution. As a dark brunette of 39 years, Bill thinks I am a much closer approximation visually, compared to Garbo and Jeanne Moreau, who did the film portrayals. That's for Saturday.

I douse the light save for a Lavender candle. I slide in beside Sleeping Beauty. She turns to hug with her face just above my chest. I am her living breathing body pillow. In case I get thirsty, there is a bottle of Perrier at the bedside. No use stumbling around and stubbing my toe in the dark. Tomorrow night, it will be my head on Roy's hairy chest. I thank the Lord for my good fortune to meet my two sleeping partners. One year ago, I had none. Most of my adult life, I had none. Love famine, followed by love feast. It all averages out. At 4 am, the bottom of the night, maximum stillness outside, a moan, a restless leg, a quickened breathing. She is reliving something, over and over, until she can fix it, until she gets it right, until she can drown the sorrow.

Friday, May 20

Dear Diary, My homemaker genius idea of the week is make a dozen hard boiled eggs, a pound of bacon, and buttered toast in advance, all just as good cold. I have 2 percolators now, one for coffee, one for tea. Just plug in one or the other while dressing. The passenger, me, can munch and sip along the way on our early Friday morning. L. saves time because no make-up. I use a little. L. wants to swipe in early to finish some online modules.

At my office, everyone is in a good mood. I have some reports to generate which takes me all the way to coffee break. We drink outside in some nice shade. We feed cookie crumbs to Sparrows and a random Pigeon. We wave to the repair crews in their golf carts. I will miss all this but I am ready take some steps up some kind of career ladder.

Susan and I both work through lunch so we can leave early. We have snacks in our desk. I make it back to MFA by 17:00. L. is ready to call it a week. A cool quiet church provides our decompression. Roy will hang with his "Bros" tonight. He must prove that he is not p-whipped.

After supper, L. wants to remodel to make it nicer for her Mom and to make space for Casey. I have room downstairs for her winter wardrobe storage. We get up a lot of dust bunnies. I find some money, 37 cents in all. L. finds a missing necklace, some socks, and a hankie. We go downstairs to launder linens and towels. There is a drink machine, an old tippy table and wobbly chairs. We share a Cherry Coke. Some of the magazines are 5 years old. We check the bulletin board advertising babysitters, dogwalkers, furniture for sale, including a dresser. We'll have to see if that works for Casey. We tear off the number. Uh oh! Was that a mouse I just saw? We go back upstairs while the towels dry. L. brings down Jager, the mini bottles. I sip mine on ice. We trade neck and shoulder rubs at my vanity. I have mine topless. In the three vanity mirrors, is my cascade from 3 angles. Mata-Hari, the night before the Firing Squad, is brushing her hair. In the left drawer is my sewing kit, scissors and ribbons. I invite L. to harvest a lock of her lover's hair..

Saturday and Sunday, May 21 and 22

Dear Diary, I have an extra ribboned lock of my perfumed hair for Roy, resting in a decorative box, enameled on the outside and red velvet on the inside. My man is waiting for me at Canton Junction when my transporter, Dave pulls in. We use our Charlie Cards. The 08:24 departure to Providence is on time for our 37-minute trip with stops at Sharon, Mansfield and Attleboro.

We taxi straight to Bill's Studio on Westminster St. Two other amateur models are there. Bill avoids the standardized look of professional models. He finishes the final pose with the first model who does not linger. The second model attempts some tragic method acting. She does well through all four poses. Bill takes a break for lunch, during which I suggest the pose of brushing my hair the evening prior to execution. He agrees to do that one last. I spend a few minutes in wardrobe and make-up. At noon, we are back to work. There is a dignified pose descending a stairway to the execution yard as a kind of warm up. The next is arms bound to a post and staring unblindfolded down the barrels of the rifles. A breeze from a large fan mimics a gust of wind. The 3rd pose is meant to be the moment of impact of the fusillade. This requires some trickery. The 4th is slumped and still bound to the post. Bill takes the longest with this one, shooting from many angles. I artlessly take direction as best I can. Meanwhile, the assistants have found props for the hair-brushing scene. They are using their standard boudoir setup. Again, Bill shoots from many angles, including above, a total of 60 shots in medium format film. Most of the outdoor shots were digital. He shakes my hand, thanks me for my time and says, "I'll call you."

We taxi back to downtown where we have a leisurely stroll along the Riverwalk. We dine at The Patio on Broadway. Roy takes my hands and states emphatically, "I thought you were the best of the lot." "That is so sweet. This is for you," I say as I pass him the box with the lock of perfumed hair, collected the night before my fake execution.

We take the 5:55 pm MBTA Commuter for our return. Along the way, I say how much I missed my man. I hold him close. We enjoy the rocking and swaying of the slow-moving train. From the elevation of Canton Station, we see storm clouds gathering. As we roll to a stop in Roy's driveway, the first thunderclaps are a startle and a shock. I reach for the shelter of my man's arms. I thank him for today. I need kisses without delay.

He carries me inside. His place is a mess. "I've been very busy," is his excuse. "I don't care. I would slum it with you anywhere," I swear and off we go to the man cave leather couch for action we do so well together. It doesn't take long to get over the top. We hitch up our jeans and proceed to the next chamber of grunge, namely the bathroom. "As you can see, I need your help but at least we got lots of hot water, enough to steam the place up," says he. "Tomorrow we clean," I promise. "Tonight, why not just wallow in it?" "That's my girl! That's the woman I love, and here's the proof." He asserts. Sure enough, that thing is at attention again.

I drag my slacker out of bed in time for 8 am Mass at the cool confines of St. Oscar's. We remember to offer prayers for Sylvia. We do the coffee and donuts downstairs after Mass. I say that we are visiting from St. Theresa in West Roxbury. We grab the Sunday Globe at 7 Eleven on the way home. Roy needs his run. That gives me 20 minutes to tidy the kitchen. On return he gets garbage detail. He doesn't recycle. We lounge around in the kitchen 'til noon, brunching and reading.

Our pretend fight is about him being a slob and no sex until he cleans the bathroom. I supervise, drill sergeant style. Halfway through he says, "Maybe I'll just do without sex today." "I wasn't talking about just today," I reply. He leaves the toilet for last. I hand him the Lysol. After an hour of back breaking labor on hands and knees, the place is spotless. We start laundry and hit the shower. In robes we start the dryers. Dry cycle is enough time for a nap. "Can I have sex now?" he begs.

Poor boy is very tired from so many chores so I get on top. Twenty minutes on top is my Sunday work out. He starts singing "Ride the White Horse" early techno pop. I make a note never to take him to Karaoke. He remembers the lyrics, something about the white horse, no, no, no, ride the white pony and be a bitch if you wanna be rich. Makes perfect sense. I can't stop laughing. As usual, I let him roll me over for the big finish.

We have a wonderful dinner of fish sticks in the newly clean kitchen. Could I really handle this 7 days a week? We'll see when we are on our vacation. As I am packing up for departure, I remember Lindsey's boudoir nudes. I toss them on the kitchen table. He studies them carefully. He says, "Wow, you shot these?" He picks out one and says he'll keep it because she is my friend and she sure is cute but he needs bigger tits and ass like mine.

The art critic has spoken.

On our ride to my place, we do the "How did I get stuck with you?" routine. There are endless variations on that one. Then I remember about the vows. Yes, he rewrote the usual vows, but they can't be recited in public. I tell him that love and honor are ok but he can forget about the obey. Also, no "death us do part." It's forever, stuck with me forever, this life and the next. "Will there be screwing in the next life?" he wants to know because he will never get tired of screwing me. "I don't see why not," I suppose. "I'll ask the priest." I got him laughing as we pull into Heron Street.

Bob and Sylvia are already gone. We pop in on Lindsey. She is busy preparing something on her desktop. Roy has time to take a breath. The cats enjoy his visits. He says he will let us two catch up. I walk him to his truck, hug and kiss and farewell. As usual when I watch him drive away, I feel an emptiness. School is out soon. He will be around more often. L. is just finishing, as I return. I tell her about the photo shoot. She turns and smiles.

It's a bit of a wicked smile, like I have not seen before. She wants to meet me downstairs in 15 minutes. She brings her last 2 Jagers. Instead of the bathrobe, she models a sheer nightgown, one I never saw before. Has she been streaming lesbian porno? I am her sex therapist. She must undress me, push me onto the bed and say, "You're mine now."

Monday, May 23

Dear Diary, We wake up all tangled and sweaty at 2 am. We have a drink and a cool shower. The cats never stirred. We straighten the covers, blow out the candle and continue our slumber. I will miss this. It can't last forever, but what if it could? Imagine it, dream it, at least.

At 06:00, the happy weekend is in the rear-view mirror. L. hugs her pillow for an extra minute. I write, "I love you." On her back. I just noticed her pelvic dimples. I kiss each one. I look in her fridge. Nothing. We better get busy. I pull open her curtains and say "See you in 20." Sure enough, in 20 minutes, I hear the Malibu wake up. She can eat her bag breakfast while I drive. I compliment her V-Neck sweater and necklace. When she bends to my window, I see her little ones nestled in a chemise.

I feel sad without my co-pilot beside me on the traverse west to Chestnut Hill. On the slow scenic route, Jamaica Pond on the right then Arnold Arboretum Museum of Trees on the left. These days of heaven will last all summer long. There is no good reason why not.

Once again, Susan is first in the office due to my longer commute. We are seriously busy by the time Sandy and Maggie show up. I review the damage assessments on recent move outs. Susan updates our apartment status tote board. Six leases expire at the end of May. These are lacking both renewal or move out notice. Susan will take care of these. Patrick, our head of maintenance, has a meeting with Maggie at lunch.

The furnished unit for the Hennigs is nearly ready. Susan and I check it out on our lunch break. The cookie of the day is Pecan Sandies, a kind of shortbread. These disappear rapidly. I promise the Lorna Doones for tomorrow. They are nearly guilt free in terms of calories.

At 17:30, L. takes the wheel. We divert to the Green T coffee shop in Roslindale. The Green Line doesn't actually go here. If we were full Bohemian, we would walk or Charlie Card our way everywhere. The Needham Line could be our connector to here. I love the décor.

Wouldn't it be great if we had our own coffee shop someday? The smoothies we order will suffice for our dinner. We don't cook tonight, instead we choose prayer and fasting for purification.

Our next stop, conveniently near, is Holy Epiphany Russian Orthodox Church. We light a candle and make an offering for Sylvia. Roslindale could be a nexus for our future Bohemian Empire.

Back home, after our run, crunches, and locker room, I dust off my blender. We combine our fruit and veggie supply and create our first home smoothies. It tastes not quite sweet enough. I run to Star Market for supplies, including honey, while L. retreats to her office.

The dresser for sale is at apartment 12. It is blond French Provincial, a bargain at $20. We move it to my place for now. By 22:00, I am in bed asleep. We had a lot of action today.

At 02:00, I am aware of a presence beside me, a very nice presence, who let herself in to watch me sleeping. She envies my curves compared to her sleek lines. She hugs my curves until the break of dawn.

Tuesday, May 24

Dear Diary, While I make liquid breakfast, L. inspects her well-traveled, but new to her, dresser. She wants to keep this one and give her old one to Casey. Inside, she finds a bobby pin and a 1985 dime but no secret documents taped under the drawers.

Markings on the bottom indicate "Made in USA". She likes the distressed look, including scratches, dents and crayon marks. A wipe down with plain water will suffice. She sits on top, legs dangling, chasing her smoothie with hot tea. She has a light day ahead including more orientation of the interns. I drop off my girlfriend at 08:00.

I am logged in at my desk by 08:30. I have a lot of e-mails to process, including reference requests concerning previous tenants. Records go back to the 1980's on paper about all the people who came and went but left a piece of themselves behind. All morning, I keep getting Susan's mischievous grin. We walk at lunch. We compare our rings. Is it possible that either one is a Cubic Zirconia? On re-entry, our Fan Club President, Phil, entertains us with an expertly formed smoke ring.

After lunch, I have pest control notices to print for distribution by the maintenance crew. Roy phones in. We have no plans for the weekend. What should we do? A lot more of doing what comes naturally, he suggests. Works for me, but we should try to accomplish something. I should practice driving his stick shift truck. It is a 3-day weekend for him. Monday is Memorial Day. Susan volunteers to work for time and a half. I will work 4 hours on Saturday and have Monday off. Got to fit Mom in there somewhere. Play it by ear.

Homeward, I hear from L. that the interns will lighten her load during summer. She put in her vacation request partially overlapping mine. So many possibilities. We need to stop at Green T. to ponder these matters after our visit at Holy Epiphany to pray. At 6 pm, one table remains. We grab it and scan the room. It seems like a nice mixed crowd. We are in the mood for Cappuccinos. Is it possible we could be partners in a business? We write all possible small businesses on a notepad, including interior design. We put the list under our shared pillow tonight to sleep on it.

Our happy day moves on to kitten care, our lady jock action, and placement of the new to us dresser. We slide it up the stairs no problem.

We take a break. Suddenly, I want a standing up make-out session with my girlfriend. We take turns with roaming hands from behind, necking with hands reaching around and under blouses, something new. We pledge to consummate after dinner on an early to bed evening.

Wednesday, May 25

Dear Diary, Today is one of our quiet mornings with no need to speak. We have time to sip our tea and stare out the window, my arm over her shoulder, her arm around my waist. We stare at the trusty Malibu, soon to change hands. It needs a wax job and detailing. We pencil that in for Saturday afternoon.

On our commute, I tell the story of Laura Nyro and Maria Desiderio. It's a bittersweet story. Let's live much longer, we agree. We blow kisses between car and employee entrance as my young object of desire surrenders her time once more to Boston's curated world of art.

My world of properties waits for me. An empty property yields no profit. A rental should feel like home, even if temporary. I get my waiting list qualified. I keep our online ads updated.

We find ourselves adrift in afternoon dead calm doldrums partly due to the heat. Susan and I share a Rock Star on ice. We recall an experimental ergonomic desk in the storeroom. It comes with a kneeling chair. Patrick comes over to set it up. We designate this as our shared special projects desk. On what feels like an overly long day, I am finally free by 17:00.

It's time to have some fun. We make our usual diversion to Roslindale for our "Pause that Refreshes" spiritually and mentally. For interior design, L. wants to use original pieces from unknown artists instead of the typical bland mass-produced abstract wall art. The new furnished unit could be our first hanging. We could offer the Hennigs some choices.

At home, we go direct to our girls' locker room shower for two then flop for a power nap. It is cooler at my place. Upon revival, L. makes the smoothie while I serve the needs of our little ones.

We take a walk at twilight, for a few blocks, holding hands. L. goes upstairs afterwards, leaving me alone with Sherlock Holmes. After a few pages of mystery, Bill calls to let me know that he is using 2 of my photos including the seated brushing hair and the windswept facing the rifles. I update Roy. "Good choice! The guy has taste," confirms Roy. We do some of our dirty pillow talk and say goodnight.

Shortly after drifting into a semi-conscious state, I barely detect a latch turning slowly. Nearly silent footsteps cross the kitchen. There is a soft flickering light. I turn to see Lindsey, in an orange candle-lit glow, gliding toward the bed wearing her sheer negligee. My angel silently slips in beside me.

Thursday, May 26

Dear Diary, After 2 days on a liquid diet we are craving some solid food. We have 1 avocado, 2 slices of Swiss Cheese, and 2 hard-boiled eggs to share on top of the last of the English Muffins. This should keep us going. At 06:30, L. takes the wheel. Smooth Jazz is our music choice to carry us onward. We are alert but mellow. At 07:00, L. slides out and I slide over to get my kiss at the window.

I enjoy smooth sailing westbound on Huntington Avenue until I reach Boylston Street. I pull over at Dunkin's in Brookline. We miss our doughnuts and the guys deserve another treat.

I arrive at the office alongside Miss Susan. We stop at the maintenance shop. It's a thank you to Patrick for our new desk. Susan unlocks and waves me in. We get the coffee going and get booted up just as Sandy arrives. The stuff in our inboxes is knocked out by break time. Sandy takes the phone calls while Susan and I go out to stretch.

We found a stale cookie to crumble for the birds. Susan wants a hug. Next year at this time, I will be gone and she likely will be knocked up. "I will miss you, truly," says she. We do our hug just in time to entertain Phil who says he needs one too. We each give him a quick one for his unwavering devotion. At lunch we search the break-room, finding only some "Cup o' Soup" packets. I saved one English Muffin from breakfast. We try out the kneeling chair. I think I can get used to it. Roy says that women's asses get really big from sitting all day. We don't want that. Maggie will have a special project for us by Monday, we're told. Homeward bound, we divert to Whole Foods Market in Jamaica Plain to stock up. Our Church of the Day is a revisit to St. John's.

We are so organized it's not even funny. L. loves the cats while I put stuff away. We have time for a jog before a late supper. We have dessert upstairs. Jello with Cool Whip is a treat remembered from childhood. L. needs a little time alone. We make a date to meet at 10 pm for massaging and hair-brushing. We read side by side in bed, a few more pages of mystery.

Friday, May 27

Dear Diary, Finally, Friday comes around. We take our tea upstairs and gaze at first light over Upper Washington Street. I deposit my Soul Sister safely at MFA by 07:30. I find myself humming as I stop and roll my way through Brookline. It's "Ice Castles" again.

Susan and I are surprised to see that Sandy precedes us at the office. She has a meeting planned. Joni arrives soon after. Guests are expected for 3 nights in the model unit, late afternoon. We coordinate that and other holiday weekend issues.

All except Sandy leave at 15:00. L. expects to leave at 16:00. I have time to stop for gas. Uh-oh, need oil and coolant. L. can have fun with that at home. I get a slime can and check the spare. Dad got me a full-size spare. We are up in the 90's zone of city concrete heat.

We stop at Holy Epiphany for cool, dark, prayer and sanctity, hand in hand. We go straight home, all windows down. A cool shower in the upstairs locker room seems like a good idea. The kittens tag along.

L. keeps some treats for them up there. We siesta head to feet on her couch 'til twilight time. Downstairs, L. makes our cold supper while I get with Roy. He will see me bright and early to take me to work.

At the table, we start with a fruit salad of grapefruit sections, mango and watermelon. We share a can of solid albacore tuna on Kale with lemon wedges, rice crackers and soy sauce. Dessert is Peach Sorbet but we save it for later. I make a pot of Lapsang Souchong. The smoky aroma smells exotic.

L. checks with her Mom. Tomorrow is the last of her current series of chemo treatments. We have dessert and watch old Alfred Hitchcock shows in black and white. We brush, rinse, floss and get ready for some really nice kisses. On my clock radio we find some Chopin piano nocturnes. L. is on her side with her girlish arm across my tummy and her hair tickling my chin. Soon our breathing is synchronized. I wake at 02:00, thirsty. I dreamed I was at my church wedding, but the school bell rang and Roy had to go.

Saturday, May 28

Dear Diary, My hero appears at 08:00. He has a bag of mixed bagels. L. waves goodbye. I unlock at work well before 09:00. Roy has his laptop. He occupies the ergonomic desk. "Hey, get one of these for me," he demands. I process repair requests and rent e-payments. Bam! Mail hits the slot. All letters are attention to Maggie. Meanwhile, my assistant makes fresh coffee and is having fun snooping around the break room. We stash the remaining bagels in the freezer. We water the avocado trees. I leave a note for Joni. We lock up at exactly 1 pm.

Roy wants to get his foot treatment, side by side with me. Dedham Day Spa can take us as walk-ins. Let's just say that Roy was a bit overdue. He leaves a big tip. I wonder if I can learn the massage portion of this luxury. I purchase the recommended lotion. I want many choices for the reinforcement of the pleasure bond. If my man's feet hurt, even better. We add the relief of pain bond.

My coach declares and dictates further instructions on our footcare. At beginning of summer, we toss our old athletic shoes and get fitted for new. Any pairs which have sentimental value due to memories attached can be deodorized and converted to decorative uses such as door stop, book-ends or wall hanging. We shop the SAS store on Providence Highway. I find a blue walking shoe which will serve nicely on casual Friday.

What Next? I know. I summon up Derek, Roy's alter-ego. We meet by chance for dinner. I enter Oscar's. Randy is on duty. I sit alone at the bar and order. Derek appears. He says that we have to stop meeting like this, that people will talk and may he join me just the same? "If you have served your country, then yes," I challenge. Derek makes up a good story about 4 years serving in the National Guard. All during dinner, he entertains Randy and I with embellished tales of his family's history of service. He covers the tab. As we leave. I wink at Randy, who stands there scratching his head.

At home, L. and her Mom, Sylvia are taking some sun. L. is proud that she added oil and coolant to our Malibu without help. The floor mats are drying after a scrub. Her little battery-operated shop-vac sufficed for the carpets. We need not pay for detailing. Once again, she prefers the distressed look. This car has a history. Why seek to erase it? Over a span of years, with minimum care, it has withstood rough roads and severe weather, serving its owners well. For her, original paint with a patina is a plus. A bit of rust, some scratches and dings all add to the charm. I am seeing a parallel with her "Worn to Perfection" series. We share the coins found, adding up to 68 cents. Bits of candy, potato chips, chewing gum wrappers and pay at the pump gas receipts are the remainder of the historical record. Two years ago, I bought gas at the Shell Station in Walpole. Here is the proof, but what was I doing there? Just for fun, I may seek a notation recorded in our 2009 journal, Dear Diary. For now, all seek coolness indoors.

I propose shower, siesta and cold supper after which, my guest may have unlimited channel surfing. Quickly bored with that, he switches to body surfing all of the wonderful places he likes on the naked body of his soon to be wife, his love object, his sex object, his ideal.

Sunday, May 29

Dear Diary, I wake to an empty bed. Roy's truck is there. He must be running during the maximum cool part of the morning. Breakfast is ready when he returns, grinning broadly, damp to the touch, Sunday Herald in hand. He takes his coffee and gym bag to the shower, returning clean shaven in 15 minutes flat. I have already enjoyed my Dilbert and Doonesbury. He checks his sports. I check my classifieds. I circle some possibilities and put them aside.

The whole day is wide open. A pleasant 25-minute walk brings us to St, Theresa's, sneaking in a little late for the 10 am Mass. A fidgety dark-haired girl in the row just in front of us could be me 32 years ago. I am stabilized by a continuous 32 years long thread of Mass participation. Suitably renewed and with prayers offered, we escape the exiting crush. We are homeward bound arm-in-arm on the aptly named St. Theresa Avenue. The Latin School Park is on our right This leads to Maplewood St. and Grouse St., conveniently passing the Speedy Market on the way. It has just turned 11 am, so Roy can get his Dos Equis. I already have mugs in the freezer.

Nurse Lindsey and her patient, Sylvia are upstairs. They found the Sunday paper which we left on their doorstep. Sylvia likes a radio in the kitchen. Country music is playing softly on an AM station. She also likes a fan, the kind you hold in your hand. She pours mint tea from a clay pot. She needs a little nap. She likes the glider rocker, Lindsey found at second hand. We leave them to find our own private coolness downstairs.

I drain half of my frosted mug ending with a foam mustache. Roy drains his mug completely, plunks it down, wipes his mouth and exhales a satisfied, "Ahh!" The Bruins are in the Stanley Cup Finals but the first game is not until Wednesday. Today is Indy 500. Girl Power,

Danica Patrick starts in 23rd position. She stays mostly in the lead lap, finishing 6th, not too shabby. We pretty much just veg-out all afternoon until Bob pulls in. The guys talk shop while Sylvia packs up. We wave them goodbye.

We expect Casey moving in at about 18:00. This could be fun. She seems like a nice kid. Sure enough, here she comes right on time, with all of the belongings necessary to a 23-year-old stuffed into 5 suitcases. Roy grabs 2 and the rest of us grab 1. She has a check for half of June rent. Chad bought her bed for $25. She gets Lindsey's bed and old dresser and half of the closet. Lindsey likes to sleep on the couch. We leave them to arrange things as best they can manage. We agree to meet for poker later, regular poker, no stripping. We will use Monopoly money. The game is Texas Hold 'em, just like they show on ESPN. The novices catch on quickly and we are not reckless with our betting. Lindsey has been folding nearly every hand. At the one-hour mark, she shoves all in. Roy stares intently at her poker face, which is amazingly blank and half hidden by her dark mane. Roy can afford to call. L. takes the pot with Aces over Jacks Full House. We retire, each to his own quarters, upstairs or below.

Monday, May 30

Dear Diary, It's time to see Mom, the Matriarch, and Dad of course. I go early, while Roy is running. We share some iced tea on the veranda. My much-loved glider remains, a happy place from childhood memory. I stretch out and occupy the full length of it now. Do Mom and Dad suspect something? The news I bring is of such a general nature. Is that a clue which stimulates inference about life-changing developments which are not yet ready for disclosure?

I return home for late lunch. Casey is creating a Gazpacho. Roy is making cheese and sausage biscuits. We are invited upstairs where we share what we have separately prepared. Casey's contributions to the upstairs culinary workspace transform the area from Spartan minimalism to nurturing comfort zone. Her tool kit and spice rack broaden the range of recipes which can be attempted, whereas previously, they were mostly a duplication and extra clutter alongside Kelsey's wares. L. gives Casey carte blanche in the kitchen. The four of us seem like a happy family at leisure. Why not go on a picnic?

Conveniently near is Roxbury Latin School Woods Park. I have a wicker basket down below, which accommodates our light refreshments. Roy has "Deep Woods Off" bug repellent in his truck and a softball to play catch. A pleasant walk of just over a mile along Grouse St. and Maplewood leads us to our sylvan retreat where plentiful shade for coolness alternates with open areas for our pitch and catch. Roy has a team to coach. We play 'round the infield at approximate distances of a softball diamond, underhand or overhand at the throwers discretion. I play second base. Casey is at first, Lindsey at third and Roy is at home plate. I manage a toss from second to home on 1 bounce. Eventually we go successfully around the horn twice without any wild throws. The coach is proud of his team. I watch him clearing a suitable area under a tree for our "seventh inning stretch". Casey spreads our blanket. I pass the basket around. We recline creating a tableau. I imagine the view from above. This image is an emblem of the happy summer which surely must follow.

Tuesday, May 31

Dear Diary, At 2 am sleep interruption, I lack a sleeping partner to hug. L. is upstairs on her couch possibly suffering similar insomnia. The kittens follow across my shadowy world to the kitchen. While draining Perrier straight from the bottle, I peek out the window. Bunnies are hopping around out there. Our grassy areas include some clover. The kittens each get a treat. We three doze off again until 06:00 when I hear activity above. L. dresses quickly and tiptoes down to our lower-level staging area.

Kisses are on the breakfast menu. We are out the door by 06:45. The sun is well above the horizon but overnight cool and damp remains. WCRB 99.5 FM plays softly on my four-way speakers. At the MFA, we drain our tea mugs and have a standing kiss goodbye flavored with honey and lemon. Kisses alone can tide me over. We promise some kind of passion later.

I am the early bird. I nearly clear my desk before the others arrive. Sandy brings the cookie of the day which are Fig Newtons, a healthy choice. Susan looks a little weary from her weekend duty. The phone desk will keep her alert. We pop in on the hammer and wrench guys at lunch. It's good for their morale, we assume. We give them a summer fashion show which reveals more of everything compared to winter. Patrick mainly appreciates the smiles, so he says.

The early bird is released at 16:30. By 17:00, the working girls are re-united on our way to Holy Epiphany for resumption of our prayer vigil. Would it be sacrilegious to have a make out session in a dimly-lit corner of the church? If it is mostly love instead of lust, maybe it is ok. Today is mostly lust and it must wait. We pray from opposite sides of the altar, she to Mary, I to Jesus. We linger at Green-T. Some abstracts by unknown artist Sean Dempsey are hanging. These could help furnish a room.

At home, Casey has dinner ready, Rigatoni, Caesar Salad and Sangria made from her gallon jug of Gallo. We praise her skills. We three combine to tidy up then walk off some of the calorie load. At 9:30 my expected visitor appears to tuck me in, with fulfillment of desire in the process.

Wednesday, June 1

Dear Diary, The birthday girl turns 27 today. Sylvia calls first thing in the morning. A small present from me waits until after work. As usual, we are all business until then. L. gets dropped off and picked up. I am her chauffeur. I come waltzing in a little after the others but ready for action.

Roy phones in on my break. He is finishing his proposals to the School Board. We plan my triumphant return to Canton on Saturday. Joni is back on duty today. She occupies the special projects desk. She is compiling some reports for Maggie. The Hennigs move in after lunch. They will choose their wall art after they are settled in. Four pieces are required, 3 large and 1 small. Our budget is $1000. Susan gets to leave early. I stay dutifully, my full shift.

L. is waiting for me outside on arrival to MFA. She is chatting with Monica and Lydia about funny quotes from staff on the group birthday card. We excuse ourselves from Yoga but we promise the interns next week for sure. By 17:30, we inhabit the coolness at St. John's, escaping from full sun to flickering candles. We like it here but we are getting hungry.

As we park at home, Casey is waving from above. What a pleasant surprise it is to find that Kelsey is there. A cake is lit with candles. We even have the party hats. We cut the cake after dinner. We pop a cork on a bottle of Champagne and toast the guest of honor wishing her the best year ever to come. My gift in its tiny box remains to be revealed. Inside, L. finds an ankle bracelet, an item of adornment which will not interfere with the work of the artist's hands. She extends her right leg, the one she often crosses when seated, so that it will be noticeable at such times. I secure the delicate clasp. We are having so much fun that we forget about our evening stroll until it's almost too late. We manage a short one before dark.

Later, I am alone just me and my kitties but I have a date with Sherlock Holmes as he solves the case of The Veiled Ledger. Will I have a visitor tonight? I wish. I dream about it. At first light, who is hugging me? My 5 ft 2 in. dream come true.

Thursday, June 2

Dear Diary, At 06:30, L. brings coffee to Casey, who is just sitting up in bed. Casey gives her a shopping list for Whole Foods which has items not found at Star Market. We feel like Mother Hens. We want to take the youngest one under our wing. Roy is the designated Rooster. He has 3 hens now, but his duties are largely ceremonial except of course for his duties to me.

Our low-speed inbound commute is routine and without incident. "Au Revoir" to L. is at 07:15. Susan and I are booted up by 08:00. Strawberry Newtons supersede the fig variety. Little rewards tweak us through the day. The starving artist, Sean Dempsey arrives by taxi at 10:30 to display his wares. The Hennigs come to the office for a viewing. They approve. They are pleased to meet the artist in person and to be in possession of original oils. Sean walks away with his $1000 dollar check, hopefully enough to cover his June rent. Our guys will hang these, avoiding damage to walls.

Maggie may win some kind of innovative office manager award if we keep this up. One measure is lease renewal percentage. We retain our tenants. Another is eviction rate. Ours is near zero.

I report the art sales news to L. on our return drive. We took no commission but we sowed good will and built reputation in the local world of art. We do some bulk shopping for cooking oils, rice, nuts, and spices at Whole Foods in Jamaica Plain. We light candles at Holy Epiphany. We linger long enough for traffic to clear. We arrive home at 18:30. Our personal chef serves broiled chicken with mashed potatoes, peas and carrots, coleslaw, and biscuits. She likes to cook but hates to shop. I always helped Mom washing dishes. I don't mind the tidying up alongside Lindsey, my helper, who turns on the radio, same as her Mom.

Our sunset walk ensues. We meet some neighbors on promenade with their pooches. It's good to know your neighbors. City life can easily become impersonal, surrounded by many but connected to few.

The sleeping arrangements are working out nicely. My middle of night guest appears often.

Friday, June 3

Dear Diary, Our weekend well-deserved awaits us on the other side of one more shift. Inbound, we roll down the windows and crank up the volume at our island music FM station. In the passenger's seat, I am getting early morning sun on my face while in the driver's seat L. tosses her dark mane in the breeze. It definitely feels like summer. At adieu, my partner turns toward me. We clasp hands left and right. She slides out quickly and waves from the employee entrance.

Susan is the early bird. I sample her brew and watch her in action. She plans an early departure to Martha's Vineyard, therefor no lingering at lunch or breaks. By 15:30 her desk and emails are cleared. Bam! She is out the door pronto to catch the Cape Flyer to Hyannis, where someone is waiting oceanside. My anticipation is an Ocean of Love washing over me in Canton.

Meanwhile my Malibu sails eastward on its usual schedule. My ship receives a pretty young passenger at MFA. We drop anchor at St. John's seeking celestial guidance and renewing our prayer vigil. We dock at 14 Heron St., where dinner is waiting. Left over sauerkraut is perfect for Casey's Reuben sandwiches.

Our walk this evening has a destination, namely, the Venezuelan Café, the place of first encounter with Casey and Kelsey, a mere 7 weeks prior. We order exotic desserts to pass around, tasting a few bites of each, one by one. One dude tries something out of my playbook. Three unescorted babes means three chances for a base hit. He claims he is a pastry chef seeking our opinion on the desserts. He asks if we dine at the Café often. "Every seven weeks," I say. He has a business card. Is he for real? "It's a date then," says he. "In seven weeks, I will come over and bother you again." He seems about 35, maybe too old for Casey. She keeps the card. She might be slightly interested in this guy named

William Sutcliffe who could be summoned at will or at least 7 weeks hence. We finish our drinks and depart with a casual wave in William's direction. At home, we get tipsy on Sangria while listening to Delilah on I-Heart Radio. I hit the pillow first.

Saturday, June 4

Dear Diary, I am first on my feet. Lindsey and I brief each other. We take coffee and kittens upstairs to help Casey wake up. By 07:00, my weekender is packed. I hear the rumble of Roy's Jeep. My girls, now numbering four, wave to me from an upstairs kitchen window. All smiles, I toss my suitcase in the back and climb aboard.

We have no plans. The day is wide open. We want to meander on little roads, for starters. I grab the crinkled paper map of Massachusetts from the glove compartment. First stop should be Needham, that park where we kissed last winter. He lets me out at the east end and parks at the west end. We script a meeting at halfway where I run to his open arms for a big lift, a spin and a deep kiss, just like the movies. We find a bench to sit and study the map. "Find a place you never have been," I prompt. He taps his finger on Dover, MA. It's only 4 miles away. For sure, this is a meander, starting with a left on Market Tree Rd. and ending with a right on Hawthorne Lane. The Dover Town Library is open. Among the discards, I find an old hard cover of *The House of the Seven Gables.* Dad will love to have this in his library. It was last checked out in 1988. St. Dunstan's Episcopal Church is open, preparing for a wedding. Flowers are just arriving. We sneak in and sit for a spell.

From there, Roy wants to proceed by dead reckoning using only the sun for reference. If we choose Walpole St., how far wrong can we go? He chooses Pine St., the road less travelled. We end up in Medfield. Why not visit the haunted Medfield State Hospital, an abandoned insane asylum, built in 1896? Visitors may roam the grounds during daylight. We found the best views at the Charles River Gateway. The buildings are Red Brick Queen Anne style. We find the quad and stop at the boarded-up Chapel. I feel that tormented souls were truly offered asylum here and that they were well cared for at great expense. Did love ever blossom within these confines between two residents? What a thought. Suddenly we are two such, having a stolen moment and planning a life together.

Sunday, June 5

Dear Diary: The foundation of our life together is our weekends. This one is very solid in terms of romance and lust, always something new and surprising in each department. Starting Saturday night, why not fully christen the duplex by screwing in every room of the duplex. It's just after midnight when I get up for a drink and make some entries. I am a little sore already after escapades in the Man Cave and in the shower. The morning will be me on top in the bedroom, leaving only the den, kitchen and living room. If I fluff up 6 boners in 24 hours, that makes me a porno rock star. The magic words are "Fuck Me!" and boing! There it is, plus he would be willing to pay for it. He told me as much, that if I was a Call Girl, he would book me as often as possible. I suppose that is a compliment. Plus, he says I give the best blow jobs he ever had, which were a fair number, maybe 12 other girls gave it a whack, including high school and college. I should be proud of that, he says.

At breakfast, we have a checklist on the fridge. Bedroom is checked off. We get some sacred at St. Oscar's before we return to profane. We go for coffee at our favorite place, Copper City. I write on a napkin my plan for the afternoon delights which will be 2 quickies and a blow job plus he has to say how much he loves me. In the kitchen he says he loves me so much that it hurts, that I am perfect and wonderful in every way. I say, "Okay, you can fuck me now, but make it quick, you got 5 minutes, 10 minutes max." That one was standing with skirt lifted up. For the next two hours, he stays away from me in his office. He is like a boxer gone to his corner for re-hydration and recovery. At 2 pm, he summons me. I strut in naked demanding, "What do you want now? Can't you see I'm busy?" Thus, commences the action in the office but he has to do the kneeling muff dive first, telling me how much he loves me all the while. We in our undies. Why get dressed with one more round to go? On a 2-hour time-out, we sip fruit juice, veggie slices and read the paper, after which I inform him that I am ready to get fucked again.

Monday, June 6

Dear Diary: I stay overnight in Canton. Roy and I are both exhausted. We sleep deeply side by side with no more screwing. He gets coffee and a kiss at 06:55. Dave comes at 07:00 to take me home. He waits while I do a quick change. L. departs before I arrive. I say hello to Casey and thank her for the cat care.

I arrive at the office just after Susan, fully prepared for comments about me being saddle sore. It seems that Susan is also worn out. We are turned inward at breaks and lunch. We manage a hug and a bit of small talk. Intense love sometimes drains your energy. The flip side is a quiet descent from Heaven back to Earth. We go for a day without cookies. Joni and Sandy are on duty. Maggie gathers the full crew for routine business updates.

L. arrives at 17:30 to whisk me away. I stay quiet while she summarizes the weekend. Kelsey and Chad stopped by for a brief visit. Jessica stayed over for a Saturday night slumber party. She wants to learn about cameras. They did Church and Sunday brunch at Rox Diner. L. did a photo session with Jessica's Grandad in his workshop. "Hang me between Whistler's Mother and American Gothic," he suggested. We stop at Holy Epiphany and Green-T to maintain our structure.

Casey knows most of our story of woman to woman love by now. She is not surprised. Waiting for us are grilled cheese sandwiches and tomato soup, gourmet version, with croutons and bacon bits. We get laced up for our neighborhood promenade. We are known to several captive bow-wows by now.

I go home alone to prepare for tomorrow. While I am busy, Lindsey and Casey trade neck rubs and watch some TV. By 10 pm, I am in bed with Sherlock trying to guess who done it. I switch out the light after just a few pages.

Some ticklish hands trace my curves in the deep dark and total silence. At the deepest part of the night, my angel is with me. Angels come in many forms. I feel her purity, but also a vulnerability. We guard each other, all through a long, lovely summer night.

Tuesday, June 7

Dear Diary: L. wants to be a really nice room-mate for young Casey, a different kind, not boy crazy, someone she can count on, not too self-absorbed. We are establishing comfort care traditions for our routine workdays. Casey, with her cooking skills, is a nice addition. I feel younger within the college dorm style situation the three of us live in. Casey says it's fun to snooze an extra half hour while aware of her early-bird pals busy getting ready.

At drop off, L. likes to lean on my shoulder, lately. Everything is all set for our weekend excursion to Brattleboro. Roy will miss me, but he will be occupied. In the all-woman office, Susan has the special projects desk today. It is a decade-by-decade analytics special report for marketing purposes. The decade 2000 to 2009 belongs to Susan. My decade is 1990 to 1999. Whether our tenants are upward bound to home ownership and related questions will be answered. We can always be busy on this compilation during off peak hours.

L. is ready and waiting at 17:30. Her interns are a big help getting her out on time. We love our diversion to Roslindale and Holy Epiphany, followed by networking at Green-T. A new artist will hang monthly. From the menu, we experiment with Matcha concoctions. We decide to formally open our business by creating a business card and posting it on bulletin boards the same as Jessica does. We do some preliminary designs on paper napkins. Perhaps Jan Boyd can help.

Turkey from the deli, a home-made gravy, mashed potatoes, peas and cranberry sauce is dinner. My pea vines are climbing. Soon they will bloom. Left-over turkey remains for sandwiches, my domain. Lately, I choose rye bread. After clean-up, Casey wants to try Lindsey's bike. She makes two laps on our route, while Lindsey and I walk one lap. Now that there are 3 of us, we keep the locker room upstairs but strictly for showering, the same as High School. For fun, we do our measurements. Maybe we should include them on our resumes, along with height, weight, marital status and natural hair color.

Wednesday, June 8

Dear Diary, I wake to an empty bed. L. says that she was awake briefly at 4 am but she was so comfortable on her couch that she simply hugged her pillow and pretended it was me. By 0630, we have our yoga stuff packed. We grab our lunches and zoom out the door. I fill the bird feeder while L. gets the condensation off of the windows. L. is driving. We have a nice Earl Grey kiss before departure.

A quiet stop and roll accompanied by Vivaldi keeps us on an even keel. This is quality time. I kiss the hands of the artist goodbye at 0730. The jelly doughnuts have reappeared at the office just to get us over the hump on Wednesday. When Susan takes a break from her analytics, I stuff one in her face. I tell her the measurements. I am 5'6", 135, 36, 28, 38. Lindsey is 5'2", 105, 34, 26, 34. Casey is 5'4", 120, 35, 27, 36. Susan's secret guy did hers just for fun. Susan is 5'5", 132, 37, 30, 37. It turns out that I have the biggest ass but Susan has the biggest tits. We are young and super-fine. "Now you got me imagining a strip show with the four of you," laughs Roy during our hot line call.

I slave the afternoon away with filing and inventory. By 18:00 the Yoga Squad has assembled at Blissful Monkey. We have time to socialize with Monica and Lydia before class. We talk about hair and nails, matters of universal importance. I tell them about my hair guy, Roger. We plan a Spa Day in July. At the end of class, all the monkeys in class are calm, harmonized, flexible and blissful. L. and I carry this mood to St. John's. We join in spirit for 20 minutes of sanctity, promising to join in body later.

In Casey's kitchen, it's pasta night with a Caesar Salad on the side. We walk at twilight. We greet our neighborhood pooches. Casey hopes for a Golden Lab when she has a house and yard. Lindsey and I shower together downstairs. We all meet in pj's upstairs for fruit cocktail and Ginger tea. I retire to my private chambers for a few more pages of Sherlock in "The Valley of Fear". L. enters discretely to extinguish the light. Our two bodies seem to need one another and we intertwine so nicely. How could I ever give this up?

Thursday, June 9

Dear Diary, We sleep with the windows open. We never need a raucous alarm, just sounds of nature, or maybe distant traffic on Washington Street. At 06:30, we sit quietly and munch our English Muffins. Casey likes hers with peanut butter.

The calm and harmony of our yoga session remain. I drive while L. flips through her design book. On our early commutes with the windows rolled down and city parks rolling by left or right, the air smells wonderful. At red lights we glance at each other and touch hands. It is a summer morning and life is sweet. Nearing the MFA, we pull over for an ambulance to pass. Danger surrounding us makes life that much sweeter.

At goodbye, we hug. I send a whispered "I love you" into one ear. I ask if she feels it. She nods her head, scoots over to the employee entrance and waves goodbye as usual.

I meet Susan in the parking lot. Our fan club is there. He says he quit smoking. He hasn't had a puff in 2 hours. "Congrats, you can do it! Your reward will be a smile from us, at lunch. He is hoping for more, we expect.

I request the phone desk, where the day flies by. Phil gets his flirt at lunch. We nibble on celery and carrots as we walk. Our thoughts begin to wander again about one year from today what will be happening. We will be in each other's network concerning love and career. We are pretty sure of that. In the afternoon, we can select the overhead piped in music, playing at low volume. We choose Beach Music on Pandora.

At MFA, I lean on my car waiting for my darling. I see her come out. She sees me waiting and runs to my arms. We go direct to St. John's. We chill in the wonderful dark and quiet. We pray in due diligence from the very front pew. We are home at 18:30 for cat care until summoned for supper at 19:00. Waiting for us is hot deli roast beef with gravy open faced sandwich and salad of baby greens. As usual, we walk it off. We turn up the air and turn on the tv. The 3 of us can fit on Lindsey's couch. The chef is granted her choices of channels. Lindsey gets her choice of upstairs couch or downstairs bed.

Friday, June 10

Dear Diary: Fatima and Felicia are happy to stay upstairs with their new caretaker, some nights such as last night. Downstairs, the love partners are tucked in by 10 pm. All we need is just one sheet and some back tickles to bring on the sleep trance. By morning we are in closer quarters. We look at the clock. There is time to attend to all of the pleasure zones, including the fire down below. Out of breath, I stumble out of bed first, pulling the sheet off that little waif of a body, leaving her no choice but to join me in the shower. Our brew perks while climbing into our Friday dress casual. We give Casey a foot tickle to bring her back to life. It's a cloudy morning.

We take the western route. I get delivered to my office doorstep. We have time to linger in the parking lot resulting in a broad daylight make-out session. At the office door, I wave goodbye all the while making sure the blouse is buttoned.

I water the avocados, start the Pandora, and get brew going while I boot up. It's just another happy, ordinary day in the office which flies by on the wings of endless chatter about weekend plans. Susan will host her secret guy. Sandy will watch her daughter at swimming and her son at baseball. Maggie's kids are coming home from college and I am going off to Vermont with my gal pal. Roy is going camping with some of his bros who I have not met, although he does want to show me off at some point. They know he is engaged. I made some progress on my decade for analytics. I take a few late phone calls while waiting for L.

Here she comes at 17:30. Our western return route on Lagrange Street takes us to St. George Orthodox for our prayer vigil. We are getting really hungry. Casey is ready to feed us fish and chips with slaw, beans and dirty rice. She tells us her weekend plans, including a bike excursion with Chad and Kelsey. L. and I fork over $100 each so she can stock everything on her shopping list. The cat items get moved upstairs. We all need a good night's sleep. While L. is packing, I scoot downstairs to call my man. He says get ready for a lot more action from him soon.

Saturday, June 11

Dear Diary: Off we go, into the wild blue yonder. That will be Vermont. Road trip! Two girls on a road trip. Not exactly Thelma and Louise, instead we are law-abiding well within speed limits for 110 miles northwest, starting at 07:00. We proceed four miles across urban sprawl, which gets us to I-95 North for 12 more miles. Upon exit, follow the signs to Fitchburg, then Gardner, then Grange.

It's 2-lane, getting green, wild, and rugged for 80 more miles. L. knows the way, which is a path back in time. She is going back in time, a time, before a lover was ever there for her day and night. We stop and stretch at a crossroads named Erving, featuring Flis Market, a place popular with the "Leaf Peepers" in the fall. They carry specialty items, little luxuries, which L. knows her Dad will love. Another scenic 20 miles and here comes I-95 North. We're almost there. The big city is far behind. It's smooth sailing for 12 more miles to our exit on Canal St. L. indicates Brattleboro Union High School on the right. At downtown, I see a bridge crossing the Connecticut River into New Hampshire.

"We should go straight to home," L. advises. Home is on Cherry Street, not far from the river and walking distance to Brattleboro Memorial Hospital where Sylvia worked for 44 years. As we pull in, I recognize Bob's truck. Some kind of long-haired, mid-sized, mixed breed Shepherd name Scout announces our arrival. He gets his love first. Bob is preparing his grill when he hears "Daddy" and receives a big hug. Sylvia is on the screened in porch. I stay with Bob and Scout while Lindsey greets her Mom. I overhear, "I feel okay." and "Your room is ready, honey."

The room is nicely preserved from High School. Older sister, Pam was gone so L. had it all to herself. Her Class of 2002 yearbook is in the closet and some of her clothes still hang there. Pam and big brother, Tom are coming next week, from New Hampshire. There is a lot of lounging around and small talk. We need help to name our business. At supper, Bob suggests, "How 'bout: Two Dames and a Truck?"

Sunday, June 12

Dear Diary, Just after midnight, we stay up late looking at Lindsey's yearbook. She was in Photography Club and Drama Club, which she joined to overcome shyness. She managed a hint of a smile for her senior portrait in long straight hair and bangs. There in an inscription from Wesley stating, "To the Sweetest Gal I know, remember me always." followed by several hearts in red ink. Is it a coincidence that her first lover was Leslie, a rhyme and perhaps a female version of Wesley? Her girlhood home at 26 Cherry Street was built in the 1930's Craftsman Style architecture. It has the old-fashioned double hung windows. We manage to get them unstuck enough to allow a bit of a flutter in the curtains and the sound of night birds.

That disturbing dream recurs containing utterances such as "…no, no, please no…,". I try to love the pain away. In this old neighborhood, roosters remain. We rise to their refrain. I made a rhyming couplet. Ha! We hear activity downstairs and Scout is barking in the yard. We dress quickly.

Bob has his Sunday edition of The Burlington Free Press. The comics are up for grabs. My Dilbert is there. L. has her English Muffins. We want the 10:30 Mass at St. Michael's. Bob drops us off. To test drive the Malibu, he takes Sylvia on an excursion to New Hampshire. We walk home to Cherry Street passing the Vermont Center for Photography where my hostess had her first show of photo landscapes.

We find a sidewalk café on Harmony Place. Our return on foot is well synchronized with Bob. L. has a romp with scout while Bob is busy again with his grill. I sit with Sylvia and watch the action in the yard. "She never was a bit of trouble, not a bit, unlike the older one," Sylvia relates. "Good marks in school and her portfolio got her a scholarship to that prestige college in Providence." I ask about the bad dreams. "She has had those since childhood when her cat, Misty got run over right out there near our driveway. She has felt guilty about it ever since. She was calling to the cat when it crossed the street. The lady in the car felt terrible. She took Misty to the Vets, but they couldn't save her. I was on an evening shift at the time. Pam was watching over things at home. Poor thing was inconsolable for months. No other cat could replace Misty. "What kind of cat was Misty?" I ask. "Some kind of Siamese mix, I think," Sylvia sighs. "We should've kept her indoors, but she was just too good at sneaking out."

Sometimes plain old hamburgers and hot dogs are exactly what you want and that is what we had. After clean-up, Lindsey presented her Father's Day gift package in advance. Bob said that he won't peek until next Sunday. We want to start back well before sunset. Bob pronounces the Malibu fit for duty. We are waving goodbye from the car windows at just before 6 pm.

We return by way of New Hampshire's Franklin Pierce Highway, which crosses the river just north of town. From Keene, NH, we head due south on Rt. 12 back to Fitchburg, a pleasant ride, a little less rugged and wild compared to our incoming alternate. We stop to stretch at Winchendon, and Mass. State Line, which is halfway. We roll onto Heron St. by 20:30.

We notice the change in air quality which is not as fresh as Vermont. Casey is outside, eager to reconnect. She and L. go straight upstairs. I reconnect with my other girls. For a few hours, my rituals are just like it was a year ago, until somewhere in the wee hours, that little slip of a thing whom I love, reappears beside me.

Monday, June 13

Dear Diary: The working girls have got their act together. With military discipline, we are out the door daily by 06:30. An ordinary routine, safe and reliable, this is all we need to be happy. Every morning on our drive is time for a business meeting. Our business is our formal commitment to each other. We need business cards. L. sketches possible designs. We desire the advice of Jan Boyd, our Calligrapher. I like the sound of "New Horizons Interior Designs".

L. gets her head start. We wave goodbye at 07:15. I am booted up by 08:00. I send Patrick his repair requests. Joni handles the phones. Susan is on special projects. We have our staff meeting and all this is before lunch.

Joni joins us on our walk. Phil, Mr. Oral Fixation, is chewing Nicorette. We praise his perseverance. He even had a manicure to remove stains from his fingertips. "To be worthy of you, Susan," he explains with a wink. Roy calls in on afternoon break. He wants to meet in Walpole tomorrow. We exchange stories of our weekends. He proved some survival skills but got plenty bug bites. I tell him how much I miss him. Nine days apart is a lot for us. Our year of engagement is about quality time mainly, but the quantity is adding up as well. In the last hour or so, I update the waiting list and notify those at the top. I find myself trundling along through Brookline promptly at 17:00, just like all the working stiffs, back and forth, over and over, on our way to uncertain futures, but now is very good, a fact of which I am fully reminded when L. slides in beside me. She likes the name, "New Horizons". We are officially in business.

Prayer is our next duty. Holy Epiphany is the site. We want our Matcha at Green-T. The staff remembers our names. Landscapes by another unknown artist are hanging. Could some of these furnish a room. We agree, yes. We grab her contact info and price list. We want Jaime Cunningham, in our stable. We grab 3 pastries for dessert. Casey can choose her favorite.

Dinner is pasta with Casey's special Alfredo sauce. Dessert waits for after our walk. Casey has seen the Aphrodite nudes. She wouldn't mind being a fine art nude in a coffee table book. After the strip poker, she is over her shyness. L. asks her to think about what will be her mystique. Of course, Roy will want to see some of those prints as a continuing benefit from my woman network. L. takes time alone at her desk, while Casey reads in bed. I take time alone with my kittens. At 02:00 on my glowing bedside digital, my nocturnal guest sneaks in and hugs me tight. "I want as much of the not yet married you as I can get," she declares. Modest in public but max passion in private, is she. This would be enough for me, if I had never met Roy. She is so young. Could this possibly last forever, my twin destinies?

Tuesday, June 14

Dear Diary: Tea of the day is once again Earl Grey, with a drop of lemon and a drizzle of honey. Casey is sitting up and rubbing her eyes as we deliver her mug. I notify her to only cook for two since I will be missing. We munch on our muffins in the car. L. wants to drive the western route and drop me off. We find our Island Music. At drop off, we do our standing hug and kiss.

Susan and I check the model unit, which was rented over the weekend. In the office, Patrick is waiting for his work orders. He will attempt a quick turnover of 10-G and 12-Q for July 1 move-in. He has full staff for all of June. At break, we find that Maggie has added snow peas to the break room veggie tray. She informs us that 1 out of 8 units can become hypo-allergenic furnished units. Corporate expects these to be an upscale alternative to extended stay hotels and also a good option for retirees who don't want to be snowbirds.

Our alternative Tuesday continues when L. arrives at 17:00. We sail homeward along VFW Parkway. St. Theresa's hosts our prayer vigil. We don't need to rush. Roy will wait for me. I exercise my right to be late. I have time to freshen up before Dave arrives at 18:00. I promise to be home by 11 pm. "That's right. We give you a curfew, 11 pm, no later," quips Casey. "We're waiting up for you."

At the Boston View, Roy has our usual room. He brought Chinese take-out. He has a plan to move forward, namely the marriage license. I crunch away fried Won-Ton while he explains. We will apply for our marriage license one week before our vacation. There is a 3-day waiting period. We will have the license in hand when we depart. The vacation will double as a honeymoon. It will be expensive. We will combine our cash to afford it. He brought a little bottle of plum wine. We seal the deal with a toast to us, our everlasting love and our success. Of course, we consummate this deal without delay. Our mid-week meetings are precious few hours. Roy is staying the night but Cinderella must go. She has a curfew. I make it home by 11:15 pm. What is my punishment? I am grounded until Friday.

Wednesday, June 15

Dear Diary: My pretend parents saved some dessert for me, a Klondike bar. After I brushed my teeth, they tucked me in and gave me my kittens to hug. Then they went upstairs and I heard TV faintly before drifting off. Our bosses know we start late today. The interns have their tasks in progress when L. arrives.

Susan and Sandy are up and running when I arrive. I cover their breaks and lunch. On my late lunch, I check in with my man. I want to tell him how great he is, over and over and over again. I am feeling elation about life in general. Every day after work, I have a lover and a business partner waiting for me. We reunite with Monica and Lydia for Yoga. They are happy with their summer job. There is harmony all around. We are a little late to St. John's. We pray in the outside grotto, holding hands.

Wednesday is our vegetarian day for dinner. Casey makes celery stalks with cream cheese, olives and capers, a Waldorf salad with walnuts, and artichoke hearts with basil and parsley. Lime sorbet waits for us after our walk. We play a little poker with monopoly money. The kitchen radio is playing some jazz. For some reason it makes us laugh. From her seemingly inexhaustible supply, L. produces more Jager, one shot each, a generous pour, more like a jigger of Jager. We make amusing attempts at poker faces, spawning more outbursts of laughter. I obediently observe my 22:00 bedtime.

I hear activity upstairs. What are they doing? Grown-ups get to stay up late. In any case, my welcome intruder eventually shows up, still playing the Mom. She asks if I brushed my teeth. I confirm a brush, a floss and a gargle. She wants kisses, deep ones, wet ones. I remember some lyrics from the song, "Hold Me, Kiss Me, Thrill me". I whisper them. "…Kiss me, kiss me, and when you do I know that you will miss me, miss me, if we ever say adieu, so kiss me. Kiss me. Make me tell you I'm in love with you. Hold me. Hold me. Never, never, never let me go." L. whispers back to me thus. "Never, never, never let you go? Sure. Why not" She starts giggling. It must be the Jager effect.

Thursday, June 16

Dear Diary: Lindsey is clinging to me all morning. "You said never, never, never let you go," she explains. At drop off, she continues the static cling. "Just quit your job and be my intern. I can't let you go." "You quit your job and be my intern," I reply. "How much does it pay?" she demands. "All I can pay you is a car and kisses," I tell her. "That's my offer." She slowly releases me from our hug until it's a two-hand hold. "We'll talk tonight. I drive a hard bargain, mind you," says the Klingon. She giggles, turns, stops at the entrance, waves and blows a kiss goodbye. That little scene intrudes and plays in my head at break and lunch. That is her way of continuous clinging. During day, she's in my head. During the night, she's in my arms.

For now, I'm stuck with my job. I might as well enjoy that as well. The veggies are fine, but the dip is not. I can get used to them without dip. They are so refreshing and guilt free. Now everyone wants the ergonomic space age special projects desk. We will have preliminary figures next week. We multitask our way through another day.

On my way through Brookline, I see late afternoon storm clouds threatening. We pull into Green-T just in time to ride out the storm. We shelter in there during the downpour, sharing a pot of Lapsang Souchong. Holy Epiphany is our next stop. We like the cheerful yellow exterior, wood framed instead of granite. Inside, it's a more intimate space compared to our other churches. We light our candles and kneel. Can we be both ambitious and humble?

At home we build our own club sandwiches with deli items from Star Market. A fruit salad waits for us after our walk. The sidewalks are steaming from the rain but the air smells fresh. We speed up and venture a little farther than usual, all the way to Eagle St. We get at least one wolf whistle a day from passing cars in our shorts and athletic shoes, but which one of us is turning the most heads. Probably bouncy blond Casey. L. and I stay modest. Later, in the wee small hours, girl hands trace my modest curves, ticklish and tantalizing.

Friday, June 17

Dear Diary: An ambulance siren wakes us a few minutes early. Life and death struggles play out on our doorstep. We live on the edge of the abyss. We bring coffee and two cats up to Casey. She says, "See ya later, alligator." Some heavy overcast persists and so does our somber mood all along West Roxbury Parkway and Centre Street. We stop for gas at 7 Eleven. I buy a rose for my partner and one for me. At MFA, Monica and Lydia are waiting.

They wave when they see us. I get my wet kiss goodbye from L. and off she runs to meet her trainees. I detect a little jiggle at her hips under the loose slacks. Aphrodite grows one click more voluptuous.

Susan has the property manager ball rolling already as I arrive. She plans to catch the Cape Flyer again today. Roy rings in mid-morning. It is his last day to teach. He and the guys have plans. He gives me the night off. I suspect they are going to see strippers. He gets his rain check for Saturday and Sunday. After indoor lunch, Susan and I each have one move-out inspection, 10-G and 12-Q. We give Patrick a heads up on the damages. Another week is winding down. Monday coming is Sandy's birthday. Joni will bring cupcakes. I will buy a card. After clicking away business e-mails for an hour, look at that. It's almost time to close up shop. I field a few more calls, water the avocados and turn out the lights.

Weekend begins. Aphrodite is waiting for me outside. Her front porch is showing more jiggle also. We have neglected St. John. His church gets our visit. Our prayers today are prayers of thankfulness. One minor disappointment is in store. "I was lazy and didn't make nothing today," Casey informs us. "You guys see what you can create." Lindsey and I create a two-fridge rewarmed combo buffet. It turns out ok. At least we had fresh greens. We freshen ourselves and sashay on over to Sophia's Patio for dessert and a flirt at the bar. Casey gets 2 flirts. I get a wink and L. gets a stare. As we are out in public, I suppose we are fair game. The Margaritas make it all seem funny. By 22:30, we three just want some happy home TV.

Saturday, June 18

Dear Diary: I miss my man. His manly musk, otherwise known as B O, is supposed to be good for my health. Scientists have studied it. Everyone is getting up late. We leave L. alone. She is designing our business card. Casey and I shop at Star Market, enough to last the week.

Roy comes rolling in around 10:00. "The man of the house is here," I announce. He is hung over. It was strippers, just as I thought. He is unshaven. "Help me?" he pleads. We make him a blueberry smoothie. He manages one piece of dry white toast. L. joins us. We sit around my downstairs table staring at each other. "It's hot. Let's just do nothing," Roy suggests. Mommy's gonna run you a cool bath, little Roy. You soak while we do laundry. We do Roy's stuff on a separate load. His dirty things need not have an orgy with our underthings. During dry cycle, he got one of my leg shavers for his beard. He is in there with just a towel wrapped around. The Chippendale wanna-be is parading around thus while awaiting the return of his clothes. Casey and I each stuff a dollar at the waist front of the towel.

With clothing and food put away, we get restless. "Take me somewhere. You never take me anywhere," I complain to Roy. "Call the day spa," says Roy. "I'll take you there." "I wanna go too!" the others exclaim. Casey's Impala has the coolest air for transport. Newberry St. is Spa central. They can take Roy and I at Bella Sante for foot care and massage. Casey and Lindsey go to Toscana Organic European for hair and facial. All I can say to them is "Très, très chic." All Roy can say is "Wow! You two are a couple of classy dames."

We have spent enough for one day. We go home for dinner. Roy is the Chef. The others go upstairs to relax. This gives us a chance for a quickie on the sly. The bill of fare ends up being chips and salsa, mushroom soup, and ham on rye, unexpected, but oddly satisfying. The chef takes a bow. We walk it off. Frosted mugs are ready. Roy pours the Heinekens. We click glasses and wipe foam mustaches. The young ones grab 2 more beers and leave us alone. My man and I need to make up for lost time.

Sunday, June 19, Father's Day

Dear Diary: Roy leaves early. He is going up to Sanford, Maine to see his Dad. He drops me at St. Theresa's for early Mass. After Mass, I bring the Sunday Globe upstairs to the laziest gals in town. L. has been on the phone with her Dad. Casey's Dad is in California. He is some kind of journalist. They communicate by e-mail. She told him about her job and that she is very happy. L. helps me do a home-created card for my Old Man. I am probably his favorite but I let Sally think that she is.

We check my snap peas vines. There are some little pods on there. Advance Auto is open today. I find a cool looking tool bag for the trunk of his '70 Malibu. I put some Armor All in there and my card. I do my home visit early and exit early. Dad has his hands full with the grand kids.

I am back in time to rejoin my girls for a languid Sunday evening. We stretch and do a short walk on hot sidewalks. After our cool showers, we trade neck rubs. Sometimes man hands are too rough. We take turns reciting poetry. L. has a book of verse by Poe. I recite "A Dream within a Dream". Casey reads some stanzas out of "The Haunted Palace". Lindsey chooses "Annabel Lee". She says we must close our eyes. I think how I might describe her voice to others. The diction is clear, the rise and fall rhythmic. The pauses are well-chosen. The tone is plaintive. We applaud her rendition. It puts us into a trance-like state. We choose to whisper our way through the remains of the day.

I check my answer machine. Roy's message is that he will see me Thursday. I gather up the helpless felines. They want attention and they shall have it, upstairs in the poetry lounge. It seems like we should have some absinthe or something similar. Instead, we break out the real fruit popsicles from Whole Foods. To amuse ourselves, we practice sensual licking and sucking. Casey puts on quite a show. She breaks her popsicle in half. One half gets a tongue job surpassing wildest wet dreams. She takes the other half slowly deep throat, full luscious lips on entry and exit. I look at Lindsey and swallow hard. What have we gotten ourselves into here? We could learn a lot from young Casey.

Monday, June 20

Dear Diary: Mondays mean back to reality, where we must make a buck and somehow stay alive amidst the mayhem. Bee Jees sang about stayin' alive. Now I'm humming it in the car. L. is in a bad mood. She says to please don't hum that in her car. She hates that movie. She thinks it's stupid. I expect her to be moody, otherwise she would be too perfect. We can fight about the children. We have 4 children including 2 cats, 1 car, and perhaps a daughter, Casey. We need a day off for the car transactions but tonight, she says she will write a check and I will produce the bill of sale to make it official.

At drop off I want her bad mood flavored kiss because all of her moods mean something and she is entitled to them. She gives me a perfunctory sour candy kiss and a tiny sideways smile. We can have fun fights, just like with Roy. There is a bit on my plate of the full buffet of office duties. At lunch we challenge Phil about who has the best tits. He says, "That would be Susan." She gloats. Who has the best ass? "That would be Sarah," he affirms. It's just as I predicted. Susan and I are even Steven. "You two look good comin' and goin'," he adds.

Enough of torturing Phil for today. We have a job to do which is: get tenants and keep them renewing. We visit the fellas in the tools trade on afternoon break. We are two flowers blooming in the war zone they call their workshop. By 17:00, I am ready for more attitude from my young lover. She criticizes my driving. She is taking this car away from me because my driving is car abuse.

Some of Casey's pasta and two big glasses of cold Sangria get us ready for dickering on the price. She dickers me down to $2,000 and a guarantee to pay half on the first big repair. I get my check. She gets her bill of sale and signed over car title. She hugs it and says "Mine, all mine, and there will be rules. We'll talk about them later." Life needs rules. Otherwise, all is chaos. Her first rule: Some of your important stuff stays in the car but mostly my stuff. I keep your stuff hostage in case you think you can dump me some day. Second rule: All kissing in that car is you and me, exclusively.

Tuesday, June 21

Dear Diary: It's another one of our quiet mornings, back to baseline. Joni is on duty, meaning, I can get off mid-afternoon. The interns are lightening Lindsey's load. Thus, we can appear at Roslindale RMV mid-afternoon to take care of new title and registration. We celebrate at Green-T, followed by more prayers of thankfulness at Holy Epiphany.

L. drives the rest of the way home and parks. With the engine still running, she delivers a lengthy hug and a declaration. "I'm never selling this car, even after it's no longer roadworthy. It is the place of our commuting and partnership. It is a part of you which is mine forever," declares she. "That is certain, a deep part of me is yours forever," I avow.

On that happy note, we are eager to see what Casey cooks up for us tonight. While L. goes upstairs, I am on cat care duty and checking the answer machine. Roy has found us a Bronco, details to follow. He is having quality time with his Dad. Minutes later, I get to see Casey transforming 2 rotisserie chickens into Chicken Cacciatore. L. is slicing the mushrooms. The radio plays Top 40 while we dine. The clean-up crew does their duty. Katy Perry sings "Last Friday Night". By the time we return from our walk Adele is "Rolling in the Deep".

The Lady Jocks end up in bathrobes. Casey's best feature is her legs. Phil, our expert on T&A, would probably agree. L. does some peek-a-boo bath robe leg show test shots by fading window light, one foot on a chair, applying lotion, hair hanging down. The artist at work, my artist, is my main interest here. I watch how she works with her subject. Could it be that she will have 2 more shows hanging before the end of the year, namely, "Leg Show" and "Worn to Perfection"?

We call Bill, the photog from Providence. He informs us that Mata Hari will exhibit, on First Friday, August 5, at The Gelman Gallery, Downtown Providence. The prints will be pricey. We make a date to see the show. Downstairs, I slip into bed alone. Before long, I behold a vision. Illuminated by streetlights through sheer curtains, young Aphrodite stands looking down at me.

Wednesday, June 22

Dear Diary: Wednesday is Yoga day. I look forward to it. My outfit is comfort clingy cotton pink and yellow pastels. I wish I could wear it all day. L. wants to drive her car and drop me off. The feeling of well-being is possible on a daily basis with my partner beside me. All summer long we are the early birds, before heat. At work we get the ball rolling. This work pays for everything we need. These days, there is no retirement, according to Dad. Work keeps you alive. A have a partner for designing 'til the day I die and a guy who is devoted to me, the best he has ever had. What a difference a year makes.

First off, I key into the weekend rental and replenish the freebies. The housekeepers turned it over nicely but a little detail work makes it perfect. Cookie of the day is Blueberry Newtons. We have tired of the carrots and celery already. A cookie goes so much better with coffee or tea. In our breakroom, we duplicate the tea choices available to our weekenders. We have our staff meeting. Prelim. reports about tenant trends are due next week.

L. comes to get me at 17:15. Phil's chewing of Nicorette stops when he sees her. She gives him a little wave in return for his smile. I introduce L. to Maggie noting that the young woman helps me with my interior designs. Susan's little smirk indicates that she suspects much more.

For most of the way to the Blissful Monkey, we enjoy the scenic view of Arnold Arboretum and associated parks on the right. We are early, so we have time to hang out at the juice bar. They have my Matcha. A small one is okay with a pomegranate shot. I don't want to slosh. Monica and Lydia show up just in time. They had to stop at home, Burbank Apts. They are having a party this weekend. Lindsey thinks she can come. Yes, she can bring Casey. We four get lost in Vinyasa Flow for 45 minutes.

We two return to Holy Epiphany, thankful and at peace. We pray on our knees for continued recovery of Sylvia. Dinner is waiting, a nice veggie stir fry from our master chef. It looks like rain. A short walk is all we need. After clean up, I retire to my quarters for kitten care and man maintenance by phone.

Thursday, June 23

Dear Diary: The Balance of Nature requires a man, some kind of rugged hunk of beefcake in the household. For Nuns, it's the priest. This is no convent here at on Heron St. and Roy is no priest but he is coming today. He is on summer hiatus and he wants to meet me for dinner in the town where nobody knows who we are, right next door in Needham. We are getting on. We are in mid-life but somehow, we feel young there, young enough to have fun making out in a truck or on a park bench. He does not disturb my commuting rituals. They proceed as usual.

L. is having fun dropping me off and picking me up. I am in her custody. She has a parking spot in the shade behind the MFA. Her acolytes join her for lunch in the car playing music. The working women in my circle are stable in their daily routines, Monday through Friday, but weekends can be full of surprises. My man shows up at 18:00. I make him wait while I freshen up. He gets to play big brother to Lindsey and Casey during his wait. They accept him as such. They watch us drive away.

In Needham we like the atmosphere at Cappella. It feels intimate. He tells me about his time up in Maine with his Dad. His roots are in Maine. He still feels like a country boy. They drank a little whiskey on the front porch and went to bed early. He has me home early. We save the lust for Saturday.

Upstairs, the girls are at leisure. Casey modeled more leg show photos earlier. This time it was running shorts, stretching, and lacing up the cross-trainers. We watch some antenna TV stretched out on the floor. L. is in the middle. I imagine the tableau. It looks like contentment, something new, something nice and unexpected but not destined to last forever. We will remember it fondly. It's sleepy time for me but I must check on Roy. He is home alone. We do our pillow talk. I manage a few more pages of mystery. I light a candle and wait. Will the Goddess reappear? Just as the birds start singing, at the faintest first light, footsteps barely audible approach my bed. Arms reach around my waist. We have an hour to cuddle. It is enough to maintain our pleasure bond.

Friday, June 24

Dear Diary: I am totally dependent on the two people who love me. L. transports me to work. I provide 2 full tanks a month. Roy transports me to play. He provides every full tank.

I am first in the office. I want to finish my analytics report. Susan is not far behind. We share the special projects ergonomic desk. Her doughnut addiction is in relapse. Someone tempted her over the weekend. Three avocado trees are still alive. Nurture them, we must. Maybe this extra packet of flower food will help. At lunch, we go outside for some stretches in the shade. Susan is staying quietly at home this weekend to read a book and finish her report. She has been pushing herself too hard.

My transporter and I are homeward bound by 17:30. We are all smiles of freedom and elation and letting our hands ride the wind. At Green-T, we choose 3 pastries for tonight's dessert. We put the contact info of painter, Jaime Cunningham in our phones. One of her landscapes has a "Sold" sticker on it. We let our sensory overload subside at Holy Epiphany. The cool and dark dampen us down. As we prepare to rise, I turn Lindsey's face toward me and kiss her lightly on the lips. "We are starting a new chapter and I still love you," I avow. "I have been waiting for that all week," says she.

Fish Fry deluxe a la Casey waits for us. I have mine with cocktail sauce. The others prefer tartar sauce. The side dish is a sliced cucumber, tomatoes, and parsley potatoes. Casey has even made iced tea. The girl is really a treasure. I feel obliged to say the blessing. "It's the way to a man's heart," Casey reminds us. "He will always come home to dinner." It's cooling off nicely. We take our tea outside to watch the stars come out. "I had to move out. I don't share bathrooms with guys especially not Chad. You guys have been great," Casey chatters on and on. "I'll serve dessert now," she adds.

The moon has not risen. The stars are bright. "Your kisses are my dessert," I tell my partner as she melts in my arms. "I'll meet you at midnight," she promises. Crickets surround us with their summer song.

Saturday, June 25

Dear Diary: I wake up alone. The pillow beside me is still warm. I hug that pillow in the absence of L. who has silently slipped away. She wants to get some work done in her notebooks while all is quiet and after that to surprise Casey by making breakfast.

I expect Roy at 09:00. My semi-conscious form sprawls across the entire bed. Before long, 2 sets of paws wander the bodyscape I present to them. One set of whiskers tickles my left ear. One set of paws imprisons my left foot, which made the mistake of moving under the sheet. Talking to my cats helps activate my brain. I tell them that Mommy is going away for the weekend but Aunt Lindsey and Aunt Casey will take care of them.

I pack my lap-top, two changes of Tomboy play clothes and a toothbrush. By 08:30, I hear activity upstairs. I pick up my gear and go to investigate. Something smells good. L. is trying a recipe she found for potato pancakes. I nibble at one of the plain ones. The secret spices alone make it tasty. Casey tries hers with sour cream. I have mine with applesauce. The final taste tester comes rolling in late. My man likes his with crushed tomato. The four of us exercise the license to be lazy. We pretty much just stare into space until Casey turns on the radio. "Why did I come here?" Roy wonders out loud. "Oh yeah! Now I remember. It was to take custody of this one." He indicates me. I go along peacefully. I wave goodbye from below.

We go direct to disaster area duplex. To my surprise, he has done the dishes and taken out the trash. He deserves a reward. He gets to screw his girlfriend without further delay. With all of our cravings finally satisfied, we are able to get down to work, me on my marketing report, him on his school board proposals. I claim the kitchen table. He inhabits his office. We work quietly for 90 minutes, sipping on iced tea along the way. I save my report to pdf. I look over Roy's shoulder and give him a neck rub. Beyond his hope for full time School Psychologists, he is listing what teachers can do on their own, within the limits of their job description. He is focused on the Parent-Teacher conferences to include grandparents. The extended family is a stabilizing influence. Ounces of prevention wherever you can find them, could make a big difference. Roy wants to make school less stressful for all, he explains. He has extensive case history files. He has been reading about predisposers and triggers and facilitators. He has been reading about Adolescent Adjustment Disorder. He knows he cannot make the school 100% safe, but he is sure he can do something helpful for students in general, beyond just being a popular teacher and coach.

I help to take his mind off of all of that for a while, with full body massage. At sunset, we go for a jog at the High School Track. He stays behind and enjoys the view. At home, we fish out some frozen stuff. We share a shower and a beer, the last one. If our marriage is like this, that will be fine.

Sunday, June 26

Dear Diary: All we want is toast and coffee followed by early Mass before it gets hot. We go straight home. The coolest room in the house is the man cave. It's almost a sensory deprivation chamber. We sprawl at opposite ends of the leather couch. "Well, what do you want to do? He inquires. "Nothin'," say I. "Suits me," says he. We hear activity across the wall. It's a retired couple who downsized. The old man works in the garage a lot. He is a finder and destroyer of dandelions. Otherwise, he keeps to himself. What else can we do totally mindless on our day of rest? I get to drive the Jeep. It is parked in the shade. It is a Red '04 Wrangler Sport. We find that this will not be a practical vehicle for me but I do so want a truck. I manage to get her inside the garage after grinding gears and stalling out just twice. Roy bought the vehicle at 2 years old. He just made the last payment on 5-year financing. We kill the engine and he shows me the knobs and switches. I practice with the stick shift. Who knows? Maybe, just, maybe. I am home by twilight. We plan another maritime adventure for Friday.

As he drives away, I miss him already. The girls upstairs see me standing forlornly. "We'll be together again Friday," I announce after trudging up the stairs. "Five long days."

I slump to the table. "You have us now and 2 Queens beats a King," reminds Casey. "He's a pretty good guy. I understand how you feel. You get just 5 more minutes in your funk and this might help." She opens the fridge and freezer which are packed full of our favorite stuff.

"Thanks, guys," I offer as I rise to hug them.

L. tells the story of the party, keeping hold of my hand all the while. "Casey and I were like chaperones. It seems a long time since college. Nobody threw up. The music was party mood in overdrive. We had to turn it down just once. Casey won the dance contest. The apartment was deluxe, central courtyard, secure parking underneath, a condo the parents bought low and will sell high."

"Now it's time for popsicles," adds Casey. Lindsey and I exchange knowing looks. "Only 2 guys have enjoyed my tongue job and no girls…yet," She laughs her wanton woman laugh.

Monday, June 27

Dear Diary: Lindsey and I slept peacefully under cool sheets with a fan blowing gently. Our relationship has a feeling of forever. That's number one, she says. Love, the emotion, that's number two and sleeping together, that's number three in hierarchy. We have adopted each other and that is solid, no anxieties there.

I enjoy being the passenger these days, with mug of tea and morning music playing softly. I lean over. We touch hands and kiss goodbye.

Susan is inside printing. We compare demographics. Typical credit score for her decade (2000-2010) is lower than my previous decade. Could this be credit card debt nearer to max? A greater percentage of tenants are borderline in terms of ratio of monthly income to rent. In her decade, the tenants are staying longer, 3 years on average. The number of evictions is flat. Vacancy rate is flat. I think corporate is looking to serve both young and old, both blue collar and professional. The retirees in good health will be our long-term tenants. Maggie skims our reports and stuffs them in her valise. L. and I are lower middle income city dwellers. We could afford the rent here, but just barely. There is one scheduled move-out today. Susan and I do the damage report with photos. This tenant went to Nursing Home after 10 years in residence. His rent was paid on time like clockwork. I wonder how he feels about those 10 years in 4-G, in the calm waters of late life, watching the seasons go by outside his windows. We bag up the personal items left behind. There is pet damage, mainly the window blinds. Our guys can have it ready by July 5th. It will be hardwood floors, like Sheila next door in 6-G. We pay her a visit. Perhaps she will stay even longer than 10 years.

L. comes breezing in at 17:00. Homeward bound, we pay a visit to Jan Boyd. She can have our business cards next week. Saint George on Lagrange is our Church of the Day. We find a shady place to park. There is a breeze. Lindsey's hair is getting longer. She can toss it about, then finger comb it straight back. I get her tiny little smile as we sit in silence and reverence for powers higher than us.

Casey's powers with food are also higher than ours. It's pasta night, featuring Rigatoni with meat sauce and Caesar side salad. She made her own croutons. Casey has passed her probationary period. We are keeping her without a doubt. The radio comes on while the junior members of the kitchen squad do their clean-up. We tune in soft rock plus "Intelligence for Your Life" from John Tesh. We find it cool enough for a brief promenade. The neighborhood yard dogs know us by sight. They are happy to see us. I retire to the cool and dark of my lower unit. L. has some stuff to do upstairs.

Tuesday, June 28

Dear Diary: At dawn, my Angel is there beside me. I tickle her bum. She needs 20 minutes more to finish some lucid dream. I do all of the stuff that will expedite our departure in my role as personal assistant to the Artist. I started driving out. We switch seats at Chestnut Hill. Her Rockstar drink has kicked in.

We kiss goodbye as usual. Today's crew is Susan, Sandy and I. Phone calls and walk-ins are all we got. Outside, we stay in the shade and do our stretches. Our fan club, Phil, is lurking about. We don't even know where he works, exactly. He says that it's classified. For the afternoon doldrums, we stay inside and give love to the avocado trees, already two feet tall. L. shows up at 17:00. She and her interns got a lot done today, mainly dusting and breakdown of old exhibits.

Our Gothic Church is waiting for us. St. Theresa Avilla is only 1.5 miles by way of Corey St. and Centre St. Granite stays the coolest. We kneel at the altar, contrite for whatever our faults have been. L. grew up Lutheran, but she does the ritual genuflect and dip of the Holy Water. It is a matter of reverence, if nothing more. Because of these pauses, we never come home irritable.

Soon, we discover that Casey has made Reuben Sandwiches. We praise everything she makes. Dessert is cantaloupe. We are ticking away a solid foundation of ordinary days, each one delightful in its own way.

Suddenly, I simply must call my man. What is he doing? He is washing dishes, his new good habit. I tell him how great he is and how much I love him.

L. saved the greasy stuff for me to wash. Suddenly, she wants to dance. It is some song from her college days. She rarely partied in College, unless she just aced her midterms. Her moves were not very original. They were understated and trying to not be noticed. Everyone seems to loosen-up when Casey is around.

I look outside in the direction of Canton. If I sent up a flair, could Roy see it? He is over there, all alone. I trust him completely. Married life, we've had a taste of what it will be like. We say, "Yes!"

Our walks become shorter but brisker, enough to work up a sweat. Upstairs is the ladies' locker room. Casey goes first for lukewarm shower. Lindsey and I go second. We come out in out terry cloth and slippers. There is a lot of flashing. No one is shy. Later, in bed, I want to tickle some more. L. say "Don't tickle my bum. You can tickle my tits instead. I notice the nipple erection. We get each-other off no problem. After our clinch, we are sticky. I deliver the warm washcloth treatment. Nobody wants to fall asleep sticky.

Wednesday, June 29

Dear Diary: I count the summer days away. My luck was bound to change, and now it has, solid, sunrise after sunrise. It is not even first light as I watch Lindsey sleeping. What a treasure, and she is mine forever, so she says. She wants babies. We'll worry about that later. Changes are coming. Somehow, we will adjust. We got our yoga stuff packed last night. I get our lunches packed. At 06:00, baby girl has got slippers on the ground. She marches upstairs to get dressed, as is often the case. She needs quiet time alone.

Our quiet time continues outbound. On such mornings, we communicate by body language. Nothing need be said by sentences. At drop off, L. watches me walk to the door where I turn and wave goodbye. I worry about her in traffic. I get a text upon safe arrival.

At our morning huddle, Maggie reports that our marketing plan will reach out to seniors as well as young professionals. The reports prepared by Susan and I were influential in that corporate decision. We will begin networking with visiting nurses who perform wellness checks. I'm stuck with inventory in the afternoon. Last chance to order before the holiday. During routine tasks, I am prone to daydreaming. Where do I see myself one year from now? I see myself walking through the office doors to say hello to everyone. My replacement is there, sitting at my old desk. She is brand new, all eager and organized. I can be replaced at work. For Roy and for Lindsey, I cannot be replaced. I am forever.

At yoga, Monica and Lidia remark at the calmness of Lindsey and I. We tell them it is the Vinyasa Flow, but it is something more, of course. We are able to be content in a world of uncertainty. We have each other. That, at least is certain. The Moms and Dads who raised us, we watch over them. They stand between us and the abyss. Enough deep thoughts for the day. Our evening rituals lie ahead, comforting in their predictability. Veggie Wednesday, a light dinner, Jello and Cool Whip, a light dessert. Walk it off, retire early and sleep deeply.

Thursday, June 30

Dear Diary: L. is first to Rise. I slept nearly motionless, on my tummy, L. reports. At 04:00, she lay there listening to me breathing, then drifted off again. She brings me my tea. Cats want attention. They expect their share.

Malibu was overheating a bit yesterday. We fear water pump failure. Malibu gets its attention at Parkway Auto. Dave takes over from there. We sit in back on cool leather seats, like two socialites. Work cuts us slack for being late. Both workplaces prepare for 3-day weekend.

Our model unit is booked. Susan takes limited weekend hours with following Friday off. Maybe her Secret Guy will sneak up from The Vineyard to see her.

It's getting really hot. A possible brown-out? Jason, from Parkway Auto, says Malibu will be ready at 17:30. Ransom is $315 for water pump and radiator flush. The socialites can simply write a check. We know the money is there. We appreciate the quality service from our mechanics. The last move out for June is complete. We have lots of cold drinks here for our tool guys. Patrick fills an ice chest. We leave water bowls outside in the shade for cats and dogs. The squirrels go to our bird-baths. The sprinklers are in water rationing mode. The grass is on brown-out. Earthworms hide under rocks in the shade. I take care of some light filing and field a few calls. We process all pending e-mails. We chill as best we can. Dave has L. with him at 17:00. Malibu is almost finished. We settle up.

The basement laundry room is our church today. I have a holy card of St. Theresa. We pin it to the bulletin board. We offer our continued pleas on behalf of Sylvia, who sits in her empty nest, up there in Vermont, wondering how long she has got. She stays up late, watching Leno. L. will call her tonight. I go to my mission control center and check in with everyone. L. has her office time while Casey lays out cold buffet. When I join them, fans are moving the air nicely. We buffet, we siesta, iced tea in hand. Later we try on our bikinis. We would be content to run around outside under a hose. Heat makes you lazy, that's for sure. What else do we need? Popsicles! We almost forgot.

Friday, July 1

Dear Diary: Wow! That was a big yawn. L. watches me stretch. I hand her an iced Starbucks. She takes it upstairs. We are both ready in 20. Malibu is running nice and cool. In-bound we stay under old growth canopy along Lagrange and VFW Parkway. It's the start of another happy summer day. I am getting used to being the passenger in my old car. We are belted in but relaxed. We have our goodbye kiss.

I am first in the office. I call Roy about our rendezvous. He will meet me at eight. I pick an overhead feed of Smooth Jazz. On duty with me are Susan and Sandy. All of us are on auto-pilot. We dim the lights. It feels more like a cocktail lounge than a place of business. L. shows her interns some design software. Plans for the Fall Season are forming already. City-wide, mass exodus to the shorelines begins just after lunch. L. and I do our full 8. We are am home-bound by 17:00. After prayer at St. George's, we are home by 18:00.

The evening is wide open. Casey offers Sangria and Tacos. We save some for Roy. He is out there, somewhere, not far away. I pack a bag but stay in my work clothes. Roy, in his rumble-mobile, rolls in right on time. We wave him up. "Mmm…, smells good. Suddenly Tarzan hungry," he remarks. Four bites later, two Tacos are gone. "How come you never make these for me?" he complains, staring in my direction. "I'll make them every day, from now on, forever," I promise. After a few more pleasantries, I am summoned with a simple, "Jane come," and off we go on our weekend adventure in the wilds of Canton, MA.

My senses are on full alert. This is a world far afield from my weekday woman comfort zones. It's a good thing I brought my K-Y because I quickly discover that women in business suits are a big turn on for the man of the jungle. I get sleepy at my usual 10 pm. Round two must wait for tomorrow early. I am happy to find clean sheets in the bachelor bedroom. Do I detect the Febreze effect? As I drift off, I am aware of ESPN droning on in the background. Jane has a dream about redesigning Tarzan's tree house but she can't get it quite right.

Saturday, July 2

Dear Diary, I slept pretty well. It's the kind of bed one sinks into and is swallowed up deep into oblivion. It is barely light. I do not disturb the man. I stay in my robe and slippers to silently prepare his breakfast in bed. I am able to find the standard juice, toast, sausage, eggs and coffee. I sneak outside and snatch a dandelion. A skinny green olive jar becomes the vase. I deliver all on one of his bar serving trays. His first words are, "What time is it? 06:30? Are you for real? Oh well." He is soon munching and grinning. I grab a toast wedge, sip my own coffee and grin back. I see signs of much recent action in his office but not today. The office is closed for the weekend.

For sure he wants his run. I change right there in front of him to running shorts and sports bra under flimsy top. I lace up my Pumas over ankle socks. "I'll meet you outside," I announce. The duplex cohabitants, Betty and Richard, are on their porch.

They have been sharing the daily newspaper with Roy, except for the crossword. Richard keeps the crossword. We find it cool enough to do 8 blocks out and 8 blocks back in. Betty offers lemonade. I am wearing my ring. They know, but they are sworn to secrecy. "Loose lips sink ships," Richard confirms and gives me a wink. "Her parents hated me," he adds while nodding at Betty. "They simply put the fear of God into you, for your own good," Betty rejoins. We left them to their lifelong controversies.

A quickie in the shower seems right. There is no time to waste because I want to return to Medfield State Asylum. It calls to me. We fix up a picnic basket with freezer packs to keep 2 beers cold. We take Rt. 27 through Walpole, a pleasant 30-minute drive. The place gives me a wonderful feeling of tranquility. We park and walk the lanes, hand in hand. The grounds are beautifully maintained and there are no vehicles to clutter or disturb the peace. Space within the fences need not be wasted on parking lots. How wonderful it would be to recreate some of the interior designs. Interiors designed to comfort and heal. In a previous life, Dr. Roy cured me of my nightmares. After discharge, I became his Secret Girl. We had forbidden love.

Roy's Jeep becomes a horse and buggy, even better, A Surrey with a Fringe on Top, clip clop, clip clop, two trotters take us back to Canton. As I step down, the 21st Century returns.

It's not so bad here, I suppose. I handle it well enough, alternately immersed inside the world of women and the world of men. The world of men includes The Waterfall Bar and Grill, just a stone's throw from our love nest at Ames Avenue. We go there directly for dinner and reminders of what is important to men, namely, sports, beer, bar maids with boobs, and the great outdoors. It's a lovely waterfront view of Forge Pond from our table on the deck. We are looking at trees reflected in water smooth as glass and deep enough behind the dam to feed a waterfall, which once powered local industry. Canton keeps its links with the past and I am happy to link up, there to meet my savior, my hero, Dr. Roy. At twilight, we depart. He leaves his standard $20 tip. The best of the bar maids count-up nothing but twenties at quittin' time. At our future home as man and wife, we collapse on the bed fully clothed. We dive off into dreamland together.

Sunday, July 3

"Let's get these clothes off," are the first words I hear 'round about 2 am. A cold drink in my hand is the first thing I feel. How did I get naked? One of my man's powers is to get my clothes off of me without much delay. I don't notice it because these days, naked seems normal. I am a Sex Goddess. Naked is my natural state. I flaunt my tits and my ass for the pleasure of my man. My full bush pleasure zone is the place for him to plant his seed, even if he hasn't got any seed left. By 3 am, we got each-other off. We report maximum mutual satisfaction. We sit up in bed. We do the warm washcloth treatment. "That is one beautiful snug pussy," he reports. "That is a pretty well-hung dong, as far as dongs go, even in current pitiful flaccid state. I could pick it out of a dong line-up. I have seen my share," is my report. He laughs at this. He gets the reference to the Movie, "Porky's". We go for our run while still dark outside.

What do the birds in the trees think of us? We are none of their concern, I expect, except that where people are, there is likely to be some food beyond what nature provides, found as litter, or within garbage bins, or as breadcrumbs in the park or as seeds in a feeder. We go home and change for church, early Mass at St. Oscars. We stay discreetly in back, heads humbly held low. We go in peace to love and serve, as instructed.

Home means breakfast served by me wearing only panties and an apron. Roy is wearing jockey shorts and muscle shirt. I prance around the kitchen with max jiggle and some bending over. The pup tent pops up pronto. Roy proves that he can delay gratification until after clean-up. Our outfits allow easy access. Why waste time. Fun is finished in ten minutes flat.

It's not even noon. What next? We visit the neighbors. They are done with The Globe. We pull up a beach chair and hang with them a while in the shade. We want the train station. We are tired of driving. Somehow, from Canton Junction, we make our way to Needham Line at Forest Hills. From there it is a mere 46 minutes to Needham Center. There is something to see at each stop, including my favorite, Roslindale Village. We check out the new art at Green-T. We reach Needham Center on the next train in time for the blue shadows of late afternoon. We linger in the park until twilight. He buys me an ice cream. Roy has his own Uber Guy, Stanley. Casey wants to come for me in her Impala. No sooner have I waved goodbye to Roy that I burst into tears to see him go. I am just wiping the tears when Casey shows up with Lindsey along for the ride.

I re-enter a world of women. I tell about Medfield Asylum. It gives Lindsey an idea for a photo shoot. We cruise the square for a bit. We return by way of Dedham where we shop at Whole Foods, enough for a week, including lots of whole fruit popsicles. I pick up some new cat toys and treats. They might be mad at me for being away so much. At home, Casey has saved me some leftovers of Guacamole and toast points. I go downstairs to unpack and freshen up. I return in robe to linger in the kitchen where the radio is on. Me and my ice tea retire at 10.

Monday, July 4

Dear Diary, I wake up briefly, just after midnight, to get a cold drink. I keep some Perrier in the green glass bottle. Ahh.., that hit the spot. There seems to be some laughing and carrying-on upstairs. No matter, I'll hear about it later. Such a pleasure, just to sleep in my own bed. Kittens are there. I am never alone. Six am and all is quiet. Tea is brewing. I have a text from Roy. He is going fishing, going to prove that he is not p-whipped. His bros ask about me. Does she do this or that, or any special skill in bed? "She is very nice," that is all he says about me. Respect, this is respect for his lady. WBZ, AM 620, news, weather, sports, gets my brain ready, for something, who knows what. Mom and Dad, that's it. I can trundle on over there and give Old Dad a squeeze. He loves me. I am his favorite. I tell Mom not to worry and such.

"Casey prayed with me," I find out over grapefruit juice at the upstairs breakfast nook. They we hot, so they went to the laundry room chapel. They washed in cold water, delicate. They hung them up to dry. "She seems very innocent when she prays," says Lindsey. "Look at me, I am innocent," Casey confirms. She plays the part very well. "I did a digital series. I call it Casey sleeping. She is in bed, actually sleeping, under streetlight, a few candles and some fill light from the next room." L. explains. I take a look. There she is, the girlish one, more or less covered by a silky sheet, including some close-ups. This is intimacy. "Wow, Lindsey, nice concept, and execution," is my praise for the artist. There is one extra shot where she is kneeling and praying, head tilted heavenward.

We stretch and walk the neighborhood with sun umbrellas. We have a cold brunch, mostly fruit, yogurt and mixed nuts. Dad comes to get me for my family obligations. Everyone says I seem different. I don't try to explain. Daddy brings me home at 19:30. "Bye, Sweetheart," are his last words. All four of my girls are still frisky. It looks like a slumber party is in store for us. A few fireworks sound off in the distance. We get our jammies on. We make popcorn. We watch a scary movie, *Psycho III*. Yikes!

Tuesday, July 5

Dear Diary, The heat wave continues, but it is a short week and the Malibu rolls on. We are all in a good mood. Casey seems like a catalyst enabling positive mood, keeping us from taking ourselves too seriously. Chad will be out of town, so Kelsey wants to join us somehow over weekend.

I am first in the office. Right away, I get a walk-in requesting furnished unit, one year lease. The new spruced-up model is still being cleaned. She has had her virtual tour of the Hennig's unit. She completes forms online in our business center. I provide coffee and cookies. The cleaners are just finishing-up. Sandy arrives in time to give the on-site tour. Our furnished units are pricing out better than Extended Stay America. Joni pops in next followed by Susan and Maggie. We have a full crew. We are catching up on everything. It's great when you feel yourself working at max efficiency. I am ready for a break.

L. texts me her mid-morning greeting. It seems our breaks are synchronized. Roy chimes in at lunch. He fried up his catch of trout dwelling in streams and tributaries of the Nissitissit River basin, not far from Nashua. He is having some for lunch. Do I want to learn fly fishing? I guess not. Would I ever come along? For sure! Get me some waders, a nice color, not too ugly.

I wait every day now for baby girl Lindsey to show at 17:30 and there she is, right on time, happy time, our ride home. We reconnect with St. Theresa of Avilla, patron saint of those suffering illness. Hers is our favorite Church, the coolest, the darkest, and most quiet. Disconnect from the mundane. Retreat within for a moment, then reach out in reverence to that which transcends earthly preoccupations. We light two candles. We make two offerings. We are able to maintain solemnity until the little six under the Malibu's hood goes silent at rest at our happy abode, 14 Heron Street. What has Casey cooked up today? A cold pasta salad, perfect. I pepper mine thoroughly and dose it with ground Romano. We have a baby greens side salad. The cold Sangria is fruited up slightly differently each time. Today, it tends toward lime.

Wednesday, July 6

Dear Diary, After one night alone, I find myself fully back into women's world. Rain is in the forecast. From my passenger seat I search for the clouds. At start of workday, none are in sight. Two couples appear all happy and ready to move in. Susan takes one of these. I take the other. One has a U-Haul van, local. One has traveled far, in a mini-van, Arizona plates. How can we help them be happy here? I log the little things that got overlooked in their rapid turn-over units. The utilities get turned over tomorrow. Where to go? Who to call? Where to shop? We help. They get move-in freebies, coffee, tea, snacks, coupons, pens, pencils, notepads. Enjoy your first night in your new home. It's quiet here and shaded. You will love it. We assure you. We are here to take care of you. Some apartments have mean office ladies, not us.

Maggie brought more veggies. We always have some kind of oral gratification rewards in there. Tammy, the temp, used to bring Jelly Bellies in little packets. I find one behind a box of plastic spoons. I will save it for emergency. I wait for my Malibu to reappear. It has a life of its own but it comes back for me, just slightly late. I am alone in the office. Susan has just left. L. wants to visit the storeroom again. "I can't wait until tonight," says she. "You're mine and I need you." We emerge after 20 minutes of heavy breathing, our clothes all in disarray. "We'll pick this up later," she promises.

We are late for dinner. It's deli sandwich night so nothing got cold. A sudden breeze picks up the curtains. Here comes those rain clouds. Lightning first, then the thunder. Casey hugs me in fright. The next thunderclap, she hugs Lindsey. She is a scaredy-cat. What is the cure? Some Jager, of course. She is alternately giggling or jumping out of her skin at each thunderclap. I bring up the kittens in case they are scared too. They and Casey crash out early. Lindsey and I make our bed on the floor. The storm reduces to a distant rumble. We make ourselves clean in the shower. We light a candle at the kitchen table and pray reverently for a decent interval before the tidal wave of lust overcomes us.

Thursday, July 7

Dear Diary, Tension, pressures, static charges in the atmosphere, and in the erotosphere, discharged simultaneously overnight. It was intense, but in the aftermath, sitting quietly at breakfast table, we smile upon one another, just a little smile, returning to modesty. One toasted English Muffin, with butter and apricot jam, is all we need to nibble upon.

The streets cooled off nicely overnight. We find a few branches down on Corey St. My driver maneuvers nimbly around them. We lean toward each other for our routine kiss goodbye and all is well. It's fun to be first in the office. Wake up all you little computers. Here is your plant food, avocado trees. Here is your water and four scoops, Mr. Coffee.

I have time to call Roy. He is up early. He has already mowed the lawn and had his run. He will take me away from the city tomorrow eve, where exactly is still uncertain. I hear chattering at the office doorstep. Susan and Sandy join me in the breakroom. We really have it made here, made in the shade. I update the waiting list. Four applicants remain in line for unfurnished units along with one applicant for furnished unit. We look at possible designs for the next furnished unit. Perhaps remove the kitchen peninsula. Patrick can tell us the feasibility.

At lunch, Phil is looking all tropical in his summer suit. He might almost be date-able if Susan and I are not already taken by secret guys. I get a call from Jan Boyd. Our business cards are ready. L. shows up early. The cards are eye catching green and gold. We put several on Green-T bulletin board. We re-visit Holy Epiphany for prayers of both thanks and entreaty.

Food aromas hit us on the way home from restaurants on Washington St. Casey is serving enchiladas and chiles on Spanish Rice, we soon find out. It seems we can't get enough of Sangria. We have to find some flaws in Casey because right now she is too perfect. Lindsey and I huddle and whisper. One day her room was messy. That's all we can come up with. We don't know her that well yet. If someday, devil woman, psycho-babe shows up, we take it in stride. No one's perfect. We keep that excuse handy.

Friday, July 8

Dear Diary, Friday of a short week feels like a lazy Friday. I slept ok with my lover girl beside me but straight off, I feel like a slacker. I'm glad L. likes to drive 'cause I'm too lazy to even drive the easy 3 miles to work. Some kind of mid-summer dead calm doldrums have taken over me. I throw on one of Mom's 1970's pants suits, nice and loose and no bra. The tits are free to jiggle all they want. I gargle and finger comb my hair. Without further ado, I am ready. "Have fun among the statues. Have fun with your interns. Don't forget to come and get me," I remind Lindsey as we kiss goodbye. She just shakes her head.

Sandy and Maggie are my wing-women. Not much is happening. Best for me to just woman the phones. I manage a cheerful greeting on each call. I keep some make-up in my desk. By noon the lipstick, blush and eyeliner have made me into a painted woman. I wish Susan was here with her jelly doughnuts. I feel like I got into some laughing gas. Everything seems a little unreal. Who can really predict all of the effects of the myriad female hormones in flux? When L. comes to pick me up, I tell her she is so cute I almost cannot stand it. The coolness in St. Theresa's tweaks me down a notch. I hold Lindsey's hand. That stabilizes. Sometimes the priest will make a lame joke. Nothing else amusing in church except maybe if a spoiled brat little girl is in the aisle opposite. You look at her disapprovingly and she sticks her tongue out at you.

Casey's kitchen features a monster tossed salad with all kinds of stuff in it, French bread with real butter and a mushroom soup. Wunderbar! I remember some German. I will be speaking in tongues before the night is over. It's Lindsey's turn to get her bad habit report. Casey and I huddle and whisper. We tell her she is sometimes moody, sullen, silent, irritable and crabby. She shrugs and replies, "So, what's your point?" This gets a big laugh. I want some Sangria. They say, "Sorry, we're cuttin' you off," even though I haven't had any yet. Thank God, Roy is finally here. They warn him that I am in a strange mood. He whisks me away into the world of men, hopefully to restore a balance.

Saturday, July 9

Dear Diary, Roy says sometimes stuff ferments in your gastro-intestinal system and creates endogenous alcohol. He learned it watching a forensic lab tv program. Wonderful! Whatever I ate, give me some more.

We went to bed early. I am up before dawn watching my man sleep while I write in our book, Dear Diary. Already, I feel renewed. The kitchen is my domain. I take over, tidy up and take stock. Fruit, is there any fruit? Aha! Pineapple slices in a can. Good start. Cottage cheese, within date, unopened is good. Frozen sausages, fry 'em up. Now, I've got a yawning man, but not for long. We're going camping, I find out. Our gear is all packed. Plentiful food and beer fill a giant cooler chilled by freezer packs.

We have a key to a remote cabin, off grid, near Warren, MA, 81 miles by way of Woonsocket and Wooster, no tolls. I am the navigator. Upon arrival in Warren, we use the facilities in town then proceed on Old West River Road to O'Neil Rd. From our cabin, a path leads to O'Neil Creek. Our cabin has a propane gas range and well water. There is a bathroom with cold shower. This seems manageable. We are totally off grid though, no electricity, no cell phone tower, no land line. Roy has On-Sat on his Jeep in case of emergency. The nearest people are 5 miles away. 80 miles is a nice decent distance from the hot concrete and congestion of our normal daily lives. Watermelon, I'm having it now. The navigator gets to rest while Roy deploys all our stuff.

In the creek, we find a deep pool for a skinny dip. Roy snaps a photo of me on a rock, starkers. Naked as a Jay-bird is normal for me these days. We find a sandy area to spread our blankets and my legs. We are in the wild, the perfect place to do the wild thing. "This is what I live for, to screw my naked girlfriend in the great outdoors. Thanks doll," says Roy. It was kind of fun for me too, I must admit. Since I am the guest, Roy does all the food prep while I grab a cold shower. There is a screened porch with a glider. I wait there to be served. We do a little siesta after lunch. The late afternoon requires heavy application of Deep Woods Off. Roy gathers wood. Our fire pit is in an open area, clear of leaf litter and overhanging branches. We be roasting weenies. Potatoes bake while soaked-in-salt-water ears of corn steam on the coals. "Let's not go back. Let's just live here," implores Roy. "I can hunt and fish and chop all the wood we need. You can grow a garden." "Okay, you got me convinced," I reply with a giggle, happy to live inside that fantasy. Later, after dark, I hear some howling. "Might that be Coyotes?" I wonder. "Probably so," confirms Roy. The crickets don't care, but I do. Time to retreat under a solid roof. Rain is expected, which will make it nice to sleep.

Sunday, July 10

Dear Diary, We spend the night on a giant rustic style sleeper sofa. Two oil lamps turned down low light the way to the bathroom. A few lacewing moths flit around the dim lamps. Roy is up once. I hear him stomp on something. I think it was a spider, probably a big one. He wouldn't say. I hope he flushed it. The rain comes right around midnight. Wonderful cool fresh air pours into the cabin through half open windows. I sigh and hug my man. I murmur something like, "So nice. So, so nice." Some tree frogs begin their serenade, all part of *The Smiles of a Summer Night*. That is a movie, by Ingmar Bergman. We studied it in college, long time ago.

I record these thoughts at breakfast. Roy is cooking. Instead of a newspaper, he has a crank radio. We pull in WBZ. That fades and we find Fox Radio News and then ESPN radio, all on AM, all important stuff for guys. "Next time, we'll go fish," Roy promises. Does he mean the card game? I get the last piece of watermelon. God, that is so good. I cut up an apple for Roy. We brew campfire style coffee in one of those blue enamel chuck wagon pots with matching mugs. We move to the glider on the porch, sip and play footsie. I try to recognize the birdsongs. I am pretty sure about the Cardinal and the Red Wing Blackbird.

While it remains cool, we get on our boots. We find a path through the woods leading to a clearing at the edge of which are blackberry bushes tangled up in old wire fencing. We spot some poison ivy and stay clear. We end up back at the stream which has risen overnight. Some of the deep pools have minnows. I have a flashback. I see myself standing there naked on the shore, but where is Roy? I hope this is not a flash forward.

Near the cabin we spot a tree to climb. The branches go low enough for Roy to boost me up there. He hands me a beer, sticks one in his pocket and climbs up there beside me. We look at our cabin with a bird's eye view. There I am on the glider. Come on Roy, come on out and sit beside me, which he finally does. I just know I will cherish this memory for decades to come. I definitely want to stay here, safe and far from places where something might go wrong. I am tomboy fit enough to get back down on my own. We clean up and pack up and take one more stroll over towards the main road. We spot a Poplar suitable for carving. We carve our initials, the date, and a big heart. We go down in the history of this happy place. "Kiss me, a really good one, right here," I implore. I close my eyes. I hear leaves rattle high on our poplar. Here comes the "L" word. "I love you forever and here is the proof," he declares. It's in his kiss. He picks me up and carries to his chariot. Happiness cannot be more complete.

Our homeward bound path passes near the place I must spend the night, most every night, just a few months more. Heron St. still feels like home, more than any other roof ever over my head, but I must begin to detach. A welcoming committee is there waiting for me. Two young women and two small cats. I tell them just the nature and adventure parts. I can't gush about the emotions in front of Lindsey. That's all private between me and you, Dear Diary. Sangria, a toast is in order, "To our happy summer." It has just begun. There is some sand in my shoes, a wee bit of a tan, two little itchy bug bites, and memories to last 'til the day I die, recorded right here, preserved in their perfection. I could not ask for more. I have been blessed. I retire first. I dream of a little water-sprite, rising from a deep pool in O'Neil Creek. Shimmering, she silently beckons me to follow her deeper into her fairy-tale sylvan land.

Monday, July 11

Dear Diary, At 06:00, my dream turns to reality. My Water Sprite is under shower a few feet away. She has taken over my private bath. I peek inside and she flicks water in my face with mischievous little grin. We trade places. With our usual economy of time, we are both ready at 06:45. We meet at our parking spot where she holds the passenger door open, playing the chauffeur. The professional young women have important work in store for them.

We take a deep breath and off we go, mugs of tea snugly installed in side-by-side cup holders. I tune in the island music. I have on my Jean Nate body splash. She is sporting her White Linen. The hug and kiss goodbye are bittersweet. We have to live without our combined powers for 9 hours.

Inside, Susan is busy with a new report, namely, how many late rent payments and broken leases per year, year by year. She is happily number crunching. She is totally revitalized from her extended weekend, plus she brought jelly doughnuts. I enjoy just one. This is self-discipline. Get married and get fat? No way! The office is busy. The day flies by. Round about 5, I start watching for my business partner. Hooray! She is early, 17:20 on the wall clock. We head straight to Green-T as we are still in work mode. We agree that first step in our business plan is a website. A Facebook page will not suffice. By the end of July, we will choose a web host and design the pages. So much for today. We pray for guidance at Holy Epiphany.

Chez Casey Gourmet Kitchen has Mac 'n Cheese, green beans with bacon bits, and tomato soup with croutons waiting for us, so nurturing. We walk before dessert which is just plain watermelon. There is a big one in the fridge and we need to whittle it down. I am on the hot seat today, my accumulation of bad habits. Casey and Lindsey confer. I sometimes leave the pots and pans greasy. I don't always floss and I am a careless driver. I should go back to driving school. Instead, I mean to stay mainly navigator. I watch for hazards. I bring up my cast iron stuff which is supposed to stay greasy. So there! I am vindicated.

Tuesday, July 12

Dear Diary, Somewhere in the night I get a nice mons massage. Maybe L. wants to 3-D scan me into a statue. Those slightly rough little hands are all over me taking measurements. Later on, my tits get a tongue job. Nothing too intense, this endless fascination with all of me. I never fully waken. Just some few murmurs of pleasure encourage the ongoing attention. By 04:30, as I drink my Perrier, L. has finally drifted off, hugging her pillow tightly, one leg exposed. She is precious. I must take care of her. She could cause trouble, if I am not careful. At departure, I pretend I want to drive. My extra keys get confiscated. "Not until you go back to driving school," is my scolding.

Roy rings in at break. He wants to be my gym teacher again on our weekend and then fuck me afterwards. "Sports and screwing go together plus you play the forbidden fruit schoolgirl really well," he reminds me. Susan and I go out on the property at lunch. We spot another abandoned car, no plates. Our guys will slap a tow notice on it pronto. Sometimes, I am tempted to scan the VIN and get a Car-Fax report on these. I am sure there is some kind of sorry story linked to this junker. Any kind of abandoned item is a sad tale.

Carefree and homeward bound by 17:30 are little Lindsey and I. We make a date to get each other off full passion tonight. No need to let horniness go into the red danger zone as we did last week. We pray at St. Theresa. We pray as one thing, our combined powers of entreaty.

Stir fry is on the menu. We are really hungry. We 3 work up a sweat on our power walk then trade shoulder rubs. We have our popsicles. This is all a nice prelude to the main event. Casey says she has stuff to do. She shoos us away early but she wants the kittens. We confer on how to proceed. Does she want it romantic or raunchy? "Give it to me raunchy, just like the lesbo porno, which is kind of disgusting, but tonight I want it," she tells me. Act one is in the shower, getting all nice and clean. Act two is deep dive 69. The crotch is the main pleasure zone. Lying on our sides works best. Vibrators in the vag complete the dirty deed.

Wednesday, July 13

Dear Diary, L. runs upstairs to dress. What a night! We gave one another the max work-out. I wonder how many calories. I water my pea patch. We can harvest tonight. We have our routine quiet commute. L. tunes in classical. I feel very mellow at peace. We are braless today in peek-a-boo blouses. We cop a feel at goodbye. "Yours are bigger," L. remarks with a smile. Susan has me beat and hers are out there.

We settle in 'til noon, just a routine day. This has been my life for 7 years. Finally, it is leading somewhere. Susan and I lunch outdoors and feed some crusts to pigeons. I find out she has set a date for her wedding, namely, Saturday, Sept. 3rd of Labor Day weekend. August 31st will be her last day at Chestnut Hill. She has a job lined up on The Vineyard. She started here just after me. All that time, we have been side by side at our desks. I am sure Maggie will give her a big send-off. Our final weeks together are ticking away. "Phil will be heartbroken," I predict.

With a sigh, we return to our desks. We take care of inventory and stockroom. We take our afternoon break. Both secret guys phone in. We have some filing. Sandy sees us daydreaming and lets us go early. Susan drops me at MFA. We pass Jamaica Pond, Arnold Arboretum and Allandale Woods along the way. I wait for Lindsey in one of the galleries. She comes and gets me at 5. Homebound, we divert to Whole Foods to restock fruits, like watermelon, got to have it.

St. John Chrysostom hosts our prayer vigil from the edge of Stony Brook Reservation forested area. We clear the static and all the cares of the day. We refocus outside of ourselves. At home the new fruits overflow to my downstairs fridge. On the menu is lasagna with an antepasto. We find that Casey rang up William Sutcliffe last night. They have a rendezvous at the Venezuela Café on Friday. L. and I agree to chaperone the young and innocent one. Is he a phony or is he for real? We shall see. It's cooling off nicely for our walk. I carve the watermelon. L. has some work to do. I feel a twinge as I prepare to sleep sadly alone.

Thursday, July 14

Dear Diary, It's Bastille Day, if anyone cares. Casey is up early. She knows about it. Her maternal grand-mother is French Canadian. She can read the menu at a French Restaurant. She knows about wines and sauces but we need not worry. She won't be serving Escargot. I harvest my peas and put them in my lunch. In the car L. wants to know how much I missed her. I admit that I felt an aching emptiness. She likes that. We refuel at 7-Eleven. We are way early. We buy each other a rose bud. I remind myself that this is a romance, a very nice one, an alternative one, such as I never imagined. I stand at the office door and wave goodbye.

I stare at the empty office, summer morning. I snapshot this in my flip for a future scrapbook. Sure enough, Susan has doughnuts. I get to stuff one in her face. Coffee is ready. We take it to our desks. We snap each other working, for a future scrap book. At break, an extra box from Dunkins goes to our grease, paint and putty guys along with the usual flirts. I share my peas at lunch, juicy in the pod, a nice breath freshener. We stay inside, too hot. We wave at Phil through the break-room window. My rose is opening in a bud vase. I shut down my desktop at 17:00. Sandy will close up. My chauffeur shows up at 17:20.

She chooses the laundry room for our daily prayers. She has 2 loads to do, the place has nice memories and it is cool down there. We want to Christen that room as our first office. It is a neutral space free of distractions. We have a table and wall outlets, perfect. We pray during the wash cycle. We look at a proposed business timeline during the dry cycle. A few people come in and we chat them up. They want to know who is growing those peas. Casey serves a thin sliced filet, medium, with au jus and mashed potatoes. The salad is iceberg wedge with Thousand Island dressing and crusty French Bread. We try a different walking route. We meet new dogs in new yards. Dessert is watermelon. I make a pot of herbal tea. I retire first and wait for my wood nymph to appear in saphenous gown. We sleep deeply in every variation of the spoon position.

Friday, July 15

Dear Diary, the summer of love rolls on. Tonight, at the Venezuela Café, may be a spark or may be a fizzle for young Casey. Meanwhile, the career women have got work to do all in nice clean orderly places, bank, office, gallery, while the men are getting into all kinds of dirty messes. The pay ain't all that great for us girls but it's enough for our needs. Speaking of which, today is payday. I get cash at Speedy Mart ATM. A balance above 5K feels good and credit score above 700, this is fiscal responsibility. Today's kiss goodbye is me holding my partners face in my hands and firm on the lips, sounding something like "mmuh!" That kind. I watch L. drive away, being careful to signal and full stop before turn.

Casual Friday looks like khakis on me, safari shorts on Susan. Even Sandy is doing tan loose-fitting breathable. The ceiling fans are moving air. A handkerchief in one hand and a Gin 'n Tonic in the other would complete the picture. Someday we will all be retired and wasting away in Margaritaville, but for now Sandy has got us jumping through all our usual hoops for the full 8 hours. By 17:30, my desk is closed.

Through the break room window, I see my miss perfect driving record pulling in. She gets out to stretch as I give extra water to the Avocado trees. They are sprouting new pairs of leaves weekly. I lock up and go to the exit of the parking lot with my thumb out, hitch-hiking. Lindsey pulls up and tells me she never picks up hitch-hikers, unless they are really cute. That's me, I get picked up. Too cute to pass by.

Before getting into party mode, some reverence is due at St. Theresa, a candle, a donation, gratitude, modesty, stillness. We cross ourselves, genuflect and re-engage worldly activity. A summer evening ensemble is needed. I prepare alone, some blush, full lipstick, pin up my hair and no bra. L. and I do jeans. Casey is going with a mini. That girl does have quite the legs. We appear at the rendezvous spot at 21:00, on foot. It's cooling down nicely. We agree on a one drink limit, entering and leaving together. William appears and pours on the charm.

Saturday, July 16

Dear Diary, The threesome got back at a decent hour. L. and I mingled. Casey got a date for next Saturday. Three of the laziest gals in town are lounging around in the upstairs kitchen this morning when Roy Rogers rolls in. We feed him some scrambled and a slice of toast. He drains his coffee with a big "Ah!" and offers me his arm. Lindsey wants to meet Richard for "Worn to Perfection". We plan to mention it and see what he says.

Twenty minutes later, we are at the deserted Canton High School Track. I am suited up in running shoes, shorts and sports bra. On a treadmill, I do 15-minute miles. No pressure today. Just set a mark to beat. The track is a little tougher because of curves and wind and sinking into cinders. Roy is just behind pushing me. My splits are 3:30, 7:10, and 11:00. I sprint out trying to catch Roy for a 3:30 final lap. This is 14:30 total, not breaking any world records, obviously. We go back to the Jeep for a drink. Behind the High School is a big empty parking lot to try out clutch and brake, upshifting, downshifting, only 1st and 2nd gears. We measure progress by the amount of grinding. There is a hill. Starting on an uphill is the big challenge. I stall out twice, but get it on the 3rd try. It's getting hot. We hit the showers back at the duplex. Hanky-panky happens in there 'til the water gets cold.

It's only noon. The office needs attention. I want to create a mid-century modern look. Curtains, bookcases, one more lamp and end-table, an old-fashioned black rotary phone. Some landscapes on the wall. Then Lindsey will photograph it for our website. We find the bookshelves at estate sale, the kind with the glass roll down covers. We find the vintage phone, table and lamp at second hand. It's all on my dime. Verizon can install the phone next week. In the man cave is some touch-up stain and Old English lemon oil. The shelves bolt together and look stunning. I keep receipts. New Horizons Interior Designs is in business. Roy puts some of the business cards in wallet and desk. By now we are ravenous. Spaghetti and meatballs, seems right. I make the sauce and salad. My luscious tits are dessert.

Sunday, July 17

Dear Diary, I guess we can just be lazy and stay at home. I get used to the idea that 24 Ames Avenue is my new home. The mortgage payment here is near to what my rent is at Heron Street, but it's ownership, someday owned in full, just like Mom and Dad's house. I join Roy for his early morning run. We are done in time for 09:00 Mass. On return, we check in with Richard and Betty. "I might hang in a gallery. Imagine that!" he ponders. "Sure, bring the young lady. I'll pose for her. Why not?" That's settled. He passes on the bulk of his Sunday Herald to us. It gets re-assembled in our kitchen.

Roy makes a grand gesture. "Someday, all this will be yours," says he indicating our 5 rooms, which have regressed to their original untidiness which I witnessed on first visit. "I can't wait," I declare. "I think I'll move in today and take over." I take over the kitchen, at least. Roy says, "Be my guest." In less than an hour, the kitchen looks great and the fridge contents are cleaned out like we do at the office break room. I get us a healthy lunch from the remains. Roy watches me at work. "You know, you should apprentice somewhere, then spin off your own little niche in the business. "Great minds think alike," I tell him. After lunch we position the bookcases, get laundry going and find a dresser for my stuff. "Be sure to leave some panties in there," I get reminded.

I take a deep breath. Roy looks pretty good in his jeans. It's time for a sex break, a quick one. Is continuous screwing the best use of our time? Probably not. We need to go outside. Free throws, I make 3 of 10 today. We toss the football around. I can catch a 5-yard screen pass. I caught one on fingertips. So many talents discovered late in life. We take a beer break. Afterwards, I make zero of 10 free throws. "Those are some ass-kicking beers," Roy explains. I think we can get physical one more time before I go back to the all-woman dorm. Roy and I have bodies that fit together. It seems like our brains are working well together as well. Is playing house on our weekends enough proof? Will we ever get bored with one another? No way!

Monday, July 18

Dear Diary, I am very happy with how the weekend turned out. It was a taste of married life, followed by back to women's dorm and early to bed. I stretch, plug in the percolator, replenish cat bowls, splash water on my face and stare into the mirror. Susan has given notice. When shall I give mine? The future is not fully clear. My first idea is to stay at Chestnut Hill until November 30, then prepare for a White Winter Wedding in Church, mid-December.

Meanwhile, L. joins me for our usual quiet inbound commute, kiss and wave goodbye. It suddenly occurs to me. I will give notice after the civil wedding in August. The office is slow to get rolling today even though full staff is there. We all, me especially, seem to get bogged down in preliminaries. Sandy's team meeting at 10 am gets us into full gear, all the stats, all the goals. I have been immersed in this for 7 years. I feel good about it. Some of my ideas took hold. I wonder what it is like to live here. My special project will be a compilation of out-going tenant feedback for the last 2 years when 43 units turned over. My report will be my going away gift to my long-term employer.

On afternoon break, I check in with Roy. He is mainly working outside, making things look nicer, for me. He's feathering the nest. We have a nest. What a thought! What will it be like for L. when I actually move into that nest, when I no longer live at Heron St.? Her surprising answer is that she prefers to be in love with a married woman. She says that they are much less trouble. "We'll talk more about that later," she adds, with a confident little smile. It seems like keeping our relationship healthy will not be difficult, so let's just have more summer happiness, starting with our prayer vigil.

Casey is not feeling well, though. She went home early. It's a monthly thing, she explains. She can tolerate a bland diet tonight. Lindsey and I play Doctor, Nurse and Dietician. Poor thing, she looks pitiful. A hot water bottle may help. I have one downstairs borrowed from Mom years ago. Casey dozes off. We leave her alone. L. wants to read more poetry on our own.

Tuesday, July 19

Dear Diary, How is it that a girl is getting me wet? Days should be make-out sessions and nights for sleep. I need my sleep to recover from all of the sex I am having. I am having trouble keeping my hands off that wonderful little creature dwelling upstairs. She is extremely seductive. If we break up, she will replace me no problem. But we avoid making out on weekday mornings. Keep focused on work, which we do. The work makes everything else possible we remind ourselves.

Most days, I am the early bird. I catch the first phone call. Broken dishwasher is in 12-F. Confine your dog. Our guys will be there today. I know my days are numbered with my co-worker crew. I add socializing whenever possible. I ask Sandy how long she and her husband stayed hot for each other after wedding day. She says, "Until the kids came. Now we're mainly like pals and partners in the game of playing house." Roy and I will be different because of no kids.

Susan and I walk the property again at lunch. I really would not mind living here but it would feel kind of weird. As the afternoon drags on, I find myself staring out the break room window waiting for my girl crush. She is a little late today. I get to put the office to bed, lights out, another day in the books.

By 18:00 we are on our way, breeze in our hair, down scenic VFW Parkway. Our prayers fly up from St. Theresa's altar. Chef Casey has made Ravioli tonight from a frozen bulk stash, not Chef Boyardee, which certainly sufficed many a time in my early poverty life. She is stirring the sauce as we enter. She is feeling much better. We walk off dinner, but just a short one. I can talk business with L. during our kitchen clean-up. What if our design niche was decadent Art-Deco Boudoir? Roger Quinn could help us with that. It would be a nice cross-over with Lindsey's art photos in shimmering crystal clear high-res black and white. Our agreement about this gets celebrated in my art-ordinary bath. We get off in a wet clinch. We go to bed just sleepy. A light back rub and tickle from spoon position is all we need to nod off happy together, side by side, as we enter our dream world.

Wednesday, July 20

Dear Diary, We sleep with windows open. We wake to the sound of rain. As usual we dress separately and quickly. Our bag lunches and briefcases are packed the night before. We are in full self-discipline mode. Casey is just sitting up and rubbing her eyes as we depart. With headlights on, we take it nice and easy does it on W. Roxbury Parkway. It feels like spring again. At drop-off, we enjoy a lingering goodbye hug. I watch and wave as L. prepares to turn left on Independence Drive.

Tunes overhead is what I need now. I set the Pandora to Smooth Jazz. I relax in the dark until coffee is ready. Susan is greeted by lights up full. She is counting the days. Her position has been posted. I take some candid shots of her at her desk with my flip. I am due to get prints from my phone then restore memory for new. We pound away at our keyboards until lunch.

We make it a light lunch with stretches in a sheltered spot outside. The cool moist air is good for our skin. Deep breaths, full oxygen to the brain banishes the lethargy briefly but it ends up being a lazy afternoon, including much time in breakroom. We decide the avocado plants need a name. We label one pot Susan and the other pot Sarah Jane. We will be remembered forever here in the office. L. returns early today. She relaxes in our breakroom until I shut down my desktop. She says hi to Sandy and Susan. I get that mischievous knowing grin from Susan.

We decide that Roslindale will be every Wednesday. More structure helps our discipline. Jaime Cunningham's landscapes are still hanging. There is one that seems right for Roy's office. I write a check. A sold sticker goes up. The piece will hang until all come down. We request to meet the artist next Wednesday. At Holy Epiphany, we get hunger pangs. They go away in minutes. This is discipline. Our reward for delayed gratification is Rueben sandwiches a la Casey, pickles on the side. We are blessed. The threesome hit the pavement at sunset. A bit of sun breaks through the overcast. We are safely home by twilight. Our usual clean-up and some lounging around channel flipping conclude one more happy day.

Thursday, July 21

Dear Diary, Why am I up so early? I guess I can't wait for the day to start. L. is on the rag. Soon, so will I. The 3 of us all on the rag at the same time. We'll see how that turns out.

Meanwhile, I know I got one or two cans of fruit cocktail in the back of the fridge. I like it cold. That's all I want for breakfast. I find one. I offer to share with L. It's the kind with the cherries. She likes it. I try to get a little smile out of her every morning and this works. From an early age she pointed to it on the grocery store shelves and her Mom got it for her.

We make it a leisurely commute along Lagrange St. This was my bus route when the Malibu broke down. Susan pulls in right behind us, L. gets out for a standing hug. Susan waits at the door. "Sweet," is all she says. She wants a hug too. She is getting nervous and jittery prior to marriage. Her first try at marriage was quickly on the rocks. I tell her about me and Roy playing house instead of dating. She likes the idea of playing house this coming weekend. She will give me a full report.

Now I want my snap peas. There are some left in the fridge. By mid-morning, we are up to speed, we 3, Susan, Sandy and Sarah Jane. Once again, I see myself in the future looking fondly back on these days. I have time to write all of this because L. is late. She is stuck in traffic on Boylston. She pulls in at 18:00, parks, and sits with me for a while. We gaze westward and pray right here. We see a sky which looks as if painted by Maxfield Parrish. She says I can drive the rest of the way home.

It is my road test. I get a good score. Casey's kitchen has Chop Suey and Kikkoman Soy Sauce waiting for us. Should we worry about MSG? We are hungry and we don't care. "Accent wakes up the flavor." All of our moms used it. We can walk it off. We take our umbrellas against early evening showers. We walk to Speedy Mart for ice cream. We deserve it. We get back at dusk. Felicia and Fatima regard our ice cream bowls with great interest. They get to lick the bowls. L. wants to sleep alone during "the curse". She lets me tuck her in and read to her from my diary entry for the day we met, Thursday, January 27, 2011.

Friday, July 22

Dear Diary, Sure enough, I wake up bloody. Midol to the rescue. Was I ever late? Once during college, I was 5 days late. Phil would have married me if I had sprung the tender trap. My woman partner and I are ready for this week to be over. We order up Dave to transport us. It's a nice luxury and we can afford it. Malibu gets a rest. It's fun to hold hands in the back of his Highlander. We say goodbye at the museum.

Cramps and caffeine do not go together. I create something different, namely, herbal iced tea. Those neglected boxes of herbal tea bags in the break room cabinets get mobilized. Apple, Cinnamon and Vanilla combine nicely. I click my way through the day on auto pilot. Susan leaves early to catch the Coastal Flyer.

Sandy drops me at the MFA. L. is waiting at the back door shaded area. We are ready for an adventure together on public transportation. We always have our Charlie Cards. A 12-minute walk gets us to the Orange Line at Ruggles. The train ends at Forest Hills where we catch the 34 Bus. 18 stops later, we step out at Washington and Heron. It's like old times for Lindsey during her lonely days before me, but now I am at her side.

Fish Fry Friday is waiting for us, fish and chips just like Merry Olde England. We present ourselves freshly showered in fluffy robes. We have an orgy of squeezing lemon wedges. To go with fish of course we need a white sangria from a Pinot Grigio and Papaya Juice. A toast is in order to something, to Chef Casey and her skills for starters, to girl power, to the Moms and Dads who raised us, to St. Theresa, to the MBTA. The toasts get more and more improbable in correlation with how tipsy we become. To sober up, we go outside in slippers to look for the evening star. Is it Mars or Venus? I say it's Mars. The others say Venus. We wager upon it. Google says Venus in the western sky just after sunset is the evening star. I put a dollar in our cookie jar for my ignorance. The 3 worshipers of Venus flee inside at the first mosquito bite. I take a little time on the phone with my betrothed. L. wants to be with me Platonic and Pure. So be it.

Saturday, July 23

Dear Diary, The ladies are up early making breakfast. A man is coming. He is a pretty good guy, we all agree. He whisks me away every weekend but he takes good care of me. We save him some scrambled, sausage and toast. He says, "Thanks for sneaking me into the girls' dorm."

The photo session with Richard is all set for Sunday morning. I give the kittens their share of love. They know I am coming back. I bring more of my stuff to get the feel of moving in. Roy finds out the bad news about me on the rag. Meanwhile, can I please throw out at least one ugly thing I don't like? "Knock yourself out," says he. He's got a cheesy old particle board entertainment center. That piece of junk is condemned to destruction by my decree. The pieces are at curbside within minutes. I polish up the coffee table, which is solid oak. That will hold the TV for now. Carpet Fresh and a few minutes of vacuuming of the newly empty space are enough to keep me happy for today. "Very nice," is Roy's comment.

Where will be my main go to grocery store. Canton Market on Washington St. is walking distance. This is perfect. Off we go. Because of heat, we drive, but mostly, I will walk there. "Imagine how much time you will save, Roy. I do all of the shopping, very economical, while you are at work," I tell him. He is happy because he hates shopping, those stupid carts and plastic produce bags which you can't get open. This place is small enough that we get in and out fast. He checks out first with his stuff and me next with mine. My feminine products move into our medicine chest. I have marked my territory.

It's still early. Next is outside. He has planted rose bushes, installed a bird bath and a bird feeder, all for me. "That is so sweet! Look at me. Look at how happy I am," I declare. "Sweet!" says he. "Now I want to show you off." I freshen up, a quick change, some body splash, jeans and peak-a-boo blouse. I wear my ring. At Waterfall Bar and Grille, I get introduced as "my fiancé, Sarah Jane" to any of his pals whom we meet. He gets to hear, "Wow! Lucky guy."

Sunday, July 24

Dear Diary, I finish up my Saturday report while I watch my man sleep. One of his wise guy pals remarked, "No way! This young lady agreed to marry you? Oh, well, stranger things have happened," which got a laugh. "Being married could be very nice. Every day we are together is more proof," he tells me on our way home. We go to bed early. I deliver full body massage. "This is even better than sex," he murmurs. Of course, full body means attention to the family jewels. I have custody of the family jewels and they do not suffer neglect.

We are up at the crack of dawn for our run followed by early Mass. We tell the priest, Father John, about our plans. I lay out a brunch buffet. We have guests arriving, our first guests, Casey and Lindsey. I see the Impala pull in. I hear them talking. They knock on the wrong door. Richard points them our way. They knock on our door. I usher them in. I show what we have done with the study. L. has a nibble, gathers her stuff and goes across to meet her subject. The rest of us stay put. We would just be in the way. 45 minutes later, she returns. "I think these are going to be really good," is her only comment.

I pour the artist a grapefruit Mimosa. She spies the English muffins. She grabs one to go. The young ladies have a full day planned. We go over to get what is left of the Sunday Globe. It turns out that wife Betty acted as photographer assistant for lighting and such. They had fun with it. They are promised 2 framed 8x10's and notification about the gallery.

What next? Over to the High School to practice on the stick shift, of course. Down shifting and reverse is today's lesson. The coast is clear, a little jolting, a bit of grinding of gears, one close call with a traffic cone. The novice is not yet ready to mix with other vehicles but progress is made. Whatever guys can do, so can girls. We shoot baskets until sundown. I practice grabbing rebounds. I wear a hockey helmet in case one lands on the top of my head. I make dinner like a good wife does for her hard-working man. Roy likes pork chops simmered in sauerkraut and applesauce for dessert.

Monday, July 25

Dear Diary, I tried not to cry as Roy drove away. Catching up on dorm news distracted me from the heart-ache. Saturday Night, date Night, turned out nicely for Casey. William gets a return engagement for Saturday next. Sunday afternoon, L. was experimenting on the grounds of the asylum, Medfield State Hospital, on how to make a ghostly image, with Casey as model. One hundred years ago, a deeply troubled young woman found within those confines, asylum, love, and perhaps her first kiss. Her spirit remains there and retells her story to any who visit, who look, and who listen to signals reverberating across time.

Monday morning, 06:15, finds L. sitting at my kitchen table, quiet, mysterious, staring at me over the top of her steaming coffee cup. She is pouring it on heavy, her full mystique. The Malibu is back in action following Centre St., windows down. L. is back behind the wheel. She keeps her eyes on the road but catches me staring one time. A faint smile appears for an instant. I lay back in my shoulder harness, run my fingers through my hair, and take a deep breath of morning air. At drop off, I turn her face toward me, fingertips on her chin, for a nice wet one and a "Thanks, Honey. See you later." She waves just prior to her left turn. I am the only one who gets to kiss those lips. They are exclusively for me, by some strange twist of fate.

Here comes another Monday when I am double lovesick. Susan looks at me and rolls her eyes. She and her Secret Guy have a few issues remaining. I am not much help except to listen impartially. "Thanks a lot. Here, have a doughnut," she quips. It's her turn to stuff one in my face. Plus, I get a kiss on the cheek. We manage to plow our way through another 8 hours of the usual stuff. I get some extra work done because L. is late.

She wanted to let traffic clear while she finished some design project. Here we are again all alone in the late afternoon office. She tries the ergonomic desk. "We can pray here," is her plan. We give time out of our lives to prolong the life of another, namely, Sylvia, who is doing well as of yesterday's update. We notify Casey about our delay.

"Show me the storeroom again," is L.'s none too subtle hint. "Dinner can wait. This can't." Twenty minutes, all tangled up and topless in the storeroom, what a way to finish the workday. What if we drove around topless? It would no doubt cause a collision. We get arrested, then get topless mug shots for States Exhibit A. The men in the jury spend extra time studying Exhibit A. Sarah Jane, the nympho is out of the closet. Add exhibitionist to her rap sheet. Not to worry, Casey can come bail us out. It's a matter of civil rights. The right to be topless. Put that into the Bill of Rights.

We settle down at home in the dorm. It's pasta night. That means Red Sangria, from Pinot Noir. Life is good. Oops! I better call Mom. I promise to come over on Friday. It's getting late. We need some kind of exercise. We spot one another for girl style weak upper body push-ups and some serious crunches, 50 of each. We check our abs and arms for tone. Twenty more of each for good measure earns our reward. That's right, popsicles, not just any, the kind with real fruit.

Tuesday, July 26

Dear Diary, I wake up alone. L. was on her desktop at bedtime. She crashed on her couch. I get to drive today. L. is deep into her notebooks.

She takes only occasional interest in my driving. Arborway, Riverway and Fenway are a pleasant early morning path to navigate, typically 25 minutes max, plenty of time for our wake-up rhythms on FM radio. As we kiss goodbye at drop off, I pledge to return at 2 pm.

Joni is on duty. She will cover my early exit. I have one move out inspection at 16-M. The tenant, a guy named Walter, is getting married. He and the bride have a 2-bedroom starter picked out in Sharon. He was here four years with many happy memories. He snaps photos with his flip to prove clean and undamaged. He feels that he is leaving a part of himself behind. Love blossomed here and grew strong in every room of this 1-br bachelor pad. He liked the view from the third floor facing south. The neighbors were quiet and he had some shade for parking. He will drop his keys tomorrow morning.

After lunch, I handle a few calls and prepare to scram. I get back to the MFA right on time. We have a big shopping list at Whole Foods. We split the list in half and use the 2-cart method. We get home before Casey, which seems strange. After putting everything up, we get 2 loads of towels going. Girls use lots of towels. We pray during the wash cycle and have our business meeting during the drying. We fold at my place while Casey starts dinner. I have an ambrosia dessert planned. I can whip it up quickly after our run. I get a glass bowl chilling in my freezer. I bring the kittens upstairs.

Dinner is a family affair, a family of 5, all girls. Back by popular demand are Casey's BLTs, mushroom soup and baby greens salad. We 3 look really cute in our shorts and running shoes. We try a new circuit around Grouse and Maplewood. While the others shower, I make my Ambrosia like Mom used to make. Del Monte Tropical Fruit Salad, Walnut pieces, mini marshmallows, shredded coconut, and whipped cream, whisked up from heavy cream in a chilled bowl. I serve my masterpiece. I know Roy will love this. We chase it with Orange and Spice hot herbal tea.

We need to rest. Three ladies at leisure share two cats. I sit next to Lindsey and we share Felicia. Fatima knows her name.

She answers Casey's invitation. I call this contentment. Maybe poor Roy is all alone or maybe with his buddies watching Baseball. I excuse myself at 9 pm but I have a date with my enchantress at 10 pm or thereabouts.

Wednesday, July 27

Dear Diary, I cut up a melon at breakfast. The cottage cheese is in date, better use it up. My kitchen was never so healthy as now. We share one English Muffin with butter and apricot jam. We pack our Yoga gear. I get dropped off with my usual wet kiss goodbye.

I get a lot done before Susan even hits the door. Walter comes with his keys. His fiancé, Karen is with him. She made sure everything was perfect. They get their full deposit back. They give us a glowing review on Yelp. I give them my business card. Maggie says it's ok. I find those Jelly Bellys to reward myself. The flavor is intense. Can we get 16-M ready by July 31st? Our guys say yes. The new tenant begs to get keys on Sunday, July 31st. Sandy will come in special to hand them over. This type of stuff keeps getting us great reviews. I invite Susan to Yoga. It will help clear her mind because she is getting a little stressed. She can buy her mat and leotard in their little boutique. She says she will try it. I notify L. that Susan and I will meet her at The Blissful Monkey. Men go to bars after work. Women go to Yoga. It helps us deal with the drunken men. Ha!

Susan is perking up a bit while choosing her leotard. She chooses one in Dusty Rose crinkly cotton, which is quite flattering on that body of hers. It will be great if she joins our group. Why did I not think of this before? Lydia, Monica and Lindsey join us, all in good spirits. There are a few guys in the class. I don't think Roy would be interested in this kind of thing. "For you, honey, you have fun," I can hear him say.

L. and I make it to Green-T just in time to meet the landscape artist, Jaime Cunningham. She has my painting wrapped up nicely. We give Casey our ETA. The stillness of Holy Epiphany accepts us for our last stop of the day. Afterwards, traffic is clearing nicely. 1.7 miles and we are home. Today, fruit is the appetizer. Watermelon, my favorite. It's in season, it's cheap, it's cold and I can't get enough of it. We enjoy some broiled chicken breasts, green beans and scalloped potatoes.

An hour of sun remains for our power walk. I lag behind talking to Roy on my flip. I tell him I have a painting for his study. I also tell him about the two nice rear views I have in front of me. "I will never be tempted by the fruit of another," he promises. "I'm pretty sure about that," he adds with a chuckle. Our reward for power walking is some raspberry tarts Casey made from a recipe William gave her. These go nicely with black tea brewed in my percolator. It's a little late but I give blessing over dessert. L. has some work to do. I start another Sherlock mystery. I awake at 2 am with two girlish arms around me.

Thursday, July 28

Dear Diary, L. brings me my tea with a squeeze of lemon and a teaspoon of honey. She runs upstairs to finish dressing, which means I have 20 minutes. I go for one of Mom's gray urban minimalist pants suits with jacket and 2-button vest, instead of blouse, loose fitting for summer. This combo still flies but it's too young woman for Mom. A finger comb is all I need for my hair. I add a bit of blush add a drop of Chanel at each ear. Walking to the car, L. is staring at me. I am reminding her of someone. "Someone huggable?" "Definitely." She confirms. The jacket swallows her up in our hug. She wants me to drive so that she can stare some more. Seven miles later, I drop her at MFA. Five miles westward gets me to Chestnut Hill.

I strut my model walk across the parking lot, valise in arm. Phil is speechless. Susan keeps calling me Demi, for Demi Moore. I put on a show for her off and on throughout the day, including some tossing of the hair and bending over hands flat on desk, hips full at the rear, cleavage at the front. She takes a snap with my phone. I send it to Roy and to Mom. We are having too much fun today. Sandy has to crack the whip. At 16:30 it's all winding down. I notify L. that I am on my way.

I find her employee parking spot. She buzzes me in the back door.. She shows me the ladies locker room. A quickie make-out is in store for me. I know by now she likes to make-out in the workplace. I wait for her to finish her project. I check out the new antiquities exhibit she is designing. We are "Designing Women" just like the 80's Sit-Com. The Goodwill on Centre St. tempts us to look for more retro. We blow a few bucks on hats and accessories. I spot an old marble floor lamp needing repair. L. thinks it is suitable for boudoir. It fits in the back seat wrapped up in faded floral curtains destined for dry cleaner.

Our personal chef has been busy. Stir fry with fluffy rice smells really good. It's all in the spices. We have a chickpea side salad. We bring our Red Sangria downstairs to my woman space, where it is cooler. We switch on antenna TV. We do our push-ups and crunches during commercials. My guests bid adieu at 22:00.

Friday, July 29

Dear Diary, Whiskers awaken me at first light. Last night was about sleep, as deep as I go. I rise and rejoin those who walk the earth. Soreness from the crunches gets hydrotherapy in the shower. Uh-oh, those legs need a shave. I hear activity upstairs. This speeds me along. L. is a role model of discipline and efficiency. Jeans and a blouse, untucked, turquoise with matching ribbon for my ponytail. That works. I'll do make-up at work. Here comes my transporter. I carry our lunches and our mugs of tea. We'll knock this Friday out and then it's fun time.

Susan is already on the scene when I arrive at 07:30. She is looking classy in a French Braid. My vacation is confirmed for August 8 to 22, one week away. Now I am the one with jitters. At the end of that vacation, I will be secretly and legally married to a great guy, a dream I felt was lost to me some several months ago. Susan is working through lunch for early beach departure. In our break room, I open my bag lunch. L. has one identical, packed with love. What's in there? I made it last night. Let's see, ham and cheese on rye, carrot and celery sticks, with a pickle, wrapped in cut-rite wax paper, a plum, and a Hostess Cupcake. I can see her little smile at each found item.

Roy likes his hot lunch at the School Cafeteria. The nice cafeteria ladies, maybe like his Mom, dish it out for him. I call. I send my love. Next week, I am all his. I will be waiting for the rumble of his truck Saturday Morning, starting another happy weekend of playing house.

I return from my reverie and it's back to business. "Bye Susan. Have fun," I wish her this and wave farewell until Monday. 5 pm finds me wistfully gazing at the parking lot. Here comes my lover, my other lover, to pray once more at St. Theresa's. At home, Dad comes to pick me up. My roomies promise to save me some of the home-made Guacamole. I promise Mom we can hang out some more during my vacation. I tell Dad and Mom about my business. I tell them about the asylum. Dad says there is book about it. They both like the ponytail. Later we 3 roomies stay up late happily sipping Sangria.

Saturday, July 30

Dear Diary, I've got to bring more stuff to my new home. Let's pack two suitcases with my winter clothes, a toothbrush, and some more undies. At first light, L. is still sleeping. She has taken over the center of the bed, lying on her side with one little foot exposed and her face covered by soft dark hair. Fatima is beside her. Felicia is at my feet. They both look at me expectantly. They join me in the kitchen where I brew tea and prepare French Toast. I make some extra for Roy. The aroma is enough to prompt L. to sit up in bed. She gathers robe and slippers, yawns, stretches and slips into the bathroom. She always starts her day with a gargle and cold water splashed in her face.

When I hear activity upstairs, I text Casey and invite her to join the party. "Nice surprise," says she upon arrival. We find out that William will cook for Casey tonight at his condo near Back Bay. They have already agreed that the occasion will not become an overnight. Roy shows up at 08:30 in a crumpled summer suit and a straw hat. I point to his seat and serve up his portion. He sits there grinning at us, forearms flat on the table, fork in left hand and knife in right hand. He pours his maple syrup. I give his plate a dusting of powdered sugar. "Mighty tasty, honey," is his compliment. "All I need now is a kiss," he continues. A few moments later, we are waving goodbye from outside.

We go direct to our duplex. I put away my stuff. We were both up early. Seems like we just want to go back to bed. He tells me how much he missed me, how it was an aching and an emptiness, empty arms, empty rooms. All he had was some naked pictures of me to stare at. We make up for lost time. By 11:00, we are back on our feet. "We need beer," he says.

Grocery shopping is perfect for a weekend of just being together. Shaw's is only 1.2 miles away. He gets what he wants and I get what I want. We pay extra for paper bags. We minimize packaging and therefor trash as well. The fridge and cabinets are his and hers for now. We shoot baskets. Wow, I nailed a jump shot from the corner, swish. Dinner is a doctored up frozen Pizza. We run. We have beers while we watch the sun go down.

Sunday, July 31

Dear Diary, We watched old time TV until late. We fell asleep on the couch. I wake up at 01:00 and turn off TV. Roy remains relatively inert. I make a cup of chamomile tea and sit in the recliner. I listen to night sounds including far away traffic and the nearby refrigerator compressor. A night light glows faintly in the bathroom and a street light filters through curtains. Will the kittens like it here? Will I have any woman friends here in town? Maybe at Church? I look down at my ring. I doze off pondering my impending married life.

At first light, I hear activity in the bathroom. Roy has his running gear on. He wants me to have my beauty sleep. I have breakfast started when he gets back. The biscuits are rising in the oven while Roy showers. We make it to St. Oscar's in time for 09:00 Mass. Our church wedding should be right here in my new parish. Back home we ask Richard and Betty to tell us about their wedding performed by a Ship's Captain, 45 years ago, which reminds Richard that the anniversary is coming up soon. He only forgot once and there was hell to pay. It is too nice a day to go back inside so we take a Sunday drive to Sharon just 3.4 miles South on a scenic route.

At the turn for Route 27, Roy pulls over. I get my road test. The coast is clear. After a shaky start, I manage my upshifts and downshifts for the remaining 2 miles into Post Office Square. We sit on a park bench and watch the passersby. I wear culotte style short shorts allowing some nice sun on my legs. I tell about the couple, Walter and Karen, soon to be living in Sharon. We passed an ice cream stand on the way here. Roy wants to buy me an ice cream cone double scoop and watch my tongue action. I manage probably a weak imitation of Casey's sensual technique.

Roy has some stuff to do in his office while I make dinner. "Dinner's ready, honey," I croon for the first time. "Coming," says he. Stuffed Idaho potatoes, nuked instead of baked, with sour cream, bacon bits, broccoli florets, and cheddar cheese is the dish which aims to please. Sliced pears in wine sauce is the final touch which earns my tanned legs lotion and kisses up and down.

Monday, August 1

Dear Diary, I got home a little late last night. Lights were out already upstairs but Felicia and Fatima are still active. They greet me at the door. They share a can of Fancy Feast. Turkey is their favorite. How will they adapt when I move to Canton? How will Roy adapt to cats wanting to be in bed with us? I get up middle of the night for my mineral water. By 06:30, L. has let herself in. She helps speed me along. She even made the lunches today. I find out that she did a lot of printing in the darkroom on Sunday. Casey had her date with William. They went shopping Saturday afternoon in the Impala. Jessica came along. One more routine week lies ahead. I get dropped off at 07:15.

Susan seems happy. We go about our business as usual. I take care of phone messages responding to our print ads. Susan follows-up on e-mails from web advertising. Joni greets the walk-ins. Sandy is in a meeting with Maggie. I have time to check in with Roy on my break. Soon he will be a big part of every day.

We have cool, cloudy weather, perfect for a walkabout at lunch. The junk car is gone. Landscapers are digging and trimming. Hydrangeas continue to bloom. I like the blue ones. So do the bees. Roy planted Rose bushes for me. That's true love. 5 o'clock finally rolls around and I stare through the break room window, waiting for the nose of the Malibu to turn into our empty parking lot, with a really cute girl at the wheel so that we can enjoy the fun part of our day.

Our church of the day is St. Theresa's. We go in there retaining some serious mood. We let go of our own selfish little interests. We are tiny in the grand scheme of things. In the upstairs kitchen we have pasta night. I am so happy I could be content with a dry crust of bread and tap water. The daily Sangria seems to stimulate lots of carefree idle chatter and teasing. We have time to stretch and run. With my longer legs and training from Roy, I take the lead. During kitchen clean-up, I sneak in a mini-make-out with L. Freshly showered and in fluffy robes, the track team assembles at my place for antenna TV. Languishing there, we make quite a nice tableau.

Tuesday, August 2

Dear Diary, There is someone walking around naked in my apartment. I rub my eyes and squint in the dim light. It's a girl, my favorite tomboy woman child. Seeing that it's only 5:45 am, I pull her back into bed for a cuddle. I nuzzle some soft dark hair for a 10-minute power nap. Duty calls. She slips away. She will be back in 20 and I better be ready. I grab a random blouse and skirt. I go with the ponytail again. I am almost ready when my transporter returns. She watches me as she munches her rye toast and raspberry jam.

By 06:05, we are turning left onto Washington St. Why am I so lazy all of the sudden? It has been a long hot summer. Hot means go slow. Happy means go slow, don't want it to end, just go on like this forever. At my destination, she puts the Malibu in park. I come around to the driver's side window. I like to see L. looking up at me, hands on the wheel. I lean over, to take my smouch, flavor of raspberry.

I stay in slow-motion as I power-up desktops and Mr. Coffee. Here comes Susan with more jelly doughnuts. Maybe she has a connection at Dunkin's. Maybe she gets day-old free. I understand how Elvis got addicted. Susan and I are the short timers, 4 weeks for her, 4 months for me. We get a going-away party, for sure. We roll onward each to her own married destiny. Time marches on, 4:30 going on 5 pm. Residents are happy, Applicants are all lined up. Sandy sets us free early.

L. arrives at 5. She completed her tasks early. We can trundle on homeward with plenty of time to spare. She wants to pray in Hancock Woods Park. We pray standing silently, on a tree-lined path, holding hands. We kiss on the park bench as we did once before. Why do so many people want to kiss me? Well, it's just two, I guess, not counting Mom and Dad.

Dinner is blinis otherwise known as crepes. The culinary virtuosity of young Casey continues to amaze. We have time for an extra-long walk in the neighborhood, close to a full mile. On return, we deal cards and practice our poker faces. I bluff my way to one large pot.

Wednesday, August 3

Dear Diary, Boing! I pop up in bed like bread in a toaster. I want to cram as much action as possible into today, first light to last. I grab one cat in each hand, touch noses with each and carry them to their sad empty food bowls. Microwavable soup bowls and sandwiches get packed, granola and fruit cocktail is laid out, and coffee is perking, all by 06:20, when I hit the shower.

On return, L. is filling her cereal bowl. I go behind, give her shoulders a squeeze and kiss her on the top of the head. We make it out the door by 06:50. We both have peek-a-boo blouses today. How many will get caught looking besides each other? I keep having comical ideas like National Go to Work Topless Day. My front porch is destined to be decent exposure for many years to come.

It's too cold in the office. Who turned the temp down to 64? The topless workers need to wear a Cardigan, unbuttoned, of course. I demolish my stack of folders by 10 am when I make fresh coffee. I stretch and go outside while it is dripping. I stay in the shade. I take some deep breaths. I want to see what Roy is doing. He is remodeling his man-cave. There is one doughnut left from yesterday I split it with Susan. At lunch we go on our walkabout. We pledge to keep in touch during my vacation.

Once again, we meet our yoga crew at Blissful Monkey. Susan says she feels less frazzled afterward. I wonder if Yoga somehow prepares you to pray. Next stop is Holy Epiphany where we stay among the candles contemplating the saints and how they transcend the mundane. This may inspire L. in her art.

At Green-T, a surrealist named Timothy Wexler is on display. His bio explains that he paints dream images described to him by others. L. wants to post a review at the café website. She makes some notes on the 2 largest paintings, including the prices.

At home we stay in and do crunches and pushups before our dinner. The bill of fare is an iceberg lettuce wedge, roast beef with gravy, mashed potatoes and baby carrots. We sip a budget brand Merlot. We skip dessert until bedtime when the last of the watermelon is served, this time with a budget sparkling rose.

Thursday, August 4

Dear Diary, My bed is empty. L. snuck away about 05:00. Casey is going in early because of a special meeting on new software. We three have breakfast upstairs at 06:30. L. has made bag lunches. She says don't look 'til lunch time. For a change, the Impala rolls out first with the Malibu not far behind.

Inbound, L. tunes in to WCRB, 99.5 FM. In my office parking lot, we pause extra minutes to enjoy "Chanson du Matin" by Edward Elgar. We sigh and kiss goodbye, once on the lips and once more blown from my hand as I stand forlornly alone, but not for long because here comes Susan in her Pontiac G6.

We open up together. During boot-up, we do our make-up side by side. Why try to improve on perfection? It's fun. Anyway, we got our best faces forward for the first walk-ins. Susan goes to show the model. Roy phones in. He is drinking coffee and staring at his office landscape chosen by me and recently hung. "It suggests adventure," is his comment. His opinion may be helpful prior to purchases from now on. I search and find that August 4 is National Single Working Women's Day. By lunchtime, all of our tallies are up to date.

I go to see what surprises L. has put in the bag. She or somebody made Rice Krispy Treats. The pickles are Gherkins. The fruit is a banana. The sandwich is peanut butter and jelly on wheat. I can tell that this stuff was assembled with love, including a napkin. I text my delight and smiley face to the creator of this throwback lunch. At 16:00, another happy day in the office is winding down. We should dine out.

Lindsey and Casey agree to step out to Sophia's Grotto. The 3 early risers meet at home for a power nap, a shower and quick change. We choose an inside table. We trade tastes of our entrees, Ravioli, Mussels, Deep Dish Personal Pan Pizza. We see Concord Grape Granita being served at the next table. We all want that for a light dessert. We chase our espresso with mineral water. Moscato waits for us at home, where we offer toasts to Art, to Amore and to Single Working Women. Casey takes her call from William. L. joins me below for prayer and blessed sleep.

Friday, August 5

Dear Diary, The bed is still warm where L. just departed. Two cats stare at me as I towel off after showering. Coffee is ready. That is all I want. My blouse is cross buttoned. L. fixes it. I pick some cat hair off of her slacks. Inbound, I stare at threatening dark clouds. Heavy rain hits us at my drop off. We wait it out in the office. Why waste the opportunity? The lights stay off. We lock the door. Kissing and clinging for a few short minutes gets us enough relief to make it through the day. We hear Susan unlocking. We let her catch us in the act. "You two," is all she says as she shakes her head. The rain has let up.

L. waves goodbye. I blow her a kiss. Typing, filing, phone, walk-ins and repair dispatch, I catch Susan looking at me as we handle our daily routine. She just winks. We stay inside for lunch. I explain how last year my love life was bankrupt but this year I hit the jackpot. Some of my pea pods remain in the fridge. The crunchiness and chlorophyl wake me up. Some tunes get us through the afternoon. Susan chooses the 90's on Pandora.

Five O'clock rolls around. My vacation is finally here. L. wants to get home quickly and start laundry, prayer, business meeting and making out all in one spot. Talk about multi-tasking. We two young professionals find a way to have it all and fish fry too. The White Sangria with passion fruit juice is heavenly. We don't get too many crunches done. The antenna TV slumber party breaks up after Alfred Hitchcock Hour. Casey says, "You two have fun," as she kidnaps the kittens so she won't be lonely, plus William has pledged to phone in at the midnight hour.

She will be fine. Roy is coming at 09:00. My enchantress and I have 9 hours to screw each other's brains out starting with total body massage and happy ending. We take a popsicle break. We chase it with

Perrier. We do the warm washcloth routine. We take turns at some deep muff diving. That is what she likes to call it. I tickle her tits 'til she falls asleep. An encore happens at 06:00. We snooze 'til 7. "I will miss you but I will also get a lot done while you are gone," are her parting words.

Saturday, August 6

Dear Diary, L. knows I am eloping during my vacation. An affair with a married woman is even more exciting for her, she says. She wants to take over my apartment in October. Casey wants to take over the upstairs apartment. They will babysit the cats when needed. This means I can be church married in October.

"I knew those two would come in handy," observes Roy, speaking of Lindsey and Casey. To sugar coat the pill of finances, we write budgets on bar napkins at the Waterfall Grille. We put them in my dresser drawer alongside with my underthings for future reference. "If I come home from work in a bad mood, just crack me a cold one and send me outside to shoot baskets," he advises me. He wants to order pizza and just nibble on it for the rest of the weekend. We apply for the marriage license on Monday in Canton, that is for sure. Now we can relax. I tell him that if I am ever in a bad mood, take me to dinner, get some Sangria on board, then take me home and use all of your powers to get me naked and unafraid of the annoying world out there. "Ok, but that sounds a lot more complicated than what you do for me," he notices. "But it is guaranteed to work, and aren't I worth the trouble? say I. "Well, I guess so," he teases.

The pizza guy arrives in short order. We share one slice then go to work putting 3 suitcases of my stuff away. My man is all kind of nervous excited, so we go for a run followed by fun in the locker room. He feels better now. He phones his dad who picks up his land line on the 10th ring. He is no nonsense and not much for gassing uselessly on the phone. We update him and that's it. We water our rose bushes and fill the bird feeder. Blackbirds notice it first. Robins get their share. Some of them may be sitting on a second nesting. Some bunny rabbits appear at the edges of the lawn. Roy has some clover mixed into his fescue.

"I'm sleepy. Let's take a nap," I propose. The old broken down, sagging couch is for napping. We wake at 11 pm, hungry for more pizza. I make some veggies and dip. Roy tries my Sangria of the day, featuring a touch of tangerine.

Sunday, August 7

Dear Diary, Roy is having cold pizza for breakfast. I get to see the new man cave. He has made it less of a sports shrine and more like Hernando's Hideaway. There remains a workbench hidden by a curtain, a table for poker night and an old-timey Norge fridge full of beer and wine coolers. I could not have done better myself.

After Mass, Father John tells us about some kind of validation. Roy needs to get his Baptismal certificate. I have mine already. Saturday, October 15th is free for the church ceremony. We make a deposit. Betty wants to know everything. She tells me not to worry about my parents, especially Mom. Richard and Betty will give Roy a good recommendation. Betty invites me to try on her old wedding dress, circa 1968. Of course, Mom has hers also of similar vintage. Betty will fish hers out of a cedar chest later.

We take the paper home to look at estate sales. We locate 2 sales nearby. We have cash. We have a truck. Cheap treasure is waiting for us. Roy finds a tabletop tube radio in need of repair, vintage 1949. The dial lights up but the tubes are weak and the cord should be replaced. He knows a place in Maine which repairs these. I find matching vanity lamps. Both items are half off for last day of sale. We stay well within our budget.

Back home, more cold pizza is waiting. That spinach I got last week needs to be a salad asap. I freshen it up and make it look really nice. Later in bed, my sailor man will be strong to the finish because he ate his spinach. I return to try on Betty's wedding dress without the train. I just want to cry when I see myself in full length mirror. I never imagined how I would look. "That will do very nicely, except that now, you are too good for me," says the groom. "Don't let that stop you," Richard adds the punch line. Roy set him up perfectly for that one. L. can do the bridal portrait. So much for dresses. Time to go home sweet home. We set-up the radio in Roy's office. Can we afford a reception for 24? We will pay for the first 24. If Mom wants more, she can talk Dad into it. It'll be all right I keep telling myself.

Monday, August 8

Dear Diary, Roy had work study in college, a job in the cafeteria for lunch and dinner. He got plenty of free food. At his dorm, the guys had nothing but pizza. That was how they survived in between visits home. His bachelor survival options always included cold pizza. It dries into chewy, salty, hard rations near to petrified and never goes bad, so it seems. That is all he needs with his coffee for breakfast today. I just do yogurt with granola.

Betty's dress was a little snug. We are first in line to apply for our wedding license. We can pick it up on Thursday. He shows me his favorite fantasy house, tucked away among the trees on dead-end Danforth St. It looks like something out of Hardy Boys Mysteries. Our modest duplex is fine with me. We can save lots for retirement or just stay there forever. Why keep looking, wishing and fantasizing? What we already got is really good. The guy I got after waiting so long is just right for me. I caught him and reeled him in. He loves me and he is mine. On Friday, we make it official.

We skip lunch except for thirst quenchers. We feel like a siesta. Let's keep on consummating. We fit together so nicely, plus he is in love with my ass. The other parts are a side dish, I guess. The lust came first, then the love. Works for me! After siesta, we freshen-up and seek entertainment. Where could that be on a Monday eve? We check out Matt Kelly's Pub. Sure enough, they are having Open-Mic Monday.

There is guy with acoustic guitar. He is not too shabby. He can pick those strings for a 20-minute set. I want an Old Fashioned, like Don Draper drinks on Madmen. Roy goes for Guiness draft. Next is a rakish Poet and Philosopher. He sets you up by being serious, then all of the sudden comes a punch line. We put our quarters in line for the 8-ball table. Meanwhile, there is a singer just slightly off tune followed by a stand-up comic who saves his best 2 jokes for last and gets a nice hand from the crowd. I get striped balls. Soon, Roy has sunk all of his solids but my stripes are blocking the 8-ball. He makes a lucky shot. It's time to go home sweet home, arm in arm, under summertime stars.

Tuesday, August 9

Dear Diary, We talk about sleeping. We talk about variety. What is going to be much more fun than the typical bachelor sleeping alone or random partner? Tonight, is together 4 nights in a row. A boring routine feels safe. Sometimes you just want sleep. I think we can have the best of both worlds. Married is just adding an extra ingredient to the previous lifestyle, an extra spice, starting with a wife in the kitchen, where he is adequate but she is expert on delivering something good to eat with TLC. Strawberries decorate our cereal bowls. We peek at each other from behind his Wheaties box and my Rice Krispies box. We don't need any chatter other than, "Bye, honey. Have a nice day." I already practiced this with L. but now no packing of lunch. He likes to eat in the school cafeteria. He goes outside. I borrow his office. I look for online courses in interior design. Some formal training is indicated. This is Roy's advice and I follow it. We discuss the choices over lunch. L. can give her input as well. I am going back to school! Why did I not think of that before? I was moribund, a $10 word, I read somewhere. I was in decline. I was sinking, holding my breath. Roy popped me up to the surface, with help from "Pretty Young Thing", living upstairs, watching over me every day.

Lunchtime! The cafeteria is open. The lunch lady offers choices. I bet on Mac 'n Cheese with Tomato Soup to satisfy the outdoorsman. We suit up for an afternoon run. Can I better my time? Can I break 14 minutes for my mile? My half mile split is just under 7 minutes. I pace myself! Today is 14 minutes, 10 seconds. We both break a good sweat. Roy has access to the High School locker rooms. We shower separately. We meet in the school parking lot, carrying our gym bags. We go for a little ride. The High School Sweethearts have stolen moments alone together at a secluded spot. Jack and Diane go to Sonic for Chili Dogs by way of two-lane black top in the direction of Stoughton.

Before dark, the High School Sweethearts shoot baskets 'til the skeeters come out. I am 5 for 10 on free throws. Cold brews on the man cave leather couch leads to more Love.

Wednesday, August 10

Dear Diary, Mom is checking up on me. I tell her I will see her next week. Two more days. Please, God, don't let anything go wrong. Where is Roy? Has he left me already? No, the sun is up. His running shoes are gone. He is just gone outside. The athlete is a meat lover. Let's get the bacon, sausage and eggs going. He comes stomping in and hits the shower. The sweaty clothes are piling up. Today is our first laundry day. My man comes back freshly shaved. He gets his coffee freshly brewed. For fun, I am wearing an apron I brought with me.

On his run, Roy brought a copy of the Cape Cod Times. He likes to pick it up once a week. For Honeymoon, we can afford the Cape Colony Inn at Provincetown, 2 nights, Monday to Wednesday, next week. We phone in our booking directly. Roy avoids travel websites. Too many screw-ups. We celebrate with a Mimosa. The kitchen is a quick clean-up. Laundry should wait 'til off peak for electricity. Anyway, it seems we got a lot done before lunch. We shelter from the heat. The bedroom is my next design project. I sell Roy on all of my ideas, including a new headboard, 2 new end-tables and 2 new matching lamps. I get busy vacuuming, dusting and stripping the bed. We pull down the sad old drapes, leaving only the sheers. Under the bed and in the sliding-door closet, I find old socks, a solo cuff link and 47 cents which will be the first money in the cookie jar. I add a 10 spot from my purse.

We break for lunch of soup and salad. I have one more remodel request, that being new comforter and pillows. We hit Kohl's and the Ikea Store in Stoughton for all we need except the headboard. I pay for everything. By late afternoon the bedroom looks wonderful. I multitask dinner prep and laundry. After dinner, we have fun folding towels and sheets. We flip the mattress and re-assemble with fresh linens and new pillows. We open the windows, get the a/c on fan only and manage a full exchange of indoor air. The transformation proceeds wonderfully, the man of the house is pleased at my domestic engineering. A scented candle at my bedside table is the final touch.

Thursday, August 11

Dear Diary, I awaken to birdsong. That, and Roy has stolen all of the covers. Pancakes will be easy. Sleepyhead shows up in bathrobe and slippers. He sits there grinning. He is in time for a short stack. Sausage and bacon remain from yesterday. We finish off the tomato juice. He takes his plate to the kitchen sink and stops behind my chair to rub my shoulders and say, "That was mighty tastey, honey." We pour our second cup and sit outside for a bit to finish waking up.

We get ready to go downtown. He checks out my limited wardrobe. He picks out blouse and slacks for me. I choose that tan linen summer suit he wore one day recently. It's fun to dress each other. Barbie and Ken decide to walk to the town hall. Finding a shady route under trees, it is less than half a mile. Roy looks great in a pale green tie, loose at the collar. He slings his jacket rakishly over his right shoulder. He gives me a big grin whenever I look at him. We wait inside Town Hall in the automated break room. It's nice and cool in there. We share a Dasani. At 1300 hours, Military Time, we march upstairs and collect our documents. Our papers are in order. Roy pockets them in his suit jacket breast pocket. "This is marriage. This is serious," says he.

We march onward to The Waterfall Bar and Grill for debriefing and light lunch. We like to sit at the bar, just as we do at Oscar's. We share some deep-fried finger foods. I learn about beer such as what's a pilsner and what the heck is lagering. I learn all the good amino acids in there. I learn about hops. They got the Golf Channel up on the HDTV. I could get into it. I like the outfits which that gal Paula Creamer wears.

Our sortie ends with a homeward march. We are at liberty to indulge in afternoon delight followed by siesta. Roy wants to cook out. He does it all himself, same as bachelor days. I get to watch and learn. The briquettes have to be just right. He has cubed steaks. Baked Beans are in a little pot on the side. He slices a cannonball watermelon which he bought just for me. Later, in our new bed, I reward my hero in all of his favorite ways.

Friday, August 12

Dear Diary, We are both up at first light for a short run. Barbie and Ken dress each other again. I pick out his navy-blue blazer with yellow tie. He chooses my yellow frock with bare shoulders. I tie his tie for him. We are ready by 08:30. We proceed on foot to Town Hall. We have the rings. The JP explains the marriage contract. He checks our signatures and documents. We are husband and wife by 09:30. A clerk takes our photo with Roy's point and shoot during the kissing of the bride. We walk home arm in arm. We try to whistle in harmony. A few bars of *You are My Sunshine* turn out ok. He carries me across the threshold of the man cave where the love slave will be kept prisoner, at least until lunch.

We got a few burgers left over. He pops the cork on a bottle of Andre Champagne. The cork bounces off of the ceiling. I recover it for a souvenir. I drop a strawberry in each glass. We drain our glasses ending with a satisfied "ah…!" We stick the strawberry in each other's mouths. "Okay, here comes the boring part. You're stuck with me for 50 or more endless years, starting right now," quips husband and then yawns. "Well, I could do worse, I suppose," says the wife with resignation. Is this the happiest day of my life? "Is it a fancy, not worth thinking of, or is it at long last love?" That's a Cole Porter lyric remembered from Music Appreciation elective. "Is what I feel, the real McCoy?", I ask Roy. "It had better be," says he.

We should go dancing. Richard plays us a Fox Trot in his garage. We manage to stay on the beat. We pour them a glass of our bubbly. Betty and Richard demo how it's done, their version of the Fox Trot, cheek to cheek. It's cool in their garage which is not quite a man cave. We dance again, a slow one, surrounded by racks of tools, a lawn mower, a weed-whacker, and a spare tire. We thank our host and hostess. There are hugs all around. I spot a tear in Betty's eye. We bid them good evening. I am ready for the boring part. On goes ESPN baseball highlights. I bring more drinks nested in foam koozies. "Are you bored yet?" the husband wants to know. "Exquisitely," say I with a yawn.

Saturday, August 13

Dear Diary, What should we do today, our first full day of officially hitched? I am ready to run another mile. We have our Wheaties and get out to the track pronto before the heat sets in. With Roy as the rabbit, I sprint the last 100 yards to clock in at 13:55, a new personal best.

I am happy with my new kitchen. I just need to organize the drawers and cabinets plus a few other touches such as curtains. Roy has got a gas stove, which I prefer to the electric at my apartment. Ham and cheese omelets for lunch sounds right. The parsley flakes make it perfect. We do some snipping and watering on the rose bushes before retreating inside for siesta. It's nice to cuddle under one thin sheet with two fans blowing. The afternoon shadows lengthen.

Betty is happy to lend me her golf clubs. She hasn't touched them in years but they retain sentimental value. I find her most recent scorecard from 2005 in the zip pocket with the tees. She was 10 over par for 9 holes. She shows me the proper grip. Ponkapoag Public Golf Course is only 3 miles away right here in Canton, due south on Washington St. Roy grabs only his 3-metal and off we go. This could be really fun. First, I have fun in the pro shop picking out a skirt, a top, and a visor hat which allows my ponytail to hang down. We start on the putting green. After I start converting 4-foot putts, Coach Roy allows me on the driving range. We share one large bucket. I have the proper grip on Betty's 9-iron. I keep my head down as instructed. After a few whiffs, I make one go up in the air but off to the right. Half of the balls are gone before I finally get one about 50 yards and fairly straight. Roy lets me figure it out on my own. Then he takes over. The ball is now going so far that I can't even see where it landed except it was high in the air and way out there.

We order dinner from the grill in the clubhouse. Some of the regulars chat us up. It is very pleasant to spend 2 hours at the links. I book a lesson with a lady pro. We hit the home locker room together. Coach says that I am as just as cute as Paula Creamer. Coach wanted to do me right there on the tee box.

Sunday, August 14

Dear Diary, Roy wants his run. I make breakfast. We walk to 9 am Mass. We establish our boring happy routine. We claim the remains of the jumbled-up Sunday paper from our neighbors. Sometimes Roy has the solution to a crossword clue for Richard. We find an estate sale but decide to stay home. Roy shows me his Ebay. He thinks we should stash gold. We bid on a half eagle, $5 gold piece. It is within our budget. After shooting baskets, we come back in, think of a toast and clink frosted glasses. Our toast is to our nice helpful neighbors.

We pack one suitcase each for our Cape Cod adventure. I make us bag lunches. We will start early. As navigator, I print our roadmap and resting spots from Roy's desktop. Our route will be 114 miles, mostly 4-lane. Coach wants push-ups and crunches, a light dinner and go to bed early, just after dark. This is our marriage boot camp drills of teamwork and discipline. Now is just about sleeping. Our honeymoon suite is the place to consummate. Candles are lit. Fans are blowing. I miss my cats. Will they like it here? Will they try to get out? Will Roy get used to them wanting to be in the bedroom. They can use that old couch for a scratching post, but they mustn't claw my curtains.

I dream I am lost in a jungle at night. Cat eyes stare at me from above. The trees begin swaying. They become more like seaweed, swaying in an ocean current. Where is Roy? How did I get here? I don't need to hold my breath. I am a fish. I see a snorkeler with a camera. I am attracted to the shiny lens. I go near. I see myself reflected in the lens. I am a brightly colored tropical fish. The snorkeler looks like Roy except much younger. He takes my picture then swims away. I try to follow but the current pushes me back. I do not like this dream. I wake up crying. Roy has witnessed my little tears of joy, but this is outright blubbering. "You had a bad dream. You can tell me about it later, now go back to sleep," reassures Dr. Roy. I get up and blow my nose loudly. After a few more sniffles, my breathing slows. I settle down, holding Roy tight.

Monday, August 15

Dear Diary, At first light, the dream journalist is scribbling away. Roy pours our cereal bowls adding banana slices. I peek at him over the top of my box of Raisin Bran. He winks back at me. We set 07:00 for departure. We do a checklist like pilot and co-pilot of a 747. We fill up at Shell right around the corner, each grabbing a fresh brew. It's clear sailing 39 miles to Plymouth and our first pit stop. A Dunkin's is there at the cloverleaf for I-93, aka Pilgrims Highway. My chronometer has ticked to 09:00 by the time the pilgrims resume their journey to the Cape, first to Sagamore, then US 6, which takes us the rest of the way.

Our room at the Cape Colony Inn is not quite ready so we walk the beach. We breathe deep and welcome the difference from city air. We check in to 206, finding it bright and cheerful. We want seafood catch of the day for lunch. The desk clerk recommends the Lobster Pot, an unpretentious place on Commercial St. We grab our sailor hats from our sunset cruise of Boston Harbor not so long ago. We walk since it is only a mile and shade can be had under storefront awnings. Roy is hankering for lobster roll. All I need is the big bowl of clam chowder, New England Style with lots of oyster crackers.

On our way back to the Inn, we shop for souvenirs. I like sand dollars. Roy wants a conch, the biggest one they have. It will decorate his bookshelves very nicely and our ocean will always be there. The Inn has a very nice pool. By 3 pm, we are poolside giving each other the Coppertone treatment. Swim, 10 minutes front tan, swim, 10 minutes back tan, then cover-up. This gets me the sexiest tan lines. Roy just wants to swim. I watch him through my sunglasses doing 20 laps. This leads us to siesta time under one sheer sheet with mutual back tickles.

For our evening walk on the beach, I do shorts, sandals, and a tunic top in turquoise. I find worn smooth drift wood I can use as a walking stick. Our desk clerk recommends The Post Office Café and Cabaret for dinner. We people watch from our patio seating. Evening summer breezes provide our jeep tailwind home to ocean-side oblivion.

Tuesday, August 16

Dear Diary, Yesterday was wonderful. Maybe I have already died and gone to heaven. Is there sex in heaven? We forgot to ask Father John. Is the marriage consummated yet? Six times over if you count this morning. Those one-cup coffee brewers in our room produce max aroma. We stand on our balcony to watch the sun rise. The hotel continental breakfast is enough for us. We ask about shark sightings. With my Bay Watch lifeguard beside me, I get pounded by some waves, full immersion, but we don't swim out. Roy rinses me off with a bottled water. We sit on a towel under an umbrella and watch the Sandpipers. I lean over and draw "I Love You" pictograms in the sand. Roy adds a "too" or a "2" under each one. We fold up our umbrella and head back to get ready for lunch.

Today, we ride, thus to see some sights. We do the village before lunch and the Woods End Lighthouse after. In the max heat of afternoon, we wander among ferns and moss in the Beech Forest. Is this the jungle I saw in my dream? We watch the sun go down at The Race Point Lighthouse. Driving there requires 4x4 vehicle such as our Jeep. My outdoorsman has no problem getting us there. For dinner, we find outdoor harbor-view seating at Jimmy's Hideaway. I can't resist the Frozen Cantaloupe Daquiri. We order from the basic comfort menu, Fish and Chips for Roy, Fried Shrimp Platter for me. We share a Sea Salt Caramel Cheese Cake for dessert. We don't want this night to be over but we are ready for pleasure zone room 206.

We arrange for late check-out which is no problem on weekdays. We steam up the bathroom scrubbing each other's backs. In our robes, we inspire night air on our balcony and see that the moon has risen, nearly full, large and orange on the horizon. We stretch out in bed together. I win the flip for who can surf. I find a mystery on HBO, namely, "The Girl with the Dragon Tattoo". We have popcorn from the vending machine. This movie rates high on suspense and creepiness. Curtains closed and a little back rub before sleep provides bad dreams prevention. The clock says 01:00 and all is quiet.

Wednesday, August 17

Dear Diary, Sadly, we must depart but not before a few more hours of swimming pool and shore. Roy does his 20 laps before breakfast while I catch bonus beauty sleep. More and more, I go outside of myself and watch the two of us together like scenes from a movie. The tide rose and washed away our pictograms. I let my hair down, allowing windswept variations on how it partially reveals my happy face. The beach offers us one more souvenir, a piece of green bottle glass, worn smooth by water and sand. The relic finds a secure resting place in the palm of my hand.

In summers to come, I may simply hold this prism up to any lamplight and film clips I mentally recorded will be summoned from their treasure vault.

Our return follows the same route as the outbound path, stopping at Plymouth for a fill-up and comfort break. By 15:00, we are home sweet home. Roy goes straight to his office, the office which I designed, there to find a place to display his conch and to process 2 days of mail. He has an in basket and an out basket. I want to go in there and take a letter in shorthand. In my kitchen office, I call Roger Quinn in the hopes of making a deal on a vanity, the kind with 3 mirrors and perhaps a secret compartment. He is willing to trade a piece recently acquired for 2 more large, framed Aphrodite prints. This piece is Mid-Century Modern Mahogany but damaged. He can deliver it to Canton for a nominal fee. The reward for L. is that she can have all of my mix-and-match furniture in exchange for the prints. She wants to make the deal but I must allow her 2 weeks for printing.

Office work has made the newlyweds hungry. I make a hand-written menu on some card stock. Roy chooses the Rueben Sandwich. I make a fair imitation of that which I saw Casey create. I call Mom and say I will see her Sunday. How to drop my marriage bombshell news? I am very worried about this. I need to handle it cool and smooth and just right and ruffling not any feathers. I tell my plan to Betty. She advises me. To calm my nervous nature, shooting some baskets seems right. Swish! More consummation is even better.

Thursday, August 18

Dear Diary, My sand dollars are lined up on the kitchen window sill, you know, the place where pies are supposed to cool. My emerald ground glass prism rests in a velvet box, nestled in with my undies. This morning, I got the Wheaties and Roy got the Raisin Bran with blueberries, then he left me alone, barefoot but not pregnant. He has got to help the football team get suited for practices. He is coming home for lunch.

I tidy the house. I find my sandals and tend to my Roses. Roy's favorite from his lunch ladies at school is spaghetti and meatballs. I present this with generous amounts of grated-cheese, a Caesar Salad, Garlic Bread and Iced tea. "Mm…, smells good, honey," is my sign of appreciation. "Fit for a king!" he adds. He leans back and exhales a satisfied "Ahh.., The hungry man is satisfied." Except that he wants a hug. He wants to hug me and kiss me and squeeze me and give me anything I want. "I'll make a list," I tell him. I am the dessert, but he will save me for later. Right now, he is determined to cut the grass. He does the neighbors' patch as a courtesy. Richard comes out to inspect the handywork. Just for fun, he pays Roy with a shiny quarter. "Gee, thanks!" I hear Roy exclaim. The shiny quarter goes straight to the cookie jar.

We are overdue for a pretend fight. "You never take me anywhere," I complain. "What about Cape Cod?" he protests. "That was Monday. Today is Thursday," I remind him. "That settles it. We're going to the Waterfall Grille," he announces. "Fine," I say in a huff. "It's always the places you like." By the time we arrive on foot at the bar, I forgive the poor guy. He does his best. It's hot. We stay inside. The bar kitchen is open. I order some fries with my Red Bull. We while away the time. The Red Sox are playing the Royals. Some of the Red Sox have big bushy beards. I stroke Roy's chin so nicely clean-shaven. He smells good too. We tell Tony, the bartender, that we just got married. "My condolences," says he, the smart-ass. I want to play darts. "You throw darts like a girl," Roy observes. We are happy with our little soiree, but it's time to go home. Roy wants his dessert.

Friday, August 19

Dear Diary, On return from his run, I have a power breakfast ready for my man. I rub his shoulders when he sits down. I get a "Thanks, Honey.

You're the best." But now he is off again to his school office. I look at my driftwood. I think it's some kind of oak. I trim it and sand it a little, forming a nice hand grip. With magic marker, I inscribe the year and the beach.

My golf pro, Tonya calls to remind me of my lesson at 5 pm. She says bring a 5-Iron only. I do my at-home stretches, crunches and sit-ups. I use my Charlie Card on Bus 716 to go to Shaw's. I restock for the weekend. I am putting items away when my man comes home for lunch. I feed him soup and sandwich. I am getting nearly the full housewife experience, except for childcare, of course.

We go outside to shoot baskets. I learn how to take a pass on the run and shoot a lay-up. I twirl my walking stick like a baton then it's time to cool off and have our siesta. Feeling refreshed, I suit up for my golf lesson.

Ponkapoag Public Course is one of his happy places. He brings his 5-iron also. We take tee boxes distant from each other, but we wave occasionally. We have the sun at our backs which allows best possible view of ball flight. Tonya and I spend a lot of time on grip and mechanics. We begin with half swing before proceeding to full swing. At the end of 45 minutes, I make 6 in a row go straight. One of them went to the 100-yard marker. Tonya says I am very coach-able. I make my next appointment for September 3rd. We have dinner in the clubhouse. On our honeymoon, we have fun every day.

We arrive home at dusk. I am aware of Roy flipping channels. I see only his feet from the kitchen table where I write. A pedicure of those man feet is overdue but that is where I draw the line, doing the guy's toenails. What now? Poker, that's it!

Heads up are we at the final table. I have the monopoly money. Who's going to be on top in bed is at stake. After several hands, he goes all in on pocket jacks. I make my flush. The bedroom is on the outer wall. We can make all the noise we want to.

Saturday, August 20

Dear Diary, Coach makes me get up early in the coolness to hit the cinders. I set a new personal at 13 minutes and 45 seconds. In the girls' locker room, I ponder about what if I met Roy in High School. What if we went to separate colleges, but stayed faithful and married right after college? I will tell this tale for him.

We want our Copper City Espresso at Canton Junction train stop. We take our brew on the train to Providence, there to have lunch on our final full day before parting again. I begin to spin my yarn. I am going back for my Senior year at Providence College. We meet on weekends, twice a month, all very clandestine. We don't have much money plus we must take time to study. We help one another on term papers. We sneak around in libraries. I sneak him into my dorm room. He sneaks me into his. Young Roy has a younger me in a parallel universe. I will get him early pictures of me to look at. We do lunch at Olga's Cup and Saucer, an artsy alternative over on Point St. We sit at outdoor tables under an awning. They serve strawberry shortcake. We drop biscuit crumbs to Sparrows hopping about amongst the tables.

The commuter train is our time machine. It takes us a mere 20 miles south, but a long span of 20 years back in time, to a place where I was in full bloom and I was in love. The places have changed little or none. It feels the same. It feels Romantic with a capital R. At the train station, my man must say goodbye to the earlier me. He enters his train car alone. At Canton Junction, the latest version of me steps out of another car and we are together again in the year of our Lord 2011. "What peculiar behavior," some may say. The husband who thinks he knows me completely discovers layers of complexity he never imagined. Mysteries and secrets draw him deeper. He must think about my latest dream. The one which upset me so. I must revisit his analyst couch. It will be like the analysis of Dora by Sigmund Freud except that I will not abandon treatment. Tonight, the Doctor need only examine my body, which for the camera lens, was Aphrodite reborn and later, Mata Hari in her boudoir.

Sunday, August 21

Dear Diary, We have a fan on all night at low setting. Our percolator is on a timer. It helps us wake up. We get ready at a leisurely pace. There will be church so conveniently near and then the rest of the day will sort itself out. Father John leads us through more of the New Testament. I pray for Sylvia. She is not forgotten. We sit. We kneel. We stand. We go in peace to love and serve the Lord.

I visit with Betty in her kitchen. Her spice rack has every spice. Roy shows Richard his man cave. Each treasured item there has a story attached, about a sporting event or a wilderness adventure. By noon, in our well-lit kitchen, we study our favorite sections of the Sunday Herald. The husband gives praise to the wife's avocado toast. We shoot baskets. I swish 3 free throws in a row. Roy does 4 in a row by bank shot. I say that I let him win. In full sun beside the garage door, hangs a rusty old thermometer reading 90. We retreat to our kitchen where frosty mugs are on standby. Roy plays the bartender.

We trade back rubs. I release his tensions. He has many situations to handle, including students ages 13 to 17, a new wife who has expectations, a Jeep which needs an oil change, bills to pay, and a looming invasion by two cats. We turn and he proceeds to calm my worried mind mainly about a secret marriage about to be revealed to concerned family members. While his rough hands work my neck and shoulders, he tells me over and over how everything is going to be all right. He says he is coming with me. It's time for him to meet the parents. Like a Drill-Sargent, he gets me up on my feet and ready to go. We drive straight to Dedham. Dad is on the porch. I say, "Dad, there is someone I would like you to meet. This is Roy and we are married." While Roy and Dad get acquainted, I go to find Mom in the kitchen. I show her my ring. "We know dear," says she. "Robert found out from Darla. He tried his best to stay mum, but you should know he is no match for me." She is thrilled about the Church Wedding in October. An hour later, Roy returns me to Heron St. He stays for dinner and hugs all around.

Monday, August 22

Dear Diary, I sleep alone. My kittens are mad at me for being gone so long. I try to make it up to them. L. left me a note under my pillow saying, "Welcome Back," with a little heart. I have my Perrier and go back to sleep. Per usual, I roll out of bed at 06:00. I stare at my depleted wardrobe. L. laundered some of my stuff. I pick out a skirt and blouse which seem to match. I find leftover biscuits in the fridge and two bag lunches. That is so sweet. I have a personal assistant for a day who shows up at 06:30, smelling really nice. It's YSL, she confides. I am fragrance free. We need not have dueling fragrances. We ride under partly sunny skies. The heat wave has broken. I do my make-up in the visor mirror. We kiss goodbye, as before. I wave from the parking lot.

What am I doing here at this office? I used to work here. I vaguely remember. It seems a lifetime ago. Here comes Susan, the short-timer. She is busting out of her blouse. Is she preggers? We open the office together. We serve a few early walk-ins. She gets her update. My secret guy's no secret anymore. Lorrie Morgan sang about it. On her last day, August 31, Susan promises to dish about her secret love. I type up my resignation letter. My last day will be September 30. Maggie says that it was bound to happen, maybe even overdue. Interviews for replacements will be later this week. I am on auto-pilot in a puddle jumper plane. Two hour jumps from open to break to lunch to break to close. The avocado trees went a little wilted in my absence. I water them and talk to them nicely. Maybe they want to be misted.

L. rolls in at 17:00. She comes in to say hello. We cut the A/C and roll down windows. I find the island music on FM. I tell all about Cape Cod. The supplicants return together to the stained-glass sanctuary of St. Theresa's where we pause our preoccupation with worldly matters. Star Market is our last stop. Casey's shopping list requires just two paper bags. We are home in time for grilled cheese, baby greens, tomato soup and watermelon. We abstain from the Sangria for one day. Exercises are indoors. Aphrodite arrives at midnight. She hugs me tight.

Tuesday, August 23

Dear Diary, Kittens return to my bed. They understand that all has returned to normal. L. goes upstairs to get ready. I find one of Mom's retro ensembles. I toast some bagels. I am busy making lunches when L. returns. A fruit cup of Mandarin Oranges goes well with our tea. We don't have much to say. Just being together is enough, commuting side by side. I wear the fragrance today, my White Linen. It makes me feel very much the young female professional. Our kiss goodbye is orange flavored, lasting longer than usual.

I sigh and gather my things for another routine day. I bring plant food for the baby trees named Sarah and Susan. How big will they get? Someday they may even bloom. The walking, talking Susan is a little late. She looks sleepy. She goes straight to the coffee pot, once more with the jelly doughnuts. Joni is here to help while Sandy does interviews. We feel a little sad at how easily we can be replaced. One of the applicants is a guy. Susan and I escape at lunch according to our habit of late. We walk the property, finding all as it should be. We see the office small in the distance. It represents the past.

L. turns the corner at 17:30. She represents the future. We want Roslindale today. It seems fitting and proper that our partnership business hub should be there where we have prayer central at Holy Epiphany plus coffee and budding artist convergence at Green-T. We pledge to secure at least one job for New Horizons before the end of the year. We are getting hungry but the hunger pangs pass during our prayers.

Pasta night features linguine, artichoke salad and the triumphant return of Papaya infused Sangria. During clean-up, I wash, Lindsey dries. L. has some web page designs to show me, then she has work to do. I have a husband to call. He misses me terribly. We ring off at 21:00. I have time for more of Sherlock. I dive into the case of "The Golden Pince-Nez". Halfway through, I fall asleep with the light on. When the light clicks off, I rouse slightly. In the dim light, L. sheds her nightgown. Ticklish hands draw me close.

Wednesday, August 24

Dear Diary, Our morning proceeds as usual except that today, freshly laundered Yoga gear is stowed away in the back seat. I must drive while L. studies her designs. At drop off, during a nuzzle, close to her ear, I whisper, "Perhaps our love is the balance of nature." L. seems surprised by my poetic spontaneity. She simply replies "Indeed, likely 'tis so." We grin. We sound like early colonial times.

I rapidly change gears dealing with the concerns of the early morning walk-ins. A lady in 12-F fears that she saw a mouse, just out of the corner of her eye. The little devils are so fast. Pest control is on the way. A man in 5-M has been transferred on short notice. He wants to sublet. Such is a problem for Maggie to tackle. At lunch I find as I expected. Susan is pregnant. She almost needs a maternity wedding gown for her small private ceremony on Martha's Vineyard. Maggie already knows. The send-off party will be a baby shower. Motherhood is her destiny but surely not mine.

Per usual on Wednesday, Susan takes me to Yoga where she gets some recommendations for first trimester. Lindsey and her two sidekicks, Monica and Lydia, arrive in due course. The four of us form the back row. We are hitting our lines quite well. We set our intention for a stop at the juice bar. Celery and Grapefruit juice, what a combination! Everyone is in a good mood as we depart The Blissful Monkey. Three cars go off in three directions.

We cruise our way home due south via Centre Street and West Roxbury Parkway. Casey is waiting for us. We mustn't be late for dinner, which is roast beef. Leftovers will make deli style sandwiches. I put an apron on Lindsey. I make her a housewife on a TV sitcom. She washes. I dry. We bring votive candles to our private chapel, the laundry room, there to pray while Casey is on the phone with William. Our entreaties fly heavenward. L. wants to call her Mom before it's too late up there in Vermont. Sylvia says that she is feeling ok. She is happy to hear her little girl's voice. Her next appointment in Boston is Tuesday after Labor Day. We crash early, and stay deep down 'til first light.

Thursday, August 25

Dear Diary, Some dogs barking wake us at 05:45. L. gets her slippers on. She needs a sleepy hug before going upstairs to dress. I slam a cold coffee and trudge my way into the shower. A cool one is best for my skin. A quick blow dry, finger comb and ponytail fits my mood. I can go braless in my tunic top. Stretchy dress jeans should match ok. I am ready at 06:15. I keep the tropical fruit cocktail cold in the fridge. L. comes to share.

The air outside smells almost like Vermont. There is dew on the grass. We are on the verge of Autumn and Football. We have 5 more weeks of commuting daily. I treasure them. Drop off is way early. L. comes in to hang out a bit while I fire up the office. She takes a sip of the fresh brew, just enough to tweak her up to optimum and ready for the rest of her solo trip.

All of us girls at Chestnut Hill are up to speed by 08:00. Maggie conducts our team meeting. Evan, the guy applicant, got the job offer to replace Susan. He begins orientation next week. I wonder what Roy is doing. I phone in at lunch. He helped at football practice. He sprays some Jean Nate on my side of the bed and hugs my pillow at night.

On afternoon break, Phil is out there vaping. We get our innocent flirts from a distance. Susan avoids the vapors. A little filing fills out the rest of the afternoon. L. strolls in at 17:20. She tries out the ergonomic desk while I log out and shut down. I imagine her working beside me in our partners office. We might need a rule of no making out in the office. No making out in church. That's another good rule, except for the laundry room chapel of course. Of all of our saints, we feel most in tune with St. Theresa to channel our supplications and that is where we linger 17:45, in the front row beneath her statue. She was a member of the Carmelite Sisterhood. She stands there serenely, wearing vestments of tan and brown. Her collar is white and her cap is black. We make an offering and light our candles.

The offering in Casey's kitchen is breast of chicken from her air fryer, green beans and mashed potatoes left over from yesterday. We are grateful.

Friday, August 26

Dear Diary, Walking at dusk last night, we breathe deep and peer through branches into edge of autumn star-scapes. We question neighborhood dogs to see which ones were barking at 05:15. We suspect two mutts over on Grouse St. At 22:00, L. joins me in bed. We just want to sleep alternating spoon positions under a single sheet. Our feet are vulnerable to attack by felines who occupy the foot of the bed. Uninterrupted slumber ensues all the way to 6 am alarm. I serve up cereal, juice and hardboiled eggs on toast, sprinkled with parsley flakes. L. has the lunches and away we go. Let's get this over with. We are eager for our weekend. L. will be framing by day, socializing in cafés by night. Jessica is her tour guide. I will be feathering my new nest. There is something lively on the classical station, some ballet music vaguely familiar. L. watches me do my model walk up to the office door. I turn and wave and blow a kiss.

Susan has opened. Already phones are ringing. We are off to the races, working at max efficiency. I process early payments for September. I inspect one early move-out in 2-M and bag found items. We respond to all e-mails. We update waiting lists.

Sandy covers so that Susan and I get to go early. She drops me near the MFA on her way to meet the Coast Flyer.

L. is just finishing up some frame repairs. We exit the MFA at 16:30. We divert to Dorchester to pick up Jessica. We zig-zag 6 miles across town, passing Au Beurre Chaud Bakery where we stop to grab a bag of baguettes.

Roy is waiting for me. We have five for fish fry. I squirt lemon in my eye. Dr. Roy makes it all better. What a guy! He even helps with the dishes. I stuff my weekender. I wave goodbye until Sunday. I am torn between my sisterhood comfort zone and my brave new world in Canton. We go straight home. Roy has stocked some white wine coolers for me. These will chase the fish nicely. I strip for him then he strips for me. We lather up really well. We don our robes, two silky ones for summer. In bed flipping channels, my leg show is unbearably provocative for the 5-day celibate man bedside me.

Saturday and Sunday, August 27 and 28

Dear Diary, I have breakfast ready for the running man on his return. He likes his eggs over easy. I care for my rose bushes while he showers. I see him watching me from the bathroom window with shave cream on his face. He puts a shave cream heart on the window. We stay home today. I want to snoop everywhere. A little door opens to a crawl space. I see a spider. I close the door quickly. Roy says the spider is his security guard.

There is a fold down ladder to the attic. I look with a flashlight. I see an outside air vent and a shoe-box sitting on some 2 by 4 planks. I reach the shoe-box with a stick. I blow the dust off the lid and see papers inside. We examine the contents at Roy's desk. We find receipts from the 1980's, some newspaper clippings, some old photos and a bankbook showing a savings of $157. Betty and Richard may understand the meaning of this stash as they knew the previous owners.

I take a break from snooping to make lunch. I round up all the remaining fresh veggies for a deluxe garden salad with blue cheese dressing. I add croutons and bacon bits. I serve some of those baguettes from yesterday with butter. Suzy Homemaker is having fun. This is an easy clean-up. Vegetable scraps go to compost. Now I snoop all of the kitchen cabinets. I find a waxed checkered tablecloth, but it is for a square table-for-two. I find a rolling pin, a French Fry slicer, and forgotten onions beginning to sprout. In the back is an old mousetrap un-sprung. I leave it alone. Roy has a mini dust buster, battery operated. I get the tops of the cabinets, finding one dead roach. I sweep and damp mop. I crack the windows, set up a little electric fan and watch the curtains flutter.

I hear activity in the man cave. For a broken table leg, Roy makes a splint with two worm gear clamps. Now we have a square table. I give it a Lemon Pledge treatment and spread the checkered tablecloth. Two wobbly cane chairs, went with this. I offer Roy $10 each for them. He wants $20 each. We dicker. He accepts $25 for the pair. I pay cash. He gives me a receipt.

The newlyweds happily play house. Dinner is hamburgers, baked beans, and sliced peaches. Next, I want to snoop in the old couch. The pillow covers are removable leaving discolored naked foam. Down in the cracks I find 37 cents, lots of lint and a bobby pin. I confront Roy with the bobby pin. He has no idea how it got there except maybe I planted it. One ex-girlfriend might have been on there years ago. "Was she naked?" I want to know. "Only topless. Her tits were decent but yours are the best ever," he goes on to explain.

All this talk about tits leads us to the bedroom. The couch is temporarily out of order. From the bedroom, we hear the dryer stop. The cushion covers have become a lighter shade of brown creating a two-tone couch. It's okay for now. The final snoop is Roy's bookshelf. I find "Catcher in the Rye", a tattered discard from Roy's High School in Sanford, Maine. This will be a change from Conan Doyle. Roy has "Love in the Time of Cholera", English translation. We read side by side in bed. We play footsie. I find some nice music on my bedside clock radio. Two lamps switch off within minutes of each other. One long deep sigh invites slumber to descend over the marriage bed.

I stretch and look at the digital dial. OMG, It's 8 o'clock already. Roy gives his razor the day off on Sunday. That saves time. Okay, so we sneak into Mass a little late but we stay late to greet some parishioners and update Father John with family information of the bride and groom. Should we have a rehearsal? Mom says "for sure" to that. She wants all the pomp and circumstance. She considers me not fully, properly married yet. The husband volunteers to serve me his typical bachelor brunch including a big mess of Jimmy Dean's sausages, grapefruit halves sprinkled with brown sugar, some tube biscuits 'n jam and coffee with Bailey's Irish Cream. I am impressed.

Our neighbors trade The Herald for the shoe box left behind by The McPhersons. One of the family members remains local. He will be happy to have it. Enough fun playing house. Our Sunday scenic drive in the country is next.

We end up at Medfield State Hospital again. Their souvenir shop is open. I buy a book about the place. Then comes a very pleasant 14-mile meander along Pleasant St. and High St., back to the women's world of 14 Heron Street.

L. has the proofs of the Medfield photo shoot with Casey. They send chills up and down my spine. Roy only wants watermelon and iced tea. We serve him gladly. He looks at the photos and then at Casey, eyes wide. Our actress in residence played the part of the lost soul wonderfully. Sadly, our Sunday is drawing to a close. The wife who must work tomorrow watches the beloved husband drive off, waving cavalierly as he makes his turn. Jessica gets to ride home in Dave's Uber Toyota. She loves the leather.

All is well. We have our walk. We watch MeTV at my place, popsicles in hand, cats in attendance. Casey calls William from my phone. Roy calls to give a phone smooch goodnight. By 22:30, we are all sleepy. Fatima goes upstairs. Felicia stays with me. We set our alarms. Goodnight.

Monday, August 29

Dear Diary, Ah! A big sigh and a big stretch. Lights up full. Felicia watches me shower. It's the last week of summer. I am suited up by 06:20, right on schedule. Fresh kibble and fresh water are in the cat bowls. Fresh sand is in the scratch boxes. The sand reminds me of Cape Cod. L helps me with the lunches. She gets a pear. I get a nectarine. The Malibu gets a full tank at 7-Eleven.

The air went slightly cool overnight. I have a little jacket over my bare shoulders top. I need it because the A/C is still full blast in the office. The new guy, Evan, shows up at 08:30. He is tall, sharp-dressed, well-coiffed and he speaks Spanish. He will go far. He comes to us from Hotel Guest Services background. Susan and I show him around until Sandy arrives. He likes the ergonomic desk. Sandy takes hm to the back offices for HR stuff.

Joni joins us at 09:00. We three knock out all of the routine stuff by break time. Sitting at the break room table, I reach across and ask Susan how she feels. "Still a little nervous," she admits. I tell her about my dream in which I am a tropical fish. She smiles. "It wasn't funny when I dreamed it," I assure her. We empathize our way to lunch. On our walk, we stop in on the Hennigs, Fritz and Kitty. We tell them our news. They say stop by anytime you revisit Chestnut Hill. They are settled in for life. Abandonment is scary but so, in a way, is "settled in for life". Are we too young for that, Susan and I, I wonder? I catch myself daydreaming as the afternoon rolls along. The year has become something far beyond my expectations. A big, unexpected part of it is right around the corner.

Lindsey's hair is a little tousled this afternoon. She waves at me on arrival at 17:30. I notice that her eye level is only slightly above the steering wheel but her hands are properly at 10 and 2. She is so adorable! Certainly, others see it as well, but they have no chance, it seems.

We go straight to St. Theresa's. What would she say to us if we met her in person? For one, we could thank her for her fine example of purity. What was it like for her living in the 1500s? Was she ever in love with a man or a woman? These topics require research. What exactly was her daily life? I mean to ask the Pastor, Father Leo, about this. He should know. We maintain our reverence until L. switches off the ignition in our driveway..

We are very hungry by now. Our girl bodies have smaller gas tanks than muscle bound man bodies do. We detect the spicy aroma of stir-fry. Endive salad goes great with that. A cherry pie is cooling but dessert waits until after our walk. We make it a brisk one. We shower and return in our robes for our treat which includes a scoop of vanilla ice cream on the side.

During coffee, we toss around suggestions for Susan's Bridal Shower gift. Suddenly, I know where to shop for it. William left behind an open bottle of Cognac. We toast to secret love, mystery love, misunderstood love, and "the love that dare not speak its name". The cognac is Courvoisier. We sniff and sip from tiny aperitif glasses. At 21:00, I leave my upstairs companions for a little solitude. My face is flushed from just one shot of the elixir. On the phone, Roy can tell I am tipsy. It's more like I am high on life. I brush and floss dutifully. I splash water on my face. I record these impressions of another happy day.

Tuesday, August 30

Dear Diary, L. is sleeping on her tummy, with legs in figure 4. On the small of her back, Fatima is resting, waiting for something to happen. Both cats follow me to the kitchen. Their needs are easily met. When I return, L. is sitting up, rubbing her eyes. I hand her Perrier. She drains it in two tilts of the mini green glass bottle. I get a sleepy smile as she exits to stairs. We breakfast separately, grabbing bites and sips while choosing items to wear.

Together again in the car, we are freshly flossed, rinsed and ready for a kiss. We repeat at drop off, a perfectly natural and nice way to start the day. I unlock, start the coffee and reboot. I take my mug back outside. Susan brings her mug out there beside me, seated on a step. We don't have much to say. We just enjoy the cool morning air and check out the cloud formations. We wave to Sandy as she pulls in and act as doormen.

The office workday officially begins. We chat a little with Evan, naming things in Spanish such as "escritorio y computadora". He has more training modules so it's "Hasta luego, amigo." Susan wants the phone and walk-ins. I do the rest. At lunch, we take Evan to meet Patrick and the maintenance crew. At afternoon break, I call Kappy's

Coins & Collectibles in Norwood. He still has the items I require. I arrange a pick up that very afternoon. I need to leave early. Dave will come to get me. I text Lindsey to meet me at Perks in Norwood about 17:30.

Kappy is closed for the day but he opens just for me at 16:30. His wife has gift wrapped my items nicely. I pay cash and wait happily for Lindsey at Perk's. Cameron is there. She recognizes me. I tell her about my wedding and how I need another bridesmaid. She is available and happy to come. L. is thirsty again. We both do a nitro cold brew. We go way in the back in a dark corner to do our prayer vigil ad-lib.

Waiting for us at home is a sandwich buffet including pickles, olives, raw veggies and grapes. We walk it off until twilight as is our custom. L. has work to do. I go below to fill out my gift card and have a nice cool shower. While Sherlock follows his clues, my eyelids get heavy. Soon enough, L. appears wanting back tickles.

Wednesday, August 31

Dear Diary, Signs of autumn are perking me up. Pow!! I am up out of bed in a flash. L. gets a smack on the butt which normally she doesn't like but I can't resist. By the time she returns from above, I have hot breakfast ready and her lunch packed. The artist fixes my hair clips achieving a more stylish look. At drop off, we nuzzle on both cheeks. I grab my gift package, run to the office door and wave goodbye.

I feel very light. From the break room window, I see Susan and Evan arriving. We are all early. We settle in slowly instead of rush job. Susan shadows the new guy as he performs his main functions on our two platforms. Susan takes a call on her cell outside. I brief Evan about the going away party at lunchtime and the task I have for him. Joni is here to say goodbye and cover the phones. Maggie and Sandy arrive carrying hot boxes containing sundry take-out Italian dishes which smell wonderful.

The party gets started at 11:30. A card we all have signed features a Victorian Couple in Silhouette. It talks about "Something Old, Something New, Something Borrowed, Something Blue, and a Silver Six Pence for her Shoe". Evan, as substitute Dad, walks Susan into the break room and slips the sixpence into her shoe. My offering is his-and-hers Sterling Silver necklace lockets, circa 1926. From Sandy is two sets of baby clothes with booties, one set in pink, another in blue. From Maggie is her lace wedding veil to borrow. From Joni, is a set of eight linen table napkins in powder blue. Susan is touched so deeply that she can barely lift her glass of non-alcoholic bubbly for the toast to the soon-to-be newlyweds. This is a perfect photo-op for the break room album. We all linger at lunch until Joni needs relief. Joni lingers with Susan for a while as she packs her stuff. We discharge her early, 2 pm. There are hugs all around, noses sniffle and tears flow as we watch her go. The office will never be the same. I let out a big sigh and mindlessly click through my remaining tasks. Life goes on. I will see Susan again socially, for sure. I come out of my trance at St. Theresa's, with L. beside me, holding my hand.

Thursday, September 1

Dear Diary, Until I saw Susan actually drive away, my happy status quo was still intact. But afterward, I must have gone numb for several hours. We were such great pals, year after year. She was a solid amid uncertainty. I don't even remember what we had for dinner yesterday, something yellow, corn on the cob, perhaps. L. allows me space to grieve the loss.

We complete our morning rituals in low key fashion. I manage to deliver a little smile of appreciation at drop off. Evan has few questions. I show him once and he has got it. The day proceeds business-like. Roy is my lifeline at lunch. He reminds me of upcoming Labor Day holiday and 3-day weekend and how much fun we will have. Susan's secret guy remains unknown. I have an idea about who he is. The doughnuts are a clue. Someday, I will find out for sure. For now, "Mum's the word". "Loose lips sink ships," Grandaddy used to say.

Roy has been revealed to all. At least that ship is not sinking. He is my Captain. He is my hero, at long last. I sail away home with First Mate Lindsey on our usual late afternoon commute. The Malibu cruises smoothly along VFW Parkway. St. Theresa receives us into her Sanctuary. I offer prayers for both Sylvia and Susan.

Casey offers Shepherd's Pie with side salad of cucumbers and tomatoes. The 3 Musketeers change into jogging gear. It feels great to hit the girls' locker room shower after. My upstairs guests arrive with popsicles and Sangria, our wine placebo, since it is diluted down so much with juices. I guess I am mellowing out a bit. Old time antenna TV helps. We escape to Mayberry, RFD. We get Bewitched. We trade neck rubs. Casey wants both cats. She is lonely waiting for her William. L. stays with me. We open all of the windows so that curtains will flutter and night sounds will enter. We watch one another walk around naked. Of course, I have the most jiggle. L. has the cutest belly button. We are weary and we just want to sleep but first some tickles. A goose quill feather gives goose bumps. An ostrich plume produces total relaxation.

Friday, September 2

Dear Diary, I awaken with L. staring at me. My finger does a ski jump on her nose. I rush to get the shower first but I am on the wrong side of the bed. In robe and slippers, I rub my eyes, stare past the curtains. Sun is not up yet. I start the Java. Where are the kittens? Oh, that's right. Casey has them. In a quick 20 we are dressed and staring at each other across our bowls of oatmeal and blueberries. L. wins the staring contest. We have a cool but pleasant morning. From the passenger seat, my hand rides the wind. Here we are at drop off, time for an early morning kiss. How many more will there be like this? Just 19 more mornings before I move on. I turn, wave, and sigh.

Sandy and Evan arrive at 08:00. They work together most of the day. I mostly work the phones. Now I am the short timer. I am lonely at lunch. I check in on Sheila in 6-G. She offers me a cup of vanilla infusion tea. She loves her unit, my first design project. She will allow photos to show my future customers. I note the personal touches she has added. There is a doily on the back of her big stuffed stair. She has 2 empty walls. She says we may show her some artwork.

On return Sandy has some filing for me. I tend to the avocado trees. I call my man. I call Bill to order some prints of Mata Hari. One for Sheila and another for Roger Quinn. I wait for L. to appear and take me to Holy Epiphany. We make it there by 18:00. We visit churches like so many oases on our journey.

At home, we unload the latest framed prints of Aphrodite. I point to them and say "Mine". L. points to the furniture and says "Mine". Already she wants to re-arrange it. That can wait because we smell fish fry Friday in progress upstairs. The aroma drives the cats crazy. We shouldn't let them beg for table scraps. Isn't raw better for them? We don't even know. We take them to their fancy feast. For our cool evening, we need light jackets and flashlights. Stars appear, winking down at the fitness parade of 3 young women in varying degrees of love entanglement. Miles away, maybe Susan is walking in sand under the same. My consoler is lightly bedside me another night.

Saturday, September 3

Dear Diary, I am not quite ready when I detect the rumble of Roy's Jeep Wrangler. He comes inside to lasso me. He doesn't mind pausing for a waffle while I finish packing. Heat and humidity are predicted. A big bottle of Banana Boat aloe vera gel is the final item stuffed into my duffle bag. I model my cut-off jeans shorts. "Too much cheek?" I ask. "You are in the decent exposure category," the fashion critic replies. The kittens have already been kidnapped, so I must I go upstairs to say goodbye. Casey and Lindsey have plans. I am dispensable. As I take my

4-wheeler passenger seat, they are each holding one cat and waving one paw goodbye through the upstairs windows.

Surprise, we are going to beaches of Maine and meeting up with Roy's reclusive old man, Sam. We are northbound 76 miles to Long Sands Beach, ME. We start happily on Centre St. and Jamaica Way. We cross the Charles at North End. We cross the Mystic River on the Tobin Toll Bridge. From there it is clear sailing through to Portsmouth on Rt. 1, NE Expressway with me as navigator. We are booked at The Stones Throw Hotel and Restaurant. Good choice, Roy. Our fairytale romance continues.

We drop our luggage and find food on the boardwalk. We dip our toes in the ocean. I find a sand dollar, a nice one. Our second-floor room is ready. We have a balcony. Without delay, we hit the pool. Roy needs his 20 laps. Two laps are enough for me. While I wait for him, my sheer one-piece and I have our Coppertone time. Roy orders cocktails from the Tiki Bar, a Pina Colada for me, Heinekens from the bottle for him.

This makes a perfect prelude to siesta. Man does not live by beer alone. We turn the bed into a tangled mess. We hit the sand venturing waist deep intent on getting hit by big waves just to feel the power of the Atlantic alongside which we are as insignificant as 2 grains of sand. Outdoor dining features Fish Tacos for the Mrs. and Crab Cakes for the Mister. We go inside to the bar lounge for black coffee and Key Lime pie. By 10 pm, we find our firm bed and balcony with ocean breeze. The last thing I remember are curtains swaying gently.

Sunday, September 4

Dear Diary, 8 am is the time for Tarzan to swim 20 laps. Jane brings coffee poolside. "A guy who is married to you needs to stay in shape," says my man as he dries off and dons his bathrobe. Later, we shop souvenirs. Roy wants another big conch so that we have his and hers at the bedside. This whole being married deal, he is really getting into it and so am I. Once upon a time, I had only fantasies but the reality is far better.

Meanwhile, Sanford, Maine is a mere 25 scenic miles inland. Once more, I am navigator from a paper map. There are many twists and turns. The tree density increases as the two-lanes narrow. Sanford is pleasant enough, similar to Brattleboro. North Main St. takes us 5 miles to Emery Mills. We pick up some luxury items at One Earth Natural Foods, which is some kind of glorified general store. It turns out that Sam craves buttermilk.

By noon, we arrive at Sam's retirement cottage on Hill Top Lane. He's got every kind of fishing and wildlife an outdoorsman desires at his fingertips. After introductions, we occupy the guest rocking chairs with iced tea in hand. Sam shaves once a week, the same day he goes to town and that was yesterday, leaving him lightly grizzled today. He figured his son for a confirmed bachelor but has been proven wrong and not for the first time. He takes us on a trail tour showing the camera traps. He wants to go out to early dinner at his favorite watering hole, namely, the Iron Tails Saloon on the other side of Mousam Lake. We share an incredible deep-dish pizza at outdoor tables. We sit a mere 80 miles from Boston city life but it seems like a different planet. Sam likes to be home before dark. Back at the cabin, we get to see the latest visitors caught on camera trap, including Bobcat, Black Bear, Fox, Turkey and rarely, a Moose.

The guest bedroom needs a little airing out. There is a lumpy bed with squeaky springs, but we make do. I see a portrait of Roy's Mom, Gloria. She looks like me just a bit. At lights out, I peek through curtains to find a lovely quarter moon but the night sounds I hear are scary. "What was that?" I shudder. "Country creatures night-life," explains Roy.

Monday, September 5

Dear Diary, The men are up early conversing in low tones. What are they planning? I dress quickly. Roy has been telling about my interior design and wondering if I have any ideas about this place. "I wouldn't change a thing," I assure them. "That's my girl," says Sam. "I give my blessing to this marriage," he adds with a grin. "Take a look at what you've got, young lady. It seems to me that you got a husband who can cook. Count yourself lucky," he continues. My short-order cook, plates the pancakes and bacon. From the back of the cupboard, he pulls out 3 jars of locally made preserves instead of syrup. I go for the blueberry and the blackberry. I get to choose my coffee mug from an assortment hanging from hooks. I grab the one with the moose on it. "We drink it black here," Roy explains. "Black it shall be," I consent. I detect the presence of chicory. "Would this be 'Chock Full of Nuts?" I guess. "You would be right about that," says Sam.

I try to describe the noises I was hearing outside last night. "Some of them likely were George, sneaking around. He's a little shy. He stays mostly outside," explains Sam. George overcomes his shyness to greet me on the front porch after I fill his bowl. George is a mid-size shaggy dog of mixed breed. It seems like he and I will get along. George doesn't bark just to be barking, I am told. If he sounds off, you better go investigate. We say our farewells at mid-afternoon.

We choose express routes back to the city. Roy can't stay for supper. He has some prep for 1st day of school. He parks and gets out to deliver a lingering hug and kiss, the whole sweet sorrow at parting scene, even though it's only to be four days absence. A lot happened while I was gone. Casey is seriously going steady with William, who came for dinner on Saturday. Busy girl Lindsey got a lot of print jobs completed. She booked her next show at Galerie D'Orsay for Friday, 10/28, including "Worn to Perfection" and "Lost Souls". She did some publicity shots for Chad's actor book and she hung out at coffee shops in Dorchester with Jessica. I tell my adventures in ocean and forest. I record all of this with kittens beside me and pillow beckoning.

Tuesday, September 6

Dear Diary, We commence four more weeks of our happy routine. Everything can't last forever. We mean to enjoy every minute. Commuting partners are helping each other wake up. If I try to snooze, I hear Miss Lindsey walking about above me. Lately, we have been doing oatmeal, with berries. Today, our coffee is espresso in a demi-tasse with cookie on the side. L. is giving me one of her subtle looks as she sips. It feels like the look of love seen through the veil of her mystique.

I fill the bird feeders. We wipe the windows because nights are going below dew point. She is calm. The driver must stay calm. I close my eyes and take deep breaths. In a mere 15 minutes we roll to a stop. L. puts it in park with the motor running. She leans over for our kiss see-ya-later.

I unlock and survey the empty office. I start up Mr. Coffee. A Dunkins box with one dried out doughnut remains in the fridge. I am tempted to just leave it there in Susan's memory. Sandy and Evan come waltzing in. He is telling jokes in Spanish. He translates the punch line. In Spanish, the punch line alone makes me laugh. Okay, I guess I can do another day's worth of work. I have ideas, important ideas, such as 2 model units, both rentable on weekends. Maybe Evan can fix it so that they both stay booked at premium pricing every weekend year-round.

I show Evan inventory and filing. He is great on the phone already. At lunch I check to see that the model is clean and ready to show. Phil is outside but he is depressed, so he says. After lunch, I am simply available when Evan has questions.

I keep watching for the Malibu to reappear. At 17:45, it finally does. The office is empty. L. doesn't see me. She parks and looks for me inside where I am inviting her to the privacy of the storeroom. A married woman is her lover, just as she prefers. It turns out to be our biggest lust attack ever producing multiples just from being in a clinch with clothing loosened and kisses as deep and wet as possible. Minutes later, we sit in church praying and not feeling the least bit guilty. The flush of passion is still there on arrival home.

Wednesday, September 7

Dear Diary, I left out yesterday evening but I am awake early so let's see. It's getting dark earlier so we walked first and dined later. Casey fixed up some mix-and-match leftovers. Lindsey had work to do and I went to bed early. Sleep is important. I love to sleep but I was sleeping alone and that is less fun so here I am filling in the blanks. My 2 fur-balls watch me as I write. L. promised to pack lunches which gives me extra time to puzzle over what to wear. I find one of Mom's pants suits with a loose-fitting double-breasted jacket top.

It's fun for me to stuff some-buttered toast into Lindsey's mouth on arrival. I asked her "kiss or toast?" She said "toast," so that's what she got. She watches me with amusement as she munches. I serve up tropical fruit salad and cottage cheese. In the car we do pilot and co-pilot check list. Enough gas? Check. Lunches? Check. Yoga outfits? Check. We taxi over to Washington St. and turn left just as so many times before. I dial in 100.7 WZLX, the light-hearted morning drive show. Three songs and a few jokes later, my arrival is still way early. I offer my kiss through the rolled down driver's side window.

I grab a copy of the Globe from the vendor box outside our door. I tire of strictly online searches. We should keep a copy in the breakroom. Joni arrives next. She takes Susan's desk. Evan takes the ergonomic desk. He has lifelines left and right. We 3 lunch together while Sandy takes over. At afternoon break, I notify L. that I will Uber over to the Blissful Monkey. She and her assistants can get extra work done.

Rain begins to fall as my driver arrives in his Lexus. I have time to peek in the Goodwill Store. I have seen other designers there with checklists, mainly for decorative items. I am all suited up when the others arrive. Monica and Lydia are their usual cheerful selves. We form a pastel rainbow along the back row.

Most of our inbound is tree lined. Some fall colors are showing. Pasta night dinner is served. L. makes crazy cocktails with Jager and Gin. We giggle the evening away. My slumber partner and I depart to our downstairs sanctuary.

Thursday, September 8

Dear Diary, Am I hung over? Maybe just a little. L. brings me grapefruit juice. What to wear? A daily dilemma at the edge of a new season. I settle on a loose-fitting khaki pleated skirt and belted zip-up jacket from the 1980s, when Mom was size 6. For breakfast toaster waffles pop up. We pack soup, veggie sticks and chips for lunch. Apricot tea is infusing in our travel mugs.

I want to drive but Lindsey says, "No! Mine!" Perhaps she fought with her sister over toys once upon a time. She grins at me as her little rear end gets seated behind the wheel. She is a good driver, I must admit. Our apricot flavored goodbye kiss turns into a mini make-out, the kind we flaunted in front of Susan not so long ago. She likes my retro outfits. They are the kind older married women wore when she first started lusting. We disengage reluctantly. Duty calls. Booty calls must wait.

I spend my office hours on auto-pilot. Evan tells more jokes. So far, they are all clean jokes. Phil is still depressed but he perks up a little when a young woman named Shannon comes to interview. He pulls me aside and whispers, "Fix it so she gets hired." "I'll do my best," I promise.

L. re-appears at 17:15. We go directly to Holy Epiphany. We kneel on opposite sides of the aisle up front. We both light candles with an offering, mirror image. We skip our usual visit to Green-T. We are home earlier than usual, plenty of time before dinner to finish what we started that morning. It's intense and over quickly. We need a cold shower. She kisses the nail marks on my back. My happy year of nymphomania rolls on. Just the one great guy and the one super seductive girl upstairs are delivering all of the satisfaction I can handle.

We just burned a lot of calories. We worked up an appetite for Casey's Gazpacho, Charcuterie Board, and tropical fruit salad complemented by chilled White Zinfandel. We three low paid working girls know how to live in-style. We are good girls, law abiding, and tax paying. We are not exactly great examples of chastity, but we leave that to others. Near midnight, a cat lands on my bed and girlish hands hold me.

Friday, September 9

Dear Diary, Casual Friday means jeans, flats, and that tunic top from Cape Cod plus a little wind-breaker during morning chill. L. has moved some of her clothes down here. I watch my brunette Barbie Doll get dressed in girl trousers, white silk blouse, V-Neck sweater and loafers. She pins back her hair on one side, adds lipstick, blush, pendent earrings and some of my White Linen. She simply states that today she feels maximum girly girl. Also, she has a meeting with her boss, John Lowery. We stop at 7-Eleven for gas. I deliver a hot breath kiss goodbye on the exposed bejeweled ear. She smells heavenly.

I march inside without delay. I mean to get some serious work done pronto and be free to leave early. Sandy is with Evan all day for advanced training. I pretty much handle it all from my usual desk. At lunch, I get calls from brother James, sister Sally and Mom. She already has spoken to Father John. She will arrange everything. It will be the perfect occasion for family re-union. I must submit my guest list ASAP. The reception will be for 50 at The Knights of Columbus in Norwood. It will be a duplicate of kid-sister Sally's wedding 10 years ago, except fine-tuned by my wedding planner, Mom. Lindsey of course will be photographer.

Okay, I do a big exhale and back to work I go. Sandy lets me go at 15:00. Dave is nearby to take me to Boston MFA. I wait for L. in her work room. She shows up all excited. Mr. Lowery offered her a salaried position, an office, a raise, and flexible work hours. He thinks she should be published. He recommends Taschen, a German art book publisher. He says her interns did a great job and he was happy to have them. She lets me drive while she goes on and on.

We take time out to give thanks at St. John Chrysostom. We depart from there all serene. It's still early. Casey just got home and yes, she will be maid of honor. We all need a siesta. We 3 rendezvous in my kitchen at 19:00. Lindsey and I do our best to fix some decent Tacos and Spanish Rice. Some of Roy's cervezas remain. We tune in Hitchcock and Twilight Zone on MeTV.

Saturday, September 10

Dear Diary, We wake up at our usual time of 06:00. L. helps me pack more stuff which will stay at Canton such as half of my shoes, then she goes upstairs to pack more of her stuff to bring down here. Since she owns my old furniture, she warns me that things might be re-arranged when I get back on Sunday. The little ones just stare, trying to comprehend what changes are happening in their world of 3 caretakers and 2 beds to sleep in.

I have a light breakfast ready for my transporter. I tell him how much I missed him. It's only been 4 days, but he was busy with school. We are young. We have goals and things to accomplish. We help one another, never hinder. Summer was the time to wander aimlessly looking for adventure. We head straight home via US 1, Boston-Providence Turnpike and Neponset St., 15 minutes to cover the 10 miles. The sunroof is open but I got my sunglasses on. With windows down, we get the max road noise and wind in my hair.

Roy's tee time is 11:40. My lesson is noon. We have plenty of time to get ready. We will do better if no sex before sports. I change into my shorts and Polo shirt. Roy's gear includes some loose-fitting stretchy super light pants in pale blue. He will be sharing a cart for 9 with Jordan, the wrestling coach. For me today's lesson is more of the 5 iron then sand wedges in a shallow practice bunker. While waiting for Roy to finish, I have fun in the pro shop. I pick out an Argyle sweater. We dine in the Clubhouse with Jordan. He is a bachelor and he agrees to play the part of best man. R. is doing all of the stuff he likes to do with the added pleasure of me along for the ride, plus he wants to show me off, he says.

We are home by 4 pm. I agree not to clean anything and just slum it. Most every weekend, we can regress to college dorm room messy. That's fine with me. I do just a small laundry load. There is room in back for a clothes line. Mr. Handyman fixes it up for me. The neighbors are fenced off. They won't care. I serve spaghetti on the little square table in the man cave. We do mugs of brew, ESPN view, and overdue screwing.

Sunday, September 11

Dear Diary, There must be a rooster around here somewhere. I could swear that is what woke me. R. says he is the only rooster. We dress in crinkled whites for Mass. Our stuff tumble dried co-mingled last night. I clean the lint trap. I find a dime and 2 pennies. I deposit them in the cookie jar where a good amount is accumulating. Roy wants it for emergency beer and pizza money.

Our walk to and from church is as good as a morning run. Father John has Roy's Baptismal certificate from Holy Family in Sanford. Roger Quinn calls. He is in the area with my antique vanity. My men offload the item into the man cave carefully. It weighs a ton. Assembly of mirrors brackets is required. I put the provenance in my designated drawer of our office. I hand over his framed prints. They are well wrapped but Roy admits that he peeked. Roger covers them in heavy blankets.

Richard is pleased to swap the Sunday Herald for the weekday editions of The Globe which I pick up at work. Betty is happy to share the clothes line. She tells of her misadventures in the multitude of sand traps she has known. If there was one anywhere near, her ball would find it. It preferred sand over water. At the bachelor kitchen we do not even remove trash because overnight, it routinely attracts raccoons who make a mess of it. The trash goes out Monday morning before work.

Supper is simple soup and salad and leave the dishes. The former bachelor will do them tomorrow. Slaving in the kitchen on Sunday seems wrong. I agree. Sun is setting. I want to shoot baskets. At least I don't totally suck at that. At twilight time, my transporter whisks me away to return another day. He pauses to see what desserts may be in Casey's kitchen. He gets a hunk of apple pie a la mode to savor while he enjoys the charms of the forbidden fruit dwelling in my woman's world. I wore him out pretty well plus they are way too impossibly young for even a fantasy. Also, they lack my sophistication and my wonderful to behold hip line. I walk the man to his Wrangler. Our big kiss goodbye is all Apples and Cinnamon. L. sequestered some of my former furniture she doesn't want. She says I can buy it back.

Monday, September 12

Dear Diary, I get my one night alone to transition to the world of women. I sleepwalk to the fridge for my 2 am Perrier. The little green girl sized glass bottles look nice beside Roy's beer. I even want to design fridge interiors so that people don't get depressed when they look at the mess in there. At breakfast, I buy back my rejected furniture items for a dollar. What have we here? An ugly lamp with a 40-watt bulb, a tippy end table, and 2 wobbly kitchen chairs circa 1960. They go to my basement storage cage. Roy can cannibalize them for parts in his workshop.

Three more weeks remain of the happy routine of lesbian lovers Lindsey and Sarah Jane, one of whom has a husband on the side. Will I be punished for this? Only if Mom finds out, she will punish me with disapproval. But then, maybe she had a girl crush once upon a time and nobody will ever know. My kiss goodbye comes with a tickle starting at the knee and moving up, a prelude for tonight.

Now comes a routine day, a little of everything which I have done so many times before. Susan phones in from a public phone, area code 774. Strange. Everything is ok. People can come and visit, maybe next year. I find out that Maggie hired Shannon. She starts next week and she is single. Phil gets the good news. If she is a vaper, he has a chance for quality time.

L. comes at 17:30. She honks for me. I forgot what the Malibu horn sounds like. I make her wait. She pretends she is leaving without me. We are both in a really good mood. We get serious at St. Theresa and get giggly at home. Dinner is not ready so we go to the storage cages. I wear kitchen stove mitts in case of spiders. I have some cardboard boxes in there. L. provides proper vinyl storage crates.

Casey made chili, 4 alarm, with melted cheese on top and Pita bread on the side. For dessert is watermelon, yea! We have a half hour to strut the neighborhood, starting with slow walking and ending up fast walking. We cool down during kitchen clean-up. I freshen up alone and wait to see who might sneak in after hours. At 2 am, I have a sparkling water drinking companion.

Tuesday, September 13

Dear Diary, It's 6 am. We have got to get up. C'mon! There are hungry cats to feed. You have art to display. You have extra new responsibilities. I have tenants to satisfy. Let's go, go, go. L. was up way too late with her gallery designs. I make her breakfast and pack her lunch. I drive today and drop her off. Partners pick up each other's slack. Some cool air and a power nap inbound get my lover-girl clicking. We kiss goodbye just as we did on the other edge of summer. My treasure turns and waves. I am getting all chocked up.

I take a deep breath and guide the sedan that used to be mine southwest. The portion of the route on tree lined Lee St. is very pleasant. I show up last at the office. Sandy has me mono-tasking while Evan gets versatile with the multi-tasking. Mindless filing will make the day roll relentlessly by. Roy calls me on his lunch. I am part of his day every day. I count those days. Only two more Tuesdays follow this one.

I take a break and go talk to Maggie in her office which is fairly plush. Does she think I can make it as a partner in a small business? "You have skills. Use them wisely and do your homework on the marketing.

You are still young enough, so go for it," she advises. My partner is smart as a whip. I can't lose.

Some stuff needs to go to banker boxes and remote storage for pick up tomorrow. I stretch and take a walk on afternoon break. Are there actually any Chestnut Trees here on Chestnut Hill. Probably not. I remember something about a blight but I do love the Copper Beeches. Sandy lets me go at 16:30.

I find the Afro-Pop station. I drum my fingers to the beat all along Jamaica way, Riverway and Fenway to retrieve my package. She is ready and she wants to drive. At Green-T, landscapes by a young artist named Jeffrey Jacobson are hanging for the rest of the month. We make notes and compare our novice art critic reviews later. We do espresso and clink our demi-tasses. Stir-fry is waiting, followed by stretches and crunches.

Prayers fly up from the laundry room chapel. Another happy day draws to a close. I dream autumnal expressionist landscapes.

Wednesday, September 14

Dear Diary, Get up. Get awake. Go. No fooling around. My partner and I return to max business-like, disciplined morning mode. The more conscientious of the 2 partners is back behind the wheel. At drop off, I give her a thank you, a handshake, and a light kiss on both cheeks. While she waits to make her left onto Independence Drive, she glances briefly in my direction. I detect a subtle satisfied smile.

My mono task today is e-mails. I plow my way through them until morning break. I use this time to plan what is next for New Horizons. I keep a steno pad for this. I need contact info for the workmen who created Sheila's hypo-allergenic apartment, formerly Reggie's apartment, 6-G. I clear it with Maggie to keep the before and after photos for business use. The freshly furnished model units are already visible online. Those who inquire may verify with Maggie, my participation in their creation.

After clicking my way to lunch, I return to my purse sized steno book to formulate my amateur critique of the Jeffrey Jacobson landscapes. I want to see if I agree with L. about these. They are offered at $350 for the large ones and $175 for the miniatures, all unframed. I took a snap of the artist bio for later reference. The guy is an architect who paints as a hobby. "Get J.J. into our network!" I scribble and underline heavily. I take the last bite of my sandwich and gulp cold coffee left from morning.

Sandy releases me at 16:00. I accidentally get Todd again for transpo to The Blissful Monkey. He gives me his card. While waiting for L. to arrive, I browse the Goodwill Store for wood frames. I want to take a stab at framing in Roy's workshop. I am all suited up when Monica, Lydia, and Lindsey arrive. We make the outside world go away. We are balanced, centered and calm. We re-open to the outside world with clearer vision. We hit the juice bar. I try the celery spiced with green chili and turmeric.

We return in time for home-made pizza. Casey gives me her crust recipe. We want to walk because it smells like fall in our neighborhood. There is a reno in progress on Grouse St. I make note of the contractor.

Thursday, September 15

Dear Diary, Late last night, my partner and I offer our prayers while sitting at my kitchen table. The windows are open. Two votive candles flicker and glow red. When finished, we sit quietly and look into one another's eyes. "How do you feel about New Horizons?" I whisper. "I feel very good about it. It is the child we conceived together," she whispers back to me. We sleep topless, but not bottomless for the usual monthly reasons. From the spoon position, I feel a kiss between my shoulder blades. Two ticklish hands trace my contours lightly until they go limp and I hear the regular breathing of her peaceful slumber. Two fur balls occupy the territory in front of me. Oblivion washes over me.

To save time, we do cold coffee in the morning. The shared closet is getting crowded with Lindsey's stuff. Cheese toast will sustain us until lunch. While the engine warms, I take deep breaths followed by jumping jacks as in high school calisthenics. L. does stretches. We are ready to commute. The driver wants classical music. So it shall be. I want a wet kiss goodbye. Upon delivery, I am ready to start my workday.

I read the latest daily Herald while waiting for Sandy. I am on inventory duty all day. Order it, unpack it, count it, and file invoices. I tune out the rest of the office. I ask Phil where he lives, which is Brookline. I get his contact info. He agrees to network. He sells insurance as an independent broker. He points to his office on the 3rd floor of our building. "Stephen Sandler wanted to sell you something," he imagines.

The inbound commute diverts to Holy Epiphany and Green-T. Solitary prayers followed by art, espresso and rubbing elbows. We love it. We agree on it. We keep doin' it. Four of our business cards were on the cork board. One has been removed. Lindsey and I agree on a large landscape titled, "Farmer in the Dells." I guess Iowa. She bets Wisconsin. Horses led by a farmer in a straw hat pull a hay wagon of yesteryear. The cloudscape was in my dream 2 nights ago. I write a check. A red sold sticker goes up. What remains to do is Casey's Shepherds' Pie, a brisk walk for the well-nourished trio, dishes, locker room and sleepy-time.

Friday, September 16

Dear Diary, On casual Friday, I wear jeans and my Red Sox ball cap, with ponytail. L. dons dress slacks and a cashmere sweater which makes us an odd couple. The glamour girl must be first at work. She has meetings scheduled. At her employee entrance, I take the wheel, promising to return at 5 pm.

Sandy delegates me to phones and walk-ins. Two weeks from today is my last day. I am getting butterflies. The back pages of my steno book are for bridal party. Mom wants 4 maids of honor. Casey, Cameron, Monica and Lydia. Lindsey is photographer. Kelsey and

Chad are guests. Maggie, Sandy, Joni, Evan, Tammy and Jessica get invitations. Phil and Shannon? Maybe. James, Sally and their kids, of course. The rest of the list is up to Mom and Roy. My mind is not totally on my work. I get the overhead Pandora going. I apply some Lavender essential oil. I unwind by daydreaming that cloudscape.

I call the office of the landscape artist. I leave a message. His secretary calls me back and says that yes, it is The Iowa Dells. He thanks me for the purchase. That income will buy him more canvases and paint. Sandy releases me at 16:30. L. is waiting for me outside. She wants to drive. We don't talk shop. We only talk food, namely Casey's shopping list at Whole Foods. We divide the list. I pay for my cart. L. pays for hers. We nearly fill the trunk. We wind our way home 5 more miles following the contours of the land.

Fish fry is ready. We cart everything upstairs. Cod is the fish of the day. Last time it was Pollock. I do Tartar sauce. The others do lemon. On the side are onion rings and slaw. A rainstorm approaches. We stay inside and sip the last of the White Zin. We manage a few crunches but soon get lazy. We trade neck and shoulder rubs. We want music. L. has some Spanish Guitar on CD. I hear my phone ringing downstairs. Roy is checking on me. I tell him to make his guest list. I bring up the cats. Casey tells about a guy who played guitar for her in college. He even made up a song about her. That is so sweet. Dishes are waiting. Casey keeps the clean-up crew company plus we get coffee and dessert.

Saturday, September 17

Dear Diary, Here comes my next weekend practicing living with a husband. So far, it is all that I hoped for and surprisingly more. I detect the familiar rumbling of his heavy-duty SUV motor. It sounds like strength. It sounds like reliability. The driver will take care of me as well as he takes care of that machine. But first, he might appreciate the breakfast I have made. I want his visits to here to be associated with good stuff to eat and drink. I was up early to make buttermilk biscuits from scratch. Okay, it was Bisquick, not totally from scratch, but the buttermilk was real. Plus, he gets a neck rub. All of those active muscles benefit from my technique. "Thanks, Honey," and a smile is all I need in return.

We take the express route and "Bam!", we are in Canton. I get to start laundry while the groom makes his guest list. He puts it up on the fridge by magnet. Betty and Richard have accepted the informal invitation. They will get a formal invitation with RSVP by mail. Mom insists on jumping through all of the traditional hoops. The husband pulls up his deck chair and watches me hang clothes. He finds it very relaxing to watch me work. I find it very relaxing to watch him work as well, mainly in his workshop, where I can grab a drink and applaud the skills which I lack. There is always the possibility of a spontaneous quickie on the leather couch.

I see that my antique vanity has been re-assembled. It came with a matching chair. Roy has tightened that up. I busy myself with the dusting. In one of the drawers is a soft cover book about furniture restoration. "I found it in the bargain bin," the thoughtful husband recalls. He gets a hug around the neck. I flip to Chapter 1 which begins, "Be careful what you restore. When in doubt, do nothing except perhaps blow away the dust and store carefully. Sometimes, 'as is' will profit you the most." I sit in front of the triple mirrors of my distressed, all original antique, nearly 100 years old boudoir vanity. Who else was reflected in these mirrors? I go topless to check out the triple view. I finger comb my hair and toss it all around. I have caught the attention of the man with the tools. One particular tool is fired up to full power. From behind he kisses me on the top of my head. He has got two hands full of his favorite boobs, six hands full if you mirror multiply. Three couples in 3 mirrors rise and become one couple on the leather couch. I want a horsey ride. This gets us off quickly. There is so much we want to pack into every day.

We share a beer straight from the bottle. I quaff half. He quaffs the other. We have a little cool down siesta. We take down the laundry. He helps me fold. We pop in 2 Tombstone pizzas. "That's all I want in this crazy world, my Tombstone pizza, my beer, and you, all at the same time. The others are no good without you!" the husband declares. It's all so simple. I don't even have to cook dinner. I am ready for hoops. Bounce pass and lay-up, 10 from the right, 10 from the left. Okay, so I am far from ready for the WNBA.

We walk over to Waterfalls Bar and Grille for dessert. It is so conveniently close and hard to resist. Darts? No. Eight ball? Yes. My ass is getting noticed when I bend over the table. We sit outside as the string lights come on. I remind myself that this is bliss.

We walk home arm-in-arm at last light. I like his arm around my shoulders and my arm around his waist. Stars contrast nicely against violet sky above treetops in the west. We strip the bed and apply the freshly laundered sheets which smell wonderful because of ozone or just plain outside air. We fluff the pillows and get under just one sheet. We each get a back tickle. We want to save the passion for morning.

Sunday, September 18

Dear Diary, Six am means 3 hours until church but 20 minutes before sex. I gargle away the morning breath. I drink a glass of cold water which is recommended before sex. I stand topless on Roy's side. I yank the sheet and say, "Hey you! Are you ready to do me or not?" He exits to bathroom and closes the door. I hear the big splash. It seems to go on forever. He heard me gargle so he follows suit. He dives back in bed and says, "Okay, spread 'em." "Make me," I challenge. By the time he is done overcoming my token resistance, the pup tent has been erected. The dong finds the opening in the boxer shorts. There is a little extra friction from the shorts. I like it. The count-down to blast off is only about 3 minutes. Both of us are satisfied so why waste time?

The nice young married couple strolls along their way to church, a matter of a few blocks. It is structure for Sunday. It is all about getting up and don't be lazy, socializing, meeting parishioners, making the homily apply to our lives. We don't have to stare at each other and the four walls. People want to meet us, the happy couple, thus to remember how it once was or could be.

We trade newspapers with Richard. Betty wants to see the vanity. I show her the matching lamps from Estate Sale. Her grandmother had a pair of lamps just like mine. I serve bagels for brunch. I slice up some peaches. I unpack more of my stuff. I am halfway moved in.

I need Roy's advice about the big dilemma which is what to do about Felicia and Fatima. Should they stay with Lindsey? Should we get a dog, maybe adopt kids? These are all weighty questions. My first impression is that it will be stressful for F&F to adapt to a new home. I will see them often. It will hurt to transition them. They are that past part of my life, not this chapter.

I dissected my recent bad dream by myself and it has not returned. All of this happens in the office which we share. Many important decisions will be made here as the years go by. I put on my apron and fix up a little something for dinner while Roy watches Golf. I will never be a golf widow because I can play. By 18:30, I am delivered safely back to my weekday home but there is that same old ache when watching him drive away, 10 miles away, near but absent.

Monday, September 19

Dear Diary, You are there for me every day. The simple act of writing the day on your pages helps me to understand it better. Just as I understood the fear of abandonment in my last nightmare. I am dressed and nearly ready when L. lets herself in quiet as a mouse. She pours herself a cup of percolator Earl Grey. I read about him, the man not the tea. He was a great reformer while Prime Minister including abolition of Slavery.

L. looks at her slender silver watch as a hint. I am ready, only five minutes later than usual. Every morning, there is dew on the grass. I have permission to drive every day now on the leg between MFA and Chestnut Hill, a pleasant drive with the sun at my rear right over meandering cityscape.

Shannon is waiting outside. She does not have a key yet. She will get mine, next week. I grab my newspaper. We get acquainted in the break room during the start-up of Mr. Coffee. She is planning a career path same as me. I tell her that here is a good launching pad. She pledges to help take care of Susan and Sarah, the avocado trees. Shannon soon goes missing most of the day for administrative stuff in Maggie's office.

Roy phones in at his expected hour. I thank him profusely for a wonderful weekend. What would a bad weekend be like? One in which we are both grumpy, I suppose. But then, we would interrogate each other and find out why, just like Perry Mason and a hostile witness. Next weekend, Roy gets to be Perry Mason in a pretend husband/wife drama.

The waiting list is overdue for update. I call those highest on the list. I sell them on furnished, hypo-allergenic or regular. For October, we will have one of each. L. is creative. I am sales. We are a team. I love it. All three are pre-approved. All three are coming in to make their deposits. Yes! I can do it. I can sell! I have a few names to get pre-approved and moved up the list.

I meet lover-girl at 17:30. We turn off work. It's to be pray and then play, basement sanctuary followed by early autumn promenade. Casey does some kind of magic with a canned ham. L. does some kind of magic with her tongue.

Tuesday, Sept 20

Dear Diary, We are quietly and efficiently out the door and strapped into our transport by 06:30. I put my waffle away. No eating in Lindsey's car. It is her first car and she is protective. It is ok if I put gas into it though, regular unleaded. She does not know about the different kinds of gasoline yet. We are getting 24 mpg, mostly city driving. Her dad tells her that is very good. We do a business partners goodbye instead of lovers' goodbye.

Business first, pleasure later.

Shannon stays with Sandy all day. I shadow Evan for hints here and there. On morning break and lunch break, I think about marketing. Who will I serve? People like the Hennigs, who are down-sizing, or Sheila who was upgrading. The afternoon is slow. I can relate some of my human-interest stories, how the tenants become in a way like your children. We look at the latest Yelp reviews. Sandy replies to them, mostly with canned comments. I long to see something original for a reply. Some of them are low due to lack of weekend coverage and big lock-out charges. We discuss possible rewards for people who renew their leases.

Forgiveness of lockout charges could be a good one. Phil says hello, when we go outside. He is suddenly shy but better dressed than usual. He does double-breasted and pocket watch well. Another Tuesday ticks away until 17:00.

L. remains quiet. She has her moods. This is one that makes me wonder if she has met someone. In any case, we will stay partners. I ask her opinion about moving the cats to Canton. She wants joint custody. When we actually flip our meetings to weekends, that could be a stressful transition for the co-parents as well as the felines. L. wants the fur balls stay in their existing territory. Dogs love people but cats love places, she reminds me.

We toast our decision about cat custody. L. perks up a bit. She munches on breadsticks and helps set the table for pasta night. She is humming on our walk. She completes her crunches and stretches quicker than usual. She gets the remote. She wants to watch "Two Broke Girls". We oblige because we like to hear her giggle.

Wednesday, September 21

Dear Diary, Overnight brings mainly hugs, but morning wake-up sex is full throttle. Wow! That girl can really go at it. L. remains flushed all through breakfast but behind the wheel, the veil descends for dead serious driving and safe arrival. As I take over, I do my version of dead serious. I get a little smile.

Shannon is waiting when I arrive. It's a beautiful morning. We sit outside for a while and share the newspaper. Phil arrives in a dark blue Pontiac Solstice, 2-seater. Who would have thought? He is still playing courteous and slightly shy. If Shannon asks, I will tell her that he has been a true gentleman and very respectful. Whenever I am restless, I go outside to talk to Patrick and his maintenance crew in their garage. I tell them what a great job that they do and how I will miss them. They offer me a Coke Classic from their fridge. I will continue to network with Patrick. The days here are dwindling down. It hasn't been the same without dear girl, Susan. I volunteer to do more mindless filing to fill the late afternoon.

At 16:30, I notify L. that I am on my way. She is waiting for me outside. We have time before class to juice it up. I want more of that celery juice concoction. L. takes a taste. "All it needs is some Jager," she remarks with a grin. Monica and Kelsey appear, all perky, as usual. They wave us over to our usual spot. We let go of the outside world. We go within. We all get on the same vibe. I feel very light.

Outside, the sun is setting. Summer is definitely way over. It's in our rear-view mirror. I say goodbye to that happy time, duly recorded here. Suddenly, I just want to cry. There goes a tear-drop on this page, smearing the ink a wee bit.

As I write, L. is already asleep, on her tummy, hugging her pillow. Dinner was roast beef. We didn't want to walk in the dark. The sisterhood of three chilled for a while, practicing our poker faces, risking Monopoly money at the kitchen table. I must record this. It is all too precious. I snuff my mini desk lamp and slip silently alongside the dearest one to me in my women's world of 2011.

Thursday, September 22

Dear Diary, L. gets the bathroom first and stays one step ahead of me. I am brushing my teeth when she pretends to leave without me. When

I step outside my apartment door, she is there waiting on the steps, looking at her watch and shaking her head. For my payback I launch a tickle attack inside the car. This playfulness is uncommon in our relationship which makes it even more fun. It seems like a sign that lover-girl is happy and secure.

The longer commute to MFA compared to Chestnut Hill gives us more side-by-side time together getting on one radio beat or another plus more time to finish our mugs of tea. For many people, the commute is an ordeal. They arrive at work already stressed. For us, it is quality time.

After an extra 5 miles alone, I am ready to work. On arrival, the office is up and running. Sandy is with Shannon. Evan is on his own. My project for my final days is our latest quarterly report. I get busy on that plus answer questions from Shannon. At lunch, I stare at our greenery. The avocado trees will remain but my Orchid will come with me next week. I polish the leaves one more time and give them a nice misting. I open my bag lunch outside. I suspect that Phil can monitor this area from his office window. He shows up shortly after Shannon joins me. We three exchange small talk. It turns out he gave up the vaping, but he still has the gum, Nicorette. The ladies applaud his will-power. I make good progress on my report and sign out at 16:30.

Retracing the inbound path almost exactly, the young urban professionals are home in plenty of time for a brisk walk along the Pheasant St., Swan St., Lagrange St. and Bobolink St. loop. Soup has been simmering while we were out. Baby greens with olives are the side salad. Vanilla spice tea is infusing. Of course, the little ones are there with us underfoot during clean-up. Casey has the DVD of "Shutter Island" with Leonardo DiCaprio. I know the surprise ending but I keep quiet. We face our fears and survive the suspense, shock, creepiness and horror, shaken but not damaged. I hold my sleep partner tighter than usual.

Friday, September 23

Dear Diary, Casual Friday means no make-up. That saves me 10 minutes. L. does not need any but lately, she does lipstick and a little blush. Last weekend, she improved her fall wardrobe shopping at boutiques in Back Bay resulting in some mix and match jackets and slacks which already populate our shared closet. Her look is changing from artist colony to art director. At night, we strip away all of that to return her to all natural. Few people get to see her this way, maybe only me.

What could be more fresh or more natural for breakfast than cold milk on Kellogg's Corn Flakes with strawberries on top? There are some nuke-able cheese biscuits remaining from a few days ago. This is our morning tableau, sitting kitty corner. We have time, don't have to rush. She takes a nibble of biscuit and leans forward to catch some crumbs in her hand. In the quiet innocence of early morning, what is a word beyond adorable for what I see before me? Her Mom, Sylvia, saw the same for years sending her little girl not yet grown off to school. We offer our silent prayers for Dear Old Mom early today.

Minutes later, I wipe the rear window of our Malibu while the engine warms up. I buckle up. I use my extra pair of eyes for safety on our left turn onto Washington Street. We roll down our windows to enjoy the cool moist air. It is good for our skin.

Twenty minutes of skin freshening later, kisses on both cheeks of the dear one suffice for the farewell 'til eventide. Victorian figures of speech permeate my thoughts lately thanks to T. Hardy.

The office is ready when I make my entrance on this, my penultimate Friday. I dive into the ongoing saga of the summer quarterly report. Corporate has already showered praise on the winter and spring reports. Shannon shadows me to see how it is done. Leaning near me, I am aware of her fragrance, a necklace dangling, a wisp of her hair and some major cleavage. Are they real? Phil hopes to find out some day. Roy wants to come early Saturday just like last week. Good, that is settled. I go at 16:30 to retrieve my precious package. Power walking, fish fry, needy felines, MeTV, and late-night intimacy to follow.

Saturday, September 24

Dear Diary, Three women hear the rumble outside, the one we are expecting. Cover up, man incoming. We wave him upstairs. He is a curiosity in our world. We assume we are supposed to feed him. He burns up a lot of fuel. We share. We whipped up a big stack of hash browns. He needs protein, mainly sausages and eggs. After some joking and cheap laughs, the brute is ready to carry me off.

He slings my suitcase in the back of the Wrangler and helps me into my seat. We take the slow route through Norwood. I hand deliver some invitations Mom dropped off. The first one goes to Cameron. She will RSVP by phone message to Mom. On arrival at Canton, we ring the doorbell of Richard and Betty. They call Mom straight off. I even hear her voice on the phone. They are the first on Roy's side to RSVP. Betty lends me her 7-iron. I have time to unpack before we hit Ponkapoag Golf Course.

Jordan, the Best Man, is there waiting for Roy. He calls in his RSVP on his flip phone, then stuffs the invitation into his golf bag. They plan to to play 18. They depart the pro shop motorized and I am on my own. I get a page overhead, "Sarah Powell to the clubhouse". My 7-iron and I are about to get a workout, including a swing mechanics review and 2 large buckets smacked off the deck, no tee. My first divot is the size of a toupee but Tonya is very patient with me. Before we are done, my 7 is sending balls out past 100 yards fairly straight, some of them even go kind of high in the air. Roy and Jordan check on me after 9. We rehydrate. I borrow a putter from the pro shop and amuse myself with 4-foot putts several times around. The first ones roll 4 feet past. A couple of guys give helpful hints. After an hour, I am doinking them in routinely. I go inside for another drink. I seek ladies fall fashions. A nice, pleated plaid is just my size right off the rack. I wait for Roy in the Clubhouse Café. I am having sandwich, salad and chips when he and Jordan re-appear. They are both pleased with themselves after breaking 90. I hint about siesta. Roy takes the hint and winks at Jordan. After siesta, a quiet evening at home seems exactly right. Domestic bliss.

Sunday, September 25

Dear Diary, We do a no talking early morning just for fun. Roy watches me dress starting from naked. Eventually he has seen enough. He splashes water on his face, finds a clean shirt and offers me his arm. We are getting hungry halfway through Mass. Does Roy know any of these parishioners? It turns out he doesn't. He wasn't much of a church goer before me but with me beside him, he likes it. He likes the organ and the choir, also, plus maybe just some general uplifting of spirits.

He says he will make brunch while I finish unpacking. The bachelor brunch buffet has an odd assortment of items. I sample his skillet fried beans and dirty rice leftover from Friday. I like the fresh pineapple and sliced apple combo with cottage cheese. He remembered to get English Muffins. To pair it with honey-butter spread, that's different. How long has it been since I had fresh squeezed orange juice? Put it all together and it feels like love.

What does he want to do today? "Very simple, stay home and do nothing," says he. We can at least go trade newspapers as usual. We lounge around after brunch in our office going over Roy's wedding guest list. Robert and Darla are on there. Sam has a biker-babe girlfriend named Rita. They will come by bike.

My next hoops lesson is the jump shots. I dribble twice, pull up and shoot. The first try is an air-ball. The next goes over the backboard. I keep trying until I make a bank shot. I weary of this game plus I worry about breaking a nail.

We retreat to the man-cave. I want to see what kind of drinks he has in there. The old Norge has stuff that girls like, such as wine coolers and canned cocktails. I find an ice-cold Pina Colada. I never thanked the doting husband properly for that wonderful brunch and now is my big chance. The vanity lamps are plugged into a strip. I repeat my performance from last Sunday with enhanced lighting. It has the expected effect which is a passion eruption amongst the tools. As we zip and button back to decency, we realize that our weekend is almost over.

"Call me every day morning and night," I demand. We ride quietly back to that other place where I am needed.

Monday, September 26

Dear Diary, Fatima and Felicia need me the most. After I take custody yesterday evening, they have me all to themselves. My sleeping body is their territory, one guards the upper body, the other guards my feet. They watch me get dressed, same as Roy does. I have 3 fall outfits. I choose the cotton blend in blue with a scarf. I pin my hair up on both sides.

We have our kitchen table time out. We stare at each other above the rims of our teacups from which steam rises sufficient for soft focus. This is our last routine Monday commute. Let's just enjoy the 7 city miles we know so well. As we dive into Bellevue Hill Park, autumnal coloration is in progress. The air smells wonderful. L.'s tousle is loose and shifting in the breeze, revealing glimpses of her secret smile.

I have time to park and peak at L.'s new office. I try a leather chair, crossing and uncrossing my legs stylishly. L. closes the office door. We have a standing hug and kiss goodbye in private. I foresee many more such encounters.

On entry to my own office space, 20 minutes later, there is sudden hush. A surprise party is being planned I suspect. Nobody has started Mr. Coffee yet. Evan is on his own at Susan's old desk. Sandy allows me her office to continue my work on the quarterly report. Once again today I have the luxury of the leather office chair. There are less distraction in here. By lunchtime the report is nearly complete. I deliver all of the wedding invitations, including Shannon. I ask her point blank should I invite Phil. She says, "Sure, why not?" Mom has provided me with fill-in-the-blank invitations. Phil's name gets filled in. It's an instant "Hell, Yes!" as soon as he knows that Shannon is coming.

I escape from the office at 16:30. L. is waiting for me outside. She wants to go straight home and visit the designated prayer, laundry, and make-out room, asap. Prayer proceeds solemnly during wash. The dry cycle is for kisses in a clinch. We have time for our power walk before dinner. Casey presents a vegan creation with tofu and mushroom. Roy phones in as promised. I sit up with a book, expecting a seductive visitor.

Tuesday, September 27

Dear Diary, What to wear to make a good impression daily on my final week? The off-white Banana Republic Wrap Effect linen-silk midi is the classiest item remaining in my closet. It has bare shoulders so I match up a shawl for a wrap. English Muffins come out of the freezer. I have 8 of them toasting in the oven while Darjeeling black tea is infusing. We do two for breakfast, two more for lunch, butter or cream cheese.

The mornings are chilly now so we need some heat inside our chariot. We follow the route of maximum trees and minimum concrete including 2 miles on Arborway and 3 miles on Riverway. At goodbye, I get a big kiss and a little smile. I print copies of the quarterly. Maggie grabs them for her Tuesday meeting with corporate, otherwise known as, the suits. There was an early move-out yesterday, thus getting me out of the office so that the plot for my send-off can advance. 10-R turns out to be medium messy but no damage. The cleaners can come in after lunch.

This is the perfect opportunity to walk the premises one more time. It's very quiet because children are in school. Even the birds have taken time out. An occasional breeze rustles leaves in the treetops. I have been very happy here, all things considered. Sandy sends me packing at 16:30.

At the MFA, I have some time to get a visitor pass and wander some exhibits in the antiquities. I fill in some of the gaps in my ancient history knowledge. At 17:30, I find L. and toss her the keys. We have a shopping list at Whole Foods for Taco Tuesday. We are looking for ground Coriander, smoked Paprika, fresh Jalapenos, an English cucumber, and a bunch of parsley.

We also need avocados, white onions, a rotisserie chicken for dicing and some limes. I select mangoes just for me. We go straight home. The Chef requires our assistance chopping up stuff. I keep this list as a dated artifact within my diary pages. We omit our walk, in favor of culinary pursuits. We do stair climbing and 100 crunches instead. We pack surplus tacos in Tupperware for tomorrow. We tune in Delilah to keep us company during clean-up. Later, in my pjs, I call my man for pillow talk.

Wednesday, September 28

Dear Diary, Ah! I slept very well indeed, 4 hours alone followed by 4 hours with lover-girl. I have one remaining outfit assembled, a checked pattern in wool, consisting of skirt and sweater. One of my older bras is torpedo style retro inspired by Madonna. It gets my B-cup out there as far as it can go. I could put someone's eye out if not careful. This does not distract my transporter as we roll along our tree-lined thoroughfares. Stop and go slow is safest inside the beltline. I turn and offer my neck for a kiss goodbye, pointing to a certain spot. By surprise, girl hands grab the boobs in the process of the wet kiss on the neck. That was something special. I turn, smile and scoot over. I get one more kiss through the driver's side window. I sigh and kick 'er into gear. How can I drive when someone has just turned me into a quivering bowl of Jello?

Auto-pilot kicks in. Twenty minutes later, I switch off the ignition, grab my Tacos and go in to do my duty. The short-timer gets phone duty. At lunch Phil says, "Wow, where have you been hiding those?" I have him take a photo with my flip, a high impact low angle partial profile, from waist up, with a background of sky. I send it to Roy. He calls and says, "How am I supposed to teach a class now?" Which phone is best for photos? We'll see what L. has to say about that.

After lunch, the office is humming. By 17:00, it has wound down enough for me to go. The Yoga rendezvous happens on schedule. Monica and Lydia get their wedding invitations. At the juice bar, they ask if they can bring their boyfriends. I will notify Mom. The boyfriends can fill shortages on Roy's side. Four blissful monkeys exit and say goodbye. Two of them have time to stop at St. John's to re-enforce the spirituality. Already it is twilight. The lights are on in Casey's kitchen. Something smells good. It's roast beef, gravy, mashed potatoes, carrot coins and cucumber side salad. After clean-up, we find a box of popsicles in the back of the freezer. Casey has Patchouli incense sticks. All we need now is beaded curtains. How can I give this up? Since I know it can't last forever, I enjoy it all the more.

Thursday, September 29

Dear Diary, I am up super early. Even the little ones remain asleep. Today will be my surprise party. That seems certain. I find some nice slacks and a turtle neck folded neatly in my dresser. I spend a little extra time on hair and make-up. I pack Lindsey's bag lunch. At 06:30, I am scratching at her door with a plate of cheese toast and her tea mug. We are extra quiet because Sleeping Beauty remains in repose. We tip-toe out the door and down the slightly creaky stairs. We sip our tea while the engine warms. It is one of those mornings when we barely speak. Everything is well understood. At goodbye, L. offers me her neck where I plant a lingering one, leaving a bit of lipstick behind.

At my office, I update my waiting list one last time and stay busy on the phone. Joni comes in at noon to cover lunches. Maggie calls me into her office for some exit paperwork. I detect hot food aromas. I hear some whispering. Maggie says "Okay, you can go to lunch now." First person I see is none other than my Susan, now well into first trimester. I give her a delicate hug and burst into tears. She takes my hand and leads me to the breakroom where meatball sandwiches with melted cheese, a veggie tray and cherry cheesecake are waiting. We bring a plate to Joni at her desk. I read a card signed by everyone. Maggie presents me with a gourmet gift basket and a bonus check in advance of Christmas. Evan takes the group photo. Shannon takes another including Evan and Joni. I can't stop blubbering.

After lunch, I am pretty much useless, merely answering a scatter of questions from Shannon. L. arrives by Uber at 16:30. She is happy to escort me home on this special day. Maggie knew I would be in no condition to drive. We stop at St. Theresa mainly to offer up thanks to Divine Providence. I feel like the luckiest girl alive. We give Casey a break tonight, happy to nibble on leftovers. We have time for a short walk before dark. The air smells wonderful. We unwind with MeTV and Jager from Lindsey's endless supply until sleepy me says goodnight. Sleepy or not, I need to call my man.

Friday, September 30

Dear Diary, All of the tears were yesterday, I expect. Today is just another normal happy day on my seven-year run at Chestnut Hill. My career path is leading me somewhere new. My driver and I do otherwise boring oatmeal, loaded with blueberries. At drop off, I get a blueberry kiss. I wind my way solo cross town to the office one last time.

I turn in my key to Sandy. I shadow Shannon. Evan is mostly on his own. At lunch, Shannon meets the maintenance crew. She tells me about her earlier career in hospital labs, which she hated. She is very happy to work normal hours in a nice, clean, friendly office. My separation anxiety sets in again nearing the end of the shift. I pack up my Orchid carefully and say goodbye with hugs to all. I pledge to come back and visit.

In the Malibu, I allow the flood of memories and more tears before I finally compose myself and drive away. Music helps. Kiss 108 feeds me top 40. Inbound to MFA in the afternoon, traffic is light. The view on Fenway is pleasant. I feel okay. I have moved on, one small step. L. is waiting outside, sitting on a bench demurely. What a doll! She wants the keys and she wants Holy Epiphany and Green-T. We have our quiet prayers, offerings and lighting of candles. We are still in reverent mood when we enter the coffee shop bustle. My "Farmer in the Dells" is wrapped up and ready to go. L. says she would like to do the framing in a fashion standardized and similar to the abstracts which we sold. We put more of our cards on the cork board. We sip our Americanos. Topo Chico Mexican mineral water is our chaser. It stays extra bubbly in a heavy glass bottle. This hang-out is our milieux. We must meet here weekly.

We are home by 18:30 just in time for Cod and chips fried in canola, slaw on the side. We savor every morsel in between sips of a bargain priced Sauvignon Blanc. When Casey serves wine, somehow, we don't get buzzed. All the chatter keeps us from partaking too much, too fast. My dinner companions are about to watch a movie but I excuse myself. I have more packing to do. Around midnight, my enchantress appears. I reach out to her.

Saturday, October 1

Dear Diary, Casey is sleeping later than usual. L. comes down at 07:00 to review our game plan. We talk while I cook for the incoming hungry man. I retain a key. I continue to pay utilities until the end of the lease. Casey is sub-leasing above. Lindsey is subleasing below. Any of my remaining stuff can be put aside for use on my visits. I pay cat support for food, veterinary services, and cat litter. We will meet twice more before the wedding. She donates photographer services as a wedding gift.

The hungry man appears at 08:00 wearing a flannel shirt and jeans. The felines are happy to see him. He gets some of my standard fare fuel on board except he doesn't do oatmeal. He carts 2 suitcases and a cardboard box of my bedroom stuff to the Jeep while I say a proper goodbye to L. I remind her that we are business partners and never far away. Casey joins us. The two of them sit at my kitchen table and wave from the window.

The man with the plan has no plan, except to get me fully moved in. By 10:00 that mission is accomplished. My bonus check is safely stored in our shared desk. We sit in our shared office and make a decision. We are off to see the Canton Public Library a minor trek of a mere 3 blocks away. Books, knowledge, information, audio-visual are accessible daily. During lunch at home, we tally up our cash. Mine is slightly higher. He married me for my money, I suspect. We find 2 estate sales to possibly plunder on Sunday.

I get my running gear on. By 13:00 I am ready to hit the cinders. Coach and I do our stretches. He gives me a 1 lap head start on a mile. I keep my own stopwatch. By the start of lap 4, Coach has caught me. I eat his dust for the last lap. He cheers my kick to the finish. I beat my previous time by 5 seconds. We are having fun with this, Coach and Lady Jock do our post athletics physio in the showers at home after which, I don my apron and take over my new kitchen. I determine a plan to totally deplete all food items there before restocking a shiny new facility. All leftovers except pizza and spaghetti go down the disposal. The freezer goes to defrost. I salvage items for dinner.

Sunday, October 2

Dear Diary, For Mass, I wear the outfit from our civil wedding ceremony, with a wrap due to cool morning. We linger a bit in the church hall. We make some friendly acquaintances with other young married couples.

At Copper City we find an orphan Boston Globe, and savor some Mill Mountain Coffee. At a garage sale on Bolivar St. Roy finds some tools. I find a set of Ladies Golf clubs with Persimmon Heads. We are home by 13:00 to swap newsprint with Richard.

While Roy cuts the grass, Lindsey and I plan next weekend. We want a visit with Roger and a Spa day for Roy. Lindsey has my car, my cats, my apartment and my furniture but she doesn't have me in the way she did before. Does she feel empty or desolate or depressed? Maybe freedom from major distraction such as I, is a relief.

I move the kitchen table against the wall so it takes up less space. I bake the leftover spaghetti with extra sauce and cheese. I toss the remaining veggies into a salad. The lawn mower is out of gas. Roy is done for the day. He does a quick wash up in the kitchen sink. I let him chow down without annoying chatter. He confirms that he hates grocery shopping, the dings in your door in the parking lot, the carts with wobbly wheels, the plastic bags, the 2-year-olds having tantrums, the clean-ups on aisle 5.

"Shaw's will deliver our food, every 2 weeks," I announce. "Put your requirements on my list. I will pay for the first two weeks. We will save loads of time and annoyance." "That is one super genius idea, honey. Why did I never think of that? I probably did but was too lazy to set it up," he decides. He gets his beer and anything he forgot to put on my list at 7-Eleven when gassing up. We also agree to separate bank accounts. We got a lot settled in the course of one ordinary dinner. Saving money turns him on. I married a closet miser. He married a closet nympho. "Spend less, screw more," is our motto.

We wear each other out, shower together to save money on hot water, drain 2 bottles and hit the sheets happy and motionless 'til the crack of dawn.

Monday, October 3

Dear Diary, Roy is not a sit-down breakfast kind of guy. He is more of a grab and go, Monday through Friday. I leave a variety of stuff ready to grab. A quick goodbye and he is off to school.

I pack a shoulder bag for my first day at the library. Can I work as an intern based on my BA in business? I find a certificate programs from Fairfield University and from RISD. I have enough right now for tuition to either. I need Lindsey's advice on these topics. Meanwhile, I head to the reference librarian, Juliette to find materials I can check out. I have her list in hand when I break for lunch. Lindsey says to get *DesignSmart* software package. Their offices are in downtown Boston.

To use it properly, I might need a laptop upgrade. She said the RISD certificate program is well regarded in the industry. She says that she is getting a lot done but she misses me on her lonely commutes and in bed at night. I say that she has me fantasizing on how to arrange a slumber party on a regular basis.

After Lunch, I check out my first books. my niche will be boudoir, Classical Decadent or Art Deco. I find that interns mostly do drafting, drawing and budgets. Perhaps I can skip the internship because L. can do the drafting and drawing while I do concept and budget. Hopefully, we can do at least one project before the end of the year, even if it is volunteer.

Roy pulls over and picks me up and my bag full of books as we converge on our duplex. He wants to cook whatever meat is left on the grill. "Don't let me sit down. I'll get lazy," he advises. Inside, I spice up the last 2 cans of pork and beans. I slice up remaining apples. The cupboards and fridge are quite bare. Our first delivery from Shaw's comes tomorrow. While Roy is doing class work, I make the kitchen shine and ready for restock.

Later, we run our hot shower to cold, shiver, wrap each other up and jump into bed of the bedroom freshly designed by me. It's only 10 pm but it feels like time to douse the lights.

Some back tickles suffice to snuff out the few flickering flames of active thought.

Tuesday, October 4

Dear Diary, Roy is focused. I avoid interference with his tried-and-true work habits. He can get off to work with or without me. I just make it a little more pleasant.

Number 1 on my list is dry clean and alter my wedding dress. I pack it up nicely in a suitcase and walk the item to Canton Cleaners and Tailors, one block south on Washington St. My fitting is scheduled for

Thursday. Reversing direction for 3 blocks, I and my shoulder bag arrive at Canton Public Library for more career planning. I need an income.

Juliette finds me books about lighting. Lighting alone could provide a quick and economical method to transform an interior. I send a text to L. asking if she would help in a volunteer project to build the reputation of New Horizons. She replies, "Yes!" I plot my next move which is financial advice.

I return home to receive our food delivery. I put up the perishables. I grab my bonus check and use it to open a new account at Bank of Canton, another easy walk for me on Washington St. This money should be invested. I guess that is enough business for today.

Fun in the kitchen follows. While potatoes are on to boil, I prepare my brown gravy. I end up with roast beef from sliced deli meat, green beans, mashed potatoes and gravy. I put a big pitcher of iced tea on the table, lightly sweetened, plus slices of lemon floating amongst the ice cubes.

I mention my interest in gold. Without hesitation, the miser in Roy stops with fork halfway to mouth and says, "Yes, get some gold coins. For every one you buy, I will get one too, super idea."

One task remains. I wash while Roy wipes. He cranks up some old-time rock on his boom box to make the chore more fun. I hang up my apron and agree to throw the football around.

My task is to hit a moving target. I solve the button-hook pattern left and right with wobbly passes a little low or high but my wide receiver manages to haul them in. The high ones he calls a dying quail. Those would be picked off pronto, he warns.

Wednesday, October 5

Dear Diary, Roy is out the door already when I remember my Orchid. I must find a place for my orchid. It sat in the bedroom, forgotten since Saturday. The kitchen has the best light. A leaf polish, a misting, a bit of Miracle Gro. There, that's better. If this is a Moth Orchid, she may bloom again this year. Yesterday was hectic. Now, all I have is more library and cook dinner.

L. calls me on her lunch. She has heard about a place in Walpole for our volunteer work. It is a coffee shop in an old building, not yet remodeled. We can check it out on Sunday. We say how much we miss each other then ring off.

It is very pleasant in the little library café. This is a good time to call Mom. I tell her my fitting is tomorrow. She says that Sally's daughter, Tina will be flower girl and Jimmy's son, Alex will be ring bearer.

Back to my books, I study about LED lighting. On the way home, I find the local Dunkin's. I can't resist a dozen raspberry jelly with powdered sugar in honor of Susan. At the Shell station, I get my Perrier and Schweppe's Tonic water. I want the Norge and the main fridge forever full of thirst quenchers. Luckily, Roy has lots of ice cube trays. Now, what's for dinner? I know Roy likes Chinese. Chicken Chow Mein with water chestnuts, extra sprouts and crunchy noodles. This is all from the can, of course except that I make the veggie fried rice from scratch, a big batch of it because I know it keeps well.

After dinner we have some quality time when I am invited into the man cave. I polish up my antique irons and woods. Roy is busy organizing his tools. I get a brush and comb for my vanity which waits there for further cleaning. I don't go topless, just unbuttoned. I begin brushing my hair, flashing my bra in the process. "How am I supposed to get anything done here?" Roy demands to know. "Take five," I suggest. I unhook my bra. Under the bra and under the skirt are quick access to his favorite pieces and parts. In just a little over 5, we get our satisfaction. I retire from the scene for our separate evening diversions. At 22:00, we have a re-union between the sheets. He can't get enough of me.

Thursday, October 6

Dear Diary, Roy rises at 06:30 just a little later than I am accustomed to. I resume my long-standing 06:00 reveille. I get the bathroom first. I re-assemble my previous structure except that my commute is on foot. If I need a job, I will apply as library assistant. The pay will certainly be small but enough.

I take a lunch break as usual, expecting L. or Mom to phone in. In the pm, I hit the books until at least 15:00. Inspired by Evan, I am learning a little Spanish. I will use it on Roy. I have my fitting at 15:30. The gown suits me nicely. It will be ready on Monday.

I am home at 16:30. Pork chops and sauerkraut are in the skillet when my man returns at 17:00. He was on the football practice fields, so he freshens up while I prepare sides of home fries and baby greens. I fill a beer stein for an Octoberfest feeling. We have our usual fun with the wash and dry before I hang up my apron. I spread my books on the kitchen table and turn on Delilah. Roy does his office time. He pays the mortgage. We are free and clear in a mere 10 more years. How will we fill those 10 years, I wonder? Doing what comes naturally, I expect.

At 21:30, I resume my affair with Sherlock. So many mysteries, so little time. After a few pages, husband appears in the doorway, hands on hips. He gives me a rough hands foot massage for a few more pages. I flip open the covers on his side and point there. He gets in and tickles me 'til I give up the book and douse the light. He holds me spoon position with one of those rough hands on my belly. "I am saving you for morning," he murmurs. That is probably for the best. In a minute, I can tell he has drifted off.

I grab my pillow and pretend it is my little Love Goddess. She wants to sneak around with a married woman. It seems that Roy doesn't care, as long as he is number one. An extra-marital affair with a girl lover doesn't count. Is there a comparable love triangle in history or fiction? I will refer this question to Juliette. Did it have a happy ending, I most want to know?

Friday, October 7

Dear Diary: I wake to find Roy shaving, which he does every other day. Yesterday, I had the Don Johnson, Miami Vice, stubble look. He shaves with old fashioned Gillette double edge shaver, double edge blades, a horse-hair brush and Ivory soap in a mug. He doesn't like putting shaving cream cans or plastic disposable razors into landfill, plus it's a cheap way to go. While he is busy in there, I start the percolator. I come back to tell him I will get a job at the library. I looked at their jobs board. I can make enough as library assistant to pay for all of our food if the man pays for everything else. I knew this would be a turn-on for my closet miser. "You got a deal!" he pronounces. He hops back in the sack to seal the bargain. The porno stars that we are, we get satisfaction quickly so that nobody is delayed on his or her appointed rounds. He throws on his clothes, grabs a doughnut, gulps his coffee and tosses me a "See ya later".

By 09:30, I am at the library, filling out my application. The rest of the morning sees me compiling costs of various lighting systems. Mom is phoning details daily. I merely make notes. It's her baby. Dad has given her carte-blanche. L. has framed the "Dells". She wants to hang it at "Grounded", our volunteer project. I tell her she was in my fantasies last night. I am making her blush. I have to just imagine it.

On the way home, I stop at Shell to stock up on soft drinks, such as V8 and cold Starbucks Nitro Brew in the can. I throw my shoulder bag down in the kitchen and think about what to make. To simplify fish fry Friday, I throw a mess of Gorton's fish sticks in the oven for appetizer. I got celery and tomatoes for a salad. I open an industrial size can of Chef Boyardee Ravioli. I put the grated cheese in a little bowl to spoon it instead of shake it.

Casey would not do this kind of mismatch but I think Roy will go for it. While I finish setting the table, he is munching on the fish sticks dipped in Heinz Cocktail Sauce. We end up with left-overs for weekend. We happily wash and dry to music, do our separate office hours, find a sexy mystery movie, trade massages. Sleepy time comes for the happily married couple right around midnight.

Saturday, October 8

Dear Diary, We don't get lazy on the weekends, my man and I, just a little slower and with less urgency. We are due at "Grounds" somewhere about 10:30. Hector is the owner of the establishment. He sits down with us while we sample his Colombian. He has some silent partners on this venture, including John Lowery, Lindsey's boss. He has one year to make a go of it. He has one employee, his son, Raimon. His market is the lawyers, clerks and judges who populate the neighboring courthouse and high school students who like it as a hang-out after school. He has an apartment on the floor above. He wants a Bohemian atmosphere, without major remodeling.

Lindsey arrives in time to hear most of this. She nods and begins to survey the room. She sits down at our table and explains that she envisions minor changes to enhance the atmosphere, including original artwork, mainly landscapes. She presents as an example, "The Dells", in distressed wood frame. She knows just where to hang it. Hector agrees to the hanging which L. accomplishes in short order. She lights it with battery operated wall fixture for night. Window light is sufficient for days.

We get a handshake agreement on all of this and proceed to Inspiration Salon on Lagrange St. in the Malibu. The Wrangler is safe in all day parking. L. and I present Roy with a gift certificate for his birthday which is coming up soon. He gets 4 hours of treatments designed for men. The ladies depart for hair appointments with Roger at "Loose Ends" in Arlington. I am back in my old familiar spot with Lindsey at the wheel for a pleasant 30-minute drive through mostly parks and residential. Roger is effusively happy to see us again, two of his favorite baby dolls to give glam to. Cheerful chatter flows until finally, he is done with us at 14:30. We find a secluded place to park for one of our brazen, broad daylight make-out sessions.

Roy is all mellowed out, sipping a shot of Bourbon, when we collect him. Casey has appetizers for us as I lounge around for an hour, reconnecting with my kittens before L. takes us back to Walpole. We are home by 18:30, hungry for leftovers.

Sunday, October 9

Dear Diary, Roy has extra cash today to put in the collection plate because yesterday didn't cost him anything except a little bit of gasoline. So far, he is having fun with our Sunday promenades. Once again, we get our free discarded copy of The Globe at Canton Junction and later our free hand-off of The Herald minus the crossword. I show Betty my retro clubs, steel shaft. Hers are graphite from the 90's. She takes a few half swings with my 5-wood and some plastic balls. The shots show big back-spin and a slight fade. "We'll go out together, maybe next season," she promises.

I have corn on the cob, last of the season, soaking in salt water. Roy cranks up his grill. I haul out some ribs. I order every kind of meat I can think of with my new service from Shaw's. I do the baked beans inside. Richard encourages the grill-master. They sample the goods before they get called inside by the wives. Roy has two platters, one for ribs and one for the ears of corn which his rough hands expertly de-husked. I have melted butter in a gravy boat. We make a big mess with the butter and the barbecue sauce. Why even try to be dainty?

We need to walk it off. What better way than to walk to Shell for a restock of beer, 1 week supply. That still leaves a long evening ahead of us. What now? The man cave, of course. I finish cleaning my vanity. We find a place for it in the bedroom after we straighten the rail on one drawer. We go back to see what's there in the Norge. All of the mugs are there since the main freezer is full of meat. We toast our happy, productive, not too expensive weekend. The man finds some tunes while I make my delayed start on KP duty. We run a tub for scrubbing of backs. I get the clean water. He gets the once used bath water. There is nothing to do in the office tonight. We go outside in robe and slippers to smell the evening air. There are rabbits hopping about. I want a kiss under the stars. I must feel really good because he wants a lot more than that under the roof. I want to be on top. We need only open our robes. We leave the light on. "The better to see you with, my dear," says the wolf.

Monday, October 10

Dear Diary, For Mom, Saturday will be the main event for which she has waited an overly long time. It's all for Mom and Dad. For me, it feels anticlimactic. Roy and I are leading man and lady in a show for others to enjoy, a big party, a reason for people to come together and have fun. Some will be meeting for the first time, while others may meet for the last time. These thoughts buzz through my head as we two who are already married in civil court, do our Monday morning rituals of domestic bliss. Roy is having "Breakfast of Champions" with banana slices while I have my English Muffin with avocado. He drives off. I wave and depart within minutes on foot in the other direction.

I love my little library with Juliette always ready to help. I enjoy my walks to and from work. No longer must I refuel a vehicle plus deal with weather and traffic. L. has taken custody of the Malibu, where so many mornings were shared between us two. I do miss having her there beside me.

On my morning, I study 2 books. One is a beginner Spanish. The other is "Elements of Interior Design". I take my lunch break every day in the coffee shop, 12 to 1. All who need me can phone in. L. needs me. She misses me. The passenger seat is forlornly empty. She had fun Saturday on our design consult. She can't come to the rehearsal, but she has stocked up on film. Jessica will be her photo assistant for the wedding.

I am homeward bound at 16:00 with Ravioli on the mind but not from the can. We have big bags of frozen raviolis stashed away. Making the sauce from tomato paste is fun. I experiment with spice combinations.

After dinner is more of shooting baskets. I practice dribble and drive to the hoop. During our office hours, I spread my study materials on the kitchen table. Otherwise, we are a distraction to each other.

Roy precedes me to bed. He looks quite erudite in his half-frame glasses, reviewing a new Math textbook. He points to my side of the bed. I climb in and douse the lights. I toss you aside, Dear Diary, knowing happiness continues on the next page.

Tuesday, October 11

Dear Diary, At 06:30, Roy is extricating himself from a tangle of 2 bodies. "You were all over me like an expensive suit last night," he explains. I am glad that he altered the simile. He beats me to the shower. He is all business. I straighten his tie and kiss him goodbye. From the front door, I wave as he drives away.

Betty takes me to pick up my borrowed wedding gown. I try it on one more time. It fits perfectly. She drops me at the library and takes the gown home with her. I find a new book to study. This one is specifically interior décor. Perhaps L. will do most designing and I will specialize in décor.

Mom calls at lunch break. The guest list is complete with just 2 vegetarians, no vegans and no gluten-free requirements for the reception dinner. Live music will be provided by a string quartet. There will be a Waltz for the bride and groom. I remember enough from Cotillion when I was sweet sixteen. Roy will be a quick study. Dad has given the church organist a challenge for the final processional. He proposed it at his own wedding with Mom but it was deemed impractical. It will require an extra-long passionate deep kiss at the altar. Maybe we should practice that as well as the Waltz. All in all, we will be putting on quite a show.

Roy is late because he stopped to pick up his white tuxedo jacket. It comes with a deep blue bow tie which he must tie himself. He already has a suitable white shirt which requires cuff links. His trousers are black with a satin stripe on the out-seam.

We are not very hungry. A frozen pizza and a side salad suffice. We sip a little Chianti. We promenade around Forge Pond Loop. Upon return, we hang out in the man cave. I learn about tools. Now I know what an Allen Wrench is for. It's for those funny bolts I sometimes see on furniture. How ho-hum if sex is always in the bedroom. We use every room of the house but our favorite spot seems to be the tool room leather couch. We trade back scrubs in the shower. We start new novels chosen from Roy's library of old books to fill up a shelf. His is: *Last of the Mohicans*. Mine is *Peyton Place*. His light is out at 22:30. So is mine a matter of minutes soon after.

Wednesday, October 12

Dear Diary, I get up early to make a full traditional breakfast, leaving lots of left-over bacon, sausage and home fries. Inbound walking to my daily stacks of books, a breeze is scattering fallen leaves of Red Oaks and Red Maples. We should rake our lawn this evening, something I have not done since childhood chores growing in Dedham. I grab a knapsack full of hardcovers from the discard rack in the library lobby. Books do furnish a room. Inside are tales from far-off lands and old times.

My bag lunch happens at an outdoor table. Nobody phones in today. I imagine décor for Grounded, the Bohemian theme coffee shop in Walpole. I conjure up La Bohème, the opera and the garret apartment of Act One. Even the slightest bit of color there is a feast for the eyes. The shop has 2 tall north facing windows for pure cold light of day. The menus and prices are on a chalk board in colored chalk. I make crude sketches. The library courtyard on this autumn afternoon becomes an impressionist landscape. I close my eyes and imagine artist with easel. The artist seems to be my Lindsey, painting a romanticized version of me, seated within a theater of falling leaves.

I go back inside to study my Spanish. I compose some sentences for L., the type where the meaning is obvious. Some are simply song lyrics. I fill pages of my notebook of creative thoughts, which is becoming a parallel diary.

At home, I start raking in the back yard. Roy is working in front yard. We meet in the middle, converging our piles on a tarp which we tie up, ready to be hauled away for mulch.

Our next convergence is in the kitchen. I make the famous red beans and dirty rice which my man loves so much. Roy creates some cold side dishes of pickles, olives and celery. We quench with iced tea. We skip office hours in favor of Waltz practice. We find room in the garage for our modest vertical figures which predictably wind up horizontal on the leather couch. "I never get tired of screwing you," are his words of passion. We get steam cleaned in the shower, leaving just enough time to dive into our novels before lights out.

Thursday, October 13

Dear Diary, Pancakes make sense to me today, fortified by the leftovers from yesterday. A lazy wife would sleep in while the husband fends for himself. I like to be wide awake and fresh as a daisy when I kiss and wave goodbye. I take a breath before my own departure. Mom phones in to confirm details for the rehearsal. I stop over to chat with Betty. Last night she posed at a full-length mirror holding up her wedding dress. Richard rubbed his eyes in amazement. In soft focus, minus his glasses, he could visualize his wife in her former glory, awakening the same feelings of that earlier time.

At the library, Juliette has time to tell me about the Boston Art World. She also recommends Taschen for Lindsey's publisher. She encourages me in my conversational Spanish. She advises a little conversational French and Italian as well, enough for cocktail parties and gallery events at which phrases used by critics are often heard. At lunch I learn that Mom has a cancellation on her guest list. I offer Juliette as a substitute. Juliette confirms that she and her husband Eduardo are free to attend the reception. I print an invitation on the spot from my online template. It turns out that Juliette is expert at Waltz and Eduardo is expert at Tango. Wow! These are super VIP guests. I can barely believe my good fortune except that it falls in line with all of the other unforeseen rewards of my year 2011.

By 16:30, Suzy Homemaker has her apron on. The man of the house craves protein. All kinds of leftovers get stir fried into the dirty rice on top of sliced pepperoni with extra chili beans and hot sauce. I get a rave review for this concoction. Roy has an iron stomach, but I go easy, no seconds. We clink frosted glasses. We stretch and hit the Forge Pond Loop just before sunset. To prove his manhood, Roy carries me the last 100 yards. The fireman's carry is not all that comfortable for me so he complies when I demand, "Put me down, you brute!" I warn him to find a better kind of carry when it's time to carry across the threshold. More Waltz practice, back scrubbing and reading in bed complete our day. We save other delights for morning.

Friday, October 14

Dear Diary, What better way to start the day than a roll in the hay? We get off quickly, per usual. I have plenty of time to send Coach off to school. It's easy when your man loves his job and his commute is less than one mile. I take an umbrella to my self-schooling since there is talk of rain. I am a little distracted in my studies but I listen dutifully to my language CDs. At lunch, Casey phones in to confirm her presence tonight in the role of Maid of Honor. During afternoon, my nose is in more big, illustrated books about decorating.

I dodge some raindrops on the way home. Our Fish Fry Friday is butterfly shrimp fresh from the freezer. We are not very hungry just now. The rehearsal is "come as you are" but we freshen up a bit. Roy shaves away his 5 o'clock shadow. He lets me tie his tie. I fix my hair. We are a little early at St. Oscars. Mom and Dad arrive next, followed by Best Man, Jordan. We wait inside for Casey. Mom and Dad are paying for most of this, so they get to be directors of a theatrical production of the type at which lots of people are in attendance. We are ready to shine. When Casey, the Maid of Honor, arrives, she gets introductions all around. Mom proceeds to direct the actors who are present. We do a run through, top to bottom, of the Catholic Rite of Marriage, in this case, not including Mass. Everyone goes home to get a good night's sleep. James arrives late, from North Adams, with his wife and 2 kids. Sally is already there, from Wooster since 19:00, with her husband and 2 kids. Sam and his girlfriend, Rita, arrive on her Harley at 22:00. They bed down at the Canton Hilton Garden Inn.

At home, suddenly, Roy and I have a mighty hunger, enough to wipe out all of our La Choy chicken chow mein and noodles. We flop exhausted on the bed and undress each other. We are due at the church at 10 am. I set my alarm for 7. Around 3 am, I hear Roy in the bathroom. On return, he needs a quickie to help him get back to sleep, one more "pre-marital" screw for us two monogamous porno stars. Oops! I may be a bigamist, if you count all of my sleeping with Lindsey. I just won't advertise it.

Saturday, October 15

Dear Diary, The stars of the show have left the Dedham Knights of Columbus building. Sarah Jane and Roy are safe at home. We each had one full flute of Champagne, danced our dances, ate our cake, thanked profusely the bringers of gifts, and visited all ten tables of guests. We laughed at the jokes provided by Best Man, Jordan. They were mostly funny failures involving coaching activities. Jordan knew that eventually, some crazy woman would take his pal Roy, as is, no upgrades needed. The string quartet provided Tangos for Eduardo. He even partnered

Mom. Dad pretended to be jealous and cut in. Roy was waltzing nicely with Juliette at one point. I did not cut in. There is no jealousy during the Waltz. Casey caught the bouquet. Lindsey did not miss any photo ops. She and Jessica did a super pro job posing all of the necessary groupings.

At St. Oscar's, Tina, Sally's youngest, was artlessly adorable scattering wildflowers along my path. Alex, James' youngest, let the ring slide off of the pillow at the altar, but Jordan caught it before it hit the floor. He held up the ring for all to see and took a bow. Alex then took a bow, to everyone's delight.

The Biblical readings released tears from many in attendance. I paraphrase Genesis 2:18, Proverbs18:22, and Ecclesiastes 4:9-10. "The man, Roy was alone but God made a helper, yours truly, suitable to him because he who finds a wife, finds what is good and two are better than one so that if Roy falls, I will help him up." The marriage vows were altered suitably removing references to sickness and death waiting to tear us apart.

Dad's alternate choices of music came from his college days when he came to know the myths, mysteries, and mysticism in the works of Richard Wagner. My entrance procession floated on strains from *The Siegfried Idyll*, played by our string quartet. The kissing of the bride, and exit procession was a transcription for organ of *The Overture to The Master Singers of Nurnberg*. I must say this was quite spectacular and memorable for all. The organist may get requests for this again.

Sunday, October 16

Dear Diary, Sunday is our day of rest. We have no tasks to perform. We reappear at St. Oscar as ordinary parishioners. Some birdseed tossed at the 9 am wedding remains. Our shower when exiting was small green leaves. Roy suggested puffed rice instead of dried rice, like maybe Rice Krispies. We sit in back, unnoticed. What a difference from yesterday! We do Communion together. Are we suitably in a State of Grace? That may be a matter of opinion. What would Jesus say? Roy doesn't mind the rituals. They are fun when done together.

As usual, we end up at Canton Station poring over discarded newspapers while doing the brew provided by Copper City Espresso. We go to outdoor tables. It is lovely fall football weather. The Patriots play the Cowboys at home later today. By 11:00, we are ready to go home and greet the neighbors. We find their gift among unopened boxes. Inside are matching satin dressing gowns in Royal Blue and Gold. We are thrilled with these and will wear them tonight. Sally and James gifted beautiful crystal bedside lamps. Sam and Rita got us luxurious sheets and pillowcases. I am noticing a bedroom theme here. Are people hoping that we produce an heir, a grandchild? There is a remote possibility of this happening. Those tubes can reconnect.

During the Cowboys game, I suggest that Roy should go to the Biology lab and check his count under a microscope. He says with a wink, that he will "take it under advisement". But what if I get pregnant? He could say that I am having an affair, which I am, with a woman, but she doesn't count, I guess. During commercials, we discuss jealousy. Am I 'gonna somehow sort of like it if he acts jealous when guys flirt with me? He says that I can have one flirt a year, maybe two, with an obvious no threat to the marriage guy and vice-versa. Outbursts of jealousy would be equally tiresome to both of us, unless it's pretend. He can pretend to be jealous. Good! I am glad we got that settled. Meanwhile, though the Cowboys put up a fight, the Brady Bunch win out in the end. We promptly stroll on down to our favorite watering hole, The Waterfall Bar & Grille, for the 4 pm game.

Monday, October 17

Dear Diary, Boing! I pop out of bed first. Roy rubs his eyes which are sore from too much football watching. I bring him a cold nitro coffee in a can. He tosses the covers decisively and heads to the shower. Women appreciate a decisive man. We do our no talking breakfast. He is out the door in plenty of time. Good, now I can make our thank you list. We can knock these out tonight. I am late to the library so I spend a little less time on each subject. Juliette gets her thank you in person as well as a card written in French, her native language. She retains a slight accent which adds some spice to normal dead dry English.

I turn my brain to pause mode for lunch on the patio. Sparrows fly in, hoping for a crumb. One brazen red squirrel eyes me, hoping for something bigger and tastier in the trash can. I startle awake from a power nap, feeling refreshed. I stick to my study plan until 16:00. We have pot pies frozen. That will be easy. I am busy assembling our big salad when the man of the house arrives. He likes to do the "Hi, Honey. I'm home. What's for dinner?" routine. He peeks in the oven and says "Yum! My favorite!" I get a peck on the cheek and a grab on the ass.

Ozzie and Harriet sit down to dinner and exchange superficial pleasantries. During dessert of Cherry Pie, he confirms he is ready for thank-you cards right after we shoot some free throws. I leave the kitchen to clean up later. I am hitting about 4 out of 10 shots, still not enough to make first string.

Back inside, Roy gets seated at his desk with his stack of cards, address list and list of gifts from people on his side of the aisle. I pretend to be his secretary, except that I do not take dictation. He stretches, cracks his knuckles, and dives in. From Jordan, we got some sex toys with a smart-ass note saying, "In case the husband ever can't get it up". His note to Jordan is full of colorful language. He writes as if the person were right there in front of him. He is knocking his notes out pronto. I get busy and go halfway through my bigger stack before we quit for the night. I wash. He dries. We are ready for bed right on schedule. "Drying dishes always makes me horny," he reports.

Tuesday, October 18

Dear Diary, One of these days, I will be first out the door, on a job for New Horizons. These are some early carefree days of marriage, but something is missing. I used to take care of kittens. I must see them this weekend or we will become estranged.

Roy catches me staring while he crunches corn flakes. He offers me a penny for my thoughts. I was imagining him 30 years from now and will we still be sitting here? "I will be a silver fox," says he. "We will be living in some kind of palace by then, on easy street, but now is not too bad. Don't you agree?" he continues. "Now is very good," I agree. We kiss goodbye, like I did with Lindsey each morning. I sigh and continue with my thank you notes. I have them bundled and ready to post by 10:00. I drop them in a mailbox near the library.

Keep plugging away, day by day. Fill that notebook of decorating ideas and phrases in Spanish. Call people at lunch or just daydream. L. calls me first. The wedding film has gone to the lab. My book of 24 prints is her gift to me. Mom will pay for her book. Sam just wants one 8x10 of the bride and groom. He has a frame for it. We schedule more work in Walpole on Saturday. We promise our love will continue.

Do I have everything I need for spaghetti and meatballs tonight? My next order comes tomorrow. I will get by. I create an antepasto for an appetizer with banana peppers, provolone, salami, and olives. We dip our Italian bread in olive oil. I am perfecting my recipe for sauce. We have lemon sorbet for dessert. I never did this cooking for me alone.

After our walk, we count up our cash gifts. We agree to invest. Roy plans to convert his to gold. Mine will go to Bitcoin as Jessica's Grandaddy advises. We won't blow it on frivolous stuff.

Roy goes to correct some tests. His study is a place of both comfort and work. A Cedar fragrance in there would be nice. Aroma could be nearly as important as lighting. I wash and dry on my own, humming to myself. I am first on the bed wearing my new satin robe, book in hand, but showing plenty of leg.

Wednesday, October 19

Dear Diary, Apparently, grading tests makes Roy horny also. We were active past bedtime and didn't get much reading done. Roy is up first.

He brings me tea and toast in bed and is out the door on his own. I get to snooze, but I make it to the library by 9.

Lots of people learn lots of stuff for free at the library and I am one. Decorating with fragrance that is my thesis, perhaps not well researched up to now. My fragrance palette goes beyond plug-ins, potpourri and Febreze. First, remove the bad smells, mold, decay, fumes from drains, bleach, paint thinner and the like. You can get sick building syndrome from too new construction as well as too old. Replace with natural smells, essential oil by atomizer perhaps, but some people require totally fragrance free. Is this actually possible. Fresh air is my favorite but is this even possible in urban areas? Once again, I seek guidance from Juliette. I am sure that Lindsey can help also.

I go outside with my print-out. Some of these books, I will purchase, thus be on my shelf at home for ready reference. I text L. about weekend plans and her olfactory advice. I want an overnight at my old place. Roy will be ok with it. I think he has guy activities in mind, possibly strippers, a delayed bachelor party. If he can get couch dances from strippers, I can get physical with my female significant other. It seems like there is plenty of love to go around.

Spanish grammar occupies my afternoon hours (mis horas de la tarde). It feels like a regular workday. I mustn't get lazy. The wife of the double income household scoots home in time to start cooking. My delivery comes at 16:30. I get the fresh cut pork chops on the skillet and crack open the sauerkraut jar. I heat up those leftover home fries. I toss some baby greens. I get my expected cheerful greeting including the grabbing of my ass which he says is irresistible.

Just as I thought, Saturday is for strippers. Roy is cheap enough not to blow too much money there. He gets horny again drying dishes. We get our horniness relief as we so often do, on the leather couch in the den of iniquity man cave.

Thursday, October 20

Dear Diary, I hit the shower first and come out with a smile and a towel on my head. I make hot breakfast while Roy is in there. I sip coffee and grin while I watch him shave. He puts a dab of shave cream on my nose. I hand him his briefcase and give him a "Bye, Honey" as he walks out the door. We are newlyweds charming, delightful and happy as can be, so far. I expect him to grope me with every kiss or I will know something is wrong.

By 09:00, I am at my usual library desk brainstorming for Saturday. So far, mostly, L. will take the lead. I will present to her my ideas before meeting with Hector. His customers are lawyers and others appearing in court, mornings, lunch and recess. The building is even older than the courthouse. It should smell of respectability. It should smell old and traditional. The high ceilings, creaky floorboards and ceiling fans are ideal. I want to focus on the display cases full of sandwiches, croissants and salads. We can make the sideboard more attractive. There could be a wall where regulars hang their mugs. He needs a spacious but not conspicuous area for trash and dirty dishes, such that stuff doesn't pile up and overflow. A digital clock in 2 locations would be nice so that nobody runs late for court. Efficiency and convenience will help Hector in his one man show. We should hang at least one more painting on those drab discolored walls.

I rest my brain at lunch. My sandwiches are wrapped in waxed paper, just as in High School. I made a thermos of soup. I go to pause mode before switching to Spanish vocabulary. I want the names of foods, animals, numbers and colors. Rice is arroz.

Dinner will be tacos y arroz español. We have plenty of cervesa friá. If I start thinking in Spanish, that will help.

Roy arrives to see me browning the hamburger. "Make me 10 Tacos, Señora, por favor," He announces with a grin. He grabs his cerveza while waiting. He eats 6. I get 4. He finds a Spanish music station while I wash and he dries. We have time for just a few baskets before dark. He retires to his office. I run a bubble bath but there are no kittens to play with the bubbles. By 21:30 we are reading side by side lit by our elegant new bedside lamps.

Friday, October 21

Dear Diary, Roy hits the snooze. I prompt him, "Get up, you big lazy slug! It's the weekend!" We shower together to save time. We both do cereal. I finish the snap, crackle and pop, with blueberries. We slam matching glasses of tomato juice. I leave first today with my rucksack over my shoulder. He gets in a grope of the boobs on my way out. Getting manhandled daily is what I signed up for. I can thrive with proper handling. He watches me walk away with my usual bouncy strut. He waves from the picture window. Dunkins is there on the right, at the halfway point. This is always a temptation. I think of Susan. I must ring her up at lunch.

Today, I am looking at furniture and carpentry books. I wonder if Roy can build a sideboard with shelves for extra cups and stirrers and sugars. Juliette tells me about Fiddleheads Fine Home Consignment on Washington St. Roy can take me there tomorrow morning.

At lunch, Mom phones in. She is pleased as punch with how my church wedding turned out plus it was a wonderful family reunion. I tell her she can choose her wedding book tomorrow afternoon. I get Susan on her cell. She is a stay-at-home wife and life is good on the Vineyard. She says to just send her scans, an e-book of wedding photos. Last but not least, L. rings up. We will meet in Walpole at 11 am. I will send her furniture photos from Fiddleheads. Yes, she definitely wants a slumber party Saturday night and the kittens are doing fine.

I save my Spanish vocabulary for last. I am memorizing the colors (los colores), not the whole Crayola Box, but at least twelve of them. Also, I need more names of food. I text Roy and tell him we are having "Pescado Frito" tonight. After a while, he texts back, "No puedo esperar!". Someone is coaching him, I suspect. I stop at Shell convenience store for a six pack of Corona. Sunday is more football and we must not run out. It's beginning to rain when I get home. I have dinner ready within 30 minutes including tomato and avocado side salad. For exercise, we do dumbbells in the garage. I don't want flabby arms.

Saturday, October 22

Dear Diary, We are on our feet at 08:00, just 1 hour extra repose on our weekends. We are synchronized, pretty much. The lazier of the two gets the bathroom second. Some of Roy's exes talked about 3 bedrooms and 2 baths and how nice that would be. I didn't, to my benefit. The man wants pancakes, eggs and bacon. I get right on it. Tomorrow morning, he will be on his own. We both have stuff to do so we don't linger at the breakfast table.

He takes his second mug of coffee to the garage while I clean up. His mission is to find his bottle of Scott's Liquid Gold, which he used once on the leather couch, and some clean rags. He also found some mineral oil. That's all I need for today. I pack for my slumber party. We depart to check out Fiddleheads Consignment. I take photos in my phone of possible fixtures for approval by Hector. I find a framed print of Thomas Kincade's, *The Blessings of Autumn.* I feel sure that we can hang this today. My man, my hero, drops me in Walpole a little before 11 am. Lindsey is there waiting, leaning against the hood of the Malibu, wearing red Buffalo Plaid jacket and cap. Oh no! She is wearing the same as Roy, except he doesn't have the cap. He tries to buy it from her. No sale. I try it on. We are certain it looks cuter on the girls. L. is an inch taller in her Army boots. We are almost at eye level. I want to kiss her right now, but now is business with Hector. He approves the Scott's Liquid Gold for wood revitalization. It has a slight almond scent which is not intrusive. He approves the Kinkade. We get busy hanging it on the larger wall, a few feet from *The Dells*, by our local artist, Jeffery Jacobson. I retain ownership of these paintings with the promise to rotate them on a seasonal basis. Lindsey shows lighting options for the display case. I show sideboard options. I also propose a love seat with matching coffee table. Hector makes his choices and agrees to installation next Saturday. We get to sample 2 of the sandwiches his wife creates. All of this took barely an hour. Before we go, I write a check for my cat support. Now, I will be allowed visitation with our babies. By noon, I am feeding them and giving overdue love.

L. wants to wash clothes. I am prepared for love in the laundry room. First, we pray at our home-made Chapel of St. Theresa. Prayers can be a foreplay. Why not? We get each other off in a tight wet kiss clinch with minimum unzipping and unbuttoning. This is not far different from the couch dances Roy will be getting tonight. During dry cycle, I get a tour of the upstairs changes which transform my previous basic bachelorette digs into something more velvety burgundy drapery boudoir decadent. Tonight, will be superfine. Casey will be home later. Jessica is coming. Casey's guy, William has the night off. We have a snack and go for a stroll in my old neighborhood. I feel the flood of memories. I traded one type of happiness for another but I get to revisit the former.

It's only 3 pm. Why not drive over to Roslindale? We love it there. We see new abstracts hanging at Green-T. We make notes on the largest one. We can do our competing art critic reviews later. We wander the little downtown business area holding hands. We were here during summer. The Fall could be just as wonderful. We return home to find a roast beef dinner is in progress in Casey's kitchen. We bring a salad of baby greens and olives which Lindsey made. Jessica is making mashed potatoes and green beans. We have pumpkin pie for dessert. What a feast, our Oktoberfest but without alcoholic beverages in deference to Jessica's long-term record of sobriety.

We play spin the remote. The on button is pointing to Jessica. She gets to pick the title for movie night. She chooses *Twilight*. She never gets tired of vampires. We don't mind seeing it again. She keeps some vampire teeth in her purse just for fun. They look scary on her, for sure. Yikes! We make it a double feature with *The Hunger*, starring Catherine Deneuve, David Bowie and Susan Sarandon. Casey is able to stream it but first we make popcorn with real butter. Our vampire double feature is over by 11:30. Lindsey and I retire but Jessica and Casey party on. We hear them until about 1 am but we don't mind. We are busy making up for lost time. She says it is quality of time which matters to her.

Sunday, October 23

Dear Diary: Once more, I wake up in my former world of women. We can do everything that men do. Men need us. We don't need them. Even the cats are girl cats. L. has changed our sleeping quarters into a pleasure palace. I am a guest at what used to be my own apartment and it is quite luxurious. Felicia and Fatima remember me. They are not angry. The female humans lounge around in their jammies until church. L. likes to be seen in public with me. We have lots of quality time afterward. Roy is not coming until half time of the first football game. We do Mimosas for brunch at home. We toast to our business, our first project, even though it is pro bono. Some we may even lose money on but we build our reputation. L. has some soft dumbbells. We do our arm exercises, 25 sit-ups, and 25 push-ups. It's good for women to have muscles and be stronger than they appear to be.

We were up early, so why not go back to bed? She wants me to play with her tits. Roy saw lots of tits last night. He calls it the titty bar. Some titties got smushed in his face but he didn't get to handle any or suck on any of them. I get to do all of that with some nice little ones. To see them hanging down from above is fun. I could be happy with just nipple erections in my bedroom and do without guys boners, but it's too late. I have gotten myself in too deep. I need to just play it out.

Roy shows up at 14:30, unshaven per usual on his Sundays. He and his crew had fun. He looks a little hung over. We pour him some grapefruit juice. His appetite comes back. We make him some cheese biscuits. He notices the new look of the place. "Very nice." Is all he has to say. We get home at 15:30. The Patriots are on a bye week. We walk the waterfall loop and breath deep the cool moist air. On return, he flops on the couch. I change into my cheerleader outfit. I give him a choice of either football on the boob tube or more boobs in his face, without the restrictions imposed at the titty bar. He went home high and dry last night. I promise never to leave him high and dry, even if it requires hand, mouth and hips to finish the job. He holds back for the hips, the full treatment. I am the best he has ever had, proven again.

Monday, October 24

Dear Diary, My eyes pop open at 06:30 and what do I see? A big hunk of beefcake, on his stomach, is lying next to me. Those muscles could use a rub down. I hear some groans of pleasure. He gets a smack on the butt. I open the bathroom door, turn on the light, splash water on my face, and gargle for a sweet kiss. At kitchen duty, I am in robe and slippers and my hair is a mess. Mainly, my man needs a smile but no chatter. The table is set with 4 choices of cereal, cold milk and a bowl of blueberries. The suburban husband is ready right on time. He tosses his shoulder bag aside and takes his seat. I sip my tea and stare outside.

Some Robins are sharing the bird bath. At the door, I ask him how he feels? "About normal, for a Monday," says he. "See you at supper," say I.

Miranda, the chief librarian, motions me into her office. She is prepared to offer the open library assistant position but we must discuss the pay grade which may seem low for a college graduate but there is opportunity for advancement and good benefits. I accept the position starting next Monday. My first paycheck will be Nov. 18.

I go straight to Spanish adjectives to fill out the morning. At lunch I get a call from Shannon. Phil is amusing enough, but she doubts it will get serious. When L. calls, I tell her about my new job and ask her to frame the Jaime Cunningham landscape. We can wrap up the Walpole project next Saturday. In the afternoon, I make a list of design books I will consult again.

Meatloaf! I have never made meatloaf for me or for anyone. Mom takes a picture of her recipe and texts it to me. I am missing one or two spices. I put them on my shopping list. I am simmering a nice brown gravy when Coach reappears. "Come here, you!" is his greeting. He grabs my blouse with one hand and gropes with the other, which is a definite sign that all is well. Two nuked potatoes, stuffed with sour cream and broccoli help me satisfy the hungry man. I tell him about my job and first paycheck. "It's like I said. I married you for your money," he says with a wink. "A woman with money makes me horny," he warns.

Tuesday, October 25

Dear Diary, Roy has some stress at school, such as dealing with parents and disruptive students. I look for the tension every night and massage it away. In our bedroom, we expect many massages with happy endings. In our kitchen, we expect many quiet breakfasts with goodbye kisses flavored like some kind of jam.

My dress code at my new job is the same as at Chestnut Hill. I can mix and match all of my old stuff but perhaps I can purchase one new ensemble for my new closet, something for Fall/Winter. I have been so frugal thus far this year, but where to shop. The need to shop can be suppressed only so long. L. is more stylish in her new capacity at the museum. We should shop together on Saturday.

I focus on Spanish verbs today, transitive and intransitive. I text Roy and ask him to practice with me tonight. He texts back, "Quiero pizza esta noche, amor mio." I feel certain now that someone is coaching him. That could the basis of a pretend jealousy fight. What if we do all of our sex, love and romance talk in Spanish. That might be fun.

At home, I pull 2 Red baron pizzas from our overstuffed freezer. I doctor them up with lots of extra stuff like olives, green peppers, mushrooms and grated cheese. Pineapple stays on the side. I am proud of my creation. The second pizza stays in the oven and gets extra crispy. He tells me "Muy delicioso." I bring out the frosted mugs. He goes to his office all satisfied and mellowed out. I shop online on my laptop at my kitchen office. I find Delilah on the radio. I pinch myself. I remind myself that this is happiness. This is the "Brass Ring". This is domestic bliss. I wonder what L. is doing. By text, I find out that she is having a Jager cocktail with passion fruit juice and watching Antenna TV with Casey. After her weekend of temperance, cocktails on board tonight is no surprise.

The next time Roy sees me, I am in bed with my book. Things are getting tense in *Peyton Place*. He manages to read just one page of his book before begging for more massage.

Wednesday, October 26

Dear Diary, His massages must take longer than mine because he has more muscle mass than me. My jiggle, that's not for massage. That's for groping. Anyway, we are maintaining equivalent amounts of roaming hands activity, morning and night, leaving just enough time for a light breakfast. He has a teacher break room with stuff to snack on similar to my old break room at Chestnut Hill. He won't starve.

I make it to my daily destination with a bounce in my step on a wonderful fall morning. At my research desk, I list my final thoughts on the coffeehouse makeover. I need footpads for the tables. Some of them are tippy. Various other items are needed at hardware. I text Roy. He agrees to take me after work and we will supper at the "Waterfalls", my treat.

I sit outside at lunch and nobody calls. A little daydreaming looking at cloudscapes and treetops transitions my thoughts to Spanish adverbs. Roy and I can freely make use of nunca, mucho and siempre at home. We will amaze our friends and amuse our Spanish speaking acquaintances. I write a sample sentence for each one.

At 5 pm, Roy is meeting me at Ricky's Ace Hardware of Washington St. I made it there by bus. I find what I need. Onward we go to Fiddleheads. I have my eye on a loveseat and matching coffee table. We bargain with the seller. I get them at a good price. I whip out my checkbook. I send photos to Lindsey. A sold sign goes on them, for pickup on Saturday morning. All business is complete by 6 pm.

We get an outside table at "The Waterfalls". Eating out mid-week? We can afford it for now. Next week, Roy will pay. We just get the special, whatever it may be. Today, It's burgers stacked with lots of stuff, all of the food groups. We have ours with iced tea. Beer mugs wait at home. Roy gets teased about "Wow, I haven't thrown him out yet." I can't really throw him out of his own house, not even for flirting with strippers.

At our happy home, Roy needs office time. I pretend I am asleep when he comes to bed. He is not fooled by my act.

Thursday, October 27

Dear Diary, OMG, we have the first frost and Ebenezer Scrooge hasn't turned on the heat yet. I wake up shivering at 06:30. At some point we will activate baseboard electric heat which is nice because no dusty ductwork and noisy fans. "A penny saved is a penny earned," he reminds me with a grin. Last year he turned it on November 2nd. He wants to break his record for late turn on of heat. I admit that I get plenty of heat from his hot body. I get the coffee going, and jump back in bed. Steam is coming up from my mug as I watch the man get ready. Only one more week remains to break his record. "Come on, It will be fun, just like camping," he encourages. I agree, but only if I get my coffee and a jelly doughnut in bed every day and he steams-up the bathroom with his shower. We shake on it.

At least the library is warm. For a change up, I start in on my conversational French. I use an online translator, English to French to make some sentences. Juliette changes the translation. to make it more like how people actually speak in Paris. I check out an old French primer with cassettes. I can play them in the Malibu. I learn that gauche is not good when referring to art.

I stay inside for lunch. Nobody calls me. I stare out the window and daydream. I remember Sylvia, so fragile, way up there in Vermont, where it gets really cold. I hope she has her heat on. I make a note to resume prayer daily. It gets me out of myself and my preoccupations.

On the afternoon, my nose is in books about furniture. I need to be able to spot the quality stuff at second hand. While looking at dinner tables, I remember supper. What to cook tonight? Left-over meatloaf will make great meatballs. I got extra sauce frozen. Roy will take spaghetti any night of the week.

By 4 pm, I am marching home with a box of a dozen jelly doughnuts from Dunkin's. They are right there behind the Shell Station. It is 60 degrees in my kitchen. I sit down to dinner in my ratty old Cardigan. I enjoy the steam coming off the boiling pasta water. I do not pour precious heat down the drain. At beddy-bye, I make Roy get in first and warm up the sheets.

Friday, October 28

Dear Diary, Day 2 of the cold house begins. I will not complain or tell anyone about this. I have agreed to help break the record for first day of heat. Last winter, Roy took an infrared photo of the house. Then he added more insulation in targeted areas. Did he sneak "for warmer and for colder" into the wedding vows? He figures out ways to afford living in the pricey suburb of Canton on a teacher's salary and it is a great location for me. I may play the "ladies don't like to be cold" card, but only for leverage. I get my coffee in bed with my jelly donut on a plate while I watch the man get ready using his previous bachelor routine, without me to slow him down.

Weekend is coming. I am excited. I continue with French and Spanish. I hope I don't get them mixed up. In the café at lunch, they make grilled cheese sandwiches. That is what I will make for dinner. Lindsey phones in. She likes the love seat. She offers to store it for me if Hector doesn't want it. When she doesn't have me, she at least has my stuff. We should pose on this love seat for a photo, making the diary illustrated.

I am simmering and grilling to keep warm when Roy gets home. While he shoots some baskets, I plate our sandwiches beautifully, garnished with pickle, celery sticks and pepperoni slices.. The tomato soup is steaming in our mugs. There is apple pie in the oven, those little ones they have at Wal-Mart. I take my seat where I can stare out the window. We look sideways at each other, every so often. I wait to see what is on his mind.

The guys want to go fishing. He needs to drop me early on Saturday, like maybe 8 am. He is restless. He wants to take me to a movie and just be out in public. We can make it to the early show. I am ready in a jiffy, while he gets tickets online. Now I can't say that he never takes me anywhere. It turns out we are going to see *Fast Five*, the sequel to *The Fast and the Furious*. Paul Walker? I don't mind. "Adrenalin freaks in Brazil" is my review. Half a tub of popcorn is left over. At home, I want my back rub first, which typically includes a preoccupation with my hips, such as a spanking, something not possible with strippers.

Saturday, October 29

Dear Diary, Our Saturday dawns clear. Dave is able to transport me and my love seat, so Roy has plenty of time to pack his gear. I fill a cooler with food for the fishermen. Four guys in 2 vehicles will converge on Glenn Echo Pond, 7 miles to the east. They have a row boat and a cabin reserved. At 08:00, Roy departs to pick up Jordan. He will text me tonight if he finds a signal.

By 10:00, I am at Walpole. Dave helps me move the furniture. The love-seat goes in the northeast corner of the floor-space. Hector is not so sure it blends in but his wife Estella says "Si, quiera!" It is her touch of femininity in a mostly masculine room. The lavender color is subdued pastel. The soft velvet contrasts but does not clash. L. arrives in time to observe the overall effect. All of the ladies agree with the harmony of this item in the grand scheme. L. goes to work on the hanging of the Jaime Cunningham landscape and the display case lighting. I take care of the tippy tables with my felt adhesive feet. I tighten some of the legs with my screw drivers and Allen wrenches. The project is complete. We pose for a snapshot taken by Raimon. Lindsey and I sit primly on the love seat, knees pointed inward. Hector and Estella, the satisfied clients, stand behind us. Lindsey and I enjoy Estella's sandwich and soup combo. Hector makes us each a Cappuccino.

Shopping is next. We are thinking outlet mall. Fashions await at The Wrentham Village Premium Outlets, a trek of 16 miles to the southwest on US 1 and 495. At Saks Off 5th, I find a sheath dress in blue, stretchy and smooth material, with elbow length sleeve. It is perfect for my library gig. Banana Republic has a woolen pencil skirt and sleeveless blouse with jacket for Lindsey. This is a major upgrade for her. We are eager to get back and model for Casey. Food is waiting for us at our home base so we waste no time, arriving before dark. Our special guest tonight is Kelsey, because Chad is acting on stage in Hartford. Jessica is on a catering job and William is overseeing a new bakery. Casey has set up a luscious buffet. Four young women stay home on a Saturday night but we are all happy. Kittens join the party.

Sunday, October 30

Dear Diary, I get to revisit my old comfort zone and L. is making it even more comfy, luxurious even, partly because it's a little warmer than my new address. After some hugs and kisses, my hostess and I slumber way down deep into oblivion until rousing with whiskers in our faces. 7 am leaves us lots of time to be lazy.

Over Darjeeling tea and blueberry muffins, we look at a digital slideshow of "Worn to Perfection" and "Eternal Asylum", the two collections for Lindsey's next show at Galerie D'Orsay. She has more framing to do before next Friday's opening. I will be there sometime after the bubbly starts flowing. I was good luck last time. I reeled in

Roger Quinn. Roy will come, plus Juliette and Eduardo, I am pretty sure.

Roy phones in. He caught mostly rainbow trout, already fried and eaten under rustic conditions. Can Lindsey bring me home today, please? She says, yes. We get dressed for Church. We arrive in time for the 11 am Mass at St. Theresa. We sit humble modest and mostly unseen in the back pew. It is warming up nicely for our walk home along Lagrange St. featuring crunchy leaves underfoot. Everything is working out nicely. L. is getting a lot more done without us all over each other daily. Upstairs, Casey and Kelsey are nearly dressed. They are going to a matinee at Boston Lyric Opera. William has tickets for 3. They are taking in Verdi's Macbeth. Lady Macbeth is Soprano, Carter Scott. Now I can nag Roy about why doesn't he ever take me to the Opera. That can be a hilarious running gag.

At 4 pm, L. is driving me back to Canton on the fast and efficient 20-minute route. I am safe. I have Danica Patrick at the wheel, getting good enough performance from my old 3.1-liter V6 Chevy engine. On arrival at my new home, Roy is unloading his Jeep. We make it a pit stop. Pressure in tires is good. Oil looks dirty but engine sounds okay, for a 12-year-old car. L. wants to shoot a basket. She heaves one up there underhand style. She banks it in and gives a fist pump. She decides to quit while she is ahead. We hug and kiss on cheeks goodbye. Within 1 hour, all is back to normal in our suburban dream come true.

Monday, October 31

Dear Diary, I have goose bumps but I do not complain or make a joke. I soldier onwards to kitchen and bath. I switch from silk robe to terry cloth. My cardigan is serving me well. At breakfast, I invite Roy on a date. He can pretend that I am some cute girl but brazen and he is bachelor. I invite him on a date to Lindsey's opening at Galerie D'Orsay. I tell him I really need a date and will he be my escort? I want to impress my friends with the cute guy I got for a date. "On the hope of getting into your pants, I will go, even though we just met and you might be a psycho-babe," he admits. I in turn, agree to be just as brazen as I was on our first date.

At 08:30, I am logged in to my new work computer. In the morning, I learn the computer software and study procedures. By afternoon, I am checking out books. Clerical jobs are important and they require attention to detail. I stay focused. Lunch is now in the employee break room. From my previous weeks, I know the stacks fairly well. I do some reshelving during afternoon by Dewey Decimal System.

I have invitations for Juliette and Eduardo for Friday. She says they often go to First Friday at Back Bay.

Roy has had enough fish for a while. We revert to meatloaf, but this time with mashed potatoes, green beans and gravy. During his office hours, I give him online pages of menus from French Restaurants to print. I tell him that tomorrow he gets escargots and cuisses de grenouille. He says, "I can't wait."

I lie extra close and inquire, "Aren't you afraid? You might be sleeping with a psycho-babe. She could turn on you at any moment." "I'll handle it when it happens," he murmurs as he dozes off. I wake up thirsty at 3 am as I often did last summer. I pad to the fridge in my bare feet to get my Perrier. The thermostat says 60 degrees but I am not even shivering. Maybe my wintertime basal metabolism has kicked in. Roy was trying to explain about this and something about my thyroid. If the pipes don't freeze, I'm ok. I think about those empty asylum buildings at Medfield, cold, haunted, quiet, except a rattling window-pane.

Tuesday, November 1

Dear Diary, This is ridiculous. My commute is only 5 minutes, one quarter mile, on foot, unless I stop at Dunkin's, which I do, all because of Susan, and her damn doughnuts which got me addicted. Now Roy is addicted. He ate the last one at breakfast and it was supposed to be mine. That will be our next fight. Who ate the last powdered sugar raspberry jelly doughnut?

Anyway, the girls like them at work. It's all girls again. I am getting good at checking out books, reshelving, and helping people find things, but I have to speak quietly. It was more raucous at Chestnut Hill, unless Maggie came out to tell the hen party to stop clucking so loudly in a place of business. I make temporary library cards for new patrons. Instead of tenants, I have patrons. I find plenty to do. I will learn more next week.

L. phones in at lunch to tell me that Hector gave good feedback about our work to John Lowery. We can put the testimonial on our website plus that will also be advertising for "Grounded." I tell her that I love her and that our weekend was wonderful. We are connected by a business, by a car, by a bed that used to be mine, and by Art. If she is framing late today, she can text me. That will probably be Roy's office hours after dinner.

Of course, every afternoon, my mind turns to dinner options. At Shell, on the way home, I see they have chicken wings in their little hot food deli area. I get a bunch of these for an appetizer. I will say that they are frog's legs. Sure enough, when I serve the mock "cuisses du grenouille", Roy remarks "Hmm, tastes just like chicken. That's amazing." He might not feel the same way about escargot. We have fun at dinner. He likes it when I wear my apron. Nobody gave us "his and hers" aprons for a wedding present. He likes to see me slaving over a hot stove. I make a big pot of chili, 4-alarm. He says, "Hmm, my favorite. Wow! That is hot!" He bites on celery and drinks iced tea to put out the fire.

After more reading of our novels side by side, Roy turns over and pretends he just wants to sleep, "Really tired, honey." I demand, "Not so fast, Cowboy. I need a horsey ride. It relieves stress. Don't you know I am under a lot of stress?"

Wednesday, November 2

Dear Diary, Husband and wife do their nice quiet breakfast and kiss on the cheek goodbye. He departs with his shoulder bag. I depart with mine. Some new books come in today. I see how they are catalogued. I study my procedure book so that I will be quicker clicking around the software. I get to break my vow of silence in the lunchroom where the last jelly doughnut, one day old, is all mine. I join in the chatter about boyfriends, children, husbands, shopping. I share my recommendations at Wrentham Outlets. I take 10 minutes daily outside for private calls. I send a text to Susan to say how much I miss her, especially at lunch.

Roy precedes me home. My hero is making dinner from leftovers. My food delivery arrived at 5 pm. He stowed it away and tipped the guy well. He is pleased to never go grocery shopping again. But beer shopping, that is different, being an in and out quick affair. We decide on a Fall/Winter weekday after work routine. He shoots his baskets to de-stress. He greets the neighbors, then grabs a snack and retreats to his office 'til I get home. We have a late supper followed by projects or frolics in the man cave. Bedroom is for reading, massages and sleep.

After several weeks of marriage, I must have at least one annoying habit. What is it? I talk too much. Blah blah blah, blah blah, blah blah! Honey this, honey that. I ask questions about too much stuff. Plus, I have to be quiet at work. I make him understand the stress of just shutting my yapper in the company of the man of few words. We can both become monosyllabic, mainly grunting and reading body language. That might be fun.

Instead of talking, can I hum? Yes, I can hum with impunity? Yes, he likes to hear me humming in the kitchen, just like his Mom. Good! We got that settled. It's our period of adjustment, you see.

In the man cave, I remove the drawers from my vanity. Lemon pledge could not hurt. I don't care about resale. I am keeping this piece forever. It has history. It is elegant and it is mine. How many women's faces have reflected there and were they happy? I try to imagine them. I sit and look. My face, for sure, is happy.

Thursday, November 3

Dear Diary, We find our elective mutism to be very amusing. I whisper few words. I whisper them in his ear. Two words, "Bye, Honey." They last us 'til dinner time. Meanwhile, we both have a job to do. His job is a little more challenging, teaching "the young skulls full of mush" as Rush Limbaugh called them. Some of the young skulls come to the library. Kids love it here. We show them the wide world far beyond Canton, Massachusetts. For the older ones, it is the perfect place to do homework. We provide structure for that. They can even practice their musical instruments in special soundproof rooms. My new task is overdue notices. Some small token fines must be paid. Be organized. Be careful. Show respect for community property. This, we teach.

At lunch, I get a text from L. informing that her framing is complete. Her photos, 16 in all are at the museum waiting for transport to the gallery. I confirm my attendance, alongside Roy and Juliette. Eduardo must stay home in his studio and work.

Homeward bound at 5 pm, my full-length coat whips in the wind. I hold my hat on my head lest it fly away. At home, all I want is a hug to start me humming my way through creation of our love-nest dinner at home. Chops from the freezer, sauerkraut from the fridge, a nice brown gravy, mashed potatoes revived from earlier in the week, now reborn as au gratin. The King in his castle is served. The Queen gets appreciation. I don my cardigan and bring coffee to the chilly workshop. We turn the lights up full and get to work on our projects. The drawers are sliding smoothly. My comb and brush rest on their tray alongside an atomizer filled with Chanel No. 9. I find a strip to plug in the matching crystal lamps from yesteryear. I excuse myself but return soon after in my slippers and terry cloth robe. I brush my hair 20 strokes on each side. I toss it about but only when power tools are not in use. I sculpt my dark eye-brows. I loosen my robe. Reflections reveal 3 extra views of the B-cup boobs in the warm glow of the vanity lamps. Someone is staring. I shiver. Somebody bring me some body heat. I don't have to wait long.

Friday, November 4

Dear Diary, I found all of the body heat I needed last night, plus the "L" word. He still loves me, after all these weeks of marriage. We are going out on the town tonight. I am very excited.

Meanwhile, I keep my mind on my work. At 1 pm, I get a text from L. She is on her way to the gallery. Juliette and I have a change of clothes. We get dolled up in the library ladies' room. We pin up each other's hair, add ear-rings and necklace down into the decolletage. Roy meets us at 17:45. We get sandwiches at Canton Junction Station. The 3 of us ride the 18:22 commuter train to Back Bay. We arrive at 19:00. We taxi over to Galerie D'Orsay. We check our coats. Roy has his best sports jacket under a trench coat and a slouch hat. He looks like a detective. He doesn't say much but he listens. He lets his double escort chatter on and on. We sample the heavy hors d'oeuvres. Roy takes his flute of Champagne and wanders off on his own to make his private observations.

We find Mitzi. She has a check for Juliette which is proceeds of sales of Eduardo's figurines. We find Lindsey. She is engaged in some serious conversation. She waves and smiles. She has 2 small booths, one for each exhibition. Some of the prints have a sold sticker on them. Jessica is with the catering service.

Many of the patrons are well known to Juliette. She introduces me around. Some are interested in "New Horizons". They have heard a little about it from John Lowery. He is here and Mitzi points him out. We chat. He tells me that Lindsey is a big talent behind the lens and that I contribute to concept formation in the mind of the blossoming artist. I cross paths with Roy acting very blasé. He gets his refill and another plate of meatballs. We look at "Eternal Asylum". "That's Casey? Jeezus! She gives me goose bumps," says he. The portrait of Jessica's grandfather has sold. Some people want to know a story behind the faces in the "Worn to Perfection" series. Roy stares at the portrait of his Dad, Sam, but says nothing. Before we go, L. comes and hugs us all. We catch the 11:05 pm train from South Station putting us back at Canton by 11:45 pm.

Saturday, November 5

Dear Diary, We deliver Juliette safe to her home by 00:15. Eduardo is still working in his studio, but he is taking a break. He often works without distraction into the wee hours. We four have an Espresso and a late-night snack. We tell him about the espectáculo. He says he will attend the next one, quizás. We say buenas noches at 01:00. My escort is eager to get me home where we aim to steam up the shower, then crash.

At 08:00, the thermometer reads 60 F inside and 35 F outside. We go out for our first cold weather run, once around the loop. The stove heats up the kitchen. I fix a mess of sausage, bacon, hash browns, scrambled eggs and melon for brunch. My trusty cardigan keeps me warm enough.

I text to L. congratulations and maybe we meet tomorrow? My escort wants to go back to bed. He is insatiable. Later, we end up on the couch watching ESPN. Later still, we walk to Saturday Vigil Mass at St. Oscar's. This is an incredible amount of exercise for me in one day both on my feet and on my back. We work up a healthy appetite for more home cooking, good old-fashioned spaghetti and meatballs, big ones, not like those tiny cocktail meatballs from last night, barely big enough to stick in your ear, according to Roy. We eat by candlelight to enhance the illusion of camping out.

A hard freeze is predicted for tonight. Roy turns on his special heated thermal tape for his pipes. He does the same for the neighbors. We leave our faucets dripping as well. I get my reply text from L. who types, "Yes! Providence by train, 10:44 am, Canton Junction." I text back "Confirmed!" I ask Roy for a day off on Sunday, for shopping at Providence. He will be totally free for unlimited football watching. The freezer is stuffed full of pizzas and the Norge is well stocked with beer.

He pretends that this is a big favor to ask. He thinks carefully then relents, "Fine. Let's see. It's 10 pm now. You're mine for 12 more hours." Okay. It's exercise. It's fun and we are porno stars. Well, not exactly. He hasn't asked to tape anything yet. Why watch a tape when you got the real item, in the flesh.

Sunday, November 6

Dear Diary, I let the lazy man sleep. He is exercising his right to be lazy and unshaven on Sunday, his day of rest. He performed admirably on Friday evening. I am proud of him. I leave him some nice breakfast leftovers on the stove. I bundle up and Uber my way to Canton Junction.

As the train pulls in, I see L. pass by in her window seat. I traverse 2 cars to find her. We settle in for the 45-minute chug along to Providence. We find it way too cold for walking about. We want some hot chocolate. I take us to the Renaissance Hotel. In the lobby, we sit and sip and watch the people pass through. We ask to see a room in case we ever miss our train. We exit to Providence Place Mall without going outside. So many stores, so little time. On the first level, L. points to Adore Me. We try on lots of stuff but we need time to get over the sticker shock. On level 2, we explore more women's fashions at Aerie. It is getting harder to resist temptation. Proceeding to level 3, American Eagle Outfitters is not too pricey. I find the Buffalo Plaid cap for Roy in his size. They have it in red. L. finds a nice scarf for her Mom. Our Christmas shopping has officially begun but we are starving.

Where to eat? Please not the food court. We want P. F. Chang's from the menu. L. wants the Mandarin Crunch Salad. I want the Crab Rangoon. Where is Rangoon anyway? It's in Myanmar formerly known as Burma. I never knew that and I have been eating this dish all of my life. We are a little giggly from the plum wine. Wasting no time, we return to Level 2 where we saw Bath and Body Works. Mom deserves a basket of her favorite creams and lotions, enough to last her a year. L. finds some stuff for Casey, Kelsey, and Jessica. We are done for the day. We pledge to return to Providence Place soon to check off the remainder of each of our Christmas lists. "We will be so busy that day, we might even miss the train home," suggests the adorable one. If so, we know where to stay. Our inbound train trundles along allowing 45 more minutes close together quality time. We kiss goodbye before I step off into the darkness.

Monday, November 7

Dear Diary, Last night was a hard freeze. We break the record for latest day with no heat except for that provided by our bodies and our kitchen stove. Last night was a "three dog night" but the body of Mr. Muscleman beside me cranks out about as much heat as three dogs so we're good. We set the thermostat at 60 F. If company comes, we will crank it up. We got to bed a little later than usual last night but it was "fall back" transition night so we got an extra hour that way. At 8 am standard time, coach is ready for his new challenges and so am I.

My new challenge is learning how to do the inter-library loan. Juliette shows me how to search the regional network of libraries. I am getting good at speaking in low tones in my workplace where written words reign supreme be they on flat screen or in bound volumes, some few thousand square feet of them. I still prefer my novels on a bookshelf instead of an e-file. Neither battery nor wall socket is required to read about small town New England Peyton Place, simply sunlight or candle.

Who will call me today, I wonder as I munch my lunch? L. texts to thank me for the shopping adventure. Monica calls to say that she and Lydia miss us at Yoga. We can meet again on Saturday. I will make it happen.

On the afternoon, I help patrons get signed in for internet access at our 12 public desktop stations or the 12 wi-fi laptop stations. When after-school students begin to trickle in, my thoughts as usual turn towards dinner.

My man and I have a double pleasure bond, sex and food. I provide both in good measure. I want more Chinese. At Shell, they have egg rolls in their hot deli fast food grab and go. I grab a dozen for the appetizer. They go good with celery sticks. When the chow mien and noodles are ready, I don't have to announce it twice. The hungry man marches to table without delay. It's dark already. I close the curtains on our intimate space. We let the dishes soak while he goes to his workshop and I do my dumbbells. I wash. He dries. He wants a back rub on the couch accompanied by Monday Night Football flickering on low volume.

Tuesday, November 8

Dear Diary, Husband and wife have their usual quiet breakfast and leave together at 08:00. He drives. I walk. I am clocked in at 08:30 on the minute with my rosy cheeks from the cold. I hang up my coat scarf and hat behind the desk. Mornings bring retirees. They read the newspapers and magazines. They check out DVDs. The new weekly magazines arrive. I get to swap them out. The New Yorker is always popular for its cartoons. I introduce myself daily to the regulars. We speak in my newly acquired hushed tones. Roy's first morning class is Algebra. I try to imagine him teaching, maintaining order, maybe even telling a joke or give a good come-back to a smart-ass. He tells the class that he has eyes in the back of his head.

Every day at lunch I think of Susan. She must be well along by now. I need to hear her voice. She has me on speaker-phone. Her guy must remain secret but maybe not forever. I start daydreaming about Christmas but first we need thanksgiving decorations. Mostly in the children's section. I now have my own key to various store-rooms. We haul out the same stuff from last year. I read the history of the library which has been on this site since 1902, the big addition built in 1962.

I watch the sun set on my brisk walk home. In the driveway, Roy tosses me a pass. I take one dribble and nail a jump-shot. We high five on my way inside. What else do I need in my kitchen? We got pretty much everything as wedding presents one of which was an air-fryer from Sally. Chicken breasts get air fried tonight. I serve them alongside lyonnaise potatoes and sauteed green beans. By now Roy has witnessed pretty much all of my culinary skills except for home-made bread. I remembered to order powdered yeast. They are coming alive in warm water as we eat. It's dark already when we sit down. After a quick clean-up, the man wants to watch me make bread while he sits at the kitchen table correcting Algebra exams. The first rise is over at 19:30. The second rise is enough at 21:00. We roll out 4 batons. They are out of the oven to cool by 22:00. We tear off crusty hunks. I want mine with apricot jam.

Wednesday, November 9

Dear Diary, At 03:00, I was dreaming about something but I can't remember what. I get up for my Perrier. I am walking around naked peeking out the windows. I saw something move out there. Should we get motion sensor flood lights? Roy rouses and says Racoons no doubt smelled my bread. We get 4 more hours. Roy is out the door first with his mouth stuffed with bread and cheese. Departure at 08:10 is fine for me. The cold air gets me fully awake.

I debut my new blue shift dress today to positive reviews. Shelving books fills my morning. Lunchroom chatter is all about Thanksgiving. Mom is inviting us for the yearly carving. I confirm, "Yes, we will be there." Instead of a daydream catnap, I go outside for fresh air. I half expect Phil to be there. Maybe Shannon has broken his heart and he has started smoking again. Re-invigorated Sarah stays at the check-out desk the remainder of the day.

Half of yesterday's dough remains in the fridge. I start it to rise straight off. I make a mess of brown gravy. I am stirring it when the outdoorsman bursts in. I throw a canned ham in the oven. We dip bread in gravy for our appetizer. I toss every kind of raw veggie we've got into our biggest wood bowl. I have a Caesar dressing ready-made. Today's loaves are baking by 20:00 and two are saved in the freezer. I had no fun cooking for one but I sure do, cooking for two. Delilah is on the radio. Teacher moves his office to the kitchen table just like yesterday. We take time out during courses. This is training day for the really big feast coming a fortnight from today. Dad liked to use such antiquated terms just for fun. I set a timer and we go to change into our terry cloth.

We detour to the office to check our financials. I still have a few thousand stashed away. My benefits kick in soon. I promise not to get sick even after they do. Mr. Miser has a few more thousands. Barring disaster, we are in good shape. A toast is in order. We finish a half bottle of Chianti. We go to bed with me tipsy but him nowhere near so.

Thursday, November 10

Dear Diary, Weeks roll along happily for the newlyweds. The husband's job is more stressful than mine. High Schools are a tumultuous cacophony inside of which the teacher works hard to maintain order. I give him silence and a neck rub to start his day, then off I go to the peaceful confines of Canton Public Library.

I get to use my IT skills today. One of the desktops has a frozen screen. I know the correct function keys get the software going again. I get to generate reports about library usage for Miranda similar to those I prepared for Maggie to deliver to "the suits" at her weekly meeting with corporate. We are non-profit but we benefit just as much from efficiency.

I stay lazy at the coffee pot for lunch, keeping the small talk threads going with all of the staff. Everyone is talking about their weekend plans. There are auditions at the Canton Community Theater for a revival if Gigi. Jenny is hoping for a small part, even if it is just a walk-on. I tell about my gallery life and amateur modeling. They all want to see the pics. I promise to bring the Mata Hari shoot but not exhibit the Aphrodite. Disapproval from even just one person could threaten my job. Could I possibly do any kind of acting? I have 2 characters in my book for casting agents to see. I will audition for Roy, no porn. He can read opposite of me. Miranda gave me a volume containing two plays, self-published by a local author. She might put it in the stacks, local author section. She wants my opinion. I take it home.

Roy tells me don't bother to cook. We get our exercise walking to our second home, our comfort zone, none other than the Waterfalls Bar and Grille. Tony, the wisecracking bartender is on duty. Roy sees wings being served. "Look honey, they have frog's legs tonight," he remarks. Tony doesn't miss a beat, "Yeah, we ran out of wings, so I fished those out of the pond, fresh caught, just for you." I triumph at the pool table when I figure out how to make a bank shot. At our table, we feed each other finger food. I try to make my lips and tongue action maximum sensual such as Casey used to do with her popsicles last summer. Last summer seems like a lifetime ago.

Friday, November 11

Dear Diary: We had fun last night. I give my man a tongue job, in the mouth, in the ear, and some other sensitive places. I have already been on his casting couch. He cast me as the girlfriend. After more auditions, he cast me as the fiancée. Finally, he put me in the leading lady role as wife, which requires many encore couch performances, no understudies allowed. Are there any sex scenes in those 2 plays? I will check it out this weekend.

I sail through my Friday on auto-pilot. I am cleared to solo on many of my clerical duties. Speed in clicking around is coming from practice. At lunch L. texts me to inform that her images will be published in Germany in a coffee table book. Depending on sales, it may be published in USA at a later date. She is over the moon thrilled out of her mind. She will get an advance and 10 personal copies. We plan to meet early tomorrow after I arrive by train. Yoga and Spa are on the agenda.

I can't wait to get home and start cooking up a storm. Upon arrival, I see that the formerly frozen loaves have risen nicely. I punch them down one more time and add grated cheese. The cheesy dough goes in the oven at 7 pm, just about the time that the ravioli is ready. We have leftover Caesar Salad. I hear the plaintive cry of hungry kittens. Am I imagining it? I look outside and see a stray, which was probably that movement I saw the other night. It looks like a young Tomcat. Roy has seen him before. He runs off so I don't have to feel guilty about failure to feed. Roy agrees to give me the day off tomorrow. Otherwise, we'll get sick of looking at each other. The cheesy bread is ready. "Honey, that is so good! Maybe I can make it myself. What do you think?" We save dessert for later in our long, lazy evening at home just us two.

I ask again about the sperm count. I am supposed to help him get a sample tomorrow morning and he will take it to the Biology Lab on the QT. That means tonight he must abstain, but the massage is the consolation prize. I get my massage too. I want the full foot treatment. Since I walk to work, saving gasoline expense, I deserve it daily.

Saturday and Sunday, November 12 and 13

Dear Diary: I don't think I need to record the exact method we used to get the semen sample. It seemed like a good amount there in a plastic screw lid cup. Dick Bothner in biology has a counting chamber. We wrap it in a warm towel inside an insulated bag. After dropping off the specimen, we exchange goodbyes at Canton Station. We wait inside until my train arrives. He looks a little sad to see me go. I board and wave from my window. He waits there on the platform until my car vanishes around the first corner. I feel guilty for leaving him alone. He says he will be working out in the gym and planning his lessons for next week. I text him and type that I miss him already.

Okay, life goes on. L. meets me at South Station. The next stop is The Blissful Monkey. Lydia and Monica are there already. They are serious seniors now and looking quite the sophisticate. I missed many sessions since September. I check myself in the mirror. I think I see some modest girl muscles. I had better stretch before getting out there. I am the oldest, possibly the least flexible. I make it through, monkey see, monkey do.

We get to try mini doses of many juices starting with a ginger spiced hot cider. The juice bar is a great place to scope the room. There are a few guys in the mix but not on the make. Guys who could be pals come in handy, just like Randy at Oscars. He will always be my pal and so will Roger. It's time to motor on over to Arlington and see if Roger wants to give us a new look. "Oh my! Look who we have here." He was getting ready to fill out a missing person's reports on the both of us. I close my eyes during my shampoo. The warm water and head massage feel wonderful. Lindsey gets her cut first. She has finer hair and less of it. She grins at me from her chair all girlish with slicked back wet hair. He is turning her into something like Gigi with optional bangs. It's a cut she can wear 3 ways. While she is in the dryer, Roger says my cut requires hedge trimmers, some kind of thinning shears where the bulk is a little too bulky. My cascade ends up full and luxurious. Roger tells us "Always a pleasure, ladies, and don't be a stranger, neither one of you."

We get home just before dark. I hang up my coat in our closet where stuff from both of us is side by side. Table lamps are casting pools of light. The place is nice and warm. It smells of Sandalwood, I think. Casey is on a date. She wants to meet us for brunch tomorrow. The little ones are waiting for us, waiting for love. L. has made a casserole. She pops it in the oven while I message Roy. He learns I am thinking about him, that I am safe indoors and that I have a new do. He will see me before dark tomorrow. For dessert, I get some of William's German Chocolate Cake. The guy is a master pastry chef. We savor it in small forkfuls. L. puts Jager in our coffee. We get a little buzzed. It doesn't take much. She wants to watch MeTV while sitting together in our jammies on her sofa which used to be mine. We trade neck rubs with a wee bit of lotion in our wonderful place, plush and fully feminine, private, except for 2 observers. It is enough for all of us just to be together. Simple pleasures connect the happiness of past to happiness present, swirled together like 2 colors of butter cream frosting on our cake. We fall asleep on our sofa with the TV playing softly. At 3 am, we light some candles, take a cool drink and move to the bed. We just want hugs and kisses, cuddles and fondles. I tell her that she is a treasure, deserving of all the nice attention anyone can think of. On that pleasant note, we drift off again into never, never land.

Nine o'clock Mass suits us. We get swallowed up in the congregation, just two of many in attendance at St. Theresa's. We walk home arm in arm. At brunch, Casey wraps up a plate of blinis for Roy. She wants to babysit. We get food. She gets 2 cats. L. wants help with her laundry. It has been piling up all week. Downstairs, we reconcile our holiday plans. We can meet on Thanksgiving weekend. She will be in Vermont for Christmas. During drying cycles, we practice our standing up kisses, her face turned upward slightly. As usual, her kisses are heavenly. We have time to linger a little longer observing action at the bird feeder. The remote starter signals my departure. The Malibu is warming up. I pack my bag. L. drives me home before dark, as promised. Roy gets his wife back and bonus blinis to boot.

Monday, November 14

Dear Diary: We got to bed early last night after I massaged the sore muscles of the body builder. The lab sample showed a very low sperm count but there were some swimmers in there. The chances of me getting knocked up are low. We decide to just roll the dice, take our chances and see what happens.

I am up at first light. I make the potato pancakes just as cheesy as the bread, providing motivation for the man to rise. By the time he is done shaving, the sausage and scrambled eggs are plated. He serves himself while I get ready. I see him out the door and take a pause. It's good we don't trip over each other. For fun, I will ask if we can get a maid.

I start my third week at my new job. I like it. It has some challenges. My first pay comes on Friday. I am the minor income but that is enough so I don't have to ask for money and document my spending. Maybe Roy will be short one day and ask for money from me. In the chatterbox lunchroom, I see the calendar with upcoming birthdays, none to worry about anytime soon. The room could benefit from some kind of plant life. I wonder about my avocado trees. Shannon sends me a photo. They are growing up fine. I should sprout two more. Guacamole for dinner, coming up.

A rolling rack full of re-shelving awaits me after lunch. I need a step stool for the top shelf. I see many titles which I wish I had time to read. Suzy Homemaker also sees that some of the shelves need to be dusted. I check the printers. One needs paper, the other needs a new ink cartridge. When they came new from the factory, someone named them "Lucy and Desi". They are due for service soon. I find some light bulbs which need to be replaced high up. I put in a work order. By 16:50, I have done enough. I log out and greet the evening staff.

I look outside. Wow! Big fluffy flakes descend. Some are on my eyelashes as I walk in our front door. They are all over my cap and shoulders. My cheeks are rosy. I stomp and find slippers and apron for KP duty. Tacos, Guac, and Spanish Rice don't take too long. More massages and Monday Night Football lie ahead.

Tuesday, November 15

Dear Diary, Roy gives mid-terms this week. Those failing will need tutoring. Tutors can use some of our library rooms after school. Some students tutor each other. Husband goes off first to get a head start on his busy day. I linger over my cottage cheese and apricots to stare at the fresh snowfall. I find the birdseed in the garage for replenishing. I march faithfully to work in my UGGs snow-boots.

Lots of returns came last evening. I inspect for damage or lateness and scan back into inventory. Jenny is there to help organize them for re-shelving. She is a local girl. She had Roy for Geometry Class her sophomore year at Canton High. She said that he is a popular teacher and that he signed her yearbook. She spent many afternoons in the study rooms here. We divide the books for shelving then proceed to the new weekly magazine refresh. We get early lunch today. I make a new pot in the Mr. Coffee. We take ours to a table outside for fresh air.

After lunch, Miranda wants to see me. She has a special project for me, namely what to do with the old card catalog cabinets. I think the museum might have some use for them or Fiddleheads. Most of them are oak. Roy may be interested. They are taking up space and gathering dust, Can I turn them into income? I am on the case. Juliette suggests Under the Bed Vintage in Stoughton. I take the rest of the day making an inventory. Other items from the old library with resale value are in storage gathering dust.

I serve up 4-alarm chili again. Roy has got the yeast germinated. More cheesy bread will be baking while he works in his office. He wants two of the cabinets. He offers $20 each. He doesn't remember Jenny. On the first rise, I do my dumbbells and sit-ups. On the second rise, I have my hot shower. While the bread is baking, Roy gets his neck and shoulder rub. Extra dough becomes hard rolls.

I dive back into my book. I remember writing book reports. I was one of the few who actually read the book. Roy finally comes to bed. We have time for perfunctory pleasure before lights out.

Wednesday, November 16

Dear Diary, Roy sat beside me today at breakfast and we both stared out the kitchen window at birds. "They're free. They don't pay taxes or rent and they get handouts from us," he observes. Off we go, marching, each to our own gigs, separate but interrelated.

I get to send overdue notices. Sometimes, a book never comes back, so sad. I get to make the display of the new additions. I do my re-shelving and suddenly, it's lunchtime. Jenny and I go outside again.

We compare Dedham High 1990 to Canton High 2008. After lunch, I am back on my special project. Miranda prints me an official City of Canton bill of sale for each buyer. I hand over the checks from Roy and Eduardo. A buyer from Stoughton is coming tomorrow to take a look at the remaining pieces.

I make a detour on my way home to Floral Scents on Washington St. They wrap two dried flower arrangements, one for home and one for work. I am still feathering the nest.

Raviolis remain plentiful in our freezer. I make my signature chopped celery, tomato and olive salad. I like to wear my sauce-stained apron and Roy likes to hear me hum. I attempt the humming chorus from Madame Butterfly. Now I am an Opera Diva. I give a silent neck rub, a take five for the teacher at his desk, then I depart, not wanting to be a distraction. His corrections are not routine since students get points for showing their work even if the final answer was incorrect. He takes a break at 7 pm, bolts his food and returns to the office space. I see him maximum focused. When he notifies me that he is almost done, I play barmaid with bottles and frosted glasses.

I hear him zipping his shoulder bag. He hangs it on the coatrack and comes to collect his reward. He plays a song from his phone. He wants a tits-in-the-face couch dance. It doesn't take long for the bulge to be obvious. I move the bottles out of the way and go at it 'til he creams his jeans. "That was pretty good, honey," says the master of understatement. I get something out of it too. I drain my bottle and exclaim "Ah!"

Thursday, November 17

Dear Diary, Sometimes the man with the plan, the man on a mission, just wants to slam that cold Starbucks Nitro Brew, a hunk of cheesy bread and kiss me goodbye on the forehead. I am left alone to stare at my songbirds and ponder life's mysteries, such as how is everything I need so conveniently close and walkable from my new home? Have I already died and gone to heaven? I give thanks. I pick one of my dried flower bouquets and carry it off to work as a way of showing thanks. It makes the breakroom a tad more cheerful since it lacks window light.

The ink cartridge has arrived for Lucy the copier/printer. I get a lesson on proper installation. I get all of the public desk-top stations booted up. I swap out the newspapers. By then, my rolling rack of books to re-shelve is ready. Jenny smiles and waves. She probably wants to know what it's like to be married to a popular teacher. Maybe she is in the same limbo that I was in, at her age. At lunch we stay inside. She tells me about some of her frustrations with guys. I tell her that I didn't solve my guy problems until I was 38. Then I met Roy in a bar, not the recommended way to meet Mr. Right.

On the way home, the sun breaks through. I march up to Sherman St. to cross Washington at a red light. I wait patiently for the walk sign. L. is probably buttoning up her office at this very moment. Maybe she will go to Yoga and meet her preferred type and go into business with her. I must keep the artist happy. Roy doesn't care. He thinks she is cute. He feels like the older brother.

Roy is late getting home. He says he had conferences with failing students. I start a pretend fight with, "Ha! A likely story." He comes back with, "Okay, but she threw herself at me. It's an occupational hazard. It didn't mean anything except maybe that she really needs to pass geometry." "Is she going to pass?" I cross examine. "Maybe, upon completing more after school tutoring, only a few more times. You understand." "I understand all too well," I say coldly. He gets the fake freeze out for almost a minute before we burst out laughing.

Friday, November 18

Dear Diary, I suddenly sit bolt upright in bed. I shake Roy by the shoulders awake. "It's time to get up and guess what? I get paid today! There it is! All of my Christmas shopping money, honey. I worked hard for it, for us. We are officially a two-income household. I will never ask you for money to buy you a present." I proclaim. "Wonderful," says he as he leans on the sink. I leave him alone while I fix a proper breakfast. "There is such a thing as too cheerful," he reminds me. "I know, but I just couldn't help myself," I explain. He waves goodbye with a slight grin on his face. He comes back in a second and grabs the last of the cheesy bread.

At 10 am, the paper checks are there. I prefer a paper check as opposed to direct deposit. It's good for record keeping and I like to bank in person with cash and checks, no debit card. I stuff the check in my purse and proceed with my routine morning tasks. The buyer from Stoughton comes after lunch. They dicker with Miranda in her office. They load up their truck. I adjust the inventory. At 4:45 pm Roy arrives followed closely by Eduardo.

They load up their stuff and reclaim their wives. Eduardo will use those drawers to organize his sculpting tools and for storage of small figurines plus the cabinets are quite attractive pieces in their own right.

Roy wants to know do I want to go to the Friday Night Canton Bull Dogs High School Football game. They are playing the Bedford Buccaneers. We have to help fill all of the home team seats. I say yes but we'll eat at home first. The pork chops have been thawing all day. I help Roy unload. While he is inspecting his new pieces, I get busy on the brown gravy and boil potatoes. I notice that my avocado pits are sprouting. He crunches a celery stick. He likes to dip them in his own private jar of queso. Bundled up sitting on hard wooden bleachers, we witness a tense low scoring game. Our fullback finally busts through on an 80-yard touchdown scamper to end the half. I stand up and cheer like a schoolgirl. I take Roy's arm walking home on a cold November night. Beers and ESPN conclude our Friday evening.

Saturday and Sunday, November 19 and 20

Dear Diary, We wake up at 7 am with no plan in mind. We aren't even hungry. Our golf course is closed for the season. I ask if I passed my wife mid-terms. Yes, I passed, A minus. I always want the minus, otherwise I am a Stepford Wife and that would be boring. I want my cat visitation or I can move the cats over to here at our duplex. He says that he will gladly take me to my cat visitation. I remind him that, in the process, he gets to visit with my cute girlfriends and to taste dishes from Casey's kitchen. We take a scenic path following MA-138/Blue Hills Avenue. He likes to see me happy in the passenger seat. I make notes of places we pass on the way, including Appleton Antique Lighting and Blue Hills Ski Area. I put images in his mind about me, adorable in ski attire. By dead reckoning, we end up in Roslindale.

We find ourselves next in Casey's kitchen, no big surprise. I throw down bagels we just bought at Green-T. Both pretty young things remain in their jammies because of slumber partying far past the previous midnight. Casey toasts all 12 in the oven and spreads a buffet of butter, cream cheese and jams. No one has much to say. Roy nibbles while he ponders his next move.

"What are you dames planning?" he wonders. "We'll think of something. Oh yeah. William is taking us out to dinner to a new place so all 3 of us dames can post glowing reviews," Casey reports. Mr. Sarcastic comments, "Wow! You guys got it rough." He pours another cup for himself. He seems to be in no great hurry. Eventually, he looks at his watch and announces his decision to go pound golf balls at Top Golf Driving Range. I whisper huddle with the other 2 ladies. On his way out the door, I grab Roy by the shirt front and plant one full on the lips. Simultaneously he gets a kiss on the left cheek from Lindsey and another on the right cheek from Casey, all 3 of us are on our toes for the triple kiss attack. I see my man blush for the first time.

The laziest gals in town got nothin' to do except play with cats and get dolled-up in time for our limo at 18:30. It's to be a French restaurant named Rochambeau, in Back Bay. This is perfect since Lindsey currently is styled like Gigi.

We show off cleavage each according to her own bounty, be it modest or full. Our bling ear-rings and necklaces are glittering. We don't want competing perfumes. All apply Casey's *YSL*, at the throat and behind the ears. Lindsey and I have faux fur wraps.

Casey's looks like genuine fox fur, perhaps an heirloom. William meets us at the cocktail lounge. He gets a group photo of the threesome of lady food critics. Maître d' Auguste seats us at a nice quiet table for four. We are prepared for 5 courses in the space of 2 hours including a powder room break at halfway point. To accommodate this bounty, Lindsey and I daintily share a plate at 3 stops along the way. Casey has a pack of Galloises Blondes cigarettes in her purse. William lights each of us with a gold lighter as we go outside. He accompanies us on a constitutional stroll along Boylston Ave. We fill our limo ride home with small talk and giddy laughter. I send the group photo to Roy. He replies that we are giving him a hard on. He adds that he is coming to get me at 4 pm tomorrow. We brew a pot of jasmine tea, turn on some lonely late-night jazz and proceed to write our reviews seated at Lindsey's downstairs kitchen table. We write them free form. Casey can proof-read and print tomorrow.

By 1 am, we are beginning to fade. Fatima and Felicia follow Casey up to her landing where she waves a cheery "Bonne Nuit." Lindsey and I get in the tub. We want another smoke but it is forbidden. Our love is not forbidden, although once upon a time, a love like ours needed maximum discretion. We barely manage a kiss or two under the sheets before we let the day slip away.

The next thing we know, it is 9 am. We lounge around, have a little fruit, and get ready for 11 am Mass. We sit serenely in a rear pew, offering prayers and thanks. We offer greetings to other parishioners. We look heavenward, where a bit of blue is peeking through. The air smells like wet snow. We spy a few sad melting snowmen along Lagrange. Casey has a very light brunch prepared, including grapefruit Mimosas. Some bacon, cucumber and spinach sandwiches on buttered rye remain when a pirate sails in aboard a red jeep. He kidnaps me at the point of a sword, but not before demolishing the remainder of those sandwiches.

Monday, November 21

Dear Diary, It was a sad and lonely duplex which sat waiting for us last evening. My woman's touch had almost disappeared in a little over one day of my absence. "Make it cheerful again," Roy pleaded. There were definite signs of the man moping around miserable and lost, such as dirty clothes, dirty dishes, and beer bottles strewn about. I comfort the pour soul. A 1-hour massage, a plate of rewarmed Spanish rice and beans, and a bit of tidying up do the trick. We were happily tucked in by 10 pm. At breakfast, biscuits are in the oven. The man grabs an extra one the way out.

My routine tasks carry me through my morning. At lunch, I read what Casey distilled from my rambling restaurant review of Rochambeau written late Saturday.

"Sumptuous setting, impeccable service, delectable dishes, and congenial atmosphere combine to create a feeling of well-being which lingers on for days. There were spirits with every course and yet no hangover. You don't even look at the bill. You do not care. It was worth it."

I ask Juliette if she has ever dined there. "Quite often," says she. On my afternoon, I clean up the storage area, update the inventory and propose auction for the remaining items.

I walk home under twilight. Tomorrow, I will carry a "torch" as they say in London. I see traffic lights twinkling red, yellow and green all up and down Washington St. Two slices from Shell Deli will be the hungry man's appetizer. Spaghetti and meatballs are under production as he hits the door. I could make this every night and he would not complain unless we run out of grated cheese.

Monday Night Football is on tap. Patriots are cruising in the fourth quarter. I show up in my flannel pjs. I walk around with beaucoup bounce. I grab the remote and demand, "Who makes you happy, Brady or I?" "Do I have to choose?" the smart-ass replies. "I'll choose for you,"

I assert as I jump his bones right there on the couch. Spontaneity keeps the sex life rocking.

Tuesday, November 22

Dear Diary, I am up first and head to the kitchen to get biscuits baking. Roy gets primary access to the bath. While I sip my tea, I see my restaurant review on yelp. Lindsey's review is all about aromas, colors, coziness and being surrounded by happy people. Casey focused on the execution of each dish, in particular the sauces. Roy grabs me, he grabs some biscuits, then he is gone. I dress at leisure and stuff my shoulder bag. Richard waves as I exit the building. He is an early riser. He grabs the morning newspaper first thing.

A scant ten minutes later, I am hanging up my coat and scarf. I switch to quiet mode and proceed with my tasks. I am pretty much on auto-pilot but still must exercise care or the location of a book could be lost. I have my 2 sprouted avocados with me. Maybe artificial light will be enough to make them grow. I search for auctions. One is coming up December 3rd, in Walpole.

Jenny and I walk outside again at lunch, which reminds me of Susan. How long will her guy remain secret? His story, I suspect, has something to do with Dunkin's. Jenny, on the other hand, is an open book. She took up acting to get over shyness. She got her part in Gigi. She must understudy two minor characters. She has the script with her lines highlighted. I agree to read opposite her on our lunches.

At 17:30, I am checking our depleted pantry. Food delivery comes tomorrow. I get some rice on to boil. The husband is reading the cast-off morning paper, sports section. He gives a thumbs up to chop suey. I have extra fortune cookies in my purse from P.F. Chang' s. Roy can't make his out. It's all in Chinese. Maybe Juliette can decode it. Mine is lucky lottery numbers. So much for wisdom of the ages. The cookies themselves go to the bird feeder.

In bed, I finish *Peyton Place*. It's slow going for my reading partner and his book. Will he play Dr. Freud again? I am frigid. Can he cure me? The Doctor says it's a phobia requiring immersion therapy. Sex every night until I start liking it.

Wednesday, November 23

Dear Diary, Where am I? Who is that hunk lying beside me? The Sarah who woke alone for so many years, is still there inside of me, doubting. It gets light earlier now and I am up at first light staring at my dream come true as if how could it be real. Maybe waffles will make it real when I see the husband stuffing one into his face and grinning at me. Waffles it is. Grab my ass. Grab a waffle and go. That was a real grope. I was groped therefor I am. These waffles taste good in my mouth, therefor I am. Let's call it a fondle. I was fondled, an indication of love. I wake all the way up. I can go to work now. I jump through all the hoops which get me paid. Jenny is a sweet kid. Juliette is a pal. Miranda gives me special projects. Mom accepted my man as good enough for me. Food gets delivered today. I have a lot to be thankful for.

The recent snowfall has melted. Some brown leaves still cling to their branches and rattle above me in a stiff breeze. I hold my hat on tight. Roy is putting groceries away when I arrive home. Dinner is simple. Roy loves that Dinty Moore beef stew in a can, a taste acquired in his college days. I doctor it up with extra veggies and spices. I wash. He dries. We wash a load of his stuff. We slip into something more comfortable. He wants his massage. I get mine, including a surprise spanking even though I wasn't a bad girl. It was a warning spanking. We hang out in the office, enjoying the new decor. His antique radio has come back from repair. We are able to tune in WOWO, Fort Wayne, Indiana. They say that AM (amplitude modulated) signal can bounce off of the stratosphere and back to earth. Richard will love this. It will awaken memories from decades before my time.

The dryer buzzes. We fold and put away the husband's wardrobe. Suddenly we want to go outside and breath the cold night air. "What star is that?" I ask, pointing to a bright one.

“Beats the hell out of me,” says my failed astronomer. “Let’s call it Asteria and make a wish,” he adds. I wish that this year I am living will just repeat, over and over, forever and ever. We mark the time, degrees above horizon, and direction of our star. We promise to look for her again tomorrow.

Thursday, November 24, Thanksgiving

Dear Diary, I pretend to remain asleep. Roy gets up at 09:00. He starts making breakfast. He brings me toast and coffee. Me being lazy gets me breakfast in bed. This is good to know. I get suited up quickly for our jog around Forge Pond Loop. I get a head start. I sprint to stay ahead of Jesse Owens but to no avail.

Our sit-down at Mom and Dad’s is 2 pm. We needn’t hurry. Mom says don’t bring anything. Sally is there already with her brood. James is at his in-laws, which is the opposite of last year. Roy brings his football and his whistle. We detour to pick up Lindsey. We are 9 in all which is a perfect fit around the heavy claw-foot dining room table. Mom says grace. She says that her heart is full. The two children are well behaved. The ladies clear while the young men go outside to toss the ball around. Roy hits his whistle to start the action. Sally’s husband Brad plays center. Brad Jr., age 9, gets to be quarterback. He launches a fair number of decent spirals to Roy, the wide receiver. Roy hits the whistle again when dessert is served.

Meanwhile, Tina has been showing her dolls to Lindsey who draws a portrait. She signs the portrait of Tina holding her favorite doll, Jasmine. Tina holds up the drawing and says, “Mommy look! I’m a model.”

We linger over coffee and dessert. The older men watch some of the 4 pm NFL game. I thank Mom profusely for her efforts. We say goodbye at 6 pm because I have to work tomorrow and so does Lindsey.

At my old home, I get a little cat visitation. Casey has cooked for William. We say hello to them upstairs. I am allowed a snifter of

Hennessy Cognac but driver Roy is not allowed. We bid adieu at 7:30 pm.

We drive serenely along Washington St. through Walpole with music playing, all nice, quiet and cozy together. Christmas lights are going up already. At home, Roy gets on the phone with his dad. We go outside and look for our star. We think we see her and make another wish. I reach in for a big hug. "Keep me forever," is my wish. "Forever and ever and ever!"

Friday, November 25

Dear Diary, I am the early bird. Roy sleeps in. He works in his office later. All I need is my cottage cheese. The streets are quiet except for cars going to Black Friday sales.

My library is open at minimum staff. I have all of my usual tasks but in smaller amount. For the retired ones who did not have family come to visit, we are their family. I say hello to all of them. I box up the Thanksgiving decorations. The weekend staff will put up the Christmas stuff.

Miranda and Juliette have the day off, but Jenny is here. We read some lines at lunch. Throughout the afternoon, we try to look busy with sweeping and dusting. The little coffee shop is closed. We brew hot tea in the break room. I study my Dewey Decimals. 800s is fiction. 900s is history, including genealogy. Juliette spends a lot of time helping with genealogy searches.

I call Roy. He had his run. He popped in on Betty and Richard. Now he is making dinner. I will be surprised. I check out a new novel, *Love in the Time of Cholera*, translated from the Spanish. There is no evening shift today, so we lock up at 5 pm.

The husband is busy with a stir fry. He made me a cheese and cracker plate for appetizer. He went out and found my favorite sparkling White Zinfandel. He sits me down and serves me a chilled glass. The stir fry turned out fine with a little Kikkoman sauce added. There is a plum wine and ice cream for dessert. I am feeling very mellow indeed. I promise him my all day Saturday. Could there be more surprises in store?

We go for a walk, just a little one. He likes to feel my arm in his. The air smells nice and it makes my cheeks rosy. He invites me to go inside and steam up the shower. He gets his back rub in the shower. He gets groped with my ticklish hands. We towel off and move it to the bed for the happy ending. Once again he proves that he never gets tired of screwing me. I signed up for it. We pour more plum wine to sip while we read. We move the antique radio to bedside. We find something nice from far away, Montreal, I think. "Ici, Radio Canada," I hear. The announcer, in a dulcet voice announces Nana Mouskouri, singing love songs.

Saturday and Sunday, November 26 and 27

Dear Diary, I get up first, but I am quiet. I don't even hum. I notice the sounds of the building we share. It is powered up. It is alive. I sip my tea and stare out the kitchen window. Some Goldfinches have come around. Their piercing cry rises above the continuous chorus of Sparrows. Traffic 2 blocks away is faintly audible.

A sleepy man eventually shows up wanting something. I offer a smile for starters. He tries a mug of my Darjeeling. "Mmm… Very nice," he comments. He sits with me a while, eventually trudging off to his shaving station. The shave is a ritual which gets him started. A waffle is all he needs prior to his run, during which I get freshened up.

I hear a bright, perky Lindsey on the phone at 10 am. We plan our overnight trip to Providence for next weekend. She is getting a lot done on her projects and I needn't worry about her. The Malibu got its oil change yesterday. She is praying every day in our private chapel.

Is it rude to visit neighbors at lunchtime? Not if you are invited. Yesterday, Roy promised to bring the little lady over. They have too many leftovers, some to eat and some to read. We find out that they do play poker but it's Five Card Stud. They play with real money, penny ante. I get Betty's recipe for gravy and for stuffing.

It's only noon. What next? We can't go back home yet lest we suffer cabin fever. We make a date to screw on the leather couch later but for now, we need more out and about in our little town. Bowling! That's it! "Take me bowling, or I'm leaving you. I mean it," I demand. I am sure that he can coach every sport except perhaps Cliff Diving. My highest score ever was 125, in college.

Luckily, the nearest lanes are another scenic drive, 7 miles on MA-27 South to Brockton. I try out my rented shoes. They slide nicely. No big surprise that coach has his own custom fitted ball and his own shoes. He gives me a 60-pin handicap per game because his average is 185. He rolls a big hook which flirts with the gutter. His first ball is a gutter ball. I say nothing. He says, "No risk, no reward." By the 5th frame, he has his hook dialed in. I continue with my 12-pound yellow house ball, rolling it straight but slow. He looks at his watch and yawns waiting for it to finally find its way to the pin deck. I make 1 strike per game. He makes 5 but he has to be careful because of the big handicap. I need a strike in the last frame to win. Oops! It's a split. "At least I didn't make any gutter balls," I remind him.

Back home we revive Betty's leftovers, which are mighty tasty. I want my horsey ride on the man-cave leather couch. I make him warm it up first with his hot body. My how time flies. By the time I am done amusing myself in the saddle, it is going on 9 pm.

We dial in Radio Canada and Coach gets his massage of his aching running, bowling and screwing muscles. The middle leg gets to rest from its labors.

There is not much to say about Sunday except for more Mill Mountain Coffee at Canton Station Copper City Espresso, The Boston Globe Sunday Edition spread out on the kitchen table, endless NFL games on TV and try not to think about Monday.

But I do think about Monday and my new career path. I fix my lunch. Grab and go breakfast is ready in the fridge. My shoulder bag is packed. My legs are shaved, armpits too. My bush is trimmed. "Very nice, honey," quote Sir Roy. "It's the most beautiful bush I have ever seen. I'm pretty sure about that." He should know. He is the strippers and naked women expert. At least he doesn't look at porn, not that I know of. There are some Playboys in the man-cave, old ones, but no Hustler. "Porn is an addiction," I warn him. "Addictions are bad," he agrees. "They could wreck a marriage and we don't want that," he adds.

I rest assured all the way to morning light, no nightmares, no 3 am thirst, just oblivion.

Monday, November 28

Dear Diary, We move at max efficiency, even the kiss good-bye is just a peck on the cheek. When I go to refill the bird-feeder, I see that stray cat run into the weeds but not too far. I see the eyes staring at me from a crouch. Some of the birds hop on the ground, putting themselves in harm's way.

The last of the Christmas decorations are going up as I arrive. There is a small tree in the children's section which they will decorate themselves. I am mostly sitting behind the main desk today. I have more software to learn. I wave to Juliette then dive into generating reports which Miranda needs. I get the moving re-shelve rack nicely organized for Jenny.

In no time it's lunch time. I change the water on Lucy and Desi, my sprouting avocados. Last week was so festive, I am not even hungry. All I need is my V-8 juice in the 12 ounce can.

I am helping in audio-visual most of the afternoon. At 4 pm, I am assigning study rooms and sound-proof music practice rooms. We have 2 upright pianos. Middle schoolers and teens have their own vending and socializing area. They need snacks after school. We provide healthy snack choices.

My walk home in the cold perks up my appetite. It feels like another Ravioli night, with baby greens, olives, and steamed broccoli. We kill the bottle of Zinfandel. I do my dumbbells and hit the tub. In my robe, I return to check on my man. His lesson plans are almost done. We trade foot massages on the couch while watching sports highlights.

In our robes and slippers, we sneak outside to look for our star but no good, we have overcast. I want a kiss outside under the winter sky, a prehistoric man and woman kiss. I want to go winter camping with my cave man in that cabin we had last summer. He agrees to check on it tomorrow. Also, I tell him about Lindsey next Saturday and how we plan to stay overnight. We bargain about it. I ask what can I do for him tonight. He shows me. He's flaccid, a pitiful sight. "Help me," he pleads. "Maybe I finally got tired of screwing you," he worries. The porno actress has no trouble fluffing up her co-star. It's a point of pride.

Tuesday, November 29

Dear Diary, Tuesday is a blank canvas. How shall I color it in? How about some brightly colored fruit for breakfast. Crammed in the back of the freezer are bags of frozen mixed berries. I wisely thawed a bag overnight. They go well on Roy's Wheaties and Sarah's waffles.

Let's add the red and green of the library seasonal décor. I wear my green pantsuit with a red cap and scarf. As Santa's helper, Sarah, hangs up her coat, she spies a big pile of returns. This will keep me busy all morning, a very pleasant morning. I can hum, but pianissimo, of course.

At noon, Jenny and I unpack our lunches. I see a script. We bolt our sandwiches and take the script to a study room. Jenny is the same size as the actress playing Gigi's rival, Lianne. No costume adjustments are needed for the understudy, if she is called upon. To read opposite her, I must read the lines of Gaston, which makes us giggle.

After lunch, I am occupied with the new numbers of the weekly and monthly periodicals. We store the periodicals for 3 years and the newspapers for one month. I suggest that the old magazines could go to auction. The old newspapers will continue to go to recycle. Miranda gives me the project of cleaning and reorganizing the back issues storage.

I ask for suggestions from Juliette because she often needs to go back there.

Before I know it, the clock on the wall says, "Time to go home." I never rush because the walk is so pleasant, even in the rain. I am all pink and fresh and glowing when I greet my man. I assess his mood and proceed accordingly.

By now, I love my new kitchen. I know where everything is. I am always well stocked. I wear my apron, just as Mom did. Taco Tuesday turns out well, as usual. All last summer, we girls had Sangria. Heavy nostalgia is pouring in all of the sudden. Roy catches me daydreaming. "Nice memories of last summer," is all I say. We review the list of the Spa services which I provide. Of course, an athletic coach needs foot care. It's one of his favorite things. No other woman ever thought to offer it, only me.

Wednesday, November 30

Dear Diary, I still expect to be tickled by cat whiskers when I wake up, but the lack of kitten care duties does save me a lot of time every morning. The man care is easy, just stay out of his way. He has a coffee pot in his office, so he does not even need that. I grab him by the shirt for the kiss goodbye, the main part of our morning ritual. We need a name for that feral cat who puts our back yard on his daily rounds. I'll just call him "Tom". I hope he catches mainly mice and not birds.

Dunkin's beckons on my way. Once a week is okay. I mean to be the anonymous donor to the break room until exposed as the bringer of temptation and ruination of diets.

Juliette shows me a plan for easy access of archived periodicals. We use the remaining surplus furniture that was destined for auction. Sweeping and dusting is now easier. We worry about spiders and mice. Which reminds me to check the snack room for wrappers, dust, crumbs and webs. I check the bathrooms also.

I have some veggies for lunch. Those are skinny things. They cancel out the fat things, such as doughnuts. Jenny is off today. I hope she is not sick. I while away the afternoon at the checkout desk. An 8th grader is typing up a book report. I give some helpful tips about the word processing. She buys a thumb drive to save her work. We sell them at no mark-up.

For dinner, I create some nice-looking deli sandwiches with chips and veggies on the side. For something hot, tomato soup delivers the final full feeling of well-being. We do ours with croutons. Roy is in a frisky mood. I get groped some more during our wash and dry. He can't resist my jiggle. He has to resist the jiggle he sees at school. To resist at home is too much to ask.

We separate for an hour. He has papers to correct. I pull out my neglected Spanish texts. We joyfully re-unite on our marriage bed by 9 pm. I get my massage tonight, starting in sitting position, then reclining. I got the hands-on from standing position a little earlier. He says it's my weekly check-up which requires me, his patient, to disrobe and get thoroughly probed.

Thursday, December 1

Dear Diary, Morning is here, woken me up and broken my sleep. My thoughts ramble on, half awake. I want cereal too. I'll do the Rice Krispies, all quietly on my own until Coach comes to the table grinning. I tell him I named the stray wild cat. His name is Tom and don't worry, he can stay outside where he belongs. "Great minds think alike," are the four words I get to hear until kiss goodbye at the door. I have a loose half hour to get professional and out the door myself for my 10-minute constitutional.

Jenny is back but she has a sore throat so she whispers and sucks on lozenges. There is a scene where her character, Liane, does not speak but does a lot of acting. We can stream it on her smart phone at lunch. My seedlings are almost ready for dirt. I must bring dirt next week. My printers need attention. There is a bad paper jam. Sarah to the rescue. The forecast is for snow. I peek outside now and then, wanting to go outside and play. Juliette shows me where the genealogy resources are and how to get people started on the apps. I help to shelve the last rolling rack of books. As I leave, high schoolers are busy with their homework and practices. That used to be me, in Dedham Library, studying hard to get into Providence College.

Roy is making grilled cheese and he wants more soup, any kind. I do the soup, vegetable beef. Celery, carrots sticks and olives look nice on the side. I could be happy if every night was the same. Teacher gets his neck rub at his desk. I want my kisses outside again. Kisses inside are boring. "Maybe you want to screw outside as well," Mr. Smart-Ass imagines. "We did, last summer, on our fishing trip," I remind him. What's left? Under water, in an airplane, and outer space. I wouldn't care if it was in the same spot, the same minute of every day, missionary only. Who I am with is what matters. "I am your life companion and after life also. You are stuck with me for all eternity," I remind Roy. "I could do worse," says he. When we go outside, he sees me with snowflakes on my eyelashes, so adorable he almost cannot stand it. Under the winter sky, I love my man.

Friday, December 2

Dear Diary, I slide silently out of bed. I get the bathroom first come, first served. If the man who hit the snooze needs it bad enough, he can barge right in. We meet in passing turning sideways in the doorway. I stick my tongue out. He swats my behind. Toaster waffles provide the grab and go. He sticks a banana in his pocket for good measure. I grab his belt at kiss goodbye. "Mine," I declare. "I have staked my claim."

I hustle straight to work. I tone down the energy. I look at all of the boxed-up magazines. Some will be bound, such as *National Geographic and Opera News*. I ask permission to have The New Yorkers because of the cartoons. Something like *Field and Stream or Popular*

Mechanics could go at auction. I mainly cover lunches and breaks today. In between, I restock the children's art area with crayons, colored pencils and sketch pads. I imagine 7-year-old Lindsey with her first sketch pad, probably drawing animals, maybe her Siamese cat, Misty.

I lunch outside alone. Those same trees that were in full glorious color a few weeks ago are now bare, except for old nests and a random Crow. The weeks are flying by. The year 2011 is dwindling away, but it is nicely archived in your many pages, Dear Diary, pages which are full of love and adventure never imagined in prior years. I sigh and return to my mundane tasks within.

My paycheck is waiting for me. This one is bigger because group health is not deducted as it was 2 weeks ago. I discuss weekend plans with Juliette. They plan to watch some Figure Skating at the Canton Ice House. They will do all of their shopping online. Eduardo despises the crassness of the Mall.

Roy wants to go out to eat at our usual place, The Waterfalls Bar and Grille. He wants steak, something like he used to grill outside last summer. I want salmon. We walk to and from. We rub elbows with the regulars. We throw darts. I got one bullseye. Roy got none. Ha! At home, Roy goes in first. Later, I knock. I sashay in playing the High Price Call Girl Escort. I am prepaid by credit card. All timid he says that he has never done this before.

Saturday, December 3

Dear Diary, "You never cease to amaze me," says the man to his not so innocent wife at their Saturday breakfast table. "Just being spontaneous," I reply with a shrug. We stare at each other and grin. He is clean shaven very nicely. Sunday is his day to go rough cut. While he was shaving, a call came in. A big change of plans is required. I get the man on board with it. Poor Lindsey is sick with fever and sore throat. She is pitiful. I go to play nursemaid as if she were my little girl or my kid sister who needs me. She's cute and I know he likes her, especially those Aphrodite nudes, plus she is unattainable. She loves only women, especially me. I will spend less money, a lot less than if we went to Providence again. It's snowing heavily. "Just take me to the train," I plead.

From Readville, Dave comes to get me. He waits while I get every kind of cold and flu remedy from CVS on Centre St., plus some canned peaches from their food aisle. I knock. The door is open. She is in bed with her laptop, a box of puffs, cough drops and ice water. The ice is the only thing which soothes the throat so far. For me, she did try to fix her hair. I have got my trusty container of Vicks Vaporub. I have got the Vicks Vapo Inhaler scented stick. I mix up a mug of Thera Flu. She has to pee almost every hour from so much fluids which is rough because of severe chills when getting out of bed. I tell her she is peeing away the toxins and pyrogens. Her birth Mom, Sylvia is giving instruction similar to mine. We do online shopping, same as Juliette and Eduardo. Amazon can deliver on Monday. Casey is gone for the weekend. The cats stare helplessly.

By 5 pm, the fever has broken. My patient wants to come to the kitchen table for chicken soup. Roy calls. I tell her he says you're just faking it. "Very amusing," I reply. I say that she almost died. This exchange gets a faint smile from the still fairly miserable patient. Her older brother had a similar sense of humor. The Theraflu is making her sleepy. She gargles with Listerine and coughs up some horrible looking stuff. She puts away her laptop and falls asleep sitting up, as do I in my chair.

Sunday, December 4

Dear Diary, I startle awake at 1 am. Felicia just jumped up on my lap. My patient remains at rest. I tip toe to the kitchen and peek through the curtains. Snow is falling heavily, big fat flakes of it soften the streetlights' glare. Fatima jumps up to the windowsill to stand watch beside me. I bring 2 bottles of Perrier to the bedside. As I settle into my armchair, my 2 fur balls each choose a preferred position, one behind my head, one in my lap. As I doze off, Nurse Sarah detects a stirring. “Thirsty,” Lindsey is saying, “Thirsty.” I offer the bottle of Perrier. She sits up straight. I feel her forehead. The fever has broken but her nightgown is drenched. She strips it off and tosses it on the floor. She sits there drinking with boobs on display but barely visible in the dark. She pulls up just her top sheet and drifts off again.

By 7 am the storm has cleared. Kitchen windows are south facing allowing patches of blue to be seen. My patient wants a little of the Starbucks cold coffee and cling peaches I told her about. She wants to sit in the chair. Her throat remains sore, so we only whisper. She finds her box of cough drops. She gets a kiss on the top of the head. She is besieged by cats but they retreat when the sneezing fit occurs. By noon, she makes it to the kitchen table. There is another attack of chills. I cover her with a fleece. She wants to work, do something. She is sure that her boss, John Lowery, will let her work from home all next week. Casey will be back to watch over her. I ring up Roy. Dave will take me to the train station this evening. His lover girl, me, will return to him. Meanwhile, I stay to take care of my lover girl. The place is a mess. I tidy up then hit the shower that used to be mine. I find one of my old robes. We take a little snooze. I tickle massage her through a fresh sheet. Does she want a pedicure?

Yes, she does, the full treatment. Her tiny, buffed nails become bright purple. We have a light dinner, bland diet. We watch some TV. Figure Skating is on. She loves the costumes and choreography. I feel sad to pack up and go. I give my report to night nurse, Casey. I kiss the pretty little feet goodbye. Trusty Dave is waiting outside. Trusty Roy is waiting at Canton Station.

Monday, December 5

Dear Diary, Here I go again, thirsty at 3 am. I stare at Roy as I drink. He looks so innocent there in front of me, flopped onto his stomach and his legs in stag leap position. I must intrude myself back into my half of the bed. At least he doesn't have sharp toenails. I make sure of that. I wish I could video monitor what he is dreaming about. I'll just go into my own dreams. At 07:00, I have no dreams to report today. I get busy with the reality of sausage links and hash browns which are always appreciated by the main breadwinner as fuel for his tank.

It's all business as usual in the land of books. Books are my responsibility to preserve against loss or damage. That is my pledge. Patrons need info or simply something nice to read or something nice to listen to. What will become of all of our CDs now that MP3s are taking over? We have CD players, cassette players and even little portable record players to lend. For now, Miranda says, it is a priority to maintain all forms of audio and video, including cassette tapes and VHS. It would be a shame to discard any of that multi-media.

At lunch, I get to chat with Juliette. We both got our Christmas shopping finished on Amazon. Jenny does a rehearsal of her non-verbal scene for us, playing Lianne in Gigi. No Tony Award but she can act. We decide that my little trees are both girl trees, so I change the names to Jenny and Juliette.

The minutes tick away. I ponder what is to be for dinner. I wonder what surprises might be in store for me at home. That's not much in the way of suspense but it is enough for me. If today, not much is happening, then I report my random thoughts to fill up the page. "Nature abhors a vacuum," someone once said. Google search tells me it was Aristotle. "Diaries abhor blank pages," according to me. I account for every day.

I get out the frozen fish and broil them to perfection. My spices keep them from smelling too fishy. We squirt fresh lemon wedges. The potatoes are little wee ones. I chop up and mix up some slaw. My man is happy. He just grins at me. He helps me clean up as usual. What a Prince I have captured!

Tuesday, December 6

Dear Diary, Crisis! Tom has killed a bird! The feathers are scattered about. I feel awful for the little bit of fluff. All it wanted was some seeds and now it is dead. "It's the law of the jungle, Honey. Tom is a predator. He doesn't eat seeds," my Naturalist observes. If it was a mouse, I wouldn't care because they try to come inside and then Tom would just be doing his job. All day long I puzzle what to do so Tom doesn't starve but neither does he kill innocent birds.

Reshelving books takes my mind off of the trauma for a while. I try to rekindle the holiday spirit, but I am still on a downer. Maybe I am seasonal-affective but I just never noticed it before. I like my job but I just feel lazy today. What was I doing last year at this time? We were decorating our office, at Chestnut Hill, of course.

At lunch I call in. Shannon answers the phone. I get some lively chatter. Here, I have to be so quiet most of the day. The traffic dangers on my inbound commute, that kept me sharp as well. I want to try driving the 4-wheel drive mode of Roy's Jeep. We'll see if he lets me. If not, I can say he loves his damn truck more than he loves me. The smart-ass will probably say, "You're right. I do. Don't come between a man and his truck."

A mystery book club will meet this afternoon. They will be reading, *The Fifth Witness* by Michael Connelly. They get refreshments, namely coffee and cookies. I line up tables and chairs in our large meeting room. Who is the English teacher at Canton High? A question spawned by my inquiring mind. I would like to meet the English Teacher. I am not sure why..

My surprise is that my hero is busy retrofitting an old umbrella to catch most of the scattering of seeds so fewer birds will be in harm's way, hopping about in the snow while a predator is on the loose. Every Tuesday may as well be Taco Tuesday. Roy could eat those every day, even if he already had them for lunch. During the drying of the dishes, I find out that the English Teacher is Miss Taralyn Davis. My services are required for head, neck and shoulder massage, followed by the usual screwing.

Wednesday, December 7

Dear Diary, Time marches on. Two cogs in the clockwork begin to turn. We both help people get educated and find out stuff they need to know. We unceremoniously get our usual fuel on board. Roy has some store-bought dirt left over from planting my roses. I have 2 shoulder bags, one with lunch and the other with dirt. I will be careful not to get them mixed up.

After I hang up my coat, I study the schedule. I know all of the staff by name now, even the part-timers. I bring the dirt, seedlings and pots to the building maintenance office. Jerry, the man on duty, says he will pot it for me as part of general building beautification and so that I don't make a mess. "Glad to help," he says. Maybe some of the children who come to the library want to learn how to grow things. We could start with cacti or bonsai trees. They can learn about pollinating. Skills grow in their fertile young minds.

After lunch, I have a nice full, well organized rolling rack to reshelve. By now I have the stacks mapped by subject matter. When I glove up and scarf up to leave, I look back at my new workplace. I can be happy here, for a good long while. Maybe not forever. It is a stepping-stone, but to where?

By 17:30, I am busy making meatballs. The sauce is simmering. The salad is Caesar, with croutons. I pull out the checkered table-cloth and linen napkins. We might as well use them. Roy looks ridiculous with his napkin tucked into his collar. He just sits there grinning at me. "Mm…, delicious honey, pass the bread and butter, please," says he as he stabs another meatball with his fork. "These are the best meatballs I have ever tasted," he adds. Something as ordinary as this, is another dose of domestic bliss.

After dinner, it's dark but we do our walk anyway, around our usual loop, arm in arm. It smells like dead leaves, melted snow and mud. Too cozy inside would put us to sleep. We haven't watched TV much lately. "You're much better than TV. I just watch you," says the husband. That is so sweet. He has turned me all to mush. We switch on the radio. The mood is romance.

Thursday, December 8

Dear Diary, I yawn and bonk Roy in the head. "Damn, that hurt," he protests. "That elbow could be a lethal weapon. The guys will think that my wife is beating me," he adds. We are both wide awake now, at any rate. I won't give up until he lets me kiss the boo-boo. By the end of breakfast, I have been forgiven. He is gone only 5 minutes and already the place feels sad and empty, probably because there are no kittens staring at me. I hurry my make-up and whoosh out the door.

I proceed at a leisurely pace on foot. I say hello to people in passing. I hear a Salvation Army bell ringer. A one block detour allows me to meet the volunteer and contribute.

Oops, I am 5 minutes late. I get the front desk all day. I log in quickly. I deal with some phone calls of a general information nature. I check lost and found for a notebook and a pair of gloves. I am allowed to have a personal drawer. I mark mine with a label maker. Inside, I find a left behind bobby pin and a penny. I review procedures on a flip ring of laminated pages. I issue some new library cards. I print my list of overdue books and suddenly it's time for lunch.

Jenny wants to sit outside. She likes to feed the pigeons. When we go to the trash can, a squirrel in there startles us. These details seem small but someday, I will re-live them. I just know that this is a magical time for me. I know it while I am living it.

On the afternoon, my exterior view is through the picture windows in the large reading room. Already at 16:30, the light is beginning to fade. I text Roy to come and get me so I can transport to home the heavy box of old New Yorkers. He shows up promptly at 5 pm. He gets to meet Jenny and Miranda. Jenny looks vaguely familiar to him.

For dinner he wants macaroni and cheese or he will die. I enhance the mac and cheese with breadcrumbs and bacon bits. I make tuna salad and toast for the side dish. So that we don't get sleepy we go to the man-cave. Roy is making something from wood. I do my dumbbells, 50 reps. We are in bed by 10 pm.

Friday, December 9

Dear Diary, At 7 am, I am dreaming about something but that dream is replaced by the reality of harmonious alarm chimes. A typical raucous alarm makes us both irritable right away to start the day. We agree on the chimes.

Roy is eager to get the ball rolling. He wants to expedite breakfast on his own. While I fix my hair, I hear him rummaging around in the fridge. He snatches one of my V-8s in a can. He makes a white bread sandwich with some leftover sausages. He pushes me out of the way so that he can brush. I get a minty kiss goodbye. I watch the man of action drive away. The sooner he goes to work, the sooner he comes home to me.

I am accustomed to my 8:30 to 5. It's going along very nicely. I call my Little Baby Doll Lindsey. Yes, she is working from home, which is not so simple with four feline eyes constantly staring at you. For the weekend, we'll play it by ear.

I work in a trance. I know something really good is in store on another magical weekend starting several hours from now. Some of my co-workers are pals. Some are matter-of-fact. I get a minute here or there to daydream. I am in a very stimulating environment. So much information at our fingertips. I help to keep it organized and readily available. In the afternoon, Juliette has a few minutes to give me a mini-tour of the historical documents, letters, maps and old books which are entombed behind locked doors in a humidity-controlled room, to be handled with gloved hands. They have some first editions which were once on the shelves, and some very old newspapers marking historical events such as Black Tuesday, 1929. I feel very light on my pathway homeward bound.

Roy has cabin fever from every night in our tiny duplex. He wants to go out. He craves the Chinese Buffet. We don't even change clothes. The Gourmet Garden is not specifically Chinese Cuisine, it is Asian fare, even better, because we can try Japanese dishes and a sip of Saki.

It was a stressful week at school. To tell me about it is to relive it. I simply provide massage, to tame the savage beast.

Saturday, December 10

Dear Diary, Late last night I got lots of chuckles from the other side of the bed during the sifting through of cartoons from *New Yorker Magazine*. During this good mood, I tell about my new designer job and this one I get paid. It's a Martini Bar in Norwood. Will he take me there please and can I stay overnight? "I suppose," he agrees. "But feed me on Sunday, then be the cheerleader on the 50-yard line." It is still my most memorable seduction. "Yes, happy to oblige, and by the time I am done, your dick will be worn out," I guarantee.

We stop at Perks. Cameron is there, another cute girl Roy gets to flirt because of me. He danced with her at our wedding reception. "If you dump me, she is my second choice," he informs me with a wink. He is having a lot of fun inside my women's network. We are enjoying the ham and cheese croissants when Lindsey arrives. She wants a chocolate one. She has her laptop and her sketchbook.

The place was a sports bar. If possible, the owner wants it to stay open during redecoration. He requires that we do it without a building permit. The budget is $12, 000. L. is the team leader. She proposes new lighting within existing wiring, new tables, improved flooring and new wall art. The old sports memorabilia has already been removed. The bar may also be resurfaced within budget. We get an advance of $6,000 and a deadline of New Year's Eve. The owner signs off on our plan. We promise an Art Deco look. We can't guarantee antiques but quality reproductions instead. Roy is an observer of Lindsey in action with me as assistant. He likes our style.

We say goodbye to Roy and go home to find what we can online in terms of lighting, furniture and wall art. I call Roger Quinn to see what he has. He might be willing to trade. We get some air by doing the vigil Mass at St. Theresa's. L. sketches at the kitchen table while I mix and match whatever I find promising in my old fridge. We do a quick change for an excursion to Venezuela Café just to rub elbows. Upon return I find that our bed is refreshed and smells of Gardenia.

Sunday, December 11

Dear Diary, Roy is coming at 4 pm. We are up at 8 am, sitting at our kitchen table in robe and slippers, drinking our Darjeeling tea. Fatima and Felicia stare out the window at the bird feeder. More snow is falling. I feel sure our Martini bar needs draperies along the street-side windows to make it cozier. The original entrance should become fire exit only. Signage directs patrons to parking and entrance in rear where there is a coat check. The Art Deco period is Prohibition. The place should be a speak-easy. L. is busy sketching. She looks up and smiles at me. She thinks the idea will fly. She will order everything on Monday. We can begin installations next weekend.

Now, how to enjoy the remainder of our time? Taking a little walk in our snow boots is invigorating. Trading back rubs with scented oils feels wonderful. Laying out a buffet for my transporter is fun. We hear his truck rumbling. We invite him into the parlor of the ladies of the evening. He samples our buffet. We sashay around languidly. When we sit, we provide a leg show. He seems in no hurry to leave. It is near to 5 pm when he bundles me up and carries me off.

The next thing I know, the call-girl wife is providing entertainment in the former bachelor pad. She does her cheerleader act culminating in a good hard fuck which wears his dick off. I am sure it will grow back. Meanwhile, he is exhausted. He has lost interest in the Sunday Night Football game between two nameless teams. They continue to bash each other about on the gridiron while we squeeze into our bubble bath, head to foot. My tits get foot fondled by the two long-fellows of the poet who don't know it. When not providing milk, tits should provide something to look at, and something to fondle. Mine provide two out of three, not bad. I am proud of my tits. Someday, they will be sagging, but for now, they are mighty fine.

My hunk flops on his stomach under a sheet. I read for a short time prior to lighting some candles. I bring cold water to the bedside. We both drink deeply. The last thing he remembers is a back tickle from his neck all the way down to his bare butt.

Monday, December 12

Dear Diary, Another December Monday is dark when I get up, and dark when I come home. We got the heat turned up to 65 F. I got my basal metabolism revved up. I am burning calories like crazy. No extra holiday poundage. No flabby arms. No cellulite. I am thankful for the convergence of all of that. I used to hibernate but not this year. The young newlyweds, in their period of adjustment, are learning how to help each other get out the door in time with some kind of fuel on board.

Sidewalks are icy, I take extra care. It's a good day for jelly doughnuts, come one, come all in the breakroom. I don't have powdered sugar in my pantry. I must add such to my weekly delivery. Mom always had some. One of our wedding presents was a Betty Crocker recipe book. I promise myself to find culinary inspiration there tonight.

My challenge today is checking in, plus reshelving. I am able to keep up plus cover checking out during lunch. One book is water damaged. You break it. You bought it. But we are not quite so mean to our patrons. I manage a little small talk with the regulars in the regular hushed tones. I check the vending machines in the teen snack area. Some are depleted. I call the serviceman for expedited restock. The High School is also on his route. Maybe what students crave is like high octane fuel.

Roy is taking a nap when I return. I wore him out yesterday. I get busy with some new sauces and enhanced brown gravy from Betty Crocker. The aromas revive my man. Roast beef, cheesy mashed potatoes and new improved gravy combine to release from the man a smile from the heart by way of the stomach. We walk first and do dessert later. It's just Jello and Cool Whip. After clean-up, I want to experiment with a crust. My kitchen is fully equipped, fully stocked, but so far under-utilized. I pop the naked crust into the oven about 9 pm. It is cooling at bedtime. My taste tester approves heartily. "Yum! That is one mighty tasty crust, honey," is his review.

We enjoy our reading and cartoon browsing until way past 10 pm. I nod off first. When I turn over, the lights are off.

Tuesday, December 13

Dear Diary, Coach is counting the days until Christmas Break. He has an extra gym class this term. He will be fitness testing today. Some boys cannot even do one pull up. Some of the girls can do several. He drags himself out the door, but not before enjoying more of my famous crust. I have two more for later. I should stuff one of them.

But first, I should get to work, no diversions. Jenny and I switch today. I recall all of miscellaneous tasks. My questions for Juliette, I ask in Spanish. She answers in Spanish and English. This becomes a daily no cost language lesson for me.

We have a donation of a vinyl record stereo system. We find a corner to set this up for use with headphones only. All of our vinyl can now be enjoyed on the premises. I spend the rest of the day straightening chairs and dusting. I may use the lemon pledge, but sparingly.

It has warmed up a bit for my hike home. The air feels wet. Hundreds of headlights and tail-lights wink at me. I trudge along, clinging to my shoulder bag. It has been a very active year for me. I am coming down the home stretch to another January 1, right where we started from, Dear Diary. I can see the finish line. Soon there will be a flood of memories.

I flop on the bed and ask Roy to undress me. "With pleasure, my dear" he consents. He takes his time. He is enjoying this, especially the nylons removal. I lay there naked for a while before hitting the shower. I let the cold water run at the end to get me totally revived.

In the kitchen, Roy has made a buffet of leftovers. He made a pot of tea for me. I haul out the second pie crust in its tin pan. The first rule of home economics is to always make extra of everything. A cup of soup would be nice, Minestrone straight from the can. It's like we are kids, Mom is away and we have to fend for ourselves. I light a candle. That makes it extra nice. The checkered tablecloth remains in place. We have nothing to say so we have a staring contest. I blink first so he gets to be on top when the bedroom action begins.

Wednesday, December 14

Dear Diary, I awake alongside a boner demanding attention. There are worse ways to wake up, such as a mouse running across the room or a flash bang invasion by a SWAT Team. My hips are positioned just right for doing what comes naturally. It helps us come alive in the morning. Later, he needs it after school to relieve stress. All I have to do is flop on the bed, let him undress me, and do a quickie in missionary. Then he will cook. On weekends, he only needs me once. Has anyone ever heard of such a thing? I intend to query Susan, the other newlywed, about this. I certainly am not going to ask Mom. But maybe that was how I was conceived. Dad screwed her every day before and after work. While Roy is innocently eating his crust, I tell him okay, it's a plan. I can handle it. This is my year of nymphomania, which is better than chastity, if you have the right partner. If you have the right two partners. Ha!

We are having an unremarkable day in the library. At lunch I am able to reach Susan while she has babe in arms. All she can say is before the baby, her guy wore her out. We were screwing like there was no tomorrow. Most of the time she did not mind. Oh well, it's like I said before. It's what I signed up for. She said I can meet her in Hyannis before the end of the year.

In the afternoon, I see someone using the record player, It's Henry, a guy who loves Opera and we have lots of Maria Callas, his favorite. For once, I don't worry about what to make for dinner. All I have to do is go home and spread 'em.

I make note that today, he wants to undress me standing up with the bonus of I get a little hot breath muff dive in the process.

After the wham bam, I return all clean to see what The Chef has prepared. Roy's version of Tacos is heavy on the ground beef and light on the lettuce. He brought home Coronas especially for tonight. He lets me wash, while he goes to his office. He gets out of drying because it would just make him horny again. The sex is finished for today. We are going to get a lot more reading done.

Thursday, December 15

Dear Diary, Her teapot is steeping while his shower is steaming. She kicks him out of the shower so he can shave on time. He chews on toast while he watches her dress. They kiss goodbye. They are a well-oiled machine.

All of the recent snow has melted. Salt gets on my street shoes so I carry a change of footwear in my shoulder bag. All of my co-workers are in a good mood today, perhaps due to Christmas Spirit. On the coat rack, mine stands out. It is throw-back, one of Mom's, fur trimmed, from before that was frowned upon. Tomorrow is Jenny's birthday. There is secret signing of her card and a donation for a gift Miranda has wrapped and stashed in her office. Surplus baked goods from home appear in the break room.

Some of our regular patrons have flown away to Florida. I make more usage reports for Miranda. They are broken down by hour and day of the week. I check the schedule for the holidays. I work a half day next Friday and the following Friday. By 16:00, teens and middle schoolers are arriving to study for finals. I help some of them who are writing term papers to do their internet searches. Some of them need tips on Power Point and Excell, my basic office skills from way back and well-polished.

Juliette and I leave at the same time. We chat about Holiday plans and say "Buenas Noches" in the parking. Her coat looks like Cashmere. There is no need to rush home. My body benefits from the evening chill. The air seems fresher in Canton compared to Dedham.

Minutes later, I am being disrobed. I could get to enjoy this. Something Roy has on simmer smells good. Meanwhile I provide my body for stress relief. Instead of slaving over a hot stove, I am slaving under a hot man as we agreed, for the common good. I retire naked to my dressing room only to reappear shortly thereafter in robe and slippers for dinner. We have pasta night, those corkscrew noodles. Roy's sauce turned out very well. He even brought us some nice Chianti. I take over the kitchen. I wash and dry with my radio on. We read. We sleep.

Friday, December 16

Dear Diary, Boing! We pop up early and have no problem getting equipped and ready for action. At kiss goodbye, I give a cheer for the weekend when we will be out and about accomplishing something plus having fun.

The winter is turning to clear and cold, but the sunshine is super bright and cheerful. The employee coat rack is in a sequestered area where we don't have to be totally hushed.

Everyone is psyched for their weekend. Jenny has rehearsals. I tell about my redecorating. New Horizons is getting business by word of mouth. I put our business card on the lobby cork board just the same.

Shopping from the cork board is the opposite of shopping online. I simply take a photo of the board, then I can study it at leisure.

During morning break, staff circulated through the break room with birthday wishes for Jenny. Miranda put together a box of sparkling bling for Jenny's role as courtesan Lianne. I have time to linger a little in there. Any time she wants to read lines opposite me, I tell her I am up for it.

Out on the floor, I try to keep busy. I check my list of busywork tasks. After lunch, I sit in Miranda's office and pick her brain about the future of the entire library system. The biggest cost is building maintenance. Second is employee salaries. A distant third is new acquisitions, paper and ink, equipment repair or replacement. To justify these expenses, we need high utilization. I volunteer for outreach activities. She says to work up a presentation and submit my ideas in January.

The sun is setting as I depart. I zoom on home to perform my domestic tasks which begin with me flat on my back as is our new custom. He likes me all flushed from my fast walk in the cold. My hips are the best hips ever and he cannot resist. He would even pay for it, he says. That's good to know. He swears that when strippers are giving him a couch dance, he is thinking about me. I told Susan. She laughed. "So romantic!" she agrees. He does pay for it or at least work for it because afterward dinner is on the table. Two hours later, we set our chime alarm for 7 am.

Saturday, December 17

Dear Diary, Roy has to hear me all animated on the phone during his Wheaties. Thankfully, for him, it was brief. L. doesn't waste time blabbing on the phone. Accordingly, I don't even waste letters when typing her name. She is most of the time just L. My man is pretty much resigned to his fate. He must return with me to Norwood for installations. The owner will be there with his wife to supervise, starting at 10 am. Deliveries will be arriving starting at 11 am. L. has arranged everything. Roy plans to meet some pals at Napper Tandy's for every kind of sports watching.

We have time to stop at Perks. Cameron is there with her usual smile on display. Cabin fever is banished. Already we are rubbing elbows. L. pulls in right behind me at our work site parking in rear. Jessica is with her wearing Jeans, work boots and a hard hat. She knows her way around a toolbox thanks to her Grand-Dad. Power tools are in the trunk. She is on duty. She is being paid cash, our first employee. Roy wants to watch us in action.

First off, A salvation army truck takes away the old tables and chairs for a big tax write off. The owners, Mr. and Mrs. Hirsch, have already sold the three big flat screen televisions. They are saving money already on cable service. The floor gets a sweep and mop. We clean the wall behind the bar in prep for hanging of a large beveled-edged metal-framed mirror. The old liquor bottles have been removed. This bar will serve only top shelf vodka, gin and vermouth to make its Martinis. Roger Quinn arrives next in a delivery van. He and his driver unveil the mirror to the awe of all. Jessica and her power tools mount a ladder to install the hangers and brackets into the brick wall. The men take the weight and the women guide the mirror. Together we slide it securely into its brackets. Mr. Hirsch turns up all of the existing lights full. The effect gets applause from all. Ten tables and 40 chairs don't take long to offload and then it's time for a break. Mrs. Hirsch has a cooler of deli sandwiches and drinks. The next delivery is the burgundy velvet draperies to cover the street-side windows. Jessica and Lindsey know just how to hang them.

Meanwhile, Mrs. Hirsch and I plot a preliminary layout of tables. Mr. Hirsch has hired a cabinet maker to reconfigure the bar and fabricate a coat-check room near the main entrance in the rear. Finally, Lindsey unveils the milk glass sconces for bar and wall lighting. These must be installed by an electrician. We promise to hang the wall art next weekend. We are finished by 3 pm. Our customers are very pleased to say the least.

Jessica has to go. We send her home by Uber after much thanks, hugs and compliments on her skills. The rest of us retire to Napper Tandy's a mere 3 blocks away. It turns out that my girl Lindsey has hung many mirrors and draperies before and that lighting was her main interest at RISD. We get a table by the fireplace just about where Roy slipped his number in my pocket. We exchange knowing glances. Roy is having Shepherds' Pie and Irish Coffee. I go for the Blackened Shrimp. L. wants the Seared Sea Scallops. Some of Roy's pals are arriving. He dismisses me in cavalier fashion. The night is young but all my lover girl and I want is quality time together at the place where our Love began.

Casey is babysitting the fur balls. We go to retrieve them. We chat for a while and exit in favor of William who waves to us as he parks. I find a mess inside my old apartment. L. has been very busy and let things go a bit. We don't care. The kitten box is clean at least, They get their love. They watch us bubble bathing. High pressure lust needs relief asap. We are not even dry before the kisses get hot and heavy. Intense action gets us tangled in the sheets. I fall out of bed trying to extricate myself. "Jager, please. I need it. It helps me get off." is her plea. "In the freezer," she tells me. We sip, chase it with Perrier, then back to business. "More!" she cries. I think she is having multiples. I hold her around her slender hips and dive deep. I have never heard her so vocal. I wonder if they can hear us upstairs. "I'll do you in a minute," she promises. One person or another has been doing me all week. "Rub my back first, please" is my desire. She works me hard, then spanks my fanny and orders me to turn over. Starting at the knee, her kisses work upward. "You're mine," she informs me. She does me better than any guy ever did. Wow!

Sunday, December 18

Dear Diary, I sit up and yawn. Three creatures are in bed with me, keeping me warm. Two of them have fur. One has hair on her head, soft, silky, shiny, shoulder length, shaded dark brunette, inviting to be stroked gently, revealing a serene face in repose. I watch the rise and fall of the breathing. Faint morning light filters through the sheer curtains. I hear sparrows active outside our window. I slip from under the sheets unnoticed. Coffee and 11 am Mass will be best for our lazy morning. She likes to be seen with me in public, arm in arm. It's okay that I am married. No one cares amongst the people in the territory we claim for our creative work. Kittens certainly don't care.

"Who loves you? Me. I do. I love you. Have you any doubt? I have been saving it up for years and now it is overflowing, all over you," I reveal as I bring her mug.

"That's sweet," says she as a smile breaks through. "Let's stay in love. It's working out very nicely, don't you think?" she continues. The talk turns to babies. "Who will have a baby, one of us or both? Casey plans to have babies with William. They have talked about it. I am envious." She is serious. We touched on this once before in passing, months ago. I tell her that there is a chance I could get knocked up. "Would you help me if I get knocked up?" she wonders. "Yes," I reply without hesitation. Both of us knocked up. How crazy would that be? She is still a virgin, medically speaking. Some skinny-hipped women pop them out no problem but where are the swimmers going to come from? Sperm bank? Anonymous volunteer, one night stand? Turkey baster? Would she let a guy do her, just to get pregnant? I am sure she could find any number of volunteers. She could pretend it was just a speculum exam which she tries to avoid also. We pray over it at St. Theresa's. Maybe others have the same prayer. Who knows? St. Theresa has no doubt heard it all over the centuries since her Beatification in 1614.

I remind her that a hungry man is coming at 4 pm. We get dressed and start having fun in our kitchen. Sure enough, there he is, unshaven but right on time.

Monday, December 19

Dear Diary, The husband has me back in his custody after an absence of 24 hours. Now I watch him sleeping. At this, my other home base, the furry things stay outdoors. I get my drink and slip back into the marriage bed. My hips and my KY are ready for the stress relief which is sure to come at the break of dawn. Predictable is good. I am always ready. He will never be grumpy in the morning ever again. I send him off with a smile on his face. I am pretty happy myself.

On my walk to work, I start thinking about fund raising for the library. My mind is racing. So much is happening. I also have an idea for Lindsey, a genius idea, I firmly believe. I can't wait to tell her. Meanwhile, I have to make it diligently, professionally, through another work day. We have full staff. It's a hen party but a quiet one, discreet and composed as befits our workplace. I have time to greet some of my retired regulars who appear bright and early. Coffee break comes. My avocado trees are growing up slowly. Lunch break comes. I go outside with Jenny. Middle Schoolers and Teens make their late afternoon appearances. Copiers and printers are copying and printing.

I surprise Juliette with some Catalan phrases instead of Spanish. Barcelona is bi-lingual, she informs me. If I go to Europe, definitely go there, she advises.

I skip my way on home prepared to do my duty. Sure enough, the possible progenitor is ready to fuck me and possibly knock me up. He likes it if I talk dirty. I tell him Lindsey and I both want to get preggers. I tell him my idea of how she can accomplish it. Her 10-year High School reunion is coming up next summer. Wesley, a guy she knows from way back, will do anything for her. The possible future father can manage one syllable per thrust. "Good, I, de, a, hon, ey," is the thrust of what he manages to communicate during the deed. I want it. I need it.

Mom will certainly be happy if I deliver. He never gets tired of screwing me, except that one time when I had to be the fluffer. We get it over with quickly and efficiently so we can relax and see what is simmering on the stove.

Tuesday, December 20

Dear Diary, Morning at home is the same deal. We have polished our act like pros. It works for us. My marching off to work in the cold is the same. My morning tasks at work are the same routine. Lunch is the same except I divulge my intent to have a baby late in my period of fertility. Yes, Jenny wants babies too, maybe just two, a boy and a girl. Miranda has two in college. Juliette has one in pre-school. I avoided my destiny for a good many years but it is not too late to bear fruit. That's me, a five-foot six fruit tree. I am flowering. Pollination efforts are underway.

Tuesday afternoon rolls around in due time. What is that tune in my head which I want to hum or whistle. The song is *Tuesday Afternoon* by the Moody Blues. I always associated that song with winter days. Normal, nothing new, routine is good. I do not crave excitement. I just keep humming along until time to go home.

I walk slowly, breathing the cold, watching the sun go down, giving the husband time to get creative with his supper prep. He undresses me gently. He wants to stare and enjoy the view. I turn slowly displaying all sides of my magnificent perfection. He wants to see my hip action when I walk. He wants to see the tits bouncing. He wants me slow and gentle today. It's been a long year and he is tired. The gravy thickens during the extra time we are taking.

We light two candles for the dinner table. We linger over our plates of roast beef, potatoes and baby greens. We finish the Chianti. I put the leftovers away. The motion detector lights come on. Peeking through the curtains, we see Tom staring up at us. Tom, the night-stalker feral cat is on patrol in his territory marked by scent. He will not come in even if we invite him. He is maybe 6 years old, a survivor of many cat fights, and the sire of many litters. What does he think of us? Birds come here because of us but they also are wary of us. We leave the dishes until tomorrow, the way that bachelors do. I dial up *Nights in White Satin* on my I-Pod. We use it as a lullaby for a winter night.

Wednesday, December 21

Dear Diary, We make sure neither one of us over snoozes, then we are on our own. Roy has home room for 9th graders at 8 am. We stay out of each other's way. When he is wearing a tie, I like to grab him by the tie to say goodbye. I know he likes it even when he has already transitioned totally to teacher mode. Would I be a good high school teacher? I could teach Office Skills or Home Economics or Cheerleading. I could teach English. I am good at spelling and grammar. I have read a lot of English Literature fiction. If we decide to home school our child, I know I could teach him or her to read and do arithmetic, maybe even teach a language. I could take them on field trips. What a thought. I can be the preschool alternative.

I certainly can teach myself more stuff. I am working at the perfect place for that. The working conditions are very good. I love my new job. Some days I feel lazy and it's hard to get up, but once I get dressed, I am eager to get in there. I am a civil servant. The pay is low, but it is enough for me.

Today is déjà vu, more of the same, but I never know when a new challenge will come, such as a software or hardware bug. We sail smoothly into the late afternoon. I help with the last bit of reshelving and log out of my desktop so that evening staff can have my station. Rose is a part timer who stays until closing. I tell her about a 10th grader who is struggling to get a term paper proofread and printed before closing. She agrees to help.

Minutes later, I agree to help in the kitchen. Roy says that he doesn't need to screw me today because his dick is worn off. First, I wash yesterday's nasty mess that was sitting in dirty dishwater all day. I set the table and find things the chef needs. He doesn't want his bachelor meal prep skills to be forgotten. His Chicken Chow Mein from a can turns out fine. His rice is a little undercooked but that is desirable, I have read. I wash. He dries, just as before and the drying makes him horny, as before. It must be something about me standing there in my apron in a dress that can be lifted up. Off we go to the pleasure room with reckless abandon and KY for the worn-out dick.

Thursday, December 22

Dear Diary, I felt some cramping overnight and sure enough, by morning I have the curse. Roy's dick gets 3 days off. "Thank God!" he swears, feigning relief. I ask if we can please sit and stare at each other this morning like other couples do. It turns out to be a blinking contest and he wins again. "You'll never beat me," he laughs. I should practice with someone, maybe Jenny.

I bring my Midol with me to keep in my personal drawer plus a toothbrush, some lozenges, my panty-liners and a makeup compact if I ever feel like powdering my nose. Other stuff, I can keep in the break room. If I have to shelter in the library during a tornado, I am all set. Speaking of monthlies, the Tampax machine in the lady's restroom is empty. They are in the supply closet with TP and paper towels.

At the check out desk, I have time to read about the banned book policy. We have *Catcher in the Rye*. No need to worry about that one nor Maya Angelou. I want to talk to Taralyn Davis about who gets to decide what is appropriate for who. Subject matter seems to outweigh how well a story is told, how important the story is and what is the moral of the story. Does forbidden subject matter protect children or make them more vulnerable?

I will ask Roy if there is a debate team at his school. I want to review the logic fallacies. I am sure he knows about them.

My ruminations shut off conveniently at 17:00. I impulse buy pizza slices and egg rolls at Shell station mini-mart. Maybe, this will suffice for tonight. Yes, it does because Roy is tossing a salad and we need nothing more. We finish the French dressing and croutons. I post a note on the fridge to take out trash tomorrow morning. We compact it down tight in our Hefty 20-gallon super strength bag. We sigh. Teacher is off tomorrow. He needs a frosted mug or two tonight. I must abstain due to the Midol on board.

For fun I get to hear about the ad hominem fallacy. It's when you argue using insults. "You're wrong because you stink," for example. We will try to avoid that kind of argument in our future fights. For now, we agree on almost everything.

Friday, December 23

Dear Diary, Lindsey is leaving for Brattleboro tomorrow afternoon. Tomorrow morning, she is hanging the artwork at the Speakeasy. Jessica will stay over on a slumber party with Casey and Kelsey tonight. L. says she will call me when she gets to Brattleboro. I leave while the man is sleeping. I say, "Goodbye, Honey." He grunts a few syllables into the pillow. He was up late submitting grades online. I saunter on over to report for my 4-hour library shift.

I am still cramping. Maybe I will be late and in suspense next month. Everyone tells me their plans for the long weekend. I plan to meet Mom for Christmas Eve Midnight Mass in Dedham. It's a family tradition. Roy will be with me. Darla and Robert will visit Sam in Maine.

Some of our regulars are on the premises. The coffee shop is open. Jenny and I do lunch there. I find out she has a date on Saturday. She rents from her parents a finished basement apartment with a private entrance. She does not do overnights with her dates but possibly a lingering late night watching an HBO movie. Like me, she doesn't have a car but she is saving up.

I get my early release at 14:30. I wonder what Roy wants to do. I find him wrapping a package for his dad. Darla promised to transport it. Richard and Betty have invited us for dinner. I have my gift for Roy waiting at Mom's house. He has his gift for me hidden somewhere. He digs out a tiny ceramic tree from last year that was tucked away in the garage rafters. We set it up in the office. Two new triples A's make it twinkle.

Dinner next door is come as you are. Roy brings two bottles of bubbly from his trip to the liquor store earlier. They do a ham and a turkey every Christmas. Tonight, we get the ham, with sweet potatoes, a cherry pie and ice cream. We hear stories of all of the cars they have owned. Once upon a time, they rode in style behind the wheel of a '61 Coupe de Ville. We experienced nothing of the '60s, but they did. The bubbly is making their stories of old times, which do not match exactly, even more entertaining. Roy and I stumble home tipsy just after midnight.

Saturday, December 24

Dear Diary, We don't have to do anything this morning. Our little Christmas tree is winking at us in tiny red, orange and yellow lights. The star on top makes a continuous white glow.

We look outside. The sun is bright. The birds seem happy. Next thing I know, my guy is getting all GQ on me, by shaving, for starters. His lathered-up face is telling me to get up because we are going out. "Here, wear this," he commands. Meanwhile, he is looking good in his dress jeans, crew sweater, wool jacket, slouch hat and rakish scarf. I do my best with my own jeans, leather jacket, gloves and boots. I flip and toss my brunette cascade. He positions my wool beret just right and delivers kisses on both cheeks. We fire up the Jeep for short drive over to where else but The Waterfall Bar and Grille, Roy's comfort zone. I like it too. We sit at outdoor tables and pretend we are in Switzerland. I start with hot chocolate. My man wants an Irish coffee. We look out over the water. Some Wood Ducks are cruising around out there. We didn't have our fish fry yesterday, so that's what we have.

We remain restless. I want to watch the skaters at The Canton Ice House. A scenic winter 1.7 miles along Bolivar St. and Waterfall Drive takes us to the arena which is brightly lit but cold so we keep our coats on. The hockey practice is finishing. Even the little girls play hockey. The figure skaters appear. The pairs do some wild stuff with their synchrony, partnership and trust in each other. We still have plenty of time to go home and pack our overnight bag for our sleepover at Dedham. We depart for the short trip before dark.

At 11 pm we get our winter gear on and head to St. Mary's of the Assumption. The night is bitter cold and clear. The bank digital thermometer reads 10 F. This is the Church of my Baptism and First Holy Communion. Sally was married here. Even on an ordinary Sunday, the place is magnificent. Now, in all of its Christmas splendor, I look up at Roy and see that he is very impressed. Then comes the heavy incense and electrifying swell of the organ. No one will fall asleep at this Mass.

Sunday and Monday, December 25 and 26

Dear Diary, At 12:45 am, we are side by side back in the Jeep, waiting for it to warm up and for traffic to clear. It takes everyone a while to settle down when we get home but by 2 am, Roy and I have walked out of our clothes and crashed into the lumpy bed of my earliest childhood recollections.

They say that smells are the oldest memories, some of which are being recalled first thing this morning. Those and the sound of barely audible chatter, which prompted little girl Sarah to find her way down there and join the group. My partner wisely grabs the shower while it is unoccupied in the 1.5 bath dwelling. We find a brunch buffet for 6 adults and 2 children. Alex the ring bearer prefers cheerios. Older sister, Jill likes the instant oatmeal. They are not fighting with each other, yet. They want to make a snowman. Dad sits on the front porch with his mug of coffee to watch over them. Soon he is joined in similar fashion by James and Roy. They occupy some matching wicker. They pass a hip flask around to enhance the coffee. "Only on Holidays," Dad claims. It's warming up a bit. The snow is getting sticky. Two misshapen figures begin to emerge. One is wearing an old hat. Passersby critique the sculptures.

Inside, I get pregnancy anecdotes from Mom and James' wife Trudy. I ask them to pray for me. I get "You'll do fine," and hugs all around. Only one NFL game is slated today of little interest to the guys but the brunch buffet gets return visits.

The children have already unwrapped their multitude of packages. Dad likes lots of hats. He looks cool in the Donegal Irish Wool hat with matching scarf and gloves. Mom loves her lotions and her illustrated hard cover "Lives of the Saints". We can learn a lot from The Saints. After all of our wedding gifts, what more could Mom and Dad think of? They thought of camping, namely his and hers high powered led rechargeable Coleman lanterns. Hang them from a tree branch or light up a tent. See your way rowing at night or light up the house in case of power failure. Modern day Jane and Tarzan are very pleased. Roy and I will gift each other at home. After a cheesecake dessert and a lot more lounging around, we depart.

The road home is near empty late Christmas night. We left the lights on at our duplex. Our neighbors have done the same. Roy and I gave ourselves a $100 limit for our gifts. He gifts me my extra set of keys for the jeep on a girl stylish key chain and beautiful bracelet in semi-precious stones. He applies it to my right wrist and kisses my hand. I gift him a rugged digital wristwatch with many functions including timing my quarter mile.

Lindsey and I already gifted matching swatches with phone finder app. I am still waiting for news from her. Just after midnight, I get a text from her saying to check my e-mail. I go to Roy's desktop and find mail with a digital album attached. Wow! The Hirsches spared no expense. They admit that they dropped 50K total on their bar upgrade, including fake gaslights for the parking lot and enclosed outdoor seating for overflow and smokers. The bar has a brass foot-rail and mahogany top. The bathrooms have new period style tiling and fixtures. The artwork is Maxfield Parrish prints in shadow-box frames. The sconces look like something right out of Edward Hopper paintings. I can view all of her photos in color or black and white. We have VIP Tickets for the grand opening when there will be catered heavy hors d'oeuvres. New Horizons shows a profit of 3K.

We can lay our heads down to sleep now. Everything was wonderful. We worked wisely and played hard. Now we sleep deeply, lightly intertwined, preceded by just a light back tickle.

Roy sleeps right through my Monday 07:00 alarm chimes. I am off. The library is closed. Roy is off all week. L. calls me. I take it in the man-cave. She is very excited on how our first paid project turned out. She also knows who will be the father of her child. It will be Wesley, the man who loves her the most. He is home for Christmas. They have met for coffee. The 10-year High School reunion will happen in June. That is when he will finally have his big chance. For one night of ecstasy, he will risk his marriage. She gives him an Aphrodite print for a keepsake.

I check on my man. He is still sleeping. I charge up our lanterns and make a buffet. We stay home today.

Tuesday, December 27

Dear Diary, The end of the year is nigh. I kiss my man goodbye and let him sleep in heavenly peace. But my motor is running. I am ready to return to the land of books on every subject waiting to be opened. I spend another happy day matching books and readers. We are back to full staff. I jump right into the periodicals and the newspapers. Our early birds keep up with current affairs. I keep back issues safely stored away in our freshly organized storage space.

We have time to exchange highlights of our holiday weekends. Jenny had fun on her date. The guy is someone she knows from Community Theater. He was using some lines on her from "Baby, It's Cold Outside". Eduardo took Juliette out on the town Christmas Eve. Miranda had a house full of grandchildren. The break room is loaded with surplus high calorie comfort foods. I knew it would be so. I did not even pack a lunch.

I wonder what my man is doing. He is in his office but remains in his robe and slippers. He is getting a head start on lesson plans for the new term. He is paying some bills. He has his AM radio on for company. He has some dough rising for bread. All in all, it is a very productive day for the stay-at-home husband.

Late in the afternoon, I am busy with dusting and replacing some light bulbs in the main reading room, the place I watch the winter daylight fade. I watch Jerry clearing snow in the parking lot. He waves. Even if I did not get this job, I would still be here, in this room, active in some way at my newest comfort zone.

I give my shift report to Rose. I bundle up to prepare for my brief blast of cold in transit to where Roy has got the home fires burning. That dough needs to be punched down. Roy watches me work. Tomorrow, I tell him, my hips will be ready for you. "Oh, thanks for reminding me," says he. "I was having so much fun I forgot all about that." Always the smart-ass is he. Dinner is Taco Tuesday, followed by my dumbbells and his wood shop. In our happiness of ordinary time, we read side by side, lights go out early, and cuddles happen while Radio Canada plays on softly.

Wednesday, December 28

Dear Diary, Roy beats me to the bathroom. He already has tea infusing. He reports cabin fever. He wants to be a patron, just a normal patron. He lets me go in first. A few minutes later, he enters to make use of the facilities since the High School Library is closed. He is on a school sports policy advisory committee and he is tired of clicking around the internet at home. I see him getting guidance from Juliette. I see him finding journals and making notes but I don't let him distract me from my work. We have lunch together in the little café. That's nice. He gets all of the info he needs but he wants to skim some newspaper sports reports after lunch. He is gone by 1 pm. Everyone says that he seems very nice. Ok, so that was different. What next?

Miranda says there will be a career seminar next week for middle schoolers. They will be coming through learning about library science as a career. The parents can learn about aptitude testing options, the possibility of late bloomers, and over emphasis on grades in an evening session given by School Psychologists. This is the kind of stuff she organizes in her office. We call it outreach.

It has been a very stimulating day, tempered by my share of routine tasks, but now the light fades. It is *"The Edge of Night"*. Grandma Powell used to have that on weekdays, after school. I still recall some of the plot lines. The fictional City of Monticello was not as nice as here.

Oh no! Crisis! We are out of butter, possibly because of all the bread we are baking. They have it at Shell mini-mart mini-dairy section. I come home with the butter. The bread is ready, but we cannot live on bread alone. Let's burn some calories first, in the bedroom, of course. I stay flat for a while so the boys don't have to swim uphill.

Pasta is waiting. The house husband has made a great sauce for dipping. His salads are looking nice. We go outside briefly. The moon is a waxing crescent and the stars are bright. Roy has installed a camera trap in the back yard. Tomorrow we can check infra-red images. What if I get camera trapped? Loads of fun!

Thursday, December 29

Dear Diary, We are both up at 07:00. R. says he does not want to get lazy over break. He means to go running on the High School Track. With his key, he can go into the locker rooms and have his long hot shower. The water pressure is somewhat better there. We feed each other toaster waffles and off we go.

So many books and so little time! Rack 'em and stack 'em. Take a pause. See who needs help. Cover someone's break. Click my way through the day.

Who did I replace here? It was Vivian, who retired and moved to Florida. She had some stories to tell but they are best not repeated.

Possibly, they were embellished quite a bit, more so with each telling. She went to Canton High School way, way back when. The old yearbooks are here. They sometimes help with genealogy. There she is in the "Senior Class of 1960". She was a cheerleader too. The Beehive hairdo was quite becoming on her. Maybe I will ask Roger for a Beehive next time. Okay, I am having too much fun. I get back to work while the clock ticks away.

I have one more task. Miranda shows me a list of perennial donors who have been inactive for 3 years. Can I follow up and update their status, such as moved away, nursing home, deceased, etc. "No deadline," she tells me. "And no pun intended," she adds. Some of the deceased become immortalized by way of their bequest.

Oops! I am a little late clocking out. R. gives me 15 minutes latitude before he worries me with a text. At the 10-minute mark, he hears me crooning "Hi Honey, I'm home. What's for dinner?" he confronts me, arms akimbo, wearing my apron and all in a huff. I apologize profusely for my inconsiderate lateness and get reluctantly forgiven. Wink, wink.

He went for the stir fry today and didn't make too much mess. He ran a six-minute mile. Not bad for a guy past his prime. I let him coach me about stretches. I don't want a hamstring injury during bedroom acrobatics. After he does his progenitor duty, we can relax, fully content with our day.

Friday, December 30

Dear Diary, The pool is open to faculty. Roy is addicted to fitness. He is off to swim 30 laps. That is almost a mile. He has the goggles. He has the Speedo. I have my shoulder bag and my change of shoes. I keep my wool cap over my ears. He has his expedition. I have mine.

After the usual morning tasks, I have time to work on my list of donors defunct in one way or another. Sadly, for 7 of the 40 on my list, I find a funeral notice. Some of my regulars know about the others. Three permanently moved away for retirement. The others receive a text invitation to the next Donor Appreciation Event asking for RSVP. Of these 5 get returned as number no longer in service. Unknown status now hangs over 25 former donors. If the library card of these donors has not been active in three years. I conclude that they no longer are participating patrons and should be removed from the donor list. The 5 names remaining get an appreciation letter which could be forwarded or returned undeliverable. Task complete. If we reactivate even one of these donors, it was worth the time.

I also need to reactivate a man who is getting stiff. His two legs came near to cramping. Now they are relaxed. Massage has the opposite effect on the middle leg. We might as well get this over with, then have a leisurely dinner after all of my tasks are complete.

The Chef is lazy. He merely bakes our remaining frozen shrimp and fish sticks. We got the Cocktail Sauce and the Tartar Sauce. I like my seafood with shredded cabbage on a bun. We are giving up beer until summer to save money because babies are expensive. Better to have a six pack of abs then a six pack of brew. I get to study the six pack of abs. I punch it to no effect. It's as solid as any boxing gym body bag. R. can be proud.

I remind my man of our VIP speakeasy tickets. We swear to drink mocktails only and keep a clear head. Darla and Robert are coming also. Dave will be the transporter. We reserve his Toyota Highlander for the four of us. It is a Gala Event in our humble lives. We haven't fought over the remote lately. I'm ready.

Saturday, December 31

Dear Diary, I yawn, a big one, this time without bonking Roy in the head. I climb on top for our last screw of the year. He is still sore from yesterday's marathon swim, so he gets to just lay there. By the time I am done, it's 08:00, which is late for us. I throw the man his robe and slippers but I grab the bathroom first. When I come out, he has two mugs in his hand, hands me mine and takes over the bath. I left him some hot water from the 30-gallon tank. I cook up a whole mess of Jimmy Dean Sausages and biscuits. There was not much action at the camera trap. We witness 1 raccoon and Tom, who came whisker close to sniff the enclosure.

We have an invitation to dinner at Darla's condo in Walpole. Robert will be there, coming directly from work. We are under another high-pressure cold front. We decide to stay inside until departure time for our soiree. While R. goes to his wood working bench, I sit in our office, coordinating with the main contacts in my women's world. L. is at home, sounding high energy. She and Jessica will appear at 10 pm by Uber. Chad and William are sharing the expense of a limo. Casey and Kelsey will be riding in style with their escorts, arriving at 10:30.

What will I wear? Something semi-formal, I think. From Mom's former wardrobe is a green silky thing with a diagonal hem and one shoulder exposed. I call to ask her when did she last wear it. "Oh, that! Let's see, possibly it was a dinner party back around 1987. I always went for a timeless look," says she. "I believe that you were 15 and we paid you to stay home and babysit Sally and James. I remember vaguely the challenge of managing the 2 brats in my custody. Roy is doing his all duded-up cowboy look with full length duster.

We arrive by Jeep in Walpole 'round about 6 pm. They have bubbly but we are abstaining. Darla's creation for dinner is a "Surf and Turf" comprised of grilled jumbo shrimp and grilled filets of grass-fed beef. Robert is fixing attractive individual salad bowls. He worked day shift, 7 am to 3:30 pm for premium pay, but took a little nap before our arrival.

The pair seem to be getting along fairly well. Robert needs a glass of wine to loosen up after the stress of hospital shift work. Darla is his employment agent, working hard to transition him to a better paying job with normal work hours. They both change after dinner. I hang with Darla while she changes. I hear some laughs coming from the guys in the living room.

I check with Dave. He is on his way. I have known him ever since Uber was invented. He has delivered me home safely on many a cold dark night. I sit in front. The others slide in back for our 15-minute passage along East St. and Washington St. to The Speakeasy. He drops us at rear parking zone. He is scheduled to return at 00:30.

We give the password that is on our VIP invitations. We check our coats. The back seating is dimly lit with low tables for four. The front room is brightly lit with seating on bar stools at high tables and at the bar. The jazz trio is playing Ragtime. A cocktail waitress in period attire serves the low tables. Three bartenders are on duty. The scene is really quite amazing. By 11:00 pm, my gang and I have found each other. Eight of us stay at low tables, while two of us circulate among the high tables.

It's all quite a blur now as I write this at 2 am in Darla's kitchen. Roy is sacked out on the couch. Robert is zonked in a Lazy-Boy. Was it the happiest day in my life? Maybe it was number 3, behind my 2 wedding days, all recorded here within the confines of this diary of many pages. I close the book on you Dear Diary of the magical year of Our Lord, 2011. You have been a faithful companion. I will come back to visit you. I will keep you as a treasure.

Epilogue

Sarah Jane has allowed me to read her 2011 Diary because there is so much of me in there. In the bittersweet year of 2012, she no longer writes her diary entries. I make this follow-up on my own as her most intimate and best-loved companion.

Despite all of his many preventive efforts, Roy fell victim to a school shooting. The boy thought the gun was not loaded but there was one in the chamber. Roy entered the locker room after gym class. He saw the gun being displayed. He still had his whistle in his mouth. He blew his whistle hard, which normally stops all action on the gymnasium floor. In this case, the boy's tragic reflex was to tighten his finger on the trigger. Roy succumbed to his wound 3 days later after a vigil during which Sarah never left his side. On his last day, he recovered his senses briefly, just long enough to squeeze her hand and whisper, "I love you."

On September 21, 2012, Sarah delivered a healthy 7-pound boy. Sarah and I share an apartment in Roslindale. I am married to Wesley. He is happy to play "The Beard". I am in my first trimester. The sonogram indicates female child.

The English teacher, Taralyn Davis, has also been permitted to read *The Diary of Sara Jane Powell.* She advises that the story is suitable for publication. We are planning a 2025 publication date, a decent interval, long enough for the children to understand the love affairs which led to their conception. Proceeds will benefit St. Theresa of Avilla Catholic Church in West Roxbury, Massachusetts.

-Lindsey Lawrence, January 1, 2013

Appendix

The Characters Mentioned in the Diary
(in order of appearance)

Phil (1): Sarah's College Boyfriend
Charlie: A Guy Sarah Rejected
Mom: Sarah's Mom
Rick: Another Guy Sarah Rejected
Charlotte (1): A Woman at Café Fresh Bagel
Charlotte (2): The Daughter of Charlotte (1)
Felicia: Sarah's Calico Cat
Roger: Sarah's Hairdresser
Robert: A Guy Mom Picked Out for Sarah
Dad: Sarah's Dad
Susan: A Co-Worker at the Chestnut Hill Office
Steven Sandler: A Guy Sarah Met Waiting in Line
Maggie: The Boss at Work
Dave: Sarah's Uber Driver on Retainer
Roy: Sarah's Secret Guy
Cameron: A Barista at Perks Coffee
Randy: A Bartender at Oscar's Restaurant
Phil (2): A Guy who Smokes in the Parking Lot
Darla: Roy's Sister
Joni: A Part-Timer at the Chestnut Hill Office

Fatima: An Abandoned Kitten
Reggie: The Tenant who has Gone Missing
Sandy: The Office Manager
James (1): Sarah's Younger Brother
Sally: Sarah's Younger Sister
Sheila: New Tenant in 6-G
Tammy: The Office Temp
Sylvia (1): The Woman in the Necklace Engraving
James (2): The Man in the Necklace Engraving
Lindsey Lawrence: An Artist living upstairs
Derek: Roy's Alter Ego
Mr. Hesse: Sarah's High School Math Teacher
Jason: Mechanic at Parkway Auto
Delores: Owner of the Lost Necklace
Dr. Desiree Allen: Lindsey's Preferred Type
Leslie: Lindsey's First Lover
Julian: Bartender at Renaissance Hotel
Anton: Waiter at Renaissance Hotel
Jessica: A Young Blonde Lindsey Met in Cambridge
Wesley: Lindsey's Prom Date in 2004
Mitzi: The Owner of Galerie D'Orsay
Jan Boyd: Calligrapher
George: New Tenant
John Lowery: Lindsey's Boss
Monica and Lydia: College Students at Yoga Class
Roger Quinn: Buyer of Antiques
The Hennigs: New Tenants in the Furnished Unit
Casey and Kelsey: Girls at Venezuela Café
Tawney: Veterinary Assistant
Sylvia (2) and Bob: Lindsey's Parents
Rosario: Waiter at Sophia's Grotto
Bill: Commercial Photographer from Providence
Chad: Kelsie's Boyfriend
Patrick: Head of Maintenance at Chestnut Hill

Sean Dempsey: A Painter of Abstracts
William Sutcliffe: A Pastry Chef
Tom and Pam: Lindsey's older Brother and Sister.
Scout: Bob's Shepherd Mix
Misty: Lindsey's Siamese Mix from Childhood
Jaime Cunningham: A Painter of Landscapes
Betty and Richard: The Duplex Co-Inhabitants
Stanley: Roy's Uber Guy
Father John: The Priest at St. Oscars
Walter: The Guy moving out of 16-M
Karen: Walter's fiancée
Timothy Wexler: A Surrealist Painter
Kappy: A Coin Store Owner in Norwood
Tony: Bartender at The Waterfall Bar and Grill
Tonya: Sarah's Golf Coach
Evan: Susan's Replacement at Chestnut Hill
Sam: Roy's Dad
Gloria: Roy's Mom (deceased)
George: Sam's Guard Dog
Shannon: A Candidate for Sarah's Job
Jordan: The Wrestling Coach and Best Man
Jeffrey Jacobson: A Painter of Landscapes
Juliette: The Reference Librarian at Canton Library
Tina: The Flower Girl
Alex: The Ring Bearer
Hector: Owner of "Grounded"
Raimon: Teenage Son of Hector
Eduardo: Juliette's Husband
Rita: Sam's Girlfriend
Miranda: Chief Librarian at Canton Public Library
Estella: Hector's Wife
Jenny: A Co-worker at Canton Public Library
Dick Bothner: Biology Teacher at Canton High
Auguste: The Maître d' at Rochambeau

Brad: Sally's Husband
Brad, Jr.: Sally's Son
Tom: The Stray Cat Lurking Behind the Duplex
Taralyn Davis: The English Teacher at Canton High School
Jerry: Maintenance Staff Member at Canton Public Library
Henry: A Guy who Loves Opera
Mr. and Mrs. Hirsch: The Owners of Speakeasy Bar
Rose: Evening Staff Member at Canton Public Library
Jill: The Elder Sister of Alex
Trudy: Wife of James, Mother of Jill and Alex
Vivian: The Library Assistant whom Sarah Replaced

www.ingramcontent.com/pod-product-compliance
Lightning Source LLC
Chambersburg PA
CBHW020307030826
48979CB00029B/2283/J

* 9 7 9 8 8 9 6 7 6 0 8 8 7 *